SILENCE OF THE STARS

IMMORTAL BELOVED

ALAIN LOUIS CAMUS

Copy-editing – Mr Neville Shaw
Final proof – Micheline François
Cover Design and Layout – Arjan van Woensel

Library of Congress Cataloguing-in-Publication Data
ISBN hard cover 978-0-6457676-5-0
ISBN paperback 978-0-6457676-1-2
ISBN e-book 978-0-6457676-3-6

Alain Francois
PO Box 22 St Marys TAS 7215
alainlouiscamu@gmail.com

Publisher
阿蘭

A catalogue record for this work is available
from the National Library of Australia.

BOOKS BY
ALAIN LOUIS CAMUS

Book One

The Tears of Apphat, Immortal Beloved

Book Two

Silence of the Stars,

Chronicles of Azizi

Book Three

The Names of the King,

Chronicles of Azizi

Book Four

Aïschah Silver Moon

Language of the Stars

DEDICATION AND ACKNOWLEDGEMENT

To my Great Grandmother Alice Camus for always being by my side, encouraging me and guiding me throughout this journey.

My mother, Blanche for her unfailing support and encouragement.

To Benjamin

I held him tight, an ephemeral cloud.
I held him on the abyss of despair,
a precipice I know too well.
Sobbing uncontrollably,
he begged me not to let him die.

I just held him.

My Love Always Benji.

In a land that is not on any of your maps, a culture based on ancient lore beyond your understanding, in a language that is barely able to be translated into yours, I exist. My name is Azizi, it means Beloved in the ancient tongue of the Desert people. I will be known as the Immortal Beloved.

Aïschah Godmother to Azizi. Her name means Silver Moon. A powerful healer and magician and a member of the Council of Elders of Naasée. (*'Aïschah Silver Moon, Language of the stars,' is a companion novella to book 1*).

Azizi Born Aldrick, son of Haakon, the chief of the Asfaine mountain village. His godmother takes him on as her apprentice into healing and magic. **Aïschah** gives him his name of 'power' – **Azizi,** meaning Beloved, to protect him from negative forces.

Elwah Prince of Naasée. Ruler of the Elders and one of the most powerful magician. Known as the sacred 'Haafiz' (Keeper) for the Sacred Sapphire of Apphat named 'Elwah' or Joy.

Faruq Cousin to **Ijlal**. His name means: 'one who distinguishes truth from falsehood.' A skilled and fierce soldier, he derives his blue eyes and serious demeanour from his father, General Giafar, brother to the Sultan of Shiraz. He led the Companions in the rescue of **Shahulm**.

Halim Shepherd from the Asfaine mountains. Friend to Azizi, born two months apart. Murdered by a Red Robe in the hire of the Sorceress.

Hasan Fierce and renowned soldier of the Naasséenes. His skill is unparalleled. He is the Captain of the Royal Guards, personal protector of the Prince Elwah of Naasée. He is also the man who initiated Azizi into the rites of Apphat.

Ijlal Prince and heir to the Kingdom of Schiraz. Leader of the 'Companions,' a band of young nobles who look for adventure and defend the citizens of the kingdom. Cousin to **Faruq**. Lover and partner of **Shahulm**.

Saeed Son of Fariqa, his name means 'happy', and 'lucky'. As a young boy, he was healed by Azizi in the desert from the sting of a scorpion. Emerald green eyes, curly red hair, he radiates strong magic. Untrained and naïve, he will seek out **Azizi** to train him into the arts of healing and magic.

Shahulm Prince and heir to the throne of Glesskerel. Abducted by the Sorceress and the forces of evil, tortured and eventually rescued by **Ijlal**, his lover and partner. Shahulm is renowned throughout the four kingdoms as the most handsome and mesmerising dancer.

The **Council of Elders** of Naasée: refer to the dictionary as an appendix for their titles and particular magic.

CHAPTER ONE

My heart heavy as a storm cloud with the memory of Halim's death, nevertheless found a rainbow of hope at Prince Shahulm's rescue, into the arms of his beloved Ijlal.

The scars inflicted upon Shahulm's body are nothing compared to the wounds of his soul. Ijlal is by his side night and day, only eating when prompted to do so. The fruit of the Shiraz tree, which flowers for the first time in seven years, is distilled and its healing properties applied.

Under the guidance of Elwah, Prince of the Naasséenes and until recently Haafiz – sacred keeper of one of the Sacred Stones, gradually Shahulm begins to recover. The nights are longest. Servants coming and going to replenish the oil lamps and attend to prince Ijlal. My sense of purpose is at an all-time low. I cannot use my powers of healing; this illness is beyond me.

The cool marble floor beneath my feet shifts as lights of torches come and go, darkness creeps back like a desert cat. Sounds recede. Incantations echo in the silence of the night and fade like fireflies at the first light of dawn. I fall into the chaotic silent world of my mind. My thoughts and prayers go unanswered. The eternal stars are silent.

I wonder, sadly, obtusely, if I had had the fruits of the Schiraz tree with me, if only one, could I have saved Halim?

A soft tune echoes fleetingly, floating like incense upon the air. I fall under its spell, sunlight on my face, green hills rolling underfoot, the softness of something gentle upon my cheek. Then the taste of salt upon my lips...

"Azizi." A whisper surfaces from an eternity. Blue sky gives way to blue ocean and gives way to his blue eyes.

"Azizi." Elwah stands before me holding me gently by the shoulders.

"Azizi, it does not good to think of how things might have been."

Tears run down my face; I rest my head upon his shoulder as he holds me in his embrace, the fragrance of all the oceans drowning me.

A WARM DESERT BREEZE gently plays with the soft window hangings, capriciously teasing them into billows and releasing them. A heavy silence lies over the palace; everyone would be resting during the Carêm. The soft tinkle of a water fountain somewhere below in the courtyard, the only audible sound in the dry desert air.

My bags are packed. Unhurriedly, convincing myself I am

making the right decision; I make my way to Elwah's room knowing he never sleeps to tell him of my resolve. I open the heavy curtain to his quarters and stop. Hasan is before his prince on bended knee, Elwah is gently chastising him.

"Hasan, understand that it is I who guided you to Azizi. Without the initiation into the mores of Apphat, I could not have passed onto him the Sacred Stone. It would have refused him."

Still Hasan remains. I understand he is overwhelmed with guilt, thinking he has robbed Elwah of the first of my manhood. Finally, Hasan still unsure looks up to his Prince's warm smile, Elwah raising him to his feet declares: "Come Hasan, you are still my fiercest and most trusted warrior; and now sacred guardian to my Beloved Azizi. I could not have wished for anyone else."

Hasan bows deeply before his prince, then turning sees me standing there.

I go to him and embracing him feel the last of his concerns melt away, like the spring snows of my mountain home. Hasan takes his leave.

Elwah looks at me and deliberately turning, stands on the balcony that faces the northern regions towards the Asfaine Mountains. "You are leaving then?"

The word choking in my heart, I answer "Yes."

"Will you not wait until morning?"

"It is cooler at night. Halim..." I struggle with his name, my chest tightens, and the sound catches at the back of my throat, "Halim taught me this, when we first made our way to the desert people."

He turns then concern in his eyes. He wraps his arms around me and holds me in his embrace. Softly he whispers, "Go then, knowing that I am watching over you."

I cannot resist kissing him, the softness of his lips like honey to my spirit. Dreamlike I walk away. I go to my god mother Aïschah. I am to be initiated into the Lore of *Muraqaba* – the Songs of *Tahannuth*, Solitude of the inner-mind.

~

The sound of my horse's hooves on the cobble stones echo in the narrow meandering streets of Schiraz.

A light in a window is still on; someone peers out and draws the curtain closed. The street widens a little towards the city ramparts.

A lonely figure on horseback stands at the gates of the city, etched against the night sapphire sky. Deliberately I approach.

Faruq's fierce gaze penetrates me. "Ijlal is saddened to hear of your departure."

I understand that even now, Ijlal will not leave Shahulm's side until he is fully recovered. "Tell my beloved brother that I will return." The horse's bit jingles loudly in the evening air. "I must go to my god mother and prepare for my next initiation. We must be ready for what is to come."

"I saw with my own eyes the sorceress reduced to ashes. Surely that is enough to restore the harmony."

I sigh, wishing it was so. "The sorceress has been destroyed, yes by her own greed. Greed still exists in the world. The Sacred Tears of Apphat disappeared. The Universe in Its wisdom has hidden the gift of harmony. It is now the task of men to restore harmony in their hearts and find the spirit within."

"I would travel with you as your companion on this journey; you but need to ask."

"I am grateful for your offer Faruq. Your place though is by your prince. Rest assured I am well looked after." I think of Elwah's gentle look as we parted.

"May The Guardian Spirit be with you on your journey. Return to us soon Azizi."

I do not say that The Spirit has not spoken to me since the Tears vanished. I no longer know Its presence, which once was as palpable as the air I breathe.

"Thank you, Faruq. I take my leave with the love of the Companions in my heart."

I urge my horse forward and as I pass by, Faruq salutes me in the way reserved for the initiates of Apphat.

The dark waves of the desert sands undulate before me as far as the eye can see.

~

Darkness envelops me, the coolness of the evening air wrapping itself like a distant and callous lover. The clear night sky offers me no comfort; the stars blindly blink at my insignificant passage upon the sand. I lose myself in the rhythm of the horse's stride and try to think of nothing.

Our return to Schiraz was uneventful, though our arrival into the Citadel was greeted with joy and clamour; the people genuinely rejoicing at the safe return of their prince, and unaware of his ordeals, were grateful that war had been avoided. Ijlal did not celebrate; his lover had been weakened and all were concerned for his well-being. I visited them every day, unsure what comfort I could bring. My healing powers were limited. Ijlal's face was tense with emotion. He had just asked me if I could heal his lover the way I had once healed Halim. I hesitated, before I answered that this technique could not be used on Shahulm as he was his lover, his star soul. Shahulm lay pale and unconscious. The rare times he opened his eyes, a faint light of recognition would appear at the sight of Ijlal, and he would slip back into unconsciousness. Occasionally his brow would bead with perspiration, and he became restless.

Although the king of Glesskerel has acquiesced to the union between his son Shahulm and Ijlal, he is nevertheless opposed to his initiation into the mores of Apphat. The alliance of the two kingdoms is tense at best if not tenuous.

The world has changed; it came to the brink of war and receded into an uncomfortable truce. Even Elwah has lost the purpose of his title as the Haafiz, Sacred Keeper of the Stone. Seemingly unperturbed, he has decided to wait until Shahulm's healing is complete and then return to his people. His future as spiritual leader is unknown, never has the Haafiz not borne the Sacred Stone within him, generations of customs and rituals thrown into chaos.

A brief gust of wind from the south overtakes me and throws my headscarf forward. I turn momentarily wondering at the sweet, strange scent of spice on the air; even the horse flares his nostrils fleetingly before resuming his steady journey. The northern star bright and large, sits over the horizon. I correct the direction my mount is taking and urge him on. It is still some hours before I will need to stop for a meal and allow the horse some rest. Once daylight appears, the sun will guide me for a while before stopping for the heat of the day. I could continue but decide that my lack of experience and the absence of visible landmarks, it is safer and more comfortable to travel at night and follow the stars. Once the rugged rocks of Gibrar are in sight, they will remain ahead and to my right hand for a whole day and night. It will then not be long before the Asfaine Mountains become visible on the horizon.

It is the onset of the season of Malkizar, only one of the moons will appear late in the sky. With a twinge of melancholy, I realise that by the time I reach my village, I will have turned twenty-three.

The dunes rise darkly against the star-studded sky, their rim delicately edged in silver, turning the desert into a work of fine filigree. I welcome the brooding silence of the wilderness and continue my journey, aiming now at a slight outcrop in the darkness. There is a well there of fresh spring water, which will be refreshing relief for both my mount and me.

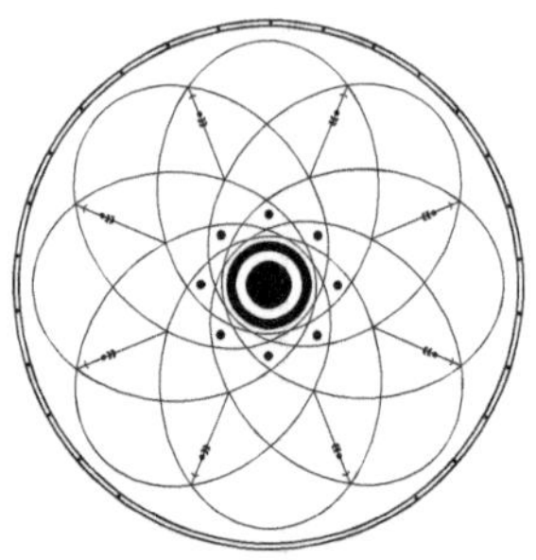

CHAPTER TWO

Some hours have passed. A lump forms in my throat at the recognition of the well I have reached; it is one that Halim had shown me on our way into the desert. It was a constant source of amazement at the time, as to how skilfully he knew his way into this barren land. Feeding the beasts first, he had explained, that many years before when the clans were at war, such wells would be poisoned, preventing their enemies from drinking, thereby weakening them. These days, the wells are clean, but it is best to always be safe, lest some unfortunate creature in its desperation for drink has fallen into it.

I sit having replenished my waterskins with fresh water. My horse is resting, his head down and eyes half closed. Using some of the dry bushes and brambles found here and there, I build a fire. I use the technique my godmother once taught me. Allowing the power to build and surge up my spine, releasing it in one gesture and burst of power, toward the brambles I gathered. Hesitating at first, knowing that what I aim to do is to look into the flames and seek Elwah; the oppressing silence of the desert is too much to bear on this night.

The fire takes hold and steady flames dance in the evening air wavering, then twisting and turning, once for a moment upright and still and then repeats their random moves. I am reminded of my first sight of Shahulm; how that young man danced like the fire to please his prince. There is no equal to him in all the kingdoms. I wonder whether he will recover his spirit. Realising that I have left my mind to wander, I focus back upon the flames and picture the blue eyes of him I want to speak with; the lover of my dreams, Elwah.

Gently, the warmth of his smile replaces the flames of the fire and I see him standing before my mind's eye.

"You are at the well of Shahreza. You have made good time."

I should not be surprised at Elwah's abilities; after all he is the Sacred Haafiz, High Priest of the Naasseenes. I return his smile and for a moment lose myself in the illusion, hoping briefly that he would hold me in his embrace. No doubt reading my every thought, Elwah raises a hand in a sacred gesture towards my heart, and I am filled with the sense of his being.

"How is Shahulm?"

"Recovering gently under the care of Ijlal."

Then sensing what lies behind my words, he adds, "You could not do anymore for him than what you have already done. Be at peace within your mind."

"Elwah, why did the stones disappear? Surely the Power from one of these could restore Shahulm to his health?"

"The power of the Tears of Apphat cannot be used lightly. Their origin in the Cosmos far surpasses individual need. You witnessed what happened to the sorceress."

"Then what is their purpose? Why have you and those before you kept guard over one of them for so long?"

Elwah sighs; his eyes take on a faraway look.

"That is a long story that one Azizi. There are many legends of the origin of the Tears of Apphat, some of which you already know, such as the creation of the two great oceans and the balance of Joy and Sorrow. Although there is some truth in those stories, like all legends they do not tell the whole truth but only allude to a part of it. Many wise men and women have pondered on the Sacred Stones. Very few have been blessed to behold one of them, each were affected in their own individual way, according to their need and their readiness."

Anticipating my question, he adds: "The stories are told in riddles to better hide the Sacred Truth and to encourage the true seekers to discover its secrets. Sacred knowledge is not freely given to those who are not ready to hear it; a true disciple must prove his worthiness through discipline. Yet once understood the riddles are almost childlike in their simplicity. Part of that simplicity, you understood in the one line the prophet had drawn on his deathbed. It confounded generations for thousands of years; yet in one instant, when confronted with the decision to release the Stone to its destiny or hold it for your personal gain, you understood, and you released it. Thus, you do not control the Power, but become an instrument of it and through which it flows freely."

A light breeze blows across the flames, momentarily distracting me. I could not understand the Power that lay behind the Sacred Stones, which at once seemed potent and benevolent and yet so cruel.

Once again, I behold Elwah's kind eyes, and for a moment I see sadness quickly dismissed with a smile. "You will understand Azizi, it is your destiny. The clouds of confusion are only momentary, they too will pass, and the clear light of wisdom will shine upon your mind. For now, though, another who like you seeks answers is seeking you out." He smiles at me.

"What do you mean?"

"Have you not sensed him? He is indeed a careful tracker. Come now Azizi, as certain as spring follows winter, so will your rejoicing emerge." With another enigmatic smile Elwah disappears from my mind.

The cool night air is fanning the glowing embers, sending small constellations of firelight into the sky. A subtle fragrance of orange blossoms hangs in the air for a moment, then disappears.

I look around and can see nothing but distant dunes. I think of Elwah's parting comment. Hasan has gone back to Naassée, besides if it were him that was seeking me out, I would have sensed him and there would be no need for stealth. Sensing no danger, I lie on the sand.

I stare at the multitude of stars above me, wondering at infinity and the power that lies within it. My mind gradually loses sense of what I am contemplating, a void opens before me engulfing me without reason.

"It would be easier for you to rearrange the stars than to comprehend my Nature."

I sit bolt upright, the voice in my ear still ringing and a

warm breath still upon my right cheek. The fire has died down completely; hours have passed. There is no one around. The horse has just stirred from its slumber. I do not remember falling asleep. Feeling somewhat subdued not wanting to interrogate what I have just heard; I make ready to eat for the morning meal before packing my things.

The sky turns an imperceptible shade of lighter cerulean; dawn is a matter of hours away. The constellation of the Fire Beast burns fiercely mid-sky, reminding me of the legend of the Princess of Baltazar, transformed by the need to defend her abducted lover. By her side a group of stars in the form of her unconscious lover, fading fast with the rush of a new day.

How I had scorned at that pretty story of love, and yet still awed at the legend of Love Transformation not seen in over one hundred years. If I had known then that a matter of months later, I would witness the Love Transformation of Ijlal into the Great Spirit Bird Hadid, in defence of his abducted lover, how I would have thought differently on matters of love. I smile wryly to myself at my past innocence in these matters. The knowledge of my Damna and the tender nights spent in the arms of my lover, lending me a sense of maturity and wisdom. I sit quietly chewing on the dried fruits and a special bread baked to last for weeks.

C H A P T E R   T H R E E

The distant and regular thuds of hooves on sand alerts me to a rider, fast approaching from the west. I stand and turn discerning the silhouette of a single horseman travelling at a reckless pace. I wonder if this is the stealthy tracker Elwah spoke of and smile at the lack of covertness, this horseman could be perceived a long way away. I wait standing.

A short time later, the rider pulls his mount to a halt a little distance away and a small figure dismounts. The rider drops the horse's reins and strides towards me. The horse obviously well trained, remains where it stands. By the slight light of early dawn, I make out a desert tribesman, whose garments I am unable to place. I notice the man takes furtive glances, almost I feel to assure himself that I am alone.

"Master Azizi?"

The horseman looks at me directly; a mixture of awe and

curiosity in his eyes is quickly averted as he lowers his gaze.

"How do you know my name?"

"Master all the people know your name; he who defeated the... the Dark One." He hesitates before uttering the last two words.

"What do you want by seeking me out?"

He swallows a little before raising his eyes. "Master, my chieftain has sent me on this quest, hearing that you were travelling alone. One of his wives has fallen ill and none can rouse her from a seeming sleep. She mutters words of dark things. Our people are afraid and seek your help." He pauses in what seems to me a well-rehearsed speech, "In return, our chief will safeguard your passage to your destination."

I look at his face and wonder at this story. Something within me stirs. By a trick of the starlight, his face is momentarily obscured. I hesitate and then ask him,

"What does your tribe trade in this arid land?"

My question unsettles him, and he turns as if seeking an answer from someone who is not there. I begin to suspect he thinks I will be asking for payment for my service.

"Salt, Master. We trade in salt from the great oceans. We take them to the plains people."

"And what do you seek in exchange?"

"Spices, cloth and herbs."

I stare at him and openly admit: "I do not know if I can heal your kinsfolk; it may be beyond my abilities."

The horseman becomes agitated, then suddenly kneels before me and taking my hands in his pleads: "Please master you must come."

A brief sense of revulsion is replaced by pity, there seems to be more than a plea for my agreement, as if he is pleading for himself. Wanting him to release me I agree.

"Very well then. How far is your tribe?"

His demeanour changes as suddenly as his plea. "It is only a two-hour ride from here." He looks at my horse, "Your horse seems rested. We should be on our way."

Reluctantly I check my belongings are secure and ready. I mount my horse and follow my impatient guide. I call after him, "What is your name?"

"Zulfikar."

A shudder runs up my spine, the name has an ominous sound to it.

Zulfikar seems to come to a decision and takes something out of his pocket; handing it to me looking only at the object he is presenting.

"Master, my Chieftain honours you with this gift. It is a talisman of his tribe, a sign of protection to bring you safely to his people."

I look at the object in his hand. It is a dark polished stone with a few markings on it I do not recognise. As soon as sighted, the markings seem to blend into the dark background. Mesmerised, I reach out for the stone and the moment I touch it, I see a flash of cobalt, Elwah's outstretched hand, which fades as quickly as it appeared. I find myself holding the talisman, a sense of dull comfort fills me that seems out of balance with my mind.

I follow my guide who has gone silent and occasionally glances back, checking that I am still following behind. There is something in his eyes that makes me feel uncomfortable, but I remind myself of the oath I took, to always use the healing power that flows through me for all those who are in need. The outline of my horse's head blurs and comes into focus alternately. A feeling of nausea stirs in my stomach, and I try to think of what I may have eaten that would cause this discomfort. Cold sweat beads on my forehead and a part of me panics at the thought of falling into a trance at the taste of salt. I gaze into the distance desperately seeking calm.

By my reckoning looking at the last fading stars and the stirring of dawn, I note that we are heading in a north westerly direction. What seems only a short dreamlike passage of time and I realise that we are approaching a settlement. I struggle to stay focussed and feel as though I have not had enough sleep. The talisman is still in my hand, alternating between feeling warm in a clammy kind of way and ice cold. Part of me feels repulsed and would like to let it go, but my hand is firmly clenched on it and will not obey my instinct.

Strands of light illuminate the horizon and I can make out a group of tents; a few palm trees mark out a small oasis. Judging where the light on the horizon is strongest indicating where the sun will rise, this must be the well near the city of *Yasad*.

As we approach the camp, I am surprised that no one comes out to greet us; an eerie silence pervades the air, not even the birds appear to be stirring yet.

As if sensing my discomfort the rider turns briefly, his face devoid of the previous doubts, his eyes burning with barely disguised hatred states quite abruptly:

"I am to take you directly to my chieftain."

He has dismounted his horse and is presently leading mine, making for a larger tent nearest the palms. I notice as I approach a large wooden pole driven into the ground, a chain attached to the pole hangs down to the ground. It has the look of something used to tie a dangerous animal.

Another shudder runs up my spine. I feel tired, my strength seems to seep out of my body.

He tethers the horses near a palm tree closest to the tent. Roughly he almost drags me off my horse and I stumble to the ground. I lean against him for support wondering at the change in his attitude. I see him take up the loose end of his keffiyeh and hold it to his face. The gesture strikes me as strange and even rude. A small voice is screaming inside my head, but I cannot comprehend what it says, the words are jumbled as if spoken through water.

We enter the tent; I collapse to the ground and Zulfikar quietly leaves the way he came. My head feels heavy and droops forward; on my knees my arms can barely hold my weight. With agonising effort, I sluggishly look around. The interior of the tent is empty; a few oil lamps are burning, smouldering heavily from their poorly trimmed wicks. The air is stale, heavy with smoke and other odours I cannot make out, but which increase my feeling of nausea. A distant recollection of my god mother's instructions on herbs that cause a state of unconsciousness, drifts into what is left of my conscious mind.

What seems an eternity passes. A movement to one side of the tent draws my attention. Lifting my head takes all my strength. A dark shape is approaches deliberately. Someone is draped in full desert garb. A large masculine hand holds the cloth tight against his face. Dark eyes peer, the man leans toward me, almost cautiously it seems.

Raising a foot, he pushes me at the shoulder, and I collapse unable to resist. The man barks an order:

"Take him outside and clear the tent of this foul smell."

Flaps of the tent are suddenly moved aside, air flowing clearing the smoke. Two men enter and each taking an arm drag me towards the wooden pole. Roughly they bind my hands together and attach these to the metal ring at the end of the chain. The chain is dragged, unable to resist, my body slides up the pole until I can barely touch the ground with my feet. The strain on my arms is only just bearable, but my breath becomes shallow, my posture making it difficult to breathe, darkness threatening to take my consciousness. The stone has fallen out of my hand and lies upon the sand at my feet. A tiny remnant of my instincts glimpses that the talisman was designed to render me servile; it was magic, dark magic of the kind that is forbidden to practice.

At the abrupt command of the large man, Zulfikar has thrown the contents of my belongings on the ground. I cannot comprehend what they are looking for. The smoke from the tent still dulls my senses.

"They are not there Master."

"Of course, they are not there fool." A soft sibilant voice, with all the darkness of foul oil makes its way from the tent to stand in front of me.

The hairs on the back of my neck rise despite my near state of unconsciousness. A woman dressed in dark clothes stands before me. Her skin is black, crisscrossed with several scars that are clearly not battle wounds but signs of initiation. My heart sinks at the sight of the three red intersecting swords emblazoned on the front of her abaya. My mind reels at the memory of seeing this on the Sorceress in my last confrontation. Her eyes black as caverns burn with a pure hatred. With a cruel twist of her mouth she orders, "They are most likely to be on him. Strip him!"

A small grimly cynical voice in my head, questions the morbid fascination these witches have, to see me naked. Zulfikar approaches me with a jubilant air of contempt and derision. Ruthlessly he pulls off my garment throwing them to the ground and leaves me naked. It is obvious that what they are looking for is not on my person.

"Do as you wish with him. He is of no consequence." The witch walks off leaving me at the hands of the henchman. The others have already broken up camp and having loaded their beasts unhurriedly move out into the desert. The last person leaves with a backward look at Zulfikar, calling out something in a foreign dialect.

"Do you know what my name means?" Zulfikar's tone is now oily, revelling with the prospect of slow torture.

I stare at him, wondering at my carelessness for letting myself be caught so easily. Another part of me wondering why Elwah would not have foreseen this and warned me. His last words running around in my head like a meaningless echo.

Zulfikar bursts out in an insane laugh, he produces a large axe, gleefully showing it off.

"My name, my name in the desert language means Spine Cleaver!"

Again, he bursts out a maniacal laugh.

That same chill down my spine, now runs in recognition of what I should have remembered when I first heard his name.

He drops the axe by his side, adding, "There will be time for that shortly." He then pulls out a long knife, the blade sharpened to a hairline's width.

He approaches deliberately and with measured sadistic steps. Leaning into me he whispers, "You may not have the Sacred Stones, but at least I can have yours, as my trophy." And with that I feel his murderous hand grab hold of my balls.

Ice fills my gut; my body begins to shake uncontrollably. I strain uselessly against my bonds, the rope cutting deeply into my wrists. Zulfikar laughs at my struggle. Suddenly his laugh turns to a shriek. He begins to scream in pain as he falls to the ground. A large white wolf is tearing him apart. A young man with hair the colour of a late sunset steps forward and stands looking on. The wolf makes short work of Zulfikar, ripping his throat in one powerful shake of his head. All his tribe have left long ago, there is no one left but this young man and I to witness the death of a notorious killer.

Surprise then shock registers as I struggle to understand what has just happened. I know that there are desert wolves, rare as they are, white ones even more rare. They are large furtive animals with broad padded paws to better protect themselves from the heat of the desert sands. But now I struggle to remember where I have seen this youth. He stands almost as tall as me. There is mischief in his pale emerald green eyes as he looks directly at me. Without a spoken word his eyes still locked with mine, he ambles over casually stepping over the bleeding body of Zulfikar, and gathering my clothes, first unties me from my bonds and offers me my robe that I may regain my modesty. A brief scent of orange blossoms and cinnamon hangs in the air and dissipates.

Allowing me room to dress, he moves a few paces and stands looking at me almost smiling. I have a sense that he is enjoying the mystery he offers. Then, casually with a shy smile lifting the hem of one of the legs of his trousers, reveals his ankle. I stare, confounded. I look down. There is a perfectly good ankle, no bracelets adorn it. His skin is pale as sheep's milk. I gasp. There right above the ankle is a small scar. Recognition hits me and I look up to stare at those emerald green eyes.

"Saeed?"

His smile turns into a glorious beam, showing off a set of perfect white teeth.

He comes over then. "Yes. Master Azizi."

"Saeed. But how did you? Where did you..." All my questions suddenly pour out. Confusion and elation mixed at the sight of my young rescuer, who was once a boy I saved from the poison of a desert scorpion. Fariqua's young man, now grown up.

His apparition is absurd, incongruous with what has just happened. The white wolf satisfied at his kill, ambles towards the Oasis, and begins to drink and wash itself. A surge of sadness wells up inside me. Relieved at my deliverance but hurt at having had my body exposed and invaded, I feel dirty. The answers can wait. Unhurriedly without a word, I walk to the edge of the oasis. The small clear pool of water reflects the morning sky and the two nakhla trees that grow on its banks. This oasis is one of the rare ones, where the water is permanent. The base is formed mostly of large rocks and pebbles. The water flows from deep inside the earth, filling this depression in the middle of the desert. Testing the water with my toes first, I don't hesitate long, and walk in fully clothed until I am chest deep in the water. My muscles relax, anxiety and sadness that has built up is released. I cry openly letting my tears wash away in the cool waters. I take my clothes off to wash those as well. I scoop up a handful of sand and scrub until all feelings of invasion have washed away.

The white wolf is looking at me unerringly, its striking blue eyes the colour of sapphires fixed on me. Its expression one of intrigue and, cocking its head to one side looks almost amused at me.

The sunlight floods the desert, dark steel blue shadows form and melt behind the surrounding dunes, moving with the rising sun. The sand begins to glow a light yellow turning now to almost brilliant white.

Saeed retrieves my clothes, wrings the water from them and lays them on the sand to dry. Opening a bag, he carries on his back; he draws out a tunic and offers it to me as I emerge from my makeshift bath. I am deeply grateful and gladly slip into it. It is a perfect size for my slight build. I smile in gratitude and Saeed in reply briefly smiles back, bows his head in acknowledgement but I perceive his cheeks begin to blush.

I look up towards the pole that still stands as stark reminder of my recent ordeal, possible mutilation and a certain death. The body of my tormentor is lying still bleeding upon the sand, disfigured by the white wolf, which sits immobile as a statue a little apart, his sapphire eyes still on me.

"Thank you, Saeed, you have saved my life. I have many questions to ask you, but first let us leave this place, I fear it is cursed for now."

Saeed picks up his bag and my belongings. Miraculously, my horse, which I thought would have been taken by the tribe's people is left behind, obviously for the use of Zulfikar the murderer.

My wrists are still sore from the bonds that held me stretched upright, holding the reins of the horse is difficult, the horse is restless, its eyes wide at the sight and smell of the white wolf. I reassure it as best as I can, finally making the decision not to mount but gently lead it away. Saeed has packed his things and gathered what is left of mine and secured them in his pack.

We move away from the oasis the rising sun on our right. We walk silently, Saeed next to me matching my pace. My heart skips a beat, realising that he has the same desert steps Halim used when we first came on a late springtime. He had shown me how to walk to maximise the efficiency in this harsh land. I notice however that Saeed, steps in a way that desert people use to hide their tracks. Anyone coming up behind us, would think that there was only one traveller with a lame horse and the possibility, that a desert wolf was carefully stalking them.

My instincts are taking over, I head towards the well of Shahreza, where I had stopped the previous night. By my reckoning it should only be an hour away. Saeed has not spoken a word and maintains a youthful but measured stride, continuing with the subtle disguise of his steps. In any case, once the wind rises later in the day, it will erase all signs of our passage. The wolf has gradually taken a position next to my horse. I notice with a slight amusement, that it has placed itself in its shadow, cleverly keeping cool. At first my horse shows signs of nervousness, staring with wide eyes and making a muffled noise shaking his head. The wolf taking no notice, keeps pace. Gradually I notice my horse becomes accustomed to its presence.

As the shadows shorten with the rising sun, it is not long before the well of Shahreza appears over the horizon.

As we reach the well, the sun is truly at its zenith. Saeed has wrapped his *shemagh* around his head and neck to best protect himself from the burning sun. He takes his pack off his back and pulls out a tightly wrapped package, around which are short flexible pieces of a strange wood. I had once seen these at a market with Hasan, they are like long tubes, strong and yet flexible enough to allow them to be bent. He unwraps a large piece of cloth and feeds those wooden tubes through tight pockets along the seams. I stare in amazement as I see him construct a makeshift tent. It has no real walls or entrance but large enough to afford at least two persons to shelter underneath it. Having seen these in the marketplace, I understand that it can also be used as a practical barrier against a strong wind.

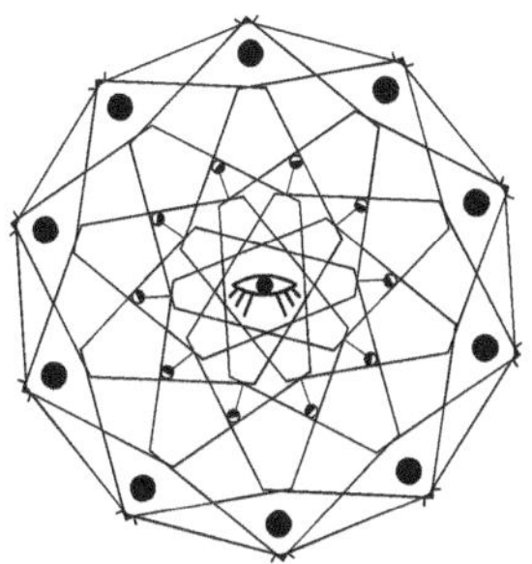

CHAPTER FOUR

We settle for a midday break, and we wait until the sun begins to sink to the horizon, making our journey cooler with the afternoon breeze. Saeed invites me to sit with him under the shelter of his makeshift tent. He offers me a piece of unleavened bread, my mouth waters just realising how hungry I am. The bread is a baked staple of the desert people, which keeps for many days. It is chewy but tasty. He looks at me openly inviting me to ask my questions.

"I am deeply grateful to you Saeed, thank you. How did you happen to appear in time and how did you know where to find me?" I cannot help but stare and admire the exquisite combination of his smooth white skin, mass of red curly hair and most strikingly, his emerald green eyes.

Saeed smiles, takes a breath, and begins, "I am happy to have returned the favour." Referring to his own rescue as a boy.

He continues, "I have recently reached the age of manhood; accordingly, our culture expects that a boy entering manhood should undertake a desert journey. This journey is not only to test my skill of survival in our land, but it is a means also for me to find my place in our society. I must gain respect as I enter our society as a responsible man. I may or may not return to my tribe once completed, but if I do, I will be welcomed not as Saeed the boy, but as an adult. I will then be given my adult name. Until then, I have cut all ties with my family and my tribe. I am not to return unless I have fulfilled my task. It was my mother's advice to seek you out for training in the arts of healing and magic. With her blessing and the permission of the tribe elders, I started on my voyage to find you a lahé ago."

I look at him both in admiration and bewilderment. If my calculations are accurate, he could not be more than fifteen, at most sixteen years old. I do not know if I could have undertaken such a journey at his age on my own. My initiation consisted of attaining certain skills as a healer and magician. It was only then that I gained my adult name.

"Saeed, you say that you left only a lahé ago. It would take a caravan twice as long to reach the oasis. I do not understand how it is that you could cover such distance in such a short time."

Saeed smiles to himself, "I travel as my ancestors have and the way I was taught – desert speed, on foot at a gentle run and without stopping."

I admired him before, now I am truly in awe of him. I cannot take my eyes off him. Saeed in return, only smiles and blushes slightly at my stare.

"Saeed, then tell me how you found me and how did you know

I would be in need of help?"

For a moment he seems in a daze, his eyes focused on something I cannot see. A small furrow of concentration forms between his eyes. He shakes his head once, his brow creases once more as if he is shaking off a thought or dream.

"I set off from our tribe's home in the *Huda* Pass and intended to make my way to the Desert City of *Ahvasar*. I thought it was most likely that travelling from *Shiraz*, you would be making your way to the Oasis of *Shahreza*. I was hoping to cut across your path and wait for you there." Saeed pauses for a moment, "But as I came out of the high cliffs of Huda pass, the light from the setting sun seemed to play a trick. An unusual white haze appeared over the sands of the desert, as if a small *habud* was forming, it seemed to be a *khamsin*."

I frown in confusion. Resuming, he explains, "a younger version of the Casim. It travelled towards the entrance to the Huda Pass. I was both frightened and mesmerised by this." Saeed pauses, he swallows hard, visibly still shaken by this sight. "Then, the sand that formed the khamsin, started to thin out. I thought it would dissipate as most small storms do. Suddenly the form of a man appeared, his loose clothes ablaze with the light of the midday sun and fluttering as if caught in a whirlwind. He walked steadily toward me. I found that I could not move. As he approached, I distinguished his features in detail; his hair is the colour of the sands, and his eyes a pure blue of the morning sky." Saeed did not need to go into any further details. I remember the first time I saw Prince Elwah, as we were preparing to enter the Huda Pass.

"He greeted me by my name and smiled in such a way that I felt immediately at ease. When he spoke, it seemed that he spoke directly to my mind. I do not remember seeing his lips move."

Saeed's face softens, he closes his eyes briefly, reliving the moment Prince Elwah appeared to him in the middle of the desert. A small pang of sadness fills my heart, thinking that when I thought I needed him, he did not or could not come to me, but instead met this young man.

Saeed again pauses for what seems an eternity. I want to hear how Elwah instructed him to find me, and a part of me desperately wants to know why he could not come to me.

Saeed's eyes refocus, "This is what he told me: 'Azizi is in grave danger. You must hurry. I tried to make him resist the charm he was being placed under, but I am not able to help him. I no longer hold one of the Tears of Apphat. The dark magic of a sorceress is too strong for me. Follow the cliffs of the Huda Pass, there along the cliffs I will send you a guardian spirit to assist you. You will then be able to cross the desert in a much shorter distance. Make haste and find him at the Oasis of Shahreza.'"

Saeed exhales deeply. "As soon as he had spoken in my mind, his form melted as a sarab in the midday sun. I set off at the best speed I could without exhausting myself. I followed the cliffs of Huda as instructed. On the second day I began to sense a presence behind me. Every time I turned to see who was following, there was just empty sand dunes. That night, the moon of Camlac was full and had risen early. I found a small hollow in the rock face where I could take a rest. Only a few moments later I felt the urge to keep moving.

As I stepped out of the hollow, I froze in shock. A large white wolf sat at the entrance. Its white fur glowing in the full moon. I knew that the cliffs along the desert edge were inhabited by wild animals, in particular small predators. There were stories of desert wolves and even legends of a large albino, white as the sands. It made no move but seemed to wait for me. Cautiously I decided to begin walking. I thought that if I started to run, it would attack for certain. It did not move but simply stared at me, its blue eyes even more eerie by the moonlight.

I heard the voice the man who had appeared to me in my mind, again telling me that he would send a guardian spirit to help me. I felt reassured. Contrary to my instincts to move away from this fearsome animal, I crouched and waited. The wolf bowing its head gently and silently, came toward me. Not more than two paces from me, it sat and looked directly into my eyes. The most extraordinary thing happened, the blue of its eyes turned to a dark brown, almost black. I briefly saw the face of a young man, which melted away as soon as it had appeared. It seemed to me that I had seen that face before but could not remember where or when. Now that the wolf sat so close to me, I noticed that around its neck, its white fur is coloured in a thin darker line, almost as if it wore a fine collar. I stood up then completely calm, realising where I had seen that face. Without a second thought I resumed my journey with a swell of energy in my heart, knowing that I had to find you quickly. The wolf easily matched my pace running on soft, silent padded paws.

As the sun rose, the wolf, which by now was running beside me, came to a complete stop and crouched low onto the sand, its long-pointed ears twitching. Crouching down beside it, I stared in the direction its ears were pointing. I made out a caravan that was making its way across the desert. It would be coming from the oasis of *Shahreza*. They were heading to the Desert city of

Ahvasar. Something about their dark clothing made me cautious and I lay still until they had passed.

At once the wolf leaped up and with one look at me started to run. I had a difficult time to keep up with its speed, and it would from time to time let me catch up. Master Azizi, the rest you know, we came upon you just in time."

A long silence follows. I stare at my rescuer, waves of emotion filling my chest. Tears well up in gratitude. "Thank you, Saeed." I pause, a question remains unanswered. "I do not understand how this wolf can be a Spirit Guardian. I am deeply grateful of its help. I know that without your intervention I would not be alive now."

Saeed stares momentarily at me, then smiles gently. "But Master yes, it is a wolf but look closely, surely you know that Spirit Guardians can sometimes inhabit an animal."

I look at the wolf and without hesitation it casually ambles and sits opposite me. It then lifts his head and looks at me directly. The piercing blue eyes are disconcerting at first. Captivated by the steady gaze of this wolf, I stare back. The air around it begins to blur, the dunes seem to recede. My body begins to float, and I hear the distant voice of my god mother reciting one of the sacred Parvus. I cannot make out which one it is. I vaguely remember a story of a fire beast and a prince in love. The faint fragrance of straw permeates the midday air. I hear a distant familiar tune. The eyes of the wolf turn a dark brown, a soft gentle face smiles back at me with pure innocence.

"Halim!" My heart explodes into tears of both sorrow and joy.

"Halim!" I call out to him, punctuated with my sobs, and he still smiles at me. Such a gentle smile that breaks my heart. How can this be, my mind reels but I don't want to lose him, so I call out to him again and again.

The image of Halim begins to fade and, in its place, the cold stare of the wolf's blue eyes. The wolf tilts its head in a quizzical fashion, a question mark at my tears.

I look up and see tears well up in Saeed's pale emerald green eyes, a look of concern on his face.

I wipe my tears away. With a twinge of embarrassment, I realise that other than Elwah or Hasan, I have not wept openly in front of someone. I look back at the wolf, which has just settled beside me, its head touching my leg. It occasionally looks up.

"Master, do you recognise this young Spirit Guardian? You call him Halim. I do not know that name."

A tightness in my heart threatens another outpouring of emotion. Breathing deliberately and deeply, I regain some control.

"Halim..." I almost choke at the word. "Halim is... was from my village."

Saeed nods and waits. "He was very dear to me. We were the same age. I met him in my forest when I had just turned thirteen. He was a shepherd," my voice falters at the memory.

"Ah," a look of comprehension and memory washes across Saeed's face. "It was him who supplied our tribes with sheep skins and dried herbs. This is how I remember his face."

A lump forms in my throat. Halim has left a legacy that will last for many years to come.

Saeed looks at me, a question forming on his face, and then he thinks better of it. I think I can guess. "He was murdered by a scarlet robe before I could do anything to save him."

A heavy silence follows. The wolf raises his head and moving forward rests it on my lap, looking at me intensely. I am not sure how to respond and an automatic gesture forms as I reach out and gently stroke him on the head. My thoughts wander. It seems that Halim's spirit has chosen to inhabit this wolf to protect me. The irony of a shepherd spirit in a wolf's skin almost makes me smile. I recall the ferocity with which it attacked my aggressor. It was the same courage and fierceness with which Halim had defended prince Ijlal and me from an attack of a Shadow in my forest.

"Master Azizi, I think it recognises you."

I do not understand how this is possible. "Did Elwah share with you any knowledge of how this came about?"

"I'm sorry master, who is Elwah?"

Of course, Saeed would not know the man that appeared to him.

"The man who gave you instructions to find me, is Prince Elwah of the *Naasseenes*. Ruler and a high priest of magic."

A nod is quickly replaced by a look of awe on Saeed's face. He visibly swallows at the news. "Oh...," is all he can manage to say. "But..."

I think the same thought has occurred to him; why couldn't Elwah come to my rescue, why choose him instead?

I give voice to his question, "I don't understand either. Why would Prince Elwah choose to send someone, and go to the trouble of finding a Guardian Spirit to inhabit the body of a wolf?"

Saeed a little flustered, looks down at the ground.

"Master Azizi, I do not know about the wolf and how the spirit of your friend came to possess the wolf. I had asked p... prince," Saeed hesitates with the title, "Elwah, why he had chosen me for this task. He answered that although he had the power to do so, his burden as Hafiz, prohibited him from taking a life. He also said that there was a destiny, which he could not intervene with."

There followed a silence, filled with more questions than answers.

"As for the wolf Master, I do not know how that came about. Perhaps it is the love that you have for Halim that drew his spirit to offer protection, where prince Elwah could not?"

The love transformation? Love? Love for Halim, certainly. But a transformation? No, I doubt that. There was no transformation. His spirit somehow found me, perhaps through Elwah's doing. My knowledge of Elwah as a high priest of magic; the powers that he has displayed in transferring the Sapphire of Joy directly into my being; even just his ability to know me and my thoughts. His knowledge of my sadness for the loss of Halim. Perhaps, his compassion is enough to make me wonder, whether somehow, Elwah managed to find Halim's spirit, and draw him back as a Guardian Spirit for my protection.

"Saeed?"

"Yes, master Azizi?"

"Please Saeed, do not call me master. I have only gained initiation to the First Order. It will be a while, before I am ordained as a master of magic and healing. Just call me Azizi."

Saeed looks down. Those unblemished white cheeks turning the colour of blushing peaches. His reaction is so like Halim when I had made the same request, that I smile at the memory.

"Saeed?"

"Yes mast... Azizi?"

"What was your plan, beyond fulfilling Elwah's direction to

rescue me?"

A long pause follows, as he reflects on his own initiation. Once more his face flushes with colour. "It was my intention to seek you." Saeed pauses, unsure how to go on, then hesitatingly, "I have come of age, not only to make my way in my tribe as a man, but... since meeting you in the desert, when you saved me from the poison of the scorpion, I have wanted to learn from you, the art of healing, and..." he looks down at his feet, he takes a deep breath and goes on, "and the art of magic."

Conflicting emotions and thoughts prevent me from responding immediately. Thinking perhaps that I would refuse him, he blurts out, "I may not be worthy, Azizi, but please consider that I will work hard to follow your instructions."

Then as another thought occurs to him, blushing this time until his face is red, he adds, "I know that to be worthy as a healer of Apphat, I will need to be initiated into the order, following the rites of the Naasseenes." There he stops and looking up from his feet to meet my eyes, "I am," he hesitates, this time he swallows hard, "I have never had relations with either a girl or man. To you, Azizi, I am willing to give myself."

He has just told me that he is a virgin, and that he wants me to initiate him into the rites of manhood, according to the rites of the Naasseenes, and the order of Apphat.

A mixture of compassion, confusing thoughts, and emotions battle within me.

My mind anxiously searches for a way to gently refuse him and not destroy him in the process. Four years have passed since I walked into the Great Desert of Keyab with Halim. I am twenty-two years old. I do not consider myself old enough or experienced enough, to initiate someone into *Damna*. I wonder also at his age, though he tells me that he has entered the required tests of manhood, he still looks young. His chin and cheeks, still showing the soft down of boyhood. Smooth unblemished, pale skinned and yet aware of his own sexuality, what the ancients in Naassée would call a *Kurus* – not quite a man but not a boy either. Although his voice has deepened, I doubt that he would be older than fifteen, perhaps sixteen at a push.

"Saeed." He looks at me with all the eagerness of youth. "Saeed, how old were you when I met you with your mother and father in the desert?"

"I had just turned thirteen."

He must have been a very young looking thirteen-year-old. I thought at the time he could have been no more than ten or twelve. Is he lying to sway me? But then I remember Niclas, the apprentice to the bookbinder, he looked no older than fifteen but in fact was twenty-five. Some men never seem to grow old until they reach their middle years. Briefly I look at him with the second sight. There is nothing in his *hala* that suggests deceit. So, that would make him seventeen.

I ask him directly, "How old are you now?"

Without hesitation he answers, "I am seventeen. On the next moon of *Elwah* I will be eighteen."

That is at least another eight *mahé* away.

Relaxing a little, having formulated a response, I smile at him and hope that my words will not be taken too harshly.

"Saeed, your virginity is a special gift, not to be squandered or given away to just anyone without due consideration. It should be a celebration of your coming of age. It is your ability to love someone intimately and give yourself unconditionally. It should be reserved for that person, who will treasure your gift as priceless and value your company for the rest of your days."

Disappointment clearly written; his face immediately falls a little. He remains silent, his eyes pleading a little.

"Saeed, although you are of an age that is considered amongst men, appropriate for *damna*, I sense that I am not the one destined to take you into that sacred ritual. As for training you into the arts of healing and magic, that is another matter." I pause. Tears are welling up in Saeed's eyes. An expression of disappointment and hurt clearly etched.

I see defeat in his eyes, his beautiful smile reminding me so much of Halim. His soft, milk like skin, that so invites to be touched, the obvious curves of the onset of manhood showing, all generate within me, clouded emotions and thoughts that battle to uphold my decision. Sensing perhaps my inner confusion, struggling to speak, he asks, "Azizi?" I nod in acknowledgement.

"Is it permitted to ask how old you were, when you were initiated into *damna*?"

I reflect, thinking back to the day Hasan took my in his loving arms.

"I was eighteen Saeed. I had just turned eighteen."

I can see that he wants to draw a comparison. I was only one year older than he is now. Hoping that my next words will not in any way appear to offer capitulation, but simply a way to acknowledge his feelings as real and true, I hesitate,

"Saeed," wiping his eyes hurriedly, he looks up, "Saeed, truly you honour me."

He smiles then, perhaps a hint of hope showing. So, I hurry to add, "Saeed, I would love you as my younger brother. Your love is too precious to me, to ask for anything else."

He looks down at his feet. Clearly not the answer he was hoping to hear.

"Master Azizi. What of training me into the art of magic and healing?"

'*Master*', there it is, that distance that places me out of reach. It brings a twist of pain to my heart. The loneliness of power.

"Saeed, I will tell you what my godmother told me, when I asked her a similar question. The knowledge of Sacred Lore is passed from *Mahjir* to apprentice. The title of *Mahjir* is only given to one who has achieved the highest level of mastery. As an apprentice, you would dedicate yourself to learn everything that is given to you. The first level will take four years unless you complete it earlier. At that point, you will be initiated into the First Order of Apphat as a Healer and Magician in training. Beyond the first order of initiation, there are two more orders to complete before being accepted as Master or Mahjir. At each stage of initiation, you will be tattooed with the mark relevant to your level of achievement."

I pause wanting all that to sink into his consciousness.

"This means Saeed, that if you decide to embark upon this path, you will be twenty-one years old when you complete your First Order, unless your understanding and gifts propel you to a shorter course. Think of this Saeed, I was thirteen when my god mother took me as her apprentice. I have only completed my First Order as a Healer and Magician of Apphat. I am uncertain that I am qualified to train another. I do not know if the Council of Elders would allow me to train someone, before I have gained the advanced level of training myself.

My training took on a different turn, when it was decided that I should protect prince Ijlal, and look for the Sacred Tears of Apphat, to defeat the sorceress."

"My mother told me of the feat that you performed in the Huda pass, to clear a barrier that was deemed insurmountable." His words take on a note of accusation, a confirmation that already, I am recognised as a powerful magician. "She was awed at the power you displayed, that of the Tears of Apphat."

I sigh at the memory, "That kind of power comes at a cost Saeed. If improperly used, or if the magician in training is not ready, it can destroy you in an instant." And then in a moment of sorrowful memory I add, "That power was useless, when it came to protect Halim from the murderous knife of a Scarlet Robe."

He is looking at me, not in awe. I suddenly find his gaze unsettling. It is not one of envy, nor of fear at the power that has flowed through me. This gaze is one of devotion. His eyes see me as I am. Azizi, Aldrik, the boy who grew up too fast to realise what love truly is.

And now, I realise, that I am such an idiot.

A flood of recent moments rush into my mind.

The gentle touch of his hands as he untied me from my bonds. The casual stare at my nakedness, the blush of his cheeks as he humbly offered me my clothes to protect my modesty. The way he took care to dry my clothes, his generosity as he offered me one of his own robes. And just now, as he offered his virginity, not to just anyone, but to me. And all I gave him in return, is a lecture on modesty and chastity that my father would have been proud of. I feel like such a fool.

Saeed is in love with me, and I have been too blind to see it.

"Oh Saeed." I go to him. I help him to his feet and gently, I enfold him in my arms. The subtle fragrance of orange blossoms envelops us both. He is a little astonished and resists me. Gradually his body relaxes, and he lets me hold him. Then softly he begins to sob and holds on to me. I hold him tighter. "Oh Saeed, thank you for your love. I have only just realised what you are telling me. I have been so blind to your feelings. Thank you."

I look at his beautiful face, tears coursing down his soft cheeks. Tenderly I wipe his tears with my thumb. Looking up he attempts a smile, his green eyes awash with tears. My heart races in my chest. He looks so fragile; I want to hold him and tell him that everything will be well. A rational part of my mind begins a subtle argument, already giving me the reasons that I should not have held him so, that I should have said nothing and let him be, that this will get complicated. I remember my godmother's advice on poisons of the heart. I tell my mind to be quiet, and I listen to my heart that only knows love.

C H A P T E R   F I V E

We sit a while, looking at each other. The communion of silence between us is not awkward as I had feared. For the most part, Saeed, looks at his hands and then occasionally looks up with a smile of pure innocence that lights up his face. Saeed's expression of total devotion and admiration threatens to undo me completely.

"Saeed?"

Completely attentive, with a serious countenance, he waits.

"Saeed, are you then willing to pursue training in Healing and Magic?"

His eyes brighten, before he answers, "yes".

Weighing my words carefully, so as not to give him false hope, or for that matter to hurt him, I continue, "As I have said, I am not sure that the Council of Elders will allow me to train, without having fulfilled a more advance level of training myself." I can see Saeed's face drop a little. "What I need to do is to speak to one of the Elders, and possibly my godmother as well, and seek their advice and permission."

A little hope returns to his eyes.

"Saeed, I do not know what decision will be made. But I can promise you this, regardless of who trains you; that I will ensure that you receive the best training and I commit myself to be with you, as often as I can throughout your instruction. I hope then to be a guide and a source of encouragement and comfort for you."

At this point, this is the best I can offer and promise. Saeed realises this now and is willing to accept. He nods his understanding. The promise of being with me often, alleviates his fear of being abandoned.

"We need to travel to Naassée and speak with the elders. I think it should only be a day's journey."

Saeed says nothing, smiles and nods his head and begins to pack our belongings.

A cool breeze rises from the east, the ocean of Elwah, bringing with it the faintest smell of salt. Saeed's head turns into the flow of air, raising his head, he sniffs the air long and deep. Turning to me, he smiles, lighting his features; truly his name does him justice. It means bright and lucky.

"The weather tonight and tomorrow will be fine."

My initial astonishment at his ability is quickly replaced with the knowledge that as a desert dweller, he will have developed a keen sense of weather forecasting. I remember his mother, Fariqa, who was able to read the weather and recognise an *Ahl Cassim* well before it manifested, even as an audible sound.

The sun has disappeared over the horizon, setting the sky

into dying embers, that quickly eclipses into a purple twilight. Constellations of stars begin to twinkle into existence in the vastness of the sky. Looking to the north, I identify the Great Fire Beast. Pointing it out to Saeed, I rest my hand on his shoulder, a thrill of satisfaction at the intimacy courses through me. I direct his gaze with my other hand, "Saeed, do you know the name of that constellation?"

He looks up, "The desert people call that one Agapé. It is a sad one."

I am curious to know how they came to name it that way. "Why is it sad, Saeed?"

"It means Sacrificial Love. It is a legend of a young girl who sacrificed herself to save her lover."

A shiver runs through me. I am astounded at the similarity of the story.

"Azizi, what do you call it?"

"It is named the Great Fire Beast." He looks at me inquiringly, and so I tell him the legend of the Princess of *Balthazar*.

He listens attentively, occasionally looking up into the sky. He sighs, turning his head to me, adds, "That is also a sad story."

We walk on in silence through the night, occasionally looking up into the sky.

"Azizi," I wait for him to continue, "Azizi, I do not know the way to Naassèe." I look up into the sky, making sure that I keep sight of the Fire Beast constellation. Calling it by the name he knows, "we must follow Agape, but as it sinks to the horizon, we need to turn and make sure that our destination lies between it and the stars that resemble a man lying down."

Reflecting on the instructions, he looks up making sure that we are on the right path. He turns then and asks, "Will this then take us to the ocean of Elwah?"

"Yes, or at least to the cliffs overlooking the ocean."

Saeed is pensive. "I have never seen the ocean of Elwah."

I consider his statement and realise that neither have I; knowing only its position and surrounds from the maps I studied with my godmother, and the writings about Naassée. "It will be the first time for me as well."

Saeed looks at me with surprise. I explain, "My journey with Halim into the desert of Keyab, to find the Sacred Tears and defeat the sorceress, was the first time I left my home in the Asfaine Mountains."

Saeed nods. While he would have accompanied his parents on some journeys, most of his time would have been spent with his maternal grandmother and the Huda tribe.

The soft squeak of the horse's hooves upon the sand and the gentle tinkling of some of the metal clips on the bridle, the only sounds accompanying us. The sun has set some hours ago. The temperature drops noticeably and although it is getting cold, I find it comfortable, a reminder of my home.

"Azizi?" He pauses considering his question. "Azizi, would you tell me of your mountain home?" He brings the horse to a stop, opens one of the large satchels and pulls out two coats made of sheep skin and wool. He hands me one and puts on the other.

A smile drifts across my face. My heart beats a little faster as I recall my beloved home in the mountains, surrounded by tall trees, moss and ferns. It will not be long now for the snows to cover the tops of the mountains. An ache of longing fills my being and settles like a nervous squirrel in the pit of my stomach. How do I describe snow to someone, who has never seen it fall from the sky or stepped into it? Or even the experience of a cold, harsh winter night, when the water turns to ice?

"Do you feel how cold it becomes here at night?" Saeed nods giving a little shiver. "Imagine then, that it becomes so cold that one coat would not be enough to keep you warm." He looks at me puzzled. "My home is in the Asfaine mountains. During the season of Malkizar, the wind begins to blow from the north, and the air cools down very quickly and stays cool for the next six *mahée*. During that time, we stay indoors as much as possible and light fires to keep warm."

Saeed's face clouds over with disbelief, "You light fires inside your house?" I laugh at his inexperience.

"Yes, we have special spaces in the house that are made of rocks. We call these fireplaces, in which we burn wood to keep the house warm." I can see that he is contemplating such a thing with difficulty. "Saeed, you have seen water, such as in an oasis in the desert and the water that flows from some rocks in the Huda Pass." He nods. "But have you ever seen the water turn to ice?"

A beautiful expression of a question mark on his face makes me smile.

"Ice Azizi? What is ice?"

"It is when the air is so cold that the water becomes solid, like a rock and it can only go back to water if it is brought near a fire, or it warms up gradually with the sun. On the coldest days, the surface of the waters of the rivers turn to ice. One can even walk on it, they are so solid."

I am certain that Saeed now thinks that I am lying to him. A look of total incomprehension written all over his face. He reflects a while, "I had heard among the elders of my tribe, those that have travelled far, that there exists a land where people live, called 'the night people'. They live in small homes made of rocks and wood and hardly ever see the sun in the sky, because it is mostly night. I had always thought those stories to be made up to frighten children, warning them not to venture too far to the north." He pauses a moment, looking at me askance, "is this the land of your home Azizi?"

"No Saeed. Although the days during the season of Malkizar are much shorter and the nights longer; the land you speak of, is much, much further north."

We keep walking, Saeed considering what I have just told him.

"Tell me more of your home Azizi. What do you yearn for the most?"

I let out a long sigh at the memory of my forest.

"I miss my forest the most Saeed." I pause gathering my thoughts on how to best describe this, in a way that will make sense to someone, who has only ever seen sand, rocks and a few trees that surround the rare oasis. "It is made up of trees." Realising that he probably does not know what I mean, I add, "You have seen those tall, strange trees, with the long fronds that grow near an oasis? When the wind blows, they make a strange dry whispering noise?"

Saeed nods, "You mean the *Nakhla*?"

I remember that Halim had called them by that name when I asked him.

"Yes. Imagine now, that in my forest there are trees, that are three, maybe four time taller than that; and that there are so many, the sunlight cannot penetrate to the ground." If Saeed was puzzled before, he now looks at me with unbridled astonishment. I can see though, that if he has a wish, it would be to see this forest of trees.

"The leaves on those trees are much smaller than the Nakhla, and of different shapes. They stay green during the season of *Elwah*, but with the onset of *Malikzar*, the leaves on some trees will turn into shades of the sunset. Not long after that, the north wind will blow through the forest and all the leaves will fall to the ground, covering it in a thick blanket of red and orange leaves." Saeed is silent, contemplating the scene conjured up by my words.

"Later in the season of Malkizar, the air cools down a great deal. Snow begins to fall and covers first the mountains, and then the forest and the land around it." I am prepared for Saeed's next question, a pang of longing in my stomach.

"Snow? Azizi, I do not know this word either."

This is going to be a challenge. I know that rain falls very rarely in the desert, but the Huda pass being so close to the ocean of Malkizar, the chance that he has experienced it at least once is high.

"Saeed, have you seen rain fall from the sky?"

"Yes, many seasons ago, about a *duwae*. Some rain fell over the Huda Pass. I remember because the younger children of my tribe had never seen it. They ran out and laughed with the coolness of the water on their bodies."

His description brought a smile at the thought of children experiencing rain for the first time in their life.

"Well, when the air has cooled so much, snow is a little like that. Except instead of water, the raindrops have turned to something like tiny wings of the night moths that are attracted to the fire. They are white, cold, and soft. As soon as they touch your face, they turn to water. When enough of those flakes touch the ground, they join to make a large blanket. Imagine a large, soft blanket made of the cotton that your clothes are made of, and it covers the whole ground. The forest then becomes silent, the sounds are muffled. Everything is quiet and mysterious. Snow is a little like that."

Saeed is focussed on imagining such an event. Finally, he looks up, "I hope to see your home in the mountains one day, Azizi."

I picture his astonishment and delight when he sees my beloved forest for the first time. Smiling at the look on his face as he first tastes the wild berries that grow in the shade of the tall trees. His look of wonder at the snow when it covers the ground and makes the world silent and reflective. With a quickening of my heart, I also imagine his marvel, when he sees for the first time the delicate blue Star flowers of my youth; the forest at the onset of the season of Elwah brimming with life. Strangely, a twinge of jealousy at wanting to protect my precious forest from anyone who does not belong there, is quickly replaced by excitement at witnessing his wonder and appreciation of the forest as I love it. The tightness in my stomach relaxes, a softening of my protectiveness gives way to a gentle thought, the possibility of developing a deep friendship with someone else. Someone who would share my love and passion of the forest and everything it holds.

I turn to look back. For a brief moment, I see Halim as I first saw him in the forest. Saeed has stopped in his tracks, the horse stands still next to him. A look of intense dreaming veils his face, his emerald green eyes unfocussed appear to stare into another world. He sighs, "Your world is filled with magic Azizi. It is no wonder that your kin are healers and magicians."

I go to him, treasuring his respect for my world. I enfold him in my arms, he is so soft that it is like holding a cloud, the gentle fragrance of orange blossom permeates the air. "I promise to take you there Saeed. I long to share with you the wonders of my home."

He holds me tight for a moment and with a small air of sadness, he lets go, turns, and leads the horse again. I follow, the wolf softly padding alongside.

The sky begins to lighten with the onset of early sunlight, the constellations begin to flicker and fade out of existence into the vastness of a light blue sky. I quickly check our direction to ensure that we have turned north towards the cave of *Gibrar* and the city of Naassée.

Keeping an eye on the horizon, I estimate that it will take no more than half a *duna* to sight the outline of the city. We should reach the outer walls by the time the sun is at its zenith. The desert air usually dry begins to change, I detect a level of moisture rising, probably due to the proximity of the ocean of Elwah. A light wind has picked up, and with it my senses pick up the inevitable scent and taste of salt. Saeed lifts his nose into the air and remarks, "we are not far from the ocean." Unexpectedly the horse he is leading makes a muffled noise and refuses to move forward. Saeed is suddenly alert, stops and looks around at the ground. Only a few steps away, a coiled snake, the colour of the sand marked with only a few dark lines, its head slightly raised is making a soft rasping sound. It must have detected the vibrations of our approach and deemed us a threat. "Azizi, this one is as poisonous as the scorpion."

"Should we wait or go around it?"

'Going around it, it may think us a threat that is circling. It could then attack without warning."

I can see how well camouflaged this creature is. If it had not raised its head and made a sound, we could easily have stepped on it.

"Azizi, could you untie the largest rod from the horse and stand behind me?"

I do not understand what he intends to do, thinking perhaps that we could use the large wooden pole to somehow either defend ourselves or attack the snake hoping it would just leave. I stand behind him.

"Pass me the pole please, Azizi."

He holds onto it with one hand and restraining the horse with the other, Saeed begins to hit the ground firmly with the base of the rod, making a rhythmical thumping sound. He also begins to softly chant a series of words at the same rhythm, using a dialect I do not understand. First, the snake stops to make its rasping sound, sluggishly uncoiling, it raises its head towards Saeed who unperturbed continues his chanting and thumping. A few seconds later, the snake completely uncoils, slithers away from us and disappears in the adjoining sand dunes.

I let out a long sigh of relief. I look at Saeed with a renewed respect for the skill and wisdom he has just displayed. He did not intend to kill the creature, only to make it move away from us. His respect for life, even a life that could so easily take his own, is deep.

He looks at me, then goes to the horse and secures the pole once more.

"When did you learn to do that Saeed?"

He smiles, "I have only just been taught this skill by one of the elders. In some ways, we are the custodians of this land, and I was taught to have respect for all its inhabitants. Even though this creature could easily kill me, it would only do so to protect itself. So, I do what I can to protect myself, but without necessarily harming it. Of course, if it came to choose between life and death, I would rather choose my life."

"Saeed, this is a magic of its own. You have a deep understanding of your land and the life within it."

He looks up at me, a shy smile lifting his cheeks as they turn a soft shade of pink.

"Thank you Azizi."

We resume our journey, and I become aware once more of the hidden dangers of this ruthless land. The sun is rising fast.

"Saeed, I think that we should be able to reach Naassée by the middle of the day. I feel we should keep going rather than rest as usual."

He nods his agreement. We walk on in silence.

C H A P T E R   S I X

The sun rises steadily, first lighting the horizon into a single shimmering line of silver, which extends to ignite the desert into a vast undulating plateau of burnished white gold. The breeze that up until now, provided a cool relief, suddenly drops and the heat of the day rises around us like a slow furnace. Saeed puts on his *shemagh* without even pausing in his step. Following his example, I reach for mine in one of the smaller satchels. Remembering how Halim taught me, I wrap it carefully around my head before placing the remnant across my face, to protect my mouth from drying and from any potential sandstorm.

"Oh!" Saeed exclaims and points to a spot on the horizon. I place myself next to him and look in the direction he is pointing. Briefly but clearly a spark lights up on the horizon.

"It must be one of the roofs of Naassée," I tell him. "I have read that the tops of the temples are giant domes, painted either white or gold depending on the function of the temple."

Saeed looks on at the horizon steadily. "We must have made good time; it does not appear to be that far."

"I hope so," I reply, thinking that perhaps what we have just seen, is a *sarab*, one of those tricks of the light in the desert.

A few hours pass in silence, Saeed seems to have picked up the pace, eager no doubt to behold the famed city of Naassée and the cliffs overlooking the ocean of Elwah. As the sun is about to reach its zenith, a clear outline of the city walls rises above the horizon. We have not stopped, and my mouth is desperate for a drink of water. I reach for my water pouch and quickly take a sip, cautious not to drink too much.

It is not long before the city becomes visible. Saeed stares in awe, unable to take his eyes off the sight emerging before us. Tall walls the colour of sand, rise from surrounding desert. Behind those walls, columns reach to the sky and in between, several domes dominate the city visible from a great distance. The domes appear to have been set on fire with the light of the rising sun. The entrance to the city of Naassée forcibly faces west, as the town itself is perched on the cliffs facing the ocean of Elwah and the rising sun. From a strategic point, the city appears that it could easily be surrounded and held to ransom. Were it not for its reputation as the home of the most feared Naasseene soldiers, in spite of its single point of defence, the city could have been sieged aeons ago. Legend states that there are secret underground passages that not only lead to the dreaded cave of Gibrar but also access the base of the cliffs and the ocean itself. This would allow the defenders to exit the city and attack from the rear of the invader.

As we approach the city along a well-trodden and maintained path, we are confronted with a tall tower, topped with a smaller white dome. The gate to the city is impressive and four guards dressed in simple leather tunics and short swords by their side wait, looking on impassively. As we reach the gate, one of the soldiers signals for us to stop and steps forward to me. His eyes briefly take in the horse and its simple cargo, rest for a moment taking in Saeed and the white wolf, before addressing me,

"What is your business here?"

"I am Azizi, I am here to meet with Mahjir Suffrah."

The soldier stands before me, his harsh look is replaced by initial confusion and then by outright disdain. He guffaws, turning to his comrades and exclaims,

"This herdsman wants an audience with the Master of Rites and Ceremonies!"

The others laugh with derision.

Saeed looks offended and is about to say something when I stop him. I am aware that our desert dress does nothing to raise our status above poor shepherds.

I reach in my inside pocket and draw out the token that Hasan gave me after *Damna*. I hold it up to the soldier, who briefly looks at it, recognises a mark. His eyes narrow and abruptly taking the token angrily asks, "Where have you stolen this?

Looking straight into his eyes, I reply, "It is not stolen, it was given to me."

"I do not believe you herdsman. You and your friend should leave now. We have no need of your kind here."

During this exchange I notice a short dark man approach, listening to the commotion. He has the dress of an initiated master. Making his way leisurely to the gate, he arrives as the soldiers are about to forcefully push us back from the city gate.

"What is the trouble guard? Who is creating this disorder?" the man speaks with an oily tone; his eyes are dark and narrow. Looking first at the guard he addressed, his eyes wander to me and then quickly to Saeed.

"Ah Mahjir Ahmad, apologies for the noise. This herds boy says that he has a meeting with Mahjir Suffrah. He presented me with this token, which he has obviously stolen from somewhere."

"May I see the token?"

The guard hands him Hasan's token. My stomach twists to see it being so poorly handled and my heart begins to beat faster in my chest. Mahjir Ahmad's eyes narrow, he raises an eyebrow in mock surprise and quickly looks up at me.

"Indeed boy, where have you obtained this token?"

"It was given to me."

"This is not an ordinary token boy. I do not believe anyone would have given you this. Unless it was stolen, and the person was trying dispose of it. Did you pay for it in the marketplace perhaps?"

Recognising his authority as Mahjir, I bow, "No Mahjir, it was not purchased. It was given to me."

His ego stroked by my gesture of respect, with an air of condescension, he appears to yield, "Very well. Then you don't mind if I consult with the owner of this token?" He turns to the soldiers with a wry smile and adds, "perhaps we can have a bit of fun?" He turns back to face me adding, "it won't be long before we know the truth of the matter." He goes to turn but not before giving a lecherous look at Saeed.

We wait patiently, Saeed would have been used to being called a poor herdsman, but now he is seething with anger at the way they have treated me.

The gate has been shut, ironically as a way of stopping us from bolting through. It is not long before I hear measured footsteps and the regular thump of a sheathed short sword accompanying those steps. A loud short order is roared from within.

The gate is flung opened, and Hasan stands there seething with fury. The soldiers initially misinterpret his anger and smiling at him, think that the joke will soon be on us. Speaking in a tone that defies contradiction, holding up the token, he barks at the guards,

"*He*! - is my Janah! Taht himayati!"

From the little I know learning the language from Ijlal, Hasan has just reproached them, declaring that I am his initiated ward and under his protection.

The soldiers' demeanour suddenly changes from bravado to utmost fear at the consequence for threatening the Janah of the Captain of the Royal Guards of Naasée.

Hasan then turns to me and steps with open arms,

"Azizi. It is so good to see you safe." He embraces me and the fragrance of patchouli envelops me like a cloud of protection. "Come, we can talk inside." He looks briefly at Saeed, then notices the white wolf, "You keep interesting company Azizi, bring them along." Without another look at the guards, he invites us to follow him.

The guards astounded and reprimanded, their heads bowed, have stepped back to let us through. I overhear one of them whisper, "How were we to know?"

As we step through the main gate and into the city itself, Saeed lets out a gasp of wonder. The road leading inside the city of Naasée is wide and beautifully paved. Numerous towers topped with golden and white domes are everywhere. The walls of the houses and shops, though made of light-coloured stones, are decorated with various signs in fresh colours.

A multitude of shop fronts decorated in such variety of colours, are opened to the streets. Vendors are selling all types of wares, fruits I have never seen and fresh herbs, the fragrance of which permeates the air. Tall slender Apphatians dominate the crowd, most of them have dark skinned and dark eyes, they speak softly. They are mostly dressed in traditional clothes, long flowing robes and scarves of intense colours. They wear strange but delicately carved ornaments. Recognising the Captain of the Royal Guards, some bow to Hasan, and then gape at us. Fingers are pointed at the white wolf, and they stare openly at Saeed, a young man with fair skin, hair the colour of a fiery sunset and eyes of green emerald. They occasionally turn their attention to me, fair skinned youth, with startling blue eyes, or so I was told by Ijlal, prince of Shiraz. The stares are followed with animated discussions behind hands, heads leaning into each other, while staring.

Leaning close to Hasan, I whisper, "It seems we are creating quite a stir, Hasan."

He turns his head to me and smiles broadly. Wrapping his arm around my shoulder, he whispers back, "You have nothing to fear." This simple gesture causes a momentary ripple of surprise with the immediate crowd.

I don't think that Saeed is aware of the impact our appearance has on the crowd. He is fully taken by the wonders of this city, looking at once in all directions. Occasionally he bows and smiles at individuals with such an innocent expression, that a smile is often returned. Suddenly a small boy breaks free from the crowd of onlookers and makes his way to Saeed, initially matching his step, he then pulls Saeed's robe. Saeed stops and looks down smiling. Understanding that the child wants him to crouch down to his level, Saeed obliges. With wonder in his eyes, the child at first touches and then strokes Saeed's hair, gazing. The mother who was momentarily distracted, calls out the boy's name, holding her hand to her mouth, unsure of what to do.

Saeed smiles back and in a gesture of pure innocence, strokes the boy's hair in return. Hasan stops and looks on with a bemused smile. The crowd smiles and some laugh at the candour of the moment. The mother tentatively steps towards her boy and taking his hand, begins to draw him away. Saeed stands and bowing to the woman, smiles at her meeting her eyes. For a moment, the woman is startled, and seeing his green emerald eyes, gasps and bows deeply.

Saeed is surprised and I am a little confused with the gesture, which intimates a deep respect. I look up inquiringly at Hasan who is looking on. Leaning to me he whispers, "Your friend's green eyes are unusual. His colouring is seen as a strong sign of magic." He looks at me and then adds, "no less magical than your blue eyes Azizi."

We make our way through the main street, heading towards a large edifice, topped with a golden dome. The crowds have thinned and with it the sounds of the marketplace recede. Every now and again, a soft but audible thud is heard, and it seems that the ground shakes slightly. Saeed sidles up to me, "Azizi, what is that sound?"

Hasan turns, "That my friend, is the sound of the waves of the Ocean Elwah crashing at the base of the cliffs below the city."

Saeed gives me a puzzling but worried look.

"I will show you in a little while. But first you need to rest. You both look as though you have travelled through the night?"

I nod to Hasan.

We arrive at the base of the imposing building with the golden dome. Two columns flank a large door, guarded by only one soldier. He is of indefinite age, very handsome in an androgenous way. His upper torso is humbly clad with a simple sleeveless shirt, revealing enough of his musculature to identify him as a slender but well-built young man. A wide leather belt crosses his chest and back and pins around his waist. He wears a leather skirt and sandals on his feet. A short sword in its scabbard is attached to a metal ring that hangs off the belt. The soldier salutes Hasan and steps away to let us through. Hasan pauses and turning to us states, "This is *Xan* my most trusted and efficient guard." The guard looks at us with a little nod of his head. "Xan, this is Azizi, my *Janah*." A significant exchange is made that Xan understands I am under Hasan's protection and by default, under his as well. Xan surprises me with a salute that I am familiar with, that of my school in *Asfaine*, his closed right fist into his open left hand, accompanied with a small bow of the head. Taken by surprise, I respond in like fashion, which seems to astonish and amuse him slightly, he glances briefly at Hasan.

Hasan chuckles a little, "Azizi, it is good that you have such good manners, but Xan is unaccustomed to have important guests greet him in such a way."

I reply, "His honour does me courtesy". Hasan nods, and

smiles at me, then adds, "and this," he hesitates, bemused and trying to think of a word, "This, is Azizi's... small but I dare say effective army." Xan openly stares at the white wolf, which pays him no heed. "Come let us go inside so that you may refresh and rest a while."

Saeed with the wolf closely on his heels step through with us.

The door opens to a small courtyard. I hear another breath of surprise from Saeed. Trees and small shrubs are planted around a medium sized fountain that is running with clear water. A path leads around the fountain to another door at the far end. This one is plain white and decorated with painted green symbols. In the old texts of runes and symbols that I read during my training; I now remember that green symbolises gentleness in balance with strength. It also signifies serenity and good health.

Entering Hasan's residence, I expected splendour befitting the captain and most trusted soldier of the Royal Guard to the regent Prince Elwah. The décor is simple, almost austere. The furnishings are simple but practical. The room we enter is large, a wide staircase to the left leads upstairs, at the far end a double glass door opens onto a balcony. A table and chairs are framed in front of the door. Judging by the orderly papers, and writing implements, I assume that to be a working desk. Being a soldier, would not preclude him from a degree of administration, such as the scheduling of the guards, or attending to minor officials who come to visit the prince.

Turning to Saeed, Hasan gestures, "Come, I promised to show the cause of the sound you heard in the streets below." Hasan opens the double doors, and a gust of air carrying the unmistakable scent of ocean suddenly floods the room. I brace myself momentarily against the fragrance of salt that immediately fills my senses.

Saeed follows and steps out and immediately steps back with a "Oooh." Hasan holds his hand out and invites him back out. Tentatively, Saeed holding on to Hasan, steps out cautiously onto the balcony, and stands in awe of the ocean. He dares to look down and at that moment, a rogue wave crashes into the base of the cliffs, the sound carrying through the rock into the chamber we stand in. The spray from the water almost makes it to the height of the balcony. Saeed's initial reaction is to almost cower at the violence of it, then quickly bursts laughing with delight. He takes a step back to the opening of the door and stands there looking out, giving a shiver every time a wave crashes into the base of the cliff. He turns to me with awe written all over his demeanour, "Azizi, the water keeps moving and yet goes on for ever!"

I nod to him smiling. Not comfortable looking down from great heights, I remain where I stand in the relative safety of the main room. I remember the first time I saw the ocean of Malkizar when staying with Ijlal and the companions in Shiraz. I was overwhelmed by its dark mysterious force and the crests of white that so resembled snow atop each wave.

Hasan chuckles lightly at the awe written all over Saeed's face. "Come, let me show you where you can refresh yourselves and take some rest."

He leads us up the stairs to another section of his dwelling and opening a door, shows us the bathing room, no less spectacular than the balcony. Gold edged marble tiles lead to a large copper bathtub that sits alongside a wall sized pane of glass, overlooking the ocean. The tub is already filled with warm steaming water, various scented herbs and oils in coloured jars sit on a small ledge above one end of the tub.

Even from the entrance, the view beyond the tub looks out over the steel grey-green ocean and a wide uninterrupted sky. White clouds are rolling in with a strong wind, allowing shafts of sunlight to pierce the air into ever shifting patterns on the water below. White horses riding the waves suddenly erupt into angry foam and crash against the cliff face, sending a shudder throughout the house.

Saeed looks at me with grave concern on his face. "I... I am not sure I want to bathe in this tub. Will it be safe?"

I smile, wanting to make him at ease. "I am sure this bathtub has been here for many years."

Hasan nods and adds, "it is secured into the very stone of the cliff."

I am not sure if that statement no matter how comforting it is meant, does anything to ease Saeed's tension. He stands fixed to the spot, wringing his hands, occasionally glancing at me. "Saeed, would you like me to bathe with you so as to ease your concerns?" Saeed stares at me, turns to Hasan who just smiles at him. Saeed nods his agreement vehemently.

"I will send my aide, Sarek, with clean cotton towels and a change of clothes for you both. Azizi, when you are done, please come and find me. I have many questions to ask you." Hasan then leaves the room, leaving a nervous Saeed and me to consider which end of the bathtub would be furthest from the window and its dizzying view.

Shedding our travel clothes, and carefully stepping into the tub, making sure that our attention does not drift to the open view, we step into the bath. Once in the warm water and my head just above the surface, the effect is immediate. My muscles relax. Saeed initially turns his head away from the window, and then bit by bit, relaxes to the point when he braves looking out. He immediately retreats away and holds onto the furthest edge of the tub, creating a small wave that threatens to overflow the tub. Understanding his instincts, not being any braver than him with heights, I take a large sea sponge, placing some of the scented ground herbs and oil on it, I gently rub his back. He visibly relaxes and allows me to tend to him. This is the first time I have seen Saeed fully naked. His milk white skin is flawless. He dunks his head below the water, surfacing like a wet dog, his red hair completely limp and framing his boyish face makes me smile. He opens his eyes, droplets of water still caught on his eyelashes, he rubs his eyes clear and looks at me smiling. I am momentarily taken aback with the pure look of innocence and the dazzling brilliance of his emerald green eyes.

Tentatively, he reaches out to the tattoo on my right wrist. A shiver runs through me at his gentle touch, "Did it hurt much, this sign of your first initiation?"

"It did but just for a brief moment."

He nods, and then reaches out to my chest, to the tattoo above my heart, "What about this one?"

"That one, yes that one hurt a lot more. It took a longer time to heal."

"What is the meaning of the various symbols?"

I pause, reflecting on my second initiation. "The whole sign means that I am accepted into the study of magic. The first sign within it means that I have been initiated into the mores and knowledge of magic as an apprentice. Once I fulfill the other stages, another mark for each phase will be placed within the circle itself. When complete, I will then be tested for the title of Mahjir." His fingers gently caress the tattoo on my chest in a sign of admiration, sending another shiver up my spine. I sense the member of my manhood begin to stir under such gentle touch. I resist the sensation, hoping also, that no fragrance of salt suddenly manifests, as that would send me into a trance. Being mostly submerged, I do not want to lose consciousness. In an effort to control the situation and express my appreciation for his concern, I hold his hand, gently kiss it and let it drift back into the water.

An aide enters the room and without any sign of embarrassment or sense of intrusion, places two towels on a wooden bench and next to that, two sets of clean clothes. The white wolf, which had been sitting outside, takes the opportunity to amble in and casually curls up in the middle of the room. Without another word or even a glance, the aide retreats and closes the door behind him.

I have never been one to take long baths and decide to step out and dry myself.

"Saeed, will you be comfortable if I dress and leave you to bathe alone?"

Saeed considers the question a moment, briefly looks at the window, shaking his head, "No. I am clean enough. I will step out also."

As he steps out, I give a short laugh, "Oh, Saeed, your skin has turned pink with the warm water."

He looks at himself and laughs such a light-hearted sound that it makes me smile.

The cotton towels are soft and slightly warm, as if they have been laid out in the sun. Hasan must be a good judge of size as my clothes fit me perfectly. But then, as I smile at the memory, Hasan has known me intimately.

Having dried himself thoroughly, Saeed still undressed reaches for his satchel and brings out a small clay bottle with a wooden stopper in it. Opening it, he splashes a few drops of liquid into an open palm and proceeds to rub himself all over with it.

The astonishing fragrance of orange flower blossoms suddenly pervades the air around us. I understand now, the fragrance that always seems to accompany Saeed.

Dressed, Saeed gives one last look at the window overlooking the ocean, has a small shiver, sighs, "I did not expect my first experience of the ocean to be this way." I smile and nod in complete agreement. Hasan certainly knows how to surprise his guests.

As we step out of the room, the same aide who delivered the towels and clothes, motions for us to follow, "My name is Sarek. Please come this way. His excellency has prepared rooms for you to rest. Master Azizi, his excellency requests a meeting with you immediately."

Saeed looks a little put out at being parted, but given that he supresses a yawn, agrees to go and rest. Much to Saeed's relief, we are shown to a room, the windows of which look out onto the streets of the market we walked through earlier. A large bed and fresh beddings are a sumptuous sight for a youth who is used to sleeping under the stars, or the rocky confines of the Huda pass. The wolf steps ahead of Saeed, sniffs around a few times and casually curls up on the rug at the base of the bed.

"Rest well Saeed. I will come to see you as soon as I have finished my meeting with Hasan."

C H A P T E R   S E V E N

The aide with a polite gesture, invites me to follow him. We pass through a series of corridors and climb a short set of stairs that opens onto a large landing with two doors. The aide goes to one door and knocks on it. Hasan gives a command to enter. The aide lets me through. "Thank you, Sarek." Sarek bows and closes the door behind me.

Hasan then steps up to me, embraces me. Releasing me, he places a hand on top of my head and brings it back to just below his eyes. He laughs out loud then, "You have grown so tall in the last four years!"

I let him take me in his arms again, luxuriating in his warm embrace.

"Come and sit a while with me." He leads me to a couch against the far wall. A window at the other end allows the late afternoon light to stream through. "This is my personal meeting room, which for practical reasons is furthest away from prying eyes and listening ears." The crest of the Prince of Naasée sits on the wall above us. "Are you hungry?" I nod, listening to the small growl my stomach just made, Hasan lets out a laugh, "I think that means yes."

Hasan goes to the door, "Sarek, could you please bring some refreshments?"

"Azizi, let me ask you some questions first." I nod waiting, "tell me about this young man with the emerald green eyes. Who is he, and how did you happen to come together?"

"Do you truly not remember him?" Hasan gives me a puzzled look. "His name is Saeed." Still no sign of recognition, I add, "He is all grown up now. Saeed is Fariqa's boy, the one I helped in the desert after he had been stung by a desert scorpion."

Recognition dawns on Hasan's face. "Oh... well. He is grown up. I do not remember him having such eyes in his youth."

"You were protecting his tribe at the time. It is unlikely that you would have had much contact with the children. It is possible that his eyes acquired that colour during late adolescence. My memory of his eyes as a young boy, they were amber, almost golden. What I remember mostly was the terror in his eyes."

'So, how did you meet with him after so many years?"

"I left Elwah to tend to Shahulm's recovery. I decided to leave and return to my godmother to prepare for my next initiation. I am to be initiated into the Lore of *Muraqaba – the Songs of Tahannuth,* Solitude of the inner mind. While crossing the desert, Elwah told me that someone was tracking me. Thinking perhaps that it was you, I wondered at the reason. I knew that Elwah had asked you to return to Naasée. Shortly after that, I had an odd experience, a kind of warning, which was quickly supressed by an unknown power. I was taken by one of the dark ones. I was about to be put to death when a white wolf accompanied by Saeed appeared, in time to kill my aggressor and release me. He and the wolf have accompanied me here."

Hasan stands up and begins pacing, occasionally stopping to listen intensely to my story.

"But Azizi, why come here. It would have been better for you to head to your beloved mountains."

"On the way here, Saeed asked to be trained into the arts of Magic and Healing, following the Rites and Lore of Apphat. He wanted me to train him, but I am not sure if that is permitted. I need to consult with one of the Elders. So, I brought him here."

I do not speak of Saeed's request for initiation using the rites of Apphat.

Hasan takes a deep breath. "Azizi, you may be in grave danger. You should not have come here. Surely my regent did not send you here?"

I shake my head. "No, he did not. But..." I am about to ask him about the danger he refers to. Hasan holds up his hand.

"What about the white wolf? How did that come about? And more importantly how is it so tame? Those creatures are cunning stalkers and calculating killers."

I nod in agreement. "I know, I have seen with my own eyes what it can do to kill a man." For a moment, Hasan stares at me. "As for how it is so tame. I suspect Elwah has something to do with that." Hasan urges me on, "Knowing of my grief for the loss of Halim and my inability to have stopped his murder, I think that somehow, Elwah has used his spiritual powers to bring

Halim's spirit as a guardian into the body of that wolf." Hasan seems unusually calm at my explanation, "Though, I think the spirit of Halim, occupies the body of the wolf only if it senses danger to myself or Saeed. It was Saeed that tracked me in the desert and on urging from Elwah, brought the wolf with him as the Sacred Guardian Spirit to protect me."

Hasan has stopped pacing, letting out a deep sigh, he comes over and wrapping me in his arms, whispers, "Azizi, I am so sorry to bring back such unhappy memories."

I am astonished that I have related those facts to Hasan, and not once did I feel the uncontrollable grief that accompanied those memories in the past.

"But Hasan, what dangers do you speak of?"

Hasan is about to speak but holds his hand up. He goes to the door and opens it. Sarek is standing at the door, holding a tray of refreshments. He bows as Hasan lets him in. It is difficult to know how long Sarek has been standing there.

"Thank you Sarek. You may retire." Sarek bows and exits, closing the door. Hasan waits a while before joining me on the couch.

"Let us have something to eat and drink while we talk." He offers me a plate, on which he has selected and placed some of the delicacies that were brought in. There is a jug of local wine, which I know from drinking with Elwah. It is sweet and has little effect on one's body.

"You are right." Hasan continues, "Elwah did send me back here to Naasée. But not for the reasons most people think. I am not here to restore order after the war that was avoided. I am here to investigate the taking of prince Elwah some five years ago."

Hasan lets the news sink in.

"Given the details that my regent conveyed to me, I believe that the taking was instigated and manipulated from within the city, and to be more precise, it was planned from within the Council of Elders."

I must look astonished, "Yes Azizi." he says with a sardonic smile. "For all the golden domes in our city and the apparent wealth and wellbeing of its population, there is a very dark undercurrent in the governing hierarchy."

I am momentarily speechless; I can feel my jaw gaping in disbelief. "But how is that possible?"

Hasan casually strides to the door and abruptly opens it. He looks down the corridor, and having satisfied himself that no one is standing near, carefully closes the door.

"You can see Azizi, how suspicious I have become. I can no longer be sure who is on my side and who is not. Out of all the soldiers under my command, there are very few who I would trust. Xan is one of them. You met him at the front door. Sarek, I am not sure of him. He still needs to demonstrate his loyalty to me. There are too many temptations for servants and soldiers who are on low salaries. Unscrupulous nobles and Elders, who receive handsome payments from the Regent's coffers are too eager to climb the social structure with bribes."

"But Hasan, how was it possible to abduct a prince so easily and what is worse," I swallow hard, "...hand him over to the sorceress?"

Hasan lets out a long sigh. "I will try and make short of this very long set of events. My work here in the city is twofold. As captain of the Royal Guard, it is my duty to protect Prince Elwah and to advise him on military issues. The prince is the figurehead of the army but the command of it, is left in my care. As such, my official title is General of Naasée. This has created much friction and unease in the past. Most of that has been resolved. The prince rules by virtue that he is the Sacred Guardian of the Sacred Tear of joy. The power of the Sapphires is well known in legend and lore. You are well acquainted with that, yes?"

I nod and let him continue. "There was an undercurrent of dissatisfaction amongst some of the newer members of the Elders Council. It was felt that choosing the next regent based solely on the concept of reincarnation of the previous Haafiz, identifying him only by virtue of the colour of his skin and his eyes, was thought to be outrageously old fashioned and inaccurate." Hasan pauses and looks at me,

I nod and say, "Some of those thoughts had occurred to me when I first read of the spiritual conventions of Naasée, but I imagined that the search for a replacement would have followed rigorous spiritual inquiries."

"Yes, you are right. The colour of skin or eyes is merely a sign. Many who have displayed those features have been dismissed out of hand when put through the thorough process of Spiritual Inquiry. The Prince of Elwah is not only a Commander, but a Spiritual leader. The Council of Elders and the population at large will always take his advice and follow his instructions on matters of magic, healing, and spirituality. There are those in the Council who have begun to question his authority as such."

I begin to understand the complexity of the situation. So why abduct the prince?

"You are probably asking yourself then, what good would come from abducting the prince?"

I nod in agreement.

"With his abduction, the Sacred Tear of Apphat also disappeared. Some of my memories of that night are clear and sharp, yet some are hazy, as if a veil has been drawn over them. You are aware in part of what I am about to tell you. For over a hundred years, the Sacred Tear of Elwah, after which the prince regent takes his title, has always been kept in a Naasée, in a room protected by royal guards and by strong magic. Entry can only be accessed by the prince and some of the high priests. You must understand that what I am about to tell you is sacred and only known to Elwah and me. As I have already told you, I am sworn to secrecy on this matter and for good reason. The Sacred Tear of Joy is given to the reigning regent through a special ceremony and only if the Haafiz is dying or dead. It is unheard of in our history, that the Haafiz can transfer the stone by any other means. That is why I was overwhelmed and astounded when I guessed that somehow, Elwah had transferred the stone to you and that you were carrying it on his behalf. I do not underestimate the power that Elwah possesses, but I do not know how it was achieved. The legend of the Sapphires is that each holds so much magic, that it can be wielded as a weapon."

I draw a quick breath in at the boldness to use one of the Sacred Stones for military purposes. But then I remember, that is precisely what the Over Lord was trying to do. I am still puzzled tough, as Hasan has just said, the stone has always been kept in a secret room.

Hasan stops pacing. He sits opposite me frowning, takes a moment, turns his head to the door, and taking a deep breath, relaxes his frown as he stares directly into my eyes.

"As I said, some of my memories are blurred as if I am not meant to remember them. On the night of Elwah's disappearance I remember doing my rounds of the palace. I had received a report from Xan, that rumours had been circulating of some strange sightings in the township. I intended to follow these up by sending a squad of soldiers to investigate. I came to an isolated part of the palace," Hasan pauses, his body shivers once, shaking his head he continues, "out of the shadows, a young woman stepped out, a young boy followed her. Both looked at me and I found I could no longer move.

Their faces were partially obscured by the hoods of their cape." Hasan pauses his face has gone pale, his eyes are misted over, the muscles of his jaw tense and relax as he releases a breath. "The light of one of the torches flared up, I could see their faces. They could have been twins except for the age difference. Their eyes are what I remember distinctly. That memory is burnt into my brain. The girl had intense blue eyes, whereas the boy's eyes were a deep blue green, like the ocean after a fierce storm. His face wavered between translucent and solid, as if he would suddenly vanish."

Hasan's body gave another shudder. "I heard the young woman's voice in my head. She urged me to find Elwah and tell him that the Sacred Sapphire was in grave danger."

I am on the edge of my seat. My skin is crawling with goose bumps. The significance of his words is obvious to me.

Hasan's body tenses once more. He looks away for what seems an eternity. Finally, releasing another breath he looks at me with such an intensity that it momentarily makes me want to step back.

"I have never spoken of this to anyone, Azizi."

I sit up and wait.

"I will not go into details as I do not know whether I am permitted to speak of this." Hasan releases another breath, "but since you have held one of the Sacred Sapphires, it is fitting that you should know their origin. After I told Elwah of what I had seen and heard of the warning, he asked me to accompany him to the sacred room."

Again, Hasan looks away and over his shoulder, as if seeking a signal from someone to go on. He swallows hard, "I witnessed the goddess Ishtar, instruct Elwah as he took the sapphire into himself. She then commanded me to protect the Haafiz and the Sacred stone as one."

I am sitting bolt upright. An energy like an audible hum, flows through my body, setting it on the edge of my seat. The silence in the room is only interrupted by the boom of the crashing waves below.

"What you are saying, if I understand you correctly: although no one other than you and Elwah knew that the Sacred Sapphire was now inside Elwah's body, one or more person decided that to acquire the Tear of Elwah, was to somehow force the prince to give it up, thinking perhaps that he carried it on his person? And to do so, they had to find the means, by which they could do that?"

Hasan smiles, nodding sadly at me. "Once those individuals heard or knew that the Sorceress had managed to obtain the Tear of Malkizar, the only means available to them, was to abduct and surrender the prince into the hands of the Over Lord who would hand him over to the sorceress?"

Hasan stands up and with measured steps goes and sits at his desk. A heavy silence fills the room, even the thud of the waves crashing appear far away.

"Yes Azizi. You are correct. It was not until much later, that the High Priests realised that the Tear of Elwah was no longer in the sacred room. They also did not count on the duplicity of the Over Lord and that once acquired, he would never hand over the Sacred Tear to the Council of Elders. Now all I must do is find the identity of the person or persons behind this attempted coup. For it is a coup for power."

A cold feeling fills me at hearing this.

"Azizi, that is why I fear for your safety. It is now common knowledge, that you were able to destroy the sorceress using the Sacred Tear of Elwah, if not both." I look up at Hasan with a shake of my head, "no, I know you did not possess both, but there are many, even some within the Council of Elders who think otherwise. They and others upon learning that Elwah had somehow surrendered the Sacred Sapphire, think that you still possess one of the Sacred Stones."

I gasp, a certain understanding begins to dawn on me. With a cold twist to my stomach, I remember that Elwah, using his exceptional power, transferred the Sacred Stone to me in a kiss that enabled me to ingest it. Hasan looks at me with a questioning look.

"That is what that wretched creature was looking for. They stripped me thinking that I held one or more of the Stones on me. It never occurred to them that if I did," momentarily I break off into a whisper, "...it would be within me." I shudder with the conclusion, "And if they had thought that, then I am sure that they would not have hesitated at slicing me open."

Another wave of cold perspiration covers me. I can feel my heart quicken at the thought. Hasan stands again and comes to me.

"Azizi, I can see the effect that this is having on you. I am truly sorry to place you in this position. But you are the only one I can trust with this information. When I have finished telling you everything I know, I will ask you to tell me who were the ones that detained you along your journey. I want to make inquiries and eliminate these people before they cause any further harm. There will be time enough for that. First, I will briefly explain how the abduction took place, or at least my guesses at it."

Encouraging Hasan to continue, I pour myself another drink. The sweetness will go a long way to relax me. Hasan takes up pacing again.

"When news broke that the Tear of Malkizar was in the possession of the sorceress, I received a message, supposedly from Elwah, asking me to investigate the appearance of Shadows in Naasée. Another urgent message came from one of my aides that a squad of royal guards had been seen taking Elwah in the direction of Gibrar. It was not until I discovered the bodies of the squad that had disappeared, that I understood that Elwah Tahir, the Sacred Haafiz of Naasée, had been abducted. No longer knowing who to trust in Naasée, I left with instructions for Sarek, to tell the Council of Elders what I suspected and that I decided to track those responsible for Elwah's abduction. I disguised myself as a freelance soldier, attaching myself to travelling caravans. I know that I left a city in turmoil, but it was vital to return Prince Elwah safely.

The Council at this point took over the administration of the city. There was little point in staying. I organised the soldiers I trusted, instructing them to avoid going to war unless my personal token was presented.

I left hurriedly and eventually picked up a faint trail, but I still did not know where the prince had been taken. That trail went cold very quickly. I heard that Giafar, the General of Shiraz was investigating some matters along the northern borders. I decided to send him a message via one of his couriers. It was not long after, that we met in the desert with your friend Halim. The rest of the story you know."

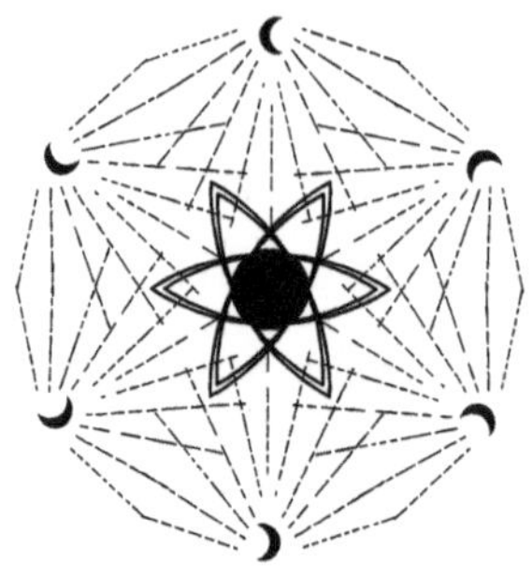

C H A P T E R   E I G H T

I sit in absolute shock at the audacity of it all. I had thought that by merely destroying the sorceress, that harmony would automatically be restored in the world. At least that was my naïve conception of my task. Now I see that my task is not yet fulfilled. I understand now Elwah's reluctance in returning to Naasée, until such time as the political situation is settled and a way to regain the Tear of Joy is achieved.

"What happened to the soldiers who delivered the prince to the Overlord?"

Hasan gives a cynical laugh, "According to my sources, once promised a reward, they were quickly eliminated by the Scarlet Robes. They did not even bother to conceal the identity of those soldiers. A warning for all I guess."

Muffled noises, then unintelligible shouts are heard outside the door. Hasan looks at me and then quickly moves to the door and opens it.

Sarek's voice cuts through authoritatively, "Please Mahjir, you cannot enter. His excellency is with a guest."

"I am the Master of Divination on the Elder's Council; I can visit any time I choose."

"What is this commotion in my household about?" Hasan's commanding voice brings everyone to silence, except for a few muffled words at the rear.

"Your Excellency," the oily tone of voice is unmistakable. It is the same voice as the Elder that stopped us at the city gates. My hairs on the back of my neck immediately rise.

"Your excellency, I am here to find out if the issue of your stolen token has been resolved. I found one of the urchins who were at the city gates, wandering in your residence and brought him along."

I immediately stand and move to the door. At the back and behind the Elder, Saeed, his eyes wide with panic, the hand of a servant across his mouth to stop him from calling out, is struggling to be let free.

"Oh, Excellency, I did not realise you had an important guest." The dark man eyes me and smiles, giving a little condescending nod. He attempts to peer around Hasan into the room. Hasan stands blocking his view.

"Mahjir Ahmad, surely you of all people would know the rules of my household. I have aides who will gladly make an appointment for you to see me. There is no call to simply barge into my house and cause a commotion."

"Excellency," the oiliness of this man's voice makes my skin crawl, "my apologies for the interruption. If you would allow me to come in and explain the situation, surely..." before Mahjir Ahmad can add another word, Hasan holds up his hand interrupting him, "You may not come in. As you can see, I am in a meeting. I order you to release this young man, he is a guest of mine. Sarek!" Sarek bows and begins to apologise, "Sarek, please escort Master Ahmad and his overzealous servant to the front gate of my house." Sarek is about to turn, Hasan adds, "and Sarek, please send the guard who is on duty to come and see me immediately after making arrangements to replace him."

Hasan then turning to Mahjir Ahmad adds, in a suave and firm tone, "Mahjir, please do me the courtesy to leave my house without any further commotion." Hasan stands there while his order is being executed. Master Ahmad is seething, but obviously knows when he has been outranked. The servant releases Saeed who collapses against the wall.

Once the corridor cleared, I rush to Saeed. He looks very frightened, I help him up, still visibly shaking, he rests against the wall taking a few deep breaths.

I guide him back inside and help sit on the couch. I pour him a drink, which he tentatively sips. He gives a small cough looking up at me.

"It's fine Saeed, it's just a weak wine. It will help you relax a little."

Hasan, still looking like a thunder cloud steps in.

"Saeed, are you hurt?"

Saeed shakes his head.

"Azizi, I need to discipline the guard who was on duty. It is very irregular that he would allow someone through without my authority and without an appointment. I will do so in the courtyard. Once I have questioned Sarek, I will ask him to stand guard at this door. You will be safe, but please stay inside."

I gesture in agreement. Hasan steps out with purpose in his step.

I would not want to be the soldier who will face Hasan's wrath.

As gently as possible, I ask "Saeed, what happened?" His eyes begin to brim with tears.

"I woke up from my rest and I forgot where I was. Disoriented, I called out for you but there was no answer. The room was dark, so I got up and went to look out into the corridor. That old man, the one who took your token at the city gates, was standing just outside my door. I was about to call out, his servant stopped me. He held his hand over my mouth and held me with my arm behind my back, forcing me to walk ahead of him. They then dragged me to this floor. The older man stopped often to listen at various doors, when suddenly, the servant who showed us to our room came running up and started shouting that they were not meant to be there."

I can see that Saeed is still upset. I fold my arms around him. He sheds a few more tears on my shoulder then resolutely, sits up, taking a deep breath, wipes his eyes and finishes his drink in one movement.

"I am better now, Azizi." He attempts a weak smile. "These people are scary Azizi. They do not seem to have any manners."

Under any other circumstances, I would find that naïve remark amusing. I bite my lips tight and comfort him some more. I am concerned now, more so than ever, to have brought this innocent young man, who has so little knowledge of politics and corruption, into this city of intrigue.

There is a soft knock at the door. I move to the door and cautiously open it. Sarek is standing there and bows to me.

"His excellency has asked me to guard this door. I am letting you know that I am here now."

"Thank you Sarek." He looks nervous. He is in his late twenties; he must have been in Hasan's service for several years. I hesitate but then resolve to ask him a question, "Sarek, thank you for your efforts to stop the intrusion earlier." Sarek bows. I cannot detect any deceit in him, so I venture to ask, "Sarek, can you remember when Master Ahmad first pushed past you downstairs, what words did he use?"

Sarek looks up a little astonished and then frowns, "His Excellency, asked me earlier how Mahjir Ahmad managed to get past me. I could not remember that. I cannot clearly remember the words; all I recall is the tone he used urged me to let him through. It was only moments later that I realised he should not be here." Sarek looks confused.

"Thank you Sarek. You are not to blame."

"I fear that I have committed a grievous fault and I have let his excellency down." He looks genuinely concerned and embarrassed.

"I will speak with His Excellency. Sarek, I don't think you have anything to fear." He looks up at me, a hint of relief in his eyes, he then bows once more, turns, and takes up his post at the door. I close the door gently.

It is as I suspect. I will have to speak to Hasan about this. I go back to sit by Saeed's side. He seems a little more relaxed.

He turns to me with one of his shy smiles. I pour him another drink.

"You must be hungry Saeed, eat some of these delicacies."

He helps himself to a few, and then to a few more. I laugh lightly. Raising his eyebrows at me, he guiltily admits "I *was* hungry." He turns to me, "What were you asking Sarek?"

"I was wondering how Master Ahmad managed to get past a loyal and attentive servant, let alone an experienced guard. I think I have my answer." Saeed looks at me quizzically. "I think Master Ahmad abused his powers. But for what purpose, I am unclear." Saeed keeps staring at me, not any the wiser, dissatisfied with my answer, he shakes his head and helps himself to more food. I smile at him reassuringly, "I will explain when Hasan returns."

Moments later, the door opens, Hasan steps in looking stern. He turns to Sarek and is about to dismiss him, when I interrupt, "Hasan, may I ask a favour?" Hasan raises an eyebrow that does little to diminish the look of fierceness, and then nods. "Would you please ask Sarek to come in? I will explain why in a moment."

Hasan opens the door a little more and gestures for Sarek to enter. If he was nervous before, the young man now looks deeply anxious. He enters, head bowed and stands by the closed door.

"Azizi? What is this about?"

"Hasan, please trust me. First, Sarek is not to blame." Sarek looks up at me, genuinely surprised that I am taking his side. "Hasan, would you please listen to Saeed for a moment." Turning to Saeed who suddenly looks very tense, "Saeed, could you please tell Hasan exactly what you told me, from the time you woke up. What was Master Ahmad doing as he was dragging you along?"

Saeed relates his words exactly.

Hasan starts to pace then stops abruptly at the part where Mahjir Ahmad was listening at various doors. He gestures for me to go on.

"Now, Sarek please repeat what you told me, regarding the words that you remember hearing from Mahjir Ahmad as he entered the house."

Sarek swallows, "I do not remember the words so much as the tone of voice Master Ahmad was using, urging me to let him through."

"Thank you Sarek."

Hasan turns to look at me. "I do not understand Azizi. What is this all about?"

I take a deep breath, "Hasan, neither your guard at the front gate to your house, nor Sarek, your trusted aide, are to blame. They are the victims of Mahjir Ahmad, who used a powerful technique to pass through unchallenged. He used what is known as the *vox imperii* or 'Command Voice'. It allows the speaker to imbue a powerful energy into the words he speaks, and take over the will of the listener, giving no choice but to obey. As such Master Ahmad has abused his power as a Magician and forced his way into your house. To what end is unclear."

If I could say that Hasan is gaping at me, it would not be far from the truth. He stands still, his jaw clenching, his large hands turning into fists until the knuckles turn white. He starts to pull out the short sword at his side, then quite deliberately, slides it back into its scabbard. His face flushes red, and it seems that he is about to explode. I don't have to look at Sarek to know that he is very uncomfortable.

Hasan softly mutters "The bastard!" He takes a deep breath and recovers his demeanour. In a voice that is calm and controlled, edged with steel that leaves no doubt how deep that steel could cut, he turns to his aide, "Sarek, thank you for your efforts. My apology for not giving you the credit of your loyalty. If ever Master Ahmad approaches you on any matter, you are to report to me immediately. I will deal with this matter and the Council of Elders in good time. You may retire Sarek."

Sarek bows to Hasan, hesitates a moment and bows to me then exits. Hasan paces around the room a few times before finally sitting opposite Saeed and me. "How dare he treat my household staff and my guests like this!" He takes another breath, and adds, "And now Azizi, you know the name of my main suspect regarding the abduction of Elwah." Hasan pauses before continuing, "Azizi, is there a way to resist that technique you speak of?"

"That technique is usually employed in case of danger or to ensure compliance from someone who needs assistance, which could be refused. The will of the individual must be very strong to resist. For most people, if the words are loaded with much energy, it would be almost impossible to resist the command. However, the custom for employing that technique is to make strong eye contact with the individual. So, the easiest way to counteract the command, is to appear submissive and look down. That will have the singular effect of becoming aware of the energy in the words, and thereby refusing in one's head to obey."

Saeed looks at me with obvious respect and perhaps a little admiration. Hasan nods and becomes withdrawn. It is obvious that something other than this incident is worrying him.

"Hasan?" Looking up, he gestures for me to go on. "Hasan, I think Master Ahmad is both ambitious and dangerous." Hasan stands up and goes to his desk and sits at it, his eyes are fixed on me. "How will you challenge Master Ahmad? Do you think that challenging him in front of the council, you could run the risk that the Elders may feel you are overstepping your authority?"

Hasan's eyes are unfocussed. Releasing a sigh, "Azizi, you are right. It will be difficult. Although I oversee the administration of the city, the rules, and laws, even the slightest decision concerning the army have always been subject to the Spiritual leadership of Elwah and the Council of Elders." His eyes wander to the Crest of the Prince of Naasée hanging on the opposite wall.

"Hasan, I think it is time for Elwah to return to his city."

Hasan suddenly looks sad. "How will we achieve that, Azizi? Returning here could still leave him vulnerable to danger. It is one thing to send a courier asking him to return. It is another to then ask him to challenge the Council of Elders. He no longer holds the Sacred Tear of Apphat. I saw with my own eyes the sapphires enveloped in a haze of light and disappear."

I think for a while, not wanting to create false hope. "Hasan, the voice I heard when the Tears disappeared, assured me that they would re-appear when they are needed." A glimmer of hope returns to Hasan's eyes.

"How many soldiers can you count on, and trust?"

Surprised by my question, Hasan frowns and then thinks. "The Royal Guards number fifty." Hasan pauses a moment before adding, "All fifty have been handpicked by me. I trust all of them." Before I could comment, "I know what you are thinking. The soldiers responsible for abducting Elwah, were not Royal guards." Hasan looks at me intently. "What are you thinking Azizi?"

"As I said, Elwah needs to be here for two reasons. First, he has the absolute authority to challenge Master Ahmad. Secondly it will re-establish his role and authority to restore order in the city and particularly the Council."

"Azizi, a royal courier will take at least a Lahé to get to Shiraz. I cannot commit my thoughts to paper, in case the courier is intercepted. And then there is the difficulty of convincing Elwah to return, let alone protecting him while on the road..."

I smile at all his concerns. Seeing me smile and remembering my abilities, Hasan stops mid-sentence and bows in a slightly mock fashion to let me go on.

"I will contact Elwah tonight and explain all that has happened. If he agrees to return, I hope then to convince Prince Ijlal and the Companions to accompany and protect him. We also need an ally on the Council of Elders and to this end, I will contact my godmother and explain the situation. I hope that she will agree to be present at the Council of Elders when Elwah appears."

Hasan is first stunned then nods, awe written on his face.

"I think we need to keep this an absolute secret and allow Prince Elwah to make an appearance unannounced. This I hope will have an unsettling effect on those Council Elders who have a guilty conscience."

Hasan stands and gently makes his way to me. He is about to kneel, and I stop him. He sits and holds my hands.

"Azizi, you are astonishing. Your powers always astound me; but I think you would make and incomparable general. Your thinking and strategies are remarkable."

"Hasan, I think we need to reflect on this a while and make sure of the detail before acting on it. I will come to you later tonight and contact Elwah so that you may be on hand if there is anything he asks that I am unsure of." I look around thinking about what I will use to focus my attention for the mind meld, I notice the large open fireplace. "Hasan, can you ask Sarek to build a fire tonight?"

Hasan readily agrees. I allow myself to smile, I think he has given up on questioning my methods, but I add, "I first saw Elwah in the flames of my home fireplace, it has since become an easy way to contact him. My godmother on the other hand, I only have to call her name in my mind and if she is not busy, she will respond."

I don't think that the last words have diminished his awe and so I jokingly punch his shoulder, "Hasan, I am still a man."

To which he responds with a mocking, "ouch!" And then embraces me exclaiming, "And I am so glad of it."

I notice Saeed has been watching this exchange. There is a little envy or perhaps some embarrassment at witnessing such intimacy. He blushes and looks away. Releasing Hasan's embrace I go to him, taking his hands in mine I pull him gently to his feet. I then wrap my arms around him and whisper, "I have not forgotten you, Saeed."

"Thank you," he whispers. He gives me a shy smile and gently releases me. "Azizi?"

"Yes, Saeed?"

"I would like to be present when you contact Prince Elwah." Thinking perhaps that he needs to justify himself, he adds, "I will be quiet and not get in your way. I just want to observe and learn."

I look at Hasan briefly who responds with a neutral smile, obviously leaving the decision to me. Turning back to Saeed, "Yes Saeed, of course you can."

The look of absolute joy and devotion on Saeed's face fills my heart. I am glad to have this young man by my side.

89

CHAPTER NINE

Saeed and I return to the room we were first shown. I do not sleep, as much as lay on the bed, studying the situation and considering what I will say to Elwah that will convince him to return.

Much later as the sky darkens to cerulean blue, Sarek knocks at the door to serve us food for our supper. He enters and lays several plates of food on the table; he then turns to me and bowing, "Master Azizi, thank you."

"Sarek, you are welcome. I could not allow your loyalty to be questioned under those circumstances."

Sarek briefly looks at me. I am aware that I was quick to answer. I am not sure if Sarek has picked up on the subtlety of my comment, that I might question his loyalty under *different* circumstances. His face remains neutral, and he gives me another bow before leaving.

I turn to Saeed, whose breath has settled in a regular soft

whisper. His relaxed features remind me so much of the first time I saw Halim asleep.

I go to him and lying close, I touch his shoulder, whispering, "Saeed? Saeed?"

He takes a breath and then opens his eyes. I smile at his still drowsy face. "It is nearly time, Saeed. Let's have some supper before we go to see Hasan."

He stretches like a small animal, cautiously gets up and goes to sit at the table where the food that Sarek has laid out for us.

I eat only a few things, preferring to have as little in my stomach for my call to Elwah. The wolf, still lying on the rug below the bed, raises its head and looks at me inquisitively. I take a few scraps of food and offer then to him. Sniffing them first, he takes them delicately and eats them. Our supper finished; we make our way to Hasan's room. The wolf follows silently on our heels.

The air in the corridors has cooled significantly. A faint whistling sound echoes as the air passes through the narrow clefts in the stone walls.

I knock softy at the door, "Come," is Hasan's only response. Opening the door, I see that torches have been lit and oil lamps are set around the room already alight. The fireplace is lit but the flames have only just caught on to the small logs.

Hasan looks up from his desk, "Azizi, Saeed, are you refreshed?" I nod my head. Saeed follows immediately behind me, shyly looks down and whispers, "yes, thank you sir."

Hasan smiles at that. "You are a friend of Azizi, please call me Hasan." Saeed blushes a little, nods his head and keeps his eyes to the floor.

The wolf following behind us, scans the room and makes its

way to the front of the fireplace where it simply settles. Hasan briefly looks at it and nods amused.

"Hasan, have you thought of what you will say to Elwah, to convince him to return?" Hasan gives me a serious look, then smiling, shakes his head.

"I thought I would leave all the talking to you." Seeing the tension in me rise, he quickly adds, "But perhaps, we should explain the situation to him first and let him decide."

I offer him a weak smile and nod. "Once I make contact with Elwah, I will ask him the questions out loud, and relay his responses, so that you can follow the conversation." Hasan affirms his understanding and sits at his desk. Saeed looks a little awed. I decide to position myself on the floor in front of the fire. The wolf lying in front of me raises his head briefly and then appears to doze off again. Saeed quietly positions himself next to me and at enough of a distance to give me room.

I relax and begin to focus on the flames in the fireplace. Letting go of my surroundings and as best as I can, I allow myself to drift away from the room and the intense attention with which Saeed is watching.

The flames take on different shapes, leaping about and the colours begin to shift and melt together, the forms blur and become one. I remember the pair of blue eyes that once manifested from the flames in my god mother's herbarium.

Elwah is standing before me, smiling his warm smile. "Azizi, I have been waiting for you."

I am filled with joy to see him. "Elwah. I have many questions, but first how is Shahulm?"

Elwah smiles, obviously anticipating my question, "See for

yourself." He turns and indicates with his open palm the other side of the room. Shahulm is standing, smiling, and supported by Ijlal who is beaming with pride and joy. My heart leaps at the sight of both. Shahulm appears to be completely recovered, the fire in his eyes has returned, his skin is back to its soft polished golden brown.

"Oh!" Is all I can say. My heart is suddenly loud in my chest, I am overcome with emotion. It is as if they are standing here in front of me. The link between my mind and that of Elwah must be clear, or by some power of his, it seems that they can see me as well.

Ijlal asks, "Are you well and safe Azizi?" I take a deep breath, to hear that resonant familiar voice, speaking my language tinged with his accent, fills me with deep sense of peace and joy.

"I am overjoyed to see you both." It is all I can do to withhold tears of joy.

Ijlal beams a smile at me, looks at Shahulm who only has eyes for his prince, "We are very happy to see you well, Azizi. Thank you for all that you have done. We hope to see you soon in person. You are always welcome in Schiraz. We leave you to speak with Elwah."

Elwah turns to me. I am about to speak when he holds his hand up, a look that reminds me of my god mother's manner when she wants to focus.

"You are in Hasan's study?"

"Yes, yes I am."

"Azizi, wait a while." And with that, Elwah the powerful, breaks the communication, again reminding me of my god mother.

The logs in the fireplace have burnt to ashes, the small languid flames are struggling to stay alive. The fire is losing its heat, smoke begins to billow up the chimney.

I am aware that Hasan and Saeed are both staring at me. The white wolf is dozing still, apparently oblivious to what is going on.

"Azizi, what is happening?" I turn to face Hasan. "I am not sure, Hasan. Elwah said to wait a while." Hasan nods and goes back to his chair.

Saeed leans into me and whispers, "Azizi, I could see and hear what you saw. How is that possible?"

Resting a hand on Saeed's shoulder, I smile at him, "Elwah has powers that I cannot even imagine. I think it was he that wished for you to see him."

Saeed looks awed and reflects in silence on what he has just experienced.

It is not long, before I sense a prickling up my spine. The white wolf suddenly whips his head up, fixing his whole attention to the centre of the room. Turning to the others, I am about to tell them that Elwah is about to make contact with me, when a column of air turning white as a light mist materialises. Before anyone can react, I already know. The mist clears and, in its stead, Elwah stands smiling.

Hasan is the first to react. Leaping from his chair he bows on bended knee before his prince. Saeed is gaping, the wolf has gone back to napping before the fire, and I am tempted to throw myself into Elwah's arms.

At that very moment, the door to the study opens suddenly. Sarek holding a bundle of firewood enters. At the sight of Elwah standing in the middle of the room, Sarek drops the wood that scatter with a thud on the floor. He stands there a moment before falling to one knee, exclaiming, "Your lordship!" Confused and perplexed, and unsure whether to keep his eyes averted, Sarek keeps staring in disbelief.

"It was not my intention to startle so many people." Elwah smiles a small ironic smile. "Please, Hasan, please stand. Sarek, it is good to see you serving your captain with such loyal attention." Elwah turns to Saeed, whose mouth has not closed. "Saeed, thank you for saving my beloved Azizi and bringing him safely into Hasan's hands."

The white wolf stands, casually ambles to Elwah and fixes him with piercing blue eyes. Elwah caresses the wolf's head and sighs.

"Now Azizi, will I be graced with an embrace?"

He does not have to ask me twice. Having recovered from his apparition, I am tempted to throw myself into his welcoming arms. Instead, I walk to him, a little unsteadily and allow him to enfold me into his embrace. Gently releasing me, Elwah goes to Sarek holding out a hand to invite him to stand. Resting his hands on Sarek's shoulders, Elwah kindly says, "Thank you Sarek. You may retire."

Sarek bows deeply, turns and leaves.

Elwah begins to gather the pieces of wood that have scattered across the floor and casually throws them into the fireplace. A moment later, Saeed realising that the prince of Naasée is doing domestic chores, bursts into action picking up the remaining logs.

Hasan turns to Elwah, "My lord Elwah, is it safe for Sarek to know?"

Elwah smiles back, "By morning, Sarek will have forgotten this night. All he will remember is that he had a pleasant and safe dream." He then turns to me, "I am sure, Azizi that you understand that it is safer and infinitely more convenient to communicate this way." I am reminded of similar words my god mother used to explain her apparition in the desert. He adds, "I am aware in part of your concerns regarding Master Ahmad. It is sad, but I think your concerns are well founded."

"But why invade my residence? What possible motive could he have for doing that? I do not remember ever offending him." Hasan's tone borders on anger.

"It is not you he's after, Hasan."

"Then who..."

"Isn't it obvious?"

Hasan looks at me briefly. "But why?"

Elwah sighs, looks at me and then Saeed, finally coming to a decision.

"Master Ahmad, thinks that Azizi is still in possession of the Sacred Tears of Apphat."

"How could I...?" Elwah holds his hand up at my interruption.

"He also thinks that you, Hasan are protecting your own interest by isolating Azizi here, in your residence."

Both Hasan and I openly stare at Elwah, unable to comprehend the enormity of this statement. Elwah looks intensely at Saeed, to the point that Saeed blushes and looks down. Elwah briefly nods and smiles to himself. Turning his attention back to Hasan, he asks, "Hasan, it is time for Azizi to know why you are charged with protecting the Haafiz. Please explain this to him now."

Hasan looks astonished, he looks at Elwah, then me and finally at Saeed and back to Elwah before asking, "Lord Elwah, are you sure...?"

"It is necessary for him to know." Looking back at Saeed he

adds, "Saeed will need to know as well. His destiny has been woven into this for many years."

Saeed gives me an inquisitive look. I cannot answer his silent question and shrug my shoulders.

Hasan visibly swallows, taking a deep breath he begins, "Many decades ago, the Tear of Apphat named Elwah was placed into the care of the High Priests of Naasée for safekeeping. It was decided, that to prevent the stone from being coveted by any one group among them, the Sacred Tear would be placed in the care of one individual. He would be named the Haafiz, or Sacred Keeper and his sole duty would be to keep and guard the Stone until it is needed.

To do so, they came up with a sacred and secret ritual that enables the Tear of Apphat to manifest physically. The stone was guarded in a sacred room protected with great magic. A tradition evolved that when a Haafiz dies, another would be sought among the people. The High priests would seek out the reincarnation of the previous Haafiz and would identify him initially by certain features: blue eyes, fair skin, and fair hair, as well as the required purity of his Hala. He would be put through a rigorous test of his abilities to ensure that this was the one sought." Hasan pauses, looks at Elwah, who with a nod grants his permission. "Recently, the goddess Ishtar instructed Elwah on how to ingest the Sacred Stone. The Sacred Tear, once ingested, has the unique effect of intensifying the Keeper's spiritual and magical abilities and when its power is called upon, the blue of his eyes takes on a greater intensity."

Hasan briefly pauses, looks at me and then goes on, "Naturally, the individual holding the Sacred Stone, would need to be protected at all times. The captain of the Royal Guards was given that duty and was initiated into the knowledge of who he was protecting and why. He was made to swear an oath of absolute devotion and secrecy."

A deep silence follows. Elwah looks at me with compassion in his eyes. Saeed is alternately looking at me and then Elwah. Hasan has paused, looking a little uncomfortable at having to disclose what he was sworn never to reveal.

"Azizi, do you remember the moment in the desert, when through sheer effort I was able to momentarily overcome the Sorceress' curse and come to you to pass on the Sacred Tear of Elwah?"

I remembered the tear he shed, the wondrous kiss and the pure joy that filled me. Eyes brimming with tears at the memory, I nod.

"Do you understand now, why I kept asking Hasan, through his dreams to guard and protect you; and how Hasan was able to identify you as the Sacred Haafiz?"

I remember an instance after a morning prayer, how Hasan had looked at me with astonishment, confusion, and then absolute devotion.

"The Sacred Stone that was then within you, not only intensified your powers, but affected the colour of your eyes. Azizi, has your god mother never explained the reason your eyes take on a more brilliant colour of blue?"

Briefly now, I remember that she looked so intensely at me, and then gave an explanation that my eyes took on a greater intensity with my growing into adulthood. An explanation I took on wholeheartedly. Yet now, I remember each time I had sought the power, how the Companions would stare at me, mumble the word 'Mahjir', shake their heads and resume their journey.

"I thought it was simply due to my family trait. That as we grow into adulthood, our eyes take on a greater depth of blue."

"In part this is true. As your abilities develop, it is reflected in the intensity of your eyes. Azizi, do you remember your first vision at the age of twelve?" I nod, I could never forget the vision that pushed me into the quest for the Sacred Tears. "Do you remember the one thing that sparked this vision?"

I think carefully to the day in the main classroom. It was late afternoon, as Delena Tobaha made us repeat time and time again, the sacred Parvus that no one seemed to be able to recite with the proper inflexions. I remember wanting the air and freedom of my forest, and then suddenly, now I remember the flash of blue light seemingly coming from a stray beam of late sunlight.

"A ray of blue light." Elwah smiles and affirms my response. "What else triggers your visions Azizi?"

"The taste of salt from my tears."

"Azizi, now think, what does the legend of the Tears of Apphat state as to their origin?"

"They are the Tears of Creation." Suddenly realisation dawns on me. "The Tears of Creation are of water and salt; their colour is blue." Reflecting on what I have just said, I add, "The ocean Elwah represents Joy, while the ocean of Malkizar represents sorrow. The waters of joy and sorrow, mix at the passage of Conflict. Yet Joy and Sorrow cannot one with the other be." I realise that I have just quoted the Sacred Parvus interpreting the secret of the Sacred Stones.

"Azizi, now remember, what words were pronounced

through you when your ability to seek the Stones of Apphat was questioned?"

As in a trance, I hear again the words spoken, this time with my own voice: "Behold my beloved, born of my tears."

"Yes Azizi, that is what you were named—beloved. Your stars at your birth aligned in the constellation of Sorrow. A child born of the Tears of Sorrow. You were born on the second hour of the second day of the second month of Malkizar. That made you a child of Stardust, a being of pure magic and light." Elwah pauses a moment before adding, "There is among the old writings, a prophesy about a child, born of the Tears, who would emerge from the land of water and ice. The rest of the prophecy is a matter of interpretation. But that part stands clear."

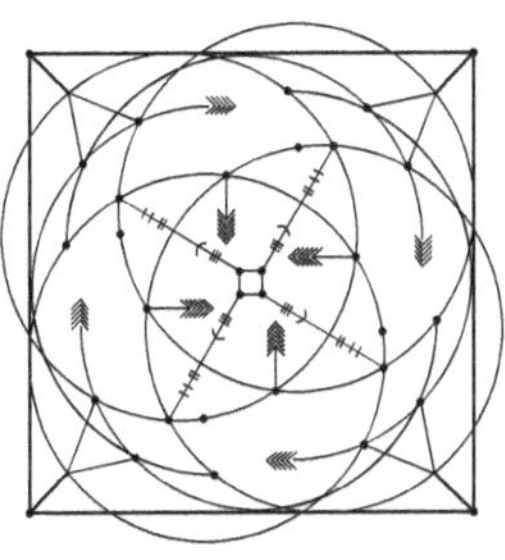

CHAPTER TEN

A hush like a heavy mantle settles in the room. A muteness I find uncomfortable. Hasan is looking at me with pride. If Saeed could look at me with more awe and devotion, I have yet to see it. I bow my head at the recognition of the facts.

"Your birth is partly the reason your being accepted the sacred Stone. Azizi, the Elders of the Council all know the legends. They are adept at reading the stars and all of them have heard of your defeat of the Sorceress. When you walked into this city, the first of the Elders to have met you was Master Ahmad. He took one look at your piercing blue eyes and your fair skin. He then sighted your friend Saeed, whose emerald green eyes speak of strong magic, and both of you were followed by a rare white wolf with intense blue eyes; Ahmad came to the wrong conclusion, that you were still holding one if not both Sacred Tears."

My legs suddenly feel weak at the revelation of so much. I

make my way to the couch and sit, a small knot of nausea settling in my stomach, I reflect on everything Elwah has just said.

"Your god mother Aïschah knew all of this. Aïschah had never taken on an apprentice. Once she had studied your birth chart, knowing that you had inherited your mother's sight, was already enough. But when you came to her with your first vision, she was certain. She took on the responsibility very few would have accepted. That of training you for your destiny. A destiny, Azizi, that is still unfolding."

The room is filled with a silence fragile as glass, threatening to shatter at the slightest noise or utterance.

Finally, taking a slow deep breath, being careful not to make too much of it, I look up at Elwah and softly, I ask, "What of the Sacred Tears now? They disappeared once the Sorceress had been defeated. Is my task not done then?"

Elwah looks at me, his eyes penetrate to very core of my being. He smiles, a warm and comforting smile.

"Azizi, you are asking me to reveal the most sacred of secrets."

My cheeks suddenly feel warm. I look at him and quickly look away. "I, no! I don't wish to know."

With a lightness in his voice he responds, "Azizi, beloved. You are entitled to know. Though I will not reveal the Sacred ritual, I can at least tell you some things that only the high priests of Naasée know, as well as a few advanced masters; including your god mother."

The news that my god mother would know such deep secrets somehow still astonishes me and yet, I know that I should not be.

Elwah settles on a chair near me. "Some things cannot be put into words, so I will need to give you some information with some mental images." With that, he holds my hand and begins: "Azizi, you have seen the love transformation for yourself. Which of the Great Guardians came to Ijlal? Remember also that you predicted this in your interpretation of Ijlal's dream."

"Hadid, Guardian of the air." An image of a giant bird, the guardian of the air, Hadid flying directly at me almost makes me fall.

"Yes. But why that particular Guardian? Why not another guardian of nature?"

"I am not sure. Is it to do with his lineage?"

"Not quite Azizi. It has to do with destiny and his star soul."

I see an image of the intertwined snakes, the amulet I had asked smith to make, floats and twist before my eyes. It begins to glow.

I look at Elwah, perplexed.

"Let me ask you another question then. What about Shahulm? If a guardian were to manifest for him, which one would it be?

Again, no immediate answer comes, and I shake my head.

"Azizi, you have seen Shahulm dance for his prince. What element of nature does he remind you of?"

The memory of seeing Shahulm dance for his prince fills my mind. My arms are covered in goose bumps, "Fire."

"Yes. Now ask yourself what keeps the element of fire burning?"

Comprehension hits me like cold icy water. "Air. Fire needs air, without it, it would extinguish."

Elwah smiles acknowledging my answers. He adds, "It was not only the fruit of the Schiraz tree that brought Shahulm back to consciousness. It was the essential presence of Ijlal and his elemental air that fed him, encouraged him, and finally brought him back to health. Without it, he would have been ill for the rest of his life and eventually perished.

In fact, I sensed that when you were still searching for him, Ijlal asked you to contact Shahulm. During your contact, on instinctual impulse, you allowed Ijlal to see Shahulm. Such is his love for him that unconsciously, Ijlal breathed his elemental air into his spirit. It caused Shahulm to open his eyes and momentarily break the sorceress' hold on him. It gave him the will to hope."

Elwah rested a moment, allowing his words to make sense.

"But Elwah, how does this relate to the Sacred Sapphires?"

He gives me the same knowing smile that my god mother often gives me when I ask a question, the answer to which I should know. He allows me a moment to reflect and when the solution does not come, he asks once more, "Who or what do you think is the Guardian Spirit of the Sacred Sapphires?"

The question hits me in the chest, my heart begins to race, a sense of expansion fills me. The question seems so obvious. It makes sense, but I have no answer for that. The stones were enveloped in light as they vanished, and a voice told me that it was not yet my time.

Almost in a whisper, I answer, "I heard the voice of its spirit, but I do not know its name."

"Its name may not be known, for it is possible that the guardian of the Sacred Tears has no name." Elwah's smile fades, a serious look in his eyes, he asks, "This, relates to the Sacred Tears. Azizi, who would be the guardian that would manifest for you?"

Considering the question, I shake my head, not knowing the answer.

"Remember your early training, Azizi, in the forest. When you became lost or frustrated, what guardians would assist you?" Memories of my beloved forest fills my mind. The sight of the spirit of the forest guiding me to the blue star flowers. The smaller woodland spirits showing me where the wild herbs grew.

"The spirits of the forest would answer your call, Azizi. This was the beginning of you harnessing your power. The power that flows through you does not originate from a specific guardian as such. You manifested some of that power in the cave, when confronting the sorceress. Even though I was semi-conscious and under the spell of the sorceress, I sensed it, and was aware of it. That power flowed at your call, and in that moment, not one but all the elementals answered your call and made manifest. Remember, the elements of air, fire and water, even earth were present. Only your training under the tutelage of your god mother allowed you to regain control.

My memory of that moment surfaces when power was unleashed at the sorceress. The sight of the Companions as they stood in awe at the manifestation of wind, water, and lighting, even the stones within the cave trembled.

How suddenly confident yet scared I was.

"Azizi, do you understand now, how the warnings of the Sacred Tears are real. Imagine you, in possession of the Tear of Elwah, but now imagine that you also held the Tear of Malkizar, all the elements of nature would answer your call. If you stood at the head of an army thus, you would be invincible. How terrifying would that be for your enemy?" Elwah pauses, "Can you now understand the motives of Master Ahmad? Are his motives based on desire and greed or are they based on the urge to protect the

Tears from misuse?"

Another fragile silence follows.

"The question remains though, were they the same motives that betrayed me to the sorceress, so that she could retrieve the Sacred Tear of Elwah from me?"

Elwah sighs.

In a soft, timid voice almost a whisper, Saeed addresses Elwah, "Master Elwah?" Elwah looks at him and smiles. "Master Elwah, what would my guardian spirit be?" Elwah considers Saeed's question, his eyes taking on a serious, slightly unfocussed look as if seeing something at a great distance.

"Young Saeed, I do not see all things clearly, as some things are hidden even from me. But this I can say. It will be necessary for you to ground and master your innate power. If you do not, I dread to see the reality of your guardian. Were your love be challenged, the power that is your guardian would easily engulf half the world." Elwah's eyes re-focus, resting on Saeed who has visibly paled at these words. A rogue wave suddenly crashes against the tower, sending a spray of foam high into the air and a shudder through the walls.

Saeed briefly looks at me, the devotion in his eyes momentarily replaced by a look of sheer terror. Casting his eyes back to the ground, his shoulders hunched, repeatedly interlacing the fingers of his hands, Saeed looks subdued.

Elwah turns to Hasan. "Hasan, I understand your concerns and the reasons you want me to return to Naasée." Hasan looks up, hope and determination in his eyes. "But do you think that my return will be celebrated and for that matter even welcomed? And what of Master Ahmad? Do you think me challenging him, without the Tear of Elwah in my possession, would he not convince the Council of Elders to usurp my position?"

Only the distant thunder of the crashing waves below the tower can be heard in the room as a vague rumble.

Hasan is unsure where to look. He holds Elwah's gaze for a moment and then looks down.

"Hasan, I am not admonishing you. Your concerns are well founded and loyal to me but more importantly to Naasée." Again, Elwah lets out a long and measured sigh. "And if it came to that, who would the Council appoint as the new Haafiz? The Tear of Elwah is not here to be transferred."

Hasan clenches his fists, his thoughts clearly etched on his face, and audible to both Elwah and my mind, *"But you are the prince of Naasée, not only by right as a reincarnated Haafiz, but by your loyalty to the people of this city, and by the power you hold."* Hasan continues out loud, "Only you can restore order to the Council of Elders. Left unchecked, some will begin a rebellion that can only lead to chaos."

"Elwah," daring to interrupt, I ask, "Regardless of their individual power, how can any of the Elders assume authority without the Sacred Tear?"

Elwah turns to me, a brooding and serious look on his face.

"This, Azizi, is the Sacred Secret I referred to earlier." He takes a deep breath and releasing it gently he goes on. "There are three ways to manifest the Sacred Tear of Elwah as well as the Sacred Tear of Malkizar. The first and most legitimate way is to wait until the Guardian chooses to manifest one or both stones. The time and place for that is always unknown. The second, is through a closely guarded secret and sacred ritual that has been handed down from high priest to high priest verbally. I hold only half of that information. For safekeeping reasons, the other half is held only by the Master of Rites and Ceremonies, Mahjir Suffrah." Elwah briefly looks at me. This is the master who conducted my first initiation. I wait for the third reason.

"The last and most disturbing way is the one the sorceress used. A ritual of black magic that forces the stone to appear. She could only muster enough strength and power for the Stone of Malkizar because the stone unwillingly responded to the energy of chaos."

It is as if the waves below have suddenly ceased their assault on the tower. I cannot even hear my own breath.

"That last way is fraught with corrupt energy and comes with a curse. The user will not be able to live long enough to benefit from its power, because the Stone of Malkizar will always call for its partner, the Stone of Elwah. What the sorceress did not know, is that when the two are joined, if the individual holding them is not spiritually prepared for the transformation that would follow, the sacred Stones' powers attack and destroy that individual." Elwah looks directly at me, "As you have witnessed, Azizi."

Turning back to Hasan, Elwah frowns a little. "Hasan, I would have to convince the council of Elders to hold this ceremony, in order to call for the stone of Elwah. There is no guarantee that they would agree to such a ritual, or that the ritual would be successful in bringing the Sacred Tear of Apphat back to Naasée and furthermore, that the Council would be unanimous in agreeing I be the one to hold it once more for safe keeping."

Both Hasan and Elwah are staring at the fireplace. Saeed is hushed and looks as though he wishes he wasn't here.

"When news broke out that you had been taken, Elwah, the rumour was that your Council of Elders were frozen into inaction." My voice, although soft, breaks the silence and with it the apparent tension. "Your army was ready to wage a holy war, but was held back by your general, Hasan. If it weren't for him, Naasée would have been lost and with it the fight to find the Sacred Tear, defeat the sorceress and release you from her curse. Only through your power was I able to gain the courage and will to search for the lost Tear of Elwah, not realising at the time that I would also find you."

Elwah is looking at me with a composed look, Hasan is watching me with a degree of pride. For a strange reason, the white wolf raises its head, ambles towards me and sits beside me, looking directly at Elwah.

Elwah smiles and emits a small laugh.

"Your army is gathering around you, Azizi."

"Elwah, I agree with Hasan. Only you can possibly have the authority and the power to bring the Council of Elders to order. Even if Master Ahmad were to convince others to side with him, they could not sway the rest of the Council. I plan to inform my god mother of what is happening. I will ask for her presence and support, which I know she will give whole heartedly." I pause briefly, gathering my thoughts. "But you must be present in person, not as you are here—a projection of yourself. You must appear in the flesh."

Elwah lets out a long sigh. I can see he is considering what I have asking him to do.

"Travelling only at night, not just for concealment but comfort, it will take at least three dahé if not a lahé to get here. And then of course there is the issue of me arriving unannounced. If I read your intention correctly Azizi, you would want me to make a surprise entrance, which means no one can know that I am on my way. There is also the issue of security once I arrive; after all," this he adds with an ironic smile, "I would not want to be abducted all over again."

I have made up mind, "I propose to ask Ijlal if he is willing, to bring the Companions to protect and accompany you. I will ask him to make sure that you travel in disguise." As an afterthought, I ask, "Do you think that Shahulm is well enough to travel?"

Elwah is pensive. Hasan is looking at me with admiration.

"I think Shahulm is well enough. There is a bit of news I have not had time to convey though." Elwah stands and takes a few paces, collecting his thoughts. "The defeat of the Over Lord has left a power vacuum at the Great Citadel. Although it was General Giafar who took the citadel, with the help of course of the army of Glesskerel and some of the soldiers of Naasée; Giafar would never claim that position. The Sultan of Schiraz will not make such a claim either, mostly for political peace. It was decided that the position of Regent of the Citadel, should be offered to Prince Shahulm. Of course, this has had the desired effect of pacifying the Lord of Glesskerel, that he readily agreed to the union of his son with Ijlal."

I am astounded at the news and overjoyed that the union between Shahulm and Ijlal has been approved. I am also excited that Shahulm will have an important role to play in establishing peace between the kingdoms.

"This is great news." I add with a slight smile, "How does Ijlal feel about his star soul as a minor king?"

Elwah smiles, "I think Ijlal is looking forward to being spoiled. But no, Ijlal is very proud to be by his side. It remains to be seen if the duties of a regent will not interfere with their relationship."

Eager to bring the conversation back on track, I address both Elwah and Hasan. "Elwah, would you ask Ijlal on my behalf and seek the Companions' protection for your return. Of course, if Shahulm is well enough to travel, then please extend the invitation to him as well." Elwah nods in agreement, "let us allow a lahé for your arrival. Hasan, as administrator of the city, will you call a meeting of the elders to coincide with Elwah's arrival?" With a note of mischief in my voice, I add, "let Elwah's return and appearance at the assembled elders be as much of an uncomfortable surprise to some. In the meantime, I will speak with my god mother and explain to her the circumstances and ask for her presence at the meeting."

Both Elwah and Hasan look at me with bemused smiles. Elwah turns to Hasan and light heartedly proclaims, "Hasan, your station as administrator may yet be usurped by this young man. Be careful and protect you position."

Hasan bows and laughing replies, "Yes Lord Elwah, I will be most careful."

I look at them both, shaking my head, joining in the amusement.

C H A P T E R   E L E V E N

It has been several duna since Elwah's presence de-materialised.

I contacted my god mother. She was already aware of many of the issues concerning dissatisfaction among the Elders for the ongoing absence of Elwah. Although initially surprised at the manner in which Master Ahmad had entered Hasan's residence, upon reflection she stated that it seemed to fit his character. She had suspected many duwae ago, when Elwah's disappearance had been known, that some of the guards of Naasée had been involved. As such, she thought at the time that there was a deeper conspiracy but said nothing and watched instead how the Elders would deal with it.

She agreed to be there for the meeting when Elwah would return and promised her confidentiality and support.

Quiet and withdrawn at first, Saeed is now asking all kinds of questions. At first, how Elwah is able to project his physical presence from so far away.

"Saeed, I can give you the same answer my god mother gave me when she materialised in the desert. She told me it was a technique of the seventh level of the seventh Mastership. One that I will eventually learn to master."

It is early morning. The sky is a bright clear blue, the sun rays beam down on the city of Naasée like a blessing. Some of the stalls in the streets and market are just beginning to open. Colourful awnings are raised, stands are laden with goods of all kinds. Shops that sell fabrics are the most colourful. My attention though is drawn by the variety of fruits and spices. The sight of boxes of fruits, golden and ripe that have matured in the late summer make my mouth water. Jars upon jars of spices, some of which I recognise, others are completely foreign to me. I am tempted to inquire and make purchases, but I am distracted by Saeed's youthful energy. I think the five-year-old sense of wonder has surfaced. There are stalls full of wooden toys, lanterns made of fine glass and painted in brilliant colours. Beautiful, handcrafted paper kites hang from display racks and decorated with mythological creatures, including one that I recognise as the fire beast. Saeed's energy and enthusiasm are contagious, I can't help smile and laugh at all the things that attract his attention.

The markets are now busy with people purchasing produce and condiments for their meals. Others are strolling through the stalls, looking for savoury treats and sweets. Merchants are calling out their wares, inviting people to look and sample their products. Beautiful young women are bargaining for a better price on expensive looking fabrics. Others are being enticed by merchants of exquisite fragrances with calls of free samples. Saeed stops at one of those merchants; instinctively I know that he is looking for oil of orange blossoms. He must be disappointed, after testing several different bottles, he replaces them all, shaking his head walks away, leaving a thwarted merchant.

I am trailing a little behind, taking time to look around, while keeping a watchful eye on Saeed, whose red hair and emerald green eyes are attracting more and more attention. A slight prickling at the back of my neck, warns me that we are being followed and watched. I stop at a stall that sells parchments and inks, the merchant seems happy for me to look and handle some of the products. Looking up I see the person that has been following us. He is asking questions from the merchant of perfumes. I cannot at first decide where I have seen this person before. A vague image of Saeed's terrified face surfaces in my memory, a hand across his mouth, an impassive face next to his holding him captive. This is Master Ahmad's servant.

Strangely, he pays very little attention to my movements apart for the occasional glance in my direction. He follows every move that Saeed is making. My heart quickens as a small anger in me begins to boil. I clench my teeth; my hands start to form fists. The reason for this servant to be following Saeed seems unsubstantiated; however, there is a shallow lewd energy about it. My reaction in some way surprises me, and yet I recognize that I want to protect Saeed's innocence. Curious to know the reason for observing and following Saeed, I decide to keep watching and if necessary, I will intervene. I am incredulous that the servant is making very little effort to conceal his actions.

Casually, I make my way to the more crowded stalls that sell the vegetables. I am inquisitive as to where these come from. This city is surrounded by desert and too far from any other major town to import such commodities. I make a note to ask Hasan about this. As I reach the nearest stall, the back of a customer seems familiar. He is negotiating a price for some of the vegetables he has just selected. With a sigh of relief, I recognise Sarek, Hasan's personal aide. Standing a little apart, I listen in on the bargaining and note how adept Sarek is at lowering the price first asked. He does so without threat or loud words, just a quiet attitude that may give the impression that he will just shop elsewhere. They agree on the price and Sarek is about to leave when I tap him on the shoulder.

"Master Azizi!"

"Good morning Sarek. I did not know that shopping for the household was also part of your duties."

He gives me a tired smiles, shrugs his shoulders saying, "I take turns with the head cook. It gets me out of the household into the fresh air and away from other duties,"

I understand that to be at Hasan's beg and call, could become tiresome after a while. I smile at him in an empathetic way.

"Sarek, would you have a moment to give me some advice?"

Sarek looks a little puzzled but nods his agreement.

"Master Ahmad's servant is following us, precisely, he is taking a particular interest in Saeed. If I point him out to you, can you at least tell me his name?"

Initial shock is quickly replaced by obvious dislike for Ahmad's servant. Sarek starts to look around. I gently place my hand on his arm to call his attention.

"I don't want to draw attention to us, let me tell you where he is at the moment."

I quickly turn and scan the market and spot Saeed and not far from him, I spot the servant.

"To my right and near the stall that sells the colourful kites, you will notice that Saeed has attracted a few onlookers. Several paces nearer to us, Ahmad's servant is casually looking at a stall with toys. He is dressed in a grey overcoat. Do you see him?"

Furtively, Sarek while pretending to look at the other goods on offer, looks up and nods his head.

"I see him. I am astounded that Master Ahmad has set his servant to follow you. His name is Tabrass." Sarek almost spits the name out with an air of utter disdain and adds, "In my tribe's language, that name means 'untrustworthy' or 'liar.'" Sarek shakes his head in disbelief. "Would you like me to report this to his excellency?"

I take a moment to reflect and come to a decision. "No, thank you Sarek. I do not think that it will change anything. I will keep an eye on Saeed, if he needs assistance, I will step in."

Sarek bows and is about to depart when I remember, "Sarek, could you tell me where to buy meat at a reasonable price? I think the wolf will need to be fed a more wholesome meal than the morsels I have been giving him." I pull out the money pouch that my father gave me. There are a few coins left.

Sarek raises a hand to gently decline payment, "Master Azizi, I can probably negotiate a better price for you. Please let me make this purchase for you as a way of thanking you for your help."

I hesitate not wanting him to be put out. With a smile Sarek adds, "His excellency has asked me to make sure that you are well looked after. I am sure that includes the white wolf."

"Sarek, I am grateful. I will thank Hasan."

Sarek smiles, bows slightly, and takes his leave.

A clamour breaks out at the outer reaches of the town. Only a distant sound at first, which builds up into a commotion. A wave of excited shouts rises from the main gate. People are turning in the direction of the sound and are at first making their way unhurriedly, and then breaking into a run. I see Sarek turn and head towards the main gate. Tabrass, Master Ahmad's servant hesitates but stays put. He must have been given strict orders not to abandon his quarry. Saeed, on the other hand looks in all directions, a clear expression of surprise on his face. Turning this way and that, he sees me, smiles, and makes his way towards me. I notice at this point that Tabrass looks away, pretending not to have seen me.

"Azizi, do you know what is happening?"

"I have no idea, Saeed. Shall we go and look?"

He nods his head vigorously with an air of excitement.

I take his hand and break out into a fast walk down the main thorough fare and as far from Tabrass as possible. I manage to mingle us into the crowd, hopefully losing the servant in the process. We follow the people who suddenly part to let a soldier dressed in the royal colours runs past us with obvious urgent news.

The main gate is in sight, the crowd is parting, lining the sides of the street, and in the distance, I see several men on horseback making their way up towards us and the main stronghold. I briefly wonder at their identity, when suddenly I realise, I am looking at young soldiers dressed in deep blue robes, a red sapphire at the collar. These are men from Schiraz. I do not recognise any of them. Desperately, I look beyond them, a young soldier, rides a powerful and elegant white stallion. He wears a golden breastplate, an unmistakable air of royalty about him, sitting straight and proud, occasionally smiling at the crowd. My heart skips a beat, Ijlal is here! Beside him, a slender person, dressed in a loose brown robe adorned with runic symbols of magic, rides a black stallion. His hood covers his head, and an odd silver mask conceals his face. I do not have time to question this person's identity, when behind them, is another young man dressed in a silver breastplate adorned with blue gems and wearing a short cape displaying the blue and gold colours of Glesskerel. He is otherwise bare headed, and his handsome looks draw gasps of admiration from the women and men alike as he passes. Shahulm accompanies his prince! My heart swells with joy and pride at the sight of them. Desperate to call out, I restrain myself and melt back into the crowd. No less than ten soldiers follow him, dressed in the same colours. Guarding the very rear of the double royal escort, dressed as a young general, Faruq, eldest son of General Giafar, brother to the Sultan of Schiraz, sits upright, scanning the crowd, his body on high alert.

Shouts of greetings from the crowd meet the strangers. Whispers run like wildfire. The words of 'Prince of Shiraz' are mixed with questions of 'who are the noble men following him?' The occasional "They are so beautiful!" The echo of those words with so many memories, pulls at my heartstrings.

Saeed is awed with the spectacle, whereas, I have withdrawn into the rear of the crowd. I do not want to be recognised and give away our advantage by acknowledging that I know them. As Faruq passes by, continuously scanning the crowd, his eyes meet mine. His initial astonishment is quickly replaced with a hint of a smile and a slight bow of his head. I briefly return his bow acknowledging recognition. A few people near me look around attempting to see who this young general has just bowed to. Immediately behind him, I recognise Husam and Fatin who are looking straight ahead. The younger companions Isamadeen, his twin Rauf, and Jamal are not among them. I assume that being the youngest, they have stayed behind in Schiraz.

I take Saeed's hand and gently draw him away from the crowd, leaning into him, I whisper, "Saeed, let us go and welcome them at Hasan's residence." With difficulty, Saeed tears himself away from the impromptu parade and follows me. As we walk away, I send out a wave of energy seeking Ahmad's servant, Tabrass. He must have been caught in the crowd as I cannot sense his presence.

~

PURPOSEFULLY MAKING OUR WAY through the crowds, we make it to Hasan's residence shortly after the arrival of the parade. Some of the crowd is still milling around, hoping for more information. The front courtyard appears to be in some chaos. All the riders have dismounted. Servants are running around, carrying the riders' belongings inside while others take hold of the horses leading them to stables. Xan, Hasan's trusted guard, looks bemused and is attempting to restore order. He directs the soldiers of Glesskerel to quarters at the rear of the main residence. Faruq is leading the Schiraz soldiers to their quarters. Sarek has returned from the markets and is leading the guests into the main residence.

As inconspicuously as possible, Saeed in tow, I make my way to a side entrance. We enter the main hall of the residence. The room is filled with the noise of animated talk. I notice the back of Hasan unhurriedly disappearing at the top of the main stairs, leading the man in the loose brown robe, still wearing his silver mask. My heart pounds, realising that this must be Elwah in disguise. I look around furtively, checking to see if anyone has noticed the stranger walking off with Hasan.

In the middle of the group, Ijlal looks up, his eyes meet mine. A broad smile spreads across his face. A swell of emotion fills me. I walk up to him and without a hint of hesitation I wrap my arms around him. "Ijlal!"

The person behind him turns, the wondrous eyes of Shahulm look at me and he smiles. My eyes tear up to see them both and have them so close to me. Shahulm looks a picture of health and vitality. The fire in him has returned. Releasing Ijlal, I go to him and embrace him. "Shahulm, it is so wonderful to see you in such good health." I recognise the familiar subtle fragrance of spices in the air around him.

"Azizi, my brother, thank you." He is still wearing the sacred talisman of the two entwined snakes I had made so many year ago.

Ijlal looks at Saeed and then back to me with an inquisitive expression.

Saeed is watching my interaction with a slight look of surprise. I am about to make the introductions when I catch a movement out of the corner of my eye and immediately sense the presence of Tabrass.

"Ijlal, let us leave this chaos and talk more privately in a room upstairs."

I take Saeed's hand in mine and lead him, Ijlal and Shahulm away.

⁓

We reach Hasan's meeting room. I knock gently on the door and wait. A moment later, the door opens enough to reveal Hasan blocking most of the interior view. He quickly scans beyond us and without a word, opens the door to let us in.

The emotion at the first sight of Elwah standing in the middle of the room, catches in my throat. His incomparable blue eyes look at me to the very core of my soul. He beams his enigmatic smile, his arms open to me, it is all I can do not to throw myself into his embrace.

Hasan closes the door and joins us. Ijlal and Shahulm both greet Elwah in a manner that indicates an ease of spirit between them. I notice that Saeed has receded in the background, a little shy with all these strangers and overwhelmed with Prince Elwah's physical presence.

I gently go to him and take his hand, leading him back to the centre of the room and introduce him: "Ijlal, this is Saeed. You have met him once before when he was but a boy."

Ijlal looks intensely at Saeed, reflecting a moment, his face suddenly lights up with a smile that could disarm a thousand foes.

"Saeed? Saeed... son of Fariqa of the Huda people?"

Saeed nods, looking a little uncomfortable.

Ijlal gently steps to him and without warning, throws his arms around Saeed, "Thank you Saeed, without you and your mother, my search for my beloved would have been in vain." Ijlal releases Saeed, who has now gone a very bright shade of red. His eyes firmly locked to the ground.

Ijlal turns to Shahulm, "My beloved, this is the boy who was instrumental in raising our plight with his mother Fariqa. She safely guided us through the Huda Pass in our search for you."

It is Shahulm's turn to stand before Saeed, who now is so self-conscious, he does not know where to turn. The sheer grace and unworldly beauty of the prince of Glesskerel go some way to relax Saeed. Shahulm takes Saeed's hands in his and softly speaks to him, "Saeed, thank you. Please be a brother to us."

Saeed is both pleased and surprised. He looks at me with his inimitable shy smile, not sure what to do. I smile at him and nod.

Turning back to Shahulm and Ijlal who stands next to him, he whispers back, "Thank you".

Then Shahulm does what the custom dictates between brothers, and kisses Saeed on both cheeks. At first taken by surprise, Saeed's body braces a little, but then the elegance and sincerity Shahulm expresses, Saeed allows himself to be so embraced. Nevertheless, the colour of his skin has remained a very ripe peach.

I see Ijlal smile, bemused at this very intimate scene, shaking his head slightly.

I look at him inquiringly.

"You two are such a pair. You Azizi, with the eyes of the blue desert sky and Saeed, with eyes of the green moss of your beloved forest."

Hasan, Elwah and Shahulm break out into a light-hearted laugh. Hasan adding, "Not to mention a wolf as white as snow with eyes of steel."

The wolf has been watching the interaction, ambles to me and looking up stares into the depth of my being. I briefly see the green hills of my mountains and a gentle pair of dark brown eyes float and disappear. My heart beats a little harder, a tender ache fills my chest, I reach out and caress his head.

Hasan breaks out into another chuckle, "The magic is very thick in this room!"

I am a little puzzled at how well-prepared Hasan is to have received so many 'guests' as he calls them. Turning to Ijlal and Shahulm, I state, "You have a veritable small army as your escort." Both look to Hasan for an explanation. Turning to Hasan I ask,

"Hasan, how did you know in advance of their arrival?"

Hasan looks at Ijlal, who smiles and nods, "I was informed two duna ago. A large Kestrel appeared on the balcony of my study and delivered a written message it held in its claw. Upon delivery into my hands, it flew off again."

Ijlal gives me a mischievous smile.

"You still have the power to transform?" I ask incredulously.

Smiling, he nods.

A soft knock at the door puts us all suddenly on high alert. Hasan gestures for us to be silent and indicating a side door, directs Elwah to it. We wait until Elwah has disappeared. Hasan goes to the door and opening it is surprised to see Faruq standing there. "Come in Faruq."

Faruq nods, takes in the room and its occupants in that unmistakable manner of his, that will not let the slightest detail escape his attention. "Hasan, your aide Sarek says to inform you that Tabrass is requesting an audience with his master, Master

Ahmad as soon as it is convenient." Faruq smiles enigmatically and adds, "I think by 'as soon as convenient', he meant as immediate as possible."

Hasan smiles and nods, "Ah, the young general who is capable of distinguishing truth from falsehood." Referring to the meaning of his name, Hasan smiles, clasping Faruq on the shoulder and adds "Faruq, if Ijlal ever tires of you, I would welcome you as general of the royal guards in an instant."

Ijlal makes a coughing sound, raising his eyebrows with a questioning look directly into his cousin's eyes. Faruq replies with a knowing smile, "Cousin, my loyalty is yours to the end of my days."

Hasan humorously acknowledges defeat and turning to Faruq asks him, "Where is Sarek now?"

"I left him at the bottom of the stairs leading to your office. He appears to be stopping anyone from accessing those stairs."

Hasan nods. "Faruq, would you please select one of your trusted soldiers to come and stand guard outside this door. Inform Sarek that this what I have requested. Also, ask him to maintain his current position. Instruct him that I have agreed to a visit from Master Ahmad immediately but that I can only see him for a short time, as I have guests to attend to."

Faruq hesitate a moment, looks at Hasan and whispers, "Perhaps that item needs to be put away." Hasan follows Faruq's gaze and seeing the silver mask that Elwah wore, lying on the desk, takes a breath and nods. "Well spotted Faruk." He takes the mask and places it in a drawer out of sight.

Faruq salutes Hasan in the typical fashion of soldiers from Schiraz, a fist upon his heart and a short bow and exits.

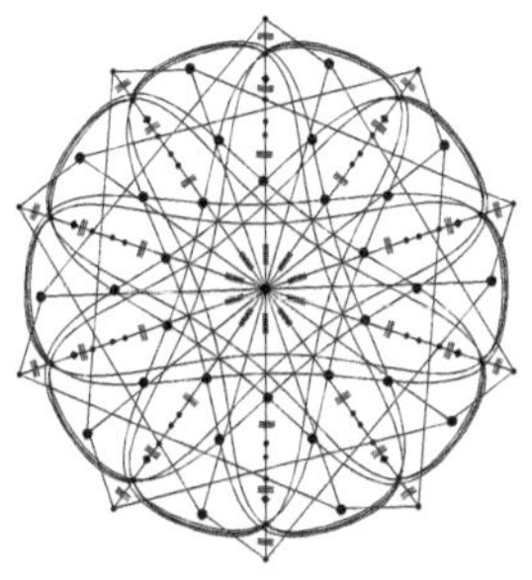

C H A P T E R   T W E L V E

Elwah re-enters the room. Hasan sighs and begins to pace in his usual manner when deep in thought.

I decide to break the silence. "Ijlal, I see that you brought a number of soldiers with you as well as three of your companions. Did you decide to leave Isamadeen, Rauf and Jamal behind because they are too young?"

Ijlal looks briefly at Shahulm who gives a slight nod, and answers, "No, Azizi. They are not left behind. Isamadeen and his twin Rauf, together with Jamal are camped outside this city and near the cave of Gibrar. I have left them as back up in case things get complicated."

I am relieved that the companions are here and always deemed equal in skill if not age. "Then Shahulm, you brought a number of soldiers from Glesskerel, was that also a strategy of protection?"

Shahulm answers with a serious look. "Not quite. Upon taking up the role of regent of the Citadel of Mina, my father insisted that given my previous experience of capture," Shahulm smiles a sad look at Ijlal at the memory, "that any movement outside the citadel, I would need to be always accompanied with men I trusted. He also appointed royal guards at the citadel from within his personal ranks."

"Between Ijlal's contingent of soldiers and your personal guards, it is any wonder that people are not thinking about an invasion." I add with a smile.

Both Ijlal and Shahulm look at Hasan.

"Azizi, that actually is part of the intention, to see what Ahmad will make of this. I want him to feel very insecure prior to his confrontation with Elwah."

"Will he suspect you then, of manipulating the Council and threatening a kind of coup?"

"Yes, Azizi. That is precisely what I think Master Ahmad will think, and possibly the other elders as well. If necessary, I want them to understand that I hold the balance of power here and that I support Prince Elwah as the rightful regent of Naasée."

A soft knock at the door and Hasan repeats his previous direction for Elwah to conceal himself.

Hasan opens the door; Faruq stands flanked by Fatin and Husam. Two of the Companions, loyal only to Ijlal and each other; the combination of 'intelligence' and 'sword edge' as their name sakes, the choice could not have been better to guard this door.

I am so happy to see them, that abandoning all caution, I rush to them to embrace them both.

Husam unexpectedly recoils from me and in a slightly mocking voice turns to Fatin and asks, "Fatin, who is this tall, strange man who seems to be so familiar with me, as to offer an embrace."

"Ah, Husam, I am not sure... although he does seem memorable."

They both look at each other and then burst out giggling at my dismay.

They then huddle around me, both throwing their arms and just about suffocate me, before releasing me with beaming smiles.

"We have been ordered to guard this door with our lives." Fatin declares in an overly dramatic tone.

Faruq shakes his head and rolling his eyes, turns to Hasan. "Hasan, I will keep company with your aide Sarek." Turning to Fatin and Husam, light heartedly says, "Do your duty you two or I will ask Azizi to turn you into goats."

As Faruq exits, Husam turns briefly to me, his hands in supplication and in mock horror mouths the words, "Please Azizi, not goats!" Bowing to us all, they turn and take their posts outside the door.

It is not long before raised voices are heard outside Hasan's door.

"I have made an appointment!" Ahamad's unmistakably arrogant tone of voice is counterbalanced by Fatin's calm assertion, "I understand Mahjir, however we have been entrusted with guarding this door to ensure that his Excellency is not unduly disturbed. Would you please give me a moment to announce your visit?"

A short knock follows, and Fatin opens the door enough to only reveal himself. "Your excellency, Mahjir Ahmad is requesting an audience."

Hasan smiles at the formality, "Thank you Fatin, please let him in."

Master Ahmad enters unceremoniously, only glancing casually

at princes Ijlal and Shahulm, and sparing me a brief look of condescending scrutiny. He marches directly to Hasan who has remained seated behind his desk. Without preamble, Ahmad addresses him, "Excellency, what is the meaning of the guards at your door, and all the foreign soldiers that have gathered in and around your residence?"

Hasan briefly looks at the princes, shakes his head once and looking directly at Master Ahmad, addresses him with a diplomatic but firm tone of voice: "Master Ahmad, even as high priest and one of the elders of the Council of Naasée, I had hoped that your manners would extend to greeting royalty with a little more decorum. As for the soldiers that are here, I had also hoped that you would understand that royalty requires protection... particularly in a time, as we have recently experienced, when heirs to kingdoms seem to vanish, abducted by forces of evil. The soldiers you refer to are personal guards of both princes."

Master Ahmad, pales a little and although seemingly calm, is seething with frustration at this address.

"As for the guards outside my door, it is to prevent any unwelcome and sudden entry without due permission." Ahmad raises a finger formulating an argument, Hasan cuts him off and adds, "Please, let me introduce you Master Ahmad. His Highness Prince Ijlal, heir to the throne of Schiraz, eldest son of his Highness the Sultan of Rashãd. And this is, His Highness Prince Shahulm, recently appointed Regent of the Citadel of Mina, eldest son, and heir to the King of Glesskerel. This is Master Ahmad, in charge of Divination and Symbols."

Master Ahmad stiffly bows to both princes before turning to Hasan.

"What then is the purpose of all these guests?"

Hasan allows himself a sardonic smile before answering, "Ah, Master Ahmad, I was going to suggest as administrator of Naasée, that you as an Elder of the Council, call a meeting of the Elders. This is to discuss the purpose of the princes' visit to our sovereignty." he adds with a mischievous smile, "and also address any other concerns you may have."

Taken aback by the last remark, Ahmad visibly relaxes a moment, before nodding his head and answering, "I will do so immediately." He bows and without a further look at anyone, exits.

Hasan is shaking his head. Ijlal looks a little amused, Shahulm raises an eyebrow before imitating Hasan.

"Not the most amiable individual, this council elder." Remarks Ijlal.

"And very few manners." Adds Saeed, which has the immediate effect of breaking the tension and sets everyone laughing. I will never get tired of watching Saeed blush.

Elwah re-appears, nodding approvingly to Hasan, "It seems that Master Ahmad's character has not improved over the years. I would venture a guess that we can expect to have a meeting of the Council of Elders tomorrow morning."

C H A P T E R   T H I R T E E N

Entering the court of assembly, I am struck by its austerity. The light is subdued, grey in texture despite a large glass dome above, the only source of natural light. The room is large, and round. Rows of individual seating rise almost all the way around, except for two doorways. The assembly of Elders and High Priests is sitting waiting for proceedings to begin. At one end, a small dais enclosed with dark wood panels and bearing the crest of Naasée stands in the centre of the seats; designated for the ruling prince of Naasée or a high priest, it partially dominates the room, allowing for all present to have a clear view. Hasan leads me and prince Ijlal unchallenged to the seats behind and slightly to the left of this dais. I hear a few whispers inquiring about the identity of the prince, most of the Elders would know of the heir to Schiraz, eldest son of Sultan Rashãd. Curious eyes follow us and keep staring. I hold my head up and stare into the void of the room. Ijlal sits, impassively looking around, unperturbed by the whispers and stares.

Master Ahmad decisively stands taking control of the gathering.

"Masters and Mages, I have many questions. Some that directly interrogate the loyalty of the General of the army."

A murmur of concern sweeps the crowd of Elders.

With perfect timing Elwah makes his entrance. A gasp of surprise ripples through the assembly; astonished and muted calls of 'Prince Elwah!' are heard. Some of the mages are standing. Elwah steps directly to the dais and takes up his position, standing and confronts Master Ahmad.

"Perhaps Master Ahmad, in my short absence you have forgotten who I am?"

The master of Divinations is about to blurt out a comment, briefly stops mid breath, looks flustered and aware that some of the Elders are staring at him, while others are looking down in embarrassment. He finally takes a breath, looking a little defiant, addresses Elwah, "Your Lordship Elwah, Custodian of Naasée," before Ahmad can say another word, Elwah cuts him off,

"Thank you, Master Ahmad, you have not forgotten. Perhaps though, it may have slipped your mind, that in my absence, His Excellency Hasan, Captain of the Royal guards is not only the General of the army sworn to protect the people and city of Naasée but also Commander in Chief, whose responsibilities include the administration of the city?"

Ahmad looks visibly annoyed. He nevertheless stares at Elwah with a challenging look.

"Your Lordship," A deep resonant voice emerges from the rear of the assembly. Elwah turns to Master Ngaway.

"Master Ngaway, master of incantation and spells. Am I correct?"

"Your Lordship." Ngaway bows.

"Please, master Ngaway, go on."

"Your Lordship. we are surprised and delighted to see you return to Naasée. I believe master Ahmad was also referring to his Excellency, general Hasan, as the captain of the Royal Guards. The general is also charged with protecting you as the Sacred Haafiz and Custodian of Naasée."

Elwah gives a small light-hearted smile. "Thank you Master Ngaway. I was wondering when we would get to that."

A heavy silence follows.

"I have no doubt that you and your peers are referring to my abduction?"

There is an audible gasp and the word abduction as a question flows through the assembly like a strong wind through tall trees.

"Your Lordship, I am... we are unaware of what you speak. We were told that you had been captured by the army of the Over Lord and handed over to the Sorceress, who would force the location of the Sacred Tear of Apphat from you."

Elwah openly stares at Master Ngaway who gradually resumes his seat, looking very unsure of himself. A silence follows so deep that an imperceptible flow of air through the chamber is heard.

I look at my godmother, she is staring at Master Ngaway shaking her head slightly in disbelief.

"Master Ngaway, before I address that particular issue, I would like to ask you a question, in your capacity as Master of Incantation and Spells of course."

"Your lordship?"

"Master Ngaway, though not strictly a spell, you are familiar with the technique of *Vox Imperii*?"

"Yes... but..." Elwah holds up his hand.

"If I were to use that technique on one of you, how would I succeed?"

I look briefly at Master Ahmad. The blood seems to have drained from his face.

"Your Lordship, it would be difficult. We are trained Mages. We could easily counter the Command Voice."

"Humour me, Master Ngaway. How would I succeed in commanding you to do something against your will or training?"

The assembly holds its breath. Ngaway finally stands again and addresses Elwah, "you would need to charge your words with considerable energy and authority."

Elwah nods his approval at the answer. "Now let me suppose that this technique has been used without consideration for the rights of the individual; suppose that it has been used to gain benefit from that individual. Would that constitute a breach of Varye? The sacred moral duty of a magician to only use spells or techniques under specific circumstances?"

Ngaway blanches and looks a little confused, "Yes, your lordship, but..."

Again, Elwah stops him. "Let me go on with my final question to you. Master Ngaway, is it possible for me to look deeply into the memory of an individual, to gain knowledge if that person has been subjected unfairly to such a technique, and in circumstance that did not warrant its use, but rather for the benefit of the person casting that spell?"

"What is this all about...?" Mater Ahmad's outburst takes

everyone by surprise. He is standing visibly shaking

"SIT DOWN!"

Elwah's command is so loaded with authority and energy that all of us check to see if we are indeed sitting. The words echo around the chamber. The energy permeates the air like a heavy mantle. Master Ahmad is seated and looking crumpled.

"That, Master Ahmad is Vox Imperii. Master Ahmad, I charge you with a breach of the Varye of the Vox Imperii. You have used that technique on the guards and servants of his Excellency Hasan, to gain unlawful entry into his residence."

An audible gasp ripples through the assembly.

"Master Ahmad? Do you deny this charge? Or perhaps you have a valid reason for acting so rashly?" Elwah, knowing that with the last words he has set a trap for the master, takes his seat, and allows himself a very faint but dry smile.

Ahmad straightens himself, stands to his full height, throwing a challenging look to the assembled masters begins,

"Elders and Masters. I begin by stating that Prince Elwah of Naasée no longer holds the title of Haafiz!" Ahmad waits a moment for his words to have the desired impact. "The Tear of Elwah is no longer with him." The elders mutter and look at each other. "The apprentice named Azizi, was given custody of the sacred tear, transferred into his possession by means unknown to us. With this tear, he is said to have vanquished the sorceress. Upon her demise, we do not know if he also took the Tear of Malkizar. It is certain that his physical attributes strongly identify him as one who is capable of possession of one of the Sacred Tears. He has recently come to this city and sought refuge in his Excellency's house. Knowing that the captain of the royal guards is the designated guardian of the Haafiz, it is my conjecture that this young man is hiding something."

He does not have the time to utter another word, when with a strong and firm voice my god mother stands and speaks, "Master Ahmad, choose your next words carefully. It sounds as though you are accusing my god son of withholding a Sacred Tear of Apphat for his own benefit and against all Varye, concerning The Tears of Apphat." My god mother's cold, piercing blue eyes could be ice daggers for all the anger and challenge with which she is now looking at Master Ahmad.

Ahmad begins to say something, stutters, and then glares at Elwah.

The master who performed my first initiation, Master Suffrah, stands and in a quiet voice addresses both the assembly and Elwah, "My Lord Elwah, it is indeed unfortunate that your return to us is amidst such turmoil. But for the sake of removing doubts, would you please confirm for us if this is true – that you are no longer in possession of the Tear of Elwah?"

"Master Suffrah, it is correct. I do not hold the Tear of Elwah"

Ahmad allows himself a look of triumph and looks smugly around at the assembly.

"Then, my Lord Elwah can you say where the Tear of Elwah is?"

"Master Suffrah, Elders and Mages of Naasée, please understand that while the sorceress met her doom, I was still under her curse and could not physically act of my own volition. Once the sorceress had been vanquished, I believe that both Tears of Apphat were taken by its Guardian Spirit and disappeared."

In another outburst of frenzy, Ahmad stands again, this time pointing his finger at me. "How can we be sure of this? As you have said, and if we are to believe you, that you were still under the curse of the witch! What reasonable person would just leave both sacred Tears of Apphat?"

"I was there, and I saw what happened." Ijlal's quite voice cuts through the tremor of dissatisfied murmurs. All eyes on Ijlal, dressed as a prince of Schiraz would be, the quiet commanding bearing of a young heir to the throne, standing, he repeats himself to the now quieted assembly, "I was there. I saw the Tears of Apphat enveloped in a bright light and disappear from sight."

"Your highness, prince Ijlal. Thank you for confirming this." Master Suffrah, briefly looks at Master Ahmad, challenging him to contradict the prince. Turning to me, Master Suffrah addresses me, "Master Azizi," he allows himself a smile at the honorific, "do you confirm what Prince Ijlal has stated and can you add anything else?"

"Mahjir," I bow in his direction, "Masters, both Tears of Apphat were enveloped in light and disappeared. As they did, I heard the voice of its Guardian Spirit say, that it was not yet my time to hold them."

A whisper like a wave of wind through tall grass, sweeps the assembly.

"Thank you Master Azizi." He turns to the assembly and in a firm voice adds, "Masters, following this young man's first initiation, I met with his godmother and the high priests, to discuss a prophesy that was made long ago. This initiate, Azizi, spoke of the prophesy while in a trance during his ordeal of admission to the ranks of Healer of Apphat and Magician in training." Master Suffrah waits for silence before adding, "It is my firm belief that Azizi, not only speaks the truth, but has revealed to us now, that the Tears of Apphat will be made manifest in the future. Furthermore, he will play an important role upon their appearance."

Like a cloudless sky the silence in the room is now filled with light. A beam of sunlight strikes through the dome and directly lights up the dais and Prince Elwah.

A hush has descended into the Council room.

Pointing to the dais now lit by a beam of golden light, Master Suffrah adds, "Master Ahmad, as master of divination and symbols, would you care to comment on this auspicious sign?" The quiet words of Master Suffrah bring about vigorous nods from the assembly.

"Thank you master Suffrah for your kind words." Elwah acknowledges the master of rites and ceremonies. "This brings me back to the question raised earlier. That of my abduction." Ahmad is now in a difficult position.

"Master Ahmad," Elwah pauses long enough that a wave of unease is felt, "it is my assertion that someone used the same technique of Vox Imperii on a squad of guards to abduct me and hand me over to the Over Lord."

Everyone in the room is holding their breath.

Master Ahmad, although looking uncomfortable, smirks and stares at Elwah, challenging him to prove his claim.

"Master Ahmad, you may be wondering how I could possibly demonstrate such a claim?" Elwah pauses, intent on creating as much tension as possible.

"Perhaps I can ask Master Ngaway to perform an incantation, and execute a ritual to retrieve the memories of those soldiers?"

"It is forbidden to perform such a ritual on the dead..." Master

Ahmad has only just realised that no one mentioned that the soldiers in question were murdered after the abduction.

It's the silence before the detonation of thunder. A fierce storm is brewing inside the council chamber.

"Master Ahmad, I am curious. How is it that you know this?" Elwah speaks in a very quiet voice, nevertheless tinged with power.

Ahmad is seated, his face is drained of any colour, in fact his colour is more grey than white. He just stares into the void. Everyone else is holding their breath.

"It may indeed be better to perform this ritual on your person, to see what memories you hold of those circumstances?"

A tension like the moment before lightning strikes shimmers in the room, the very air seems charged.

Ahmad is speechless, crumpled in his chair he nevertheless seems to be searching for a way out, anything that will allow him to regain the authority in the room. My godmother scans the assembly, gauging the dwindling support for Ahmad.

Master Suffrah's quite tone cuts through the tension.

"Your lordship Elwah, I am not sure I follow your thoughts. However if I understand the bare minimum, you are making a very serious accusation, and I do not comprehend how this concerns Master Ahmad?"

Elwah looking directly at Master Suffrah, takes a deep breath and releasing it slowly, focusses his energy on the assembled Elders.

"Master Suffrah, it appears that a lie has been told. I am uncertain if the origin of the lie is a single person or more." Elwah pauses, Master Suffrah deliberately regains his seat, a serious look filling his composure. "I have already made an allegation against Master Ahmad for breaching the Varye of Vox Imperii and using this technique to gain unlawful access to His Excellency Hasan's residence. I have proof of this. By his own admission, Master Ahmad accuses the young apprentice, Azizi, of dishonesty and collusion; claiming that he is in possession of one of the Sacred Tear of Apphat. I think we have established, with Prince Ijlal's testimony that this is not the case." Looking directly at Ahmad, Elwah goes on, "Master Ahmad's suspicion does not give him the right to use these techniques on a member of my staff first, without the consent of the Council of Elders; unless of course this was sanctioned?" a murmur of denial accompanied by head shakes, "and certainly not without actual proof of disloyalty? I ask, what was Master Ahmad's ultimate motive in doing so?"

Several elders are now looking at Master Ahmad with serious concern.

"If his concern extended itself to the security of The Tear of Elwah, then why was this not brought up to the Elders?"

"Masters, before my disappearance, I became fully aware of the discontent among the new members of Council, with the tradition of seeking the reincarnation of the previous Haafiz."

Master Suffrah is about to rise, Elwah holds his hand up and continues, "I now come to the point of your question Master Suffrah. The night of my disappearance, I was handed an urgent message from Hasan, stating that some of the sorceress' scarlet robes were sighted along our northern borders, near the foothills of the Asfaine Mountains. He stated in his message that he had gone to investigate. Please note masters, the message was handed to me by Tabrass, Master Ahmad's personal servant."

"I understand all of this your lordship, but I still cannot comprehend the further claim that you are making, that of deliberate abduction."

Elwah allows himself a sad smile. "Perhaps masters, rather than relying on my words alone, if I could simply transmit my memories to you all without having to rely on words and misinterpretation of the facts."

There is a brief intake of breath amongst the assembled elders. Master Suffrah nodding his head asks, "Your lordship, we know that your abilities far surpass ours, but have you recovered enough from your ordeal to enable you to do this, without unnecessarily draining your energy?"

Elwah is about to answer, when a younger voice interrupts, "As a new member to this Council, and because of my youth, I admit I have not witnessed your lordship's powers. Is it safe for our well-being and how are we to guarantee that your memories have not been tampered?"

Elwah smiles, "Master Sahir?" I look across the council chamber at a youthful man, his face heavily tattooed. The young man nods. Elwah smiles, "It is comforting to see a mage from the Huda tribe." Saeed suddenly looks up and then looks at me. I had imagined that even the Huda people would have a trained magician. However, I understood that these were trained mostly with the ability to find water and find their way through a Cassim and possibly be able to raise one at will.

Elwah continues, a mischievous tone in his voice, "In spite of your one hundred years, Master Sahir, you are looking fit and well. Your mastery is that of names and potions, am I correct?"

"One hundred years!? I am not sure I heard right. He looks no

older than me. If that is the case, then how old is Elwah?" My mind is racing I can sense Saeed's fascination for the kin of his tribe.

The 'young' master Sahir bows, acknowledging Prince Elwah's correct address.

"The answer to your question Master Sahir is simple. If all of you see my memories in unison, and you all see the same events, then my memories are accurate. However," Elwah scans the assembly meaningfully, and adds, "if one of you were to consciously attempt to manipulate those memories with your own will, all memories for all of you would be affected." Elwah waits to see the reactions, no one is moving, all eyes are fixed on him. "In order to protect myself from this incidence, should it tempt someone, the memories so thwarted, would display a shadow of the face of the individual attempting the tampering."

Elwah waits a moment. Master Ahmad looks uncomfortable.

"Does that satisfy your question, Master Sahir?"

"Your lordship." Sahir bows and takes back his seat, briefly glancing at Master Ahmad.

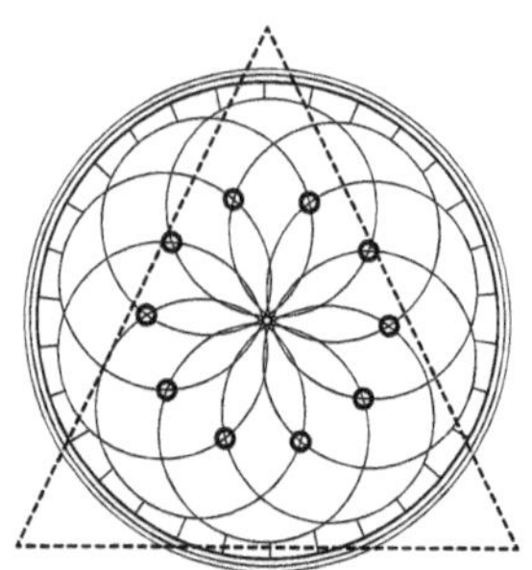

CHAPTER FOURTEEN

The images that suddenly crowd my mind almost feel like an assault on my senses. Unrelenting, they come one after the other, giving rise to strong emotions and an absolute sense of truth. I have no time to dwell on any of them. Each presents itself as an outright event in the most minute detail and yet appears for such a brief time. I am reliving Elwah's experience of the night of his abduction that took several hours and yet seem to pass in just a few moments. The views of Elwah's memories, feel personal, as if I am experiencing them myself.

Nausea almost overcomes me with each memory and the sudden lurches in time.

I experience first, the briefest scene of my god mother – a younger version of herself, sitting in her herbarium as Elwah telepathically instructs her, to *'take on an apprentice. He will play an important role in fulfilling the sacred prophecy.'* She shakes her head as waking from a dream, and then begins to draw a star chart, the scene fades away as the face of a young woman appears. I recognise her as my mother and the Lady of The Forest. The views of Elwah's memories, feel personal. I do not know if this last memory is somehow filtered from all Elwah's other memories for me alone.

Another memory of Elwah's surfaces then. The scene that unfolds is deep within the city of Naasée. It is night, there is a chill in the air. Along the shadowed stone walls, candles are lit. Hasan dressed as a general of the Royal guards is leading with a torch; the flame bends and flickers in the slight breeze of the long corridor, throwing odd shadows. Somehow, I know that it is many years ago.

I hear the words that are spoken but they have taken on a strange echo, as if expressed from a distance. "Was anything else spoken of?" Elwah asks Hasan as they are walking at a hurried pace.

"No, your lordship. She only said that everything would be explained when you see her."

The images flash by and finally Elwah and Hasan are standing in front of a very old door, decorated with strange symbols, and studded with metallic talismans bearing ancient rune-like inscriptions.

I perceive a rustle in the assembly of Elders, I understand that this door holds a special significance and wait.

Two of the royal guards are standing on either side and salute Hasan as he approaches. Hasan then opens the door allowing Elwah through, turning to the guards he instructs them in soft voice, "Prince Elwah is not to be disturbed under any circumstance." The guards nod and return to attention on either side of the door as Hasan makes his way inside the room.

The room is lit with a strange iridescent light that seem to emanate from the walls. It is as if the rocks themselves are glowing. The room is bare, except for a small single obelisk made of black obsidian. The top is slightly hollowed out and holds a stone of the purest blue I have ever withheld. I remember suddenly where I have seen that stone of pure blue.

A sudden gasp from the assembled Elders confirms that I am looking at Elwah the Sacred Stone of Joy.

In my mind, Elwah is staring at the stone. A sense of relief seems to fill him. He is about to turn to Hasan, when he pauses, raising his eyes to the far wall, a small figure wrapped in a loose hooded grey cloak is standing looking at him. I sense Elwah's nervous anticipation.

The figure's face is shadowed by the hood.

Elwah hesitates, then in a quiet voice, "You have summoned me. My servant says that you have grave warnings for the Sacred Stone."

The figure deliberately moves closer and as the light shifts, I perceive a pair of eyes of the clearest and most penetrating blue. The hood falls off as a small blue butterfly takes flight alighting on the blue sapphire and vanishes.

I am filled with a sudden frisson, "Ishtar!" I hear my godmother's awed whisper.

A small woman, whose age seems a complete anomaly and a mystery, stands there smiling a most enigmatic smile at Elwah.

'Elwah, child, I have come to warn you that the Sacred Sapphire is threatened. There is one who would take it and attempt to rule the world with it. It must be safeguarded tonight. You, also are in danger."

I sense that Elwah wants to ask a question, but the woman holds her hand, "there is no time. The Sacred Stone of Sorrow has already been forced into submission through the most evil magic. You must protect this one. You also will be taken, but fear not, for the one who will defeat the evil one and safeguard you and the stone, has already been conceived."

Elwah attempts a response, I sense in his mind the care with which he now chooses his words, close to a whisper he asks, "Sacred Ishtar, how am I to protect the Sacred Stone?"

Ishtar reaches out a hand and places her palm over Elwah's heart. He sheds a tear that falls upon the Sapphire, which begins to glow. Without further explanation, Elwah takes the Tear of Joy and placing it in his mouth allows it to dissipate in him.

Ishtar adds, "When the Sacred Stone is required, you will need to sing this sacred song to manifest it." Here, the memory blurs and I hear Elwah's voice in my head. "The song is sacred and may only be transmitted to one that is destined to sing it. It cannot be revealed here to this assembly."

Ishtar then turns to Elwah and adds, "You are no longer simply the Keeper of Elwah, you are now Elwah Tahir, the Sacred Keeper of the Sacred Sapphire. The Stone is within you. Now your servant Hasan becomes the guardian of your safety and the stone within you. Unfortunately, he will be manipulated, and he will fail in his task."

Hasan has fallen to one knee in awe and in recognition of the sacred ritual that has just played before his eyes. Upon hearing the last words pronounced of his failure, Hasan stares in disbelief that he would so easily fail in his task. Ishtar adds, "This will be necessary Hasan, everything will move according to my plan and not those of men."

Ishtar suddenly vanishes. Hasan looks up into Elwah's eyes with a look of astonishment and awe. He begins to speak stumbling over his words,

"My lord, my lord, Mahjir! Your eyes, I cannot look. It is not fitting for me."

"Come Hasan, my faithful servant. It is fitting for you if no one else. It is merely the stone within me. It simply enhances my powers. There is no need for you to hold me in awe." Elwah extends his hand and helps Hasan to his feet.

There is a discreet knock at the door. Hasan goes to the door. One of the guards looks abashed, "Your excellency, my apologies. The Master insisted."

Master Ahmad is standing there, looking a little annoyed at having been told to wait.

"Prince Elwah, I have been told that you are concerned for the safety of the Sacred Sapphire," Ahmad begins to say, craning his head to see into the room. Elwah with a generous gesture, invites him into the room. Ahmad, unceremoniously steps in past Elwah, almost pushing Hasan out of his way.

He suddenly comes to a stop, gaping at the now empty obelisk that held the Sacred Tear of Joy.

"Where is it?" His tone is more accusatory in nature than shock at the missing sapphire. "Where is the Sacred Sapphire?"

Elwah steps next to him looking at him unflinchingly into his eyes. Ahmad takes an involuntary step back at the sight of Elwah's eyes.

"You can see Master Ahmad, that it is no longer here."

Ahmad with obvious intent, looks Elwah up and down, searching for any possible way that Elwah could be hiding it on his person.

"What have you done with the Sacred Stone? It was in this room the last time the Council of Elders checked."

With a slightly mischievous smile and patting his person in an obvious, 'search me and find' attitude, Elwah states, "I can assure you Master Ahmad it is not *on* my person."

Master Ahmad looks flustered. It is all he can do to refrain himself from searching prince Elwah himself. He then turns to Hasan with a critical stare.

"General, what has happened here?"

Hasan is about to speak when Elwah raises his hand, "you do not have to accuse my servant Hasan. I can attest for you that the hand of the goddess Ishtar is at play in safeguarding the Tear of Joy. The stone is no longer kept in this room."

The face of master Ahmad is a mixture of conflicting thoughts and emotions.

"But then, but then where is it? And what of the role of Keeper?" He pauses in obvious mental conflict, "But then, oh." He catches himself mid-sentence. Ahmad turns, seemingly casually and walks out hurriedly.

Elwah turns to Hasan, with a questioning look. Hasan shrugs his shoulders.

"I do not know, my lord. I can follow him if you wish?"

"No, that won't be necessary. Although, I am curious, and I will seek him out."

The image of the room is suddenly snatched away, and

darkness pervades my senses. Lights race by and in my mind, I find myself at the northern city gates. Elwah has a slightly raised vantage point. He looks down the courtyard that gives onto the gates, and beyond to the Cave of Gibrar. The gates stand open, a group of guards stand around, they appear to be either restless or nervous.

Emerging from a lower door of the main temple, a person enters the courtyard, hurriedly making his way to the assembled soldiers. Master Ahmad is easily recognisable by his clothes and demeanour. The soldier in charge approaches Ahmad, a few inaudible words are exchanged. Master Ahmad points several times to the cave of Gibrar.

Elwah senses a presence behind him. It is unclear how long Tabrass, Master Ahmad's servant, has been standing there. He bows to Elwah,

"Lord Elwah, his excellency, general Hasan is searching for you, he requests that you return to your rooms."

Another lurch forward in time and space and I find myself inside Elwah's rooms. Shortly after arriving, Hasan enters looking on edge.

"My lord, reports have just come in that Shadows, servants of the sorceress have been seen in the streets of Naasée. I am about to go out and investigate. Please remain here. I will post my personal aide, Sarek outside your door."

My heart sinks at the thought of Shadows having infiltrated Naasée; I remember then that this is a memory of a time before they appeared in the Asfaine mountains. Already the sorceress was making a move for control, obviously searching for the second Tear of Apphat.

I am astounded at the sense of calm that Elwah has. Turning towards a window that overlooks the city, he casually strolls toward it and stops. A feeling of weariness overcomes him. He turns then and fixes his gaze upon an elaborate incense bowl that is gently emitting a small amount of incense smoke. Caught as I am in the memory of Elwah, even I can feel that the incense is designed to bewilder and calm the senses. Elwah's body gives in, and he falls into a semi-conscious state, collapsing on a chair.

Only moments later, a soft knock and the door to his room opens, Tabrass enters, carrying a large, hooded cape. Tabrass is wearing a shemagh, partly covering his face.

"Your lordship, Master Ahmad has discovered a plot to assassinate you. He has ordered that you be safeguarded out of Naasée. I am to lead you out of the city."

Tabrass helps Elwah into the cape and pulls the hood over his head, concealing his face as much as possible and leads him out of the room.

As they walk down the darkened corridors out of the palace, Sarek strides hurriedly past, only glimpsing at the hooded figure being led by Tabrass. Elwah attempts to make a gesture calling for help, instead stumbles as Tabrass catches him and they walk on. The hood seems permeated with a fragrance that is distinctly like the incense burning in Elwah's room.

They finally exit into the courtyard of the palace and the city gates that face north and the cave of Gibrar. A small squad of five or so guards are standing nervously around. Upon seeing Tabrass approach they form a circle around Elwah, one of them supporting his arm. Elwah looks up into the soldier's eyes, hoping to signal that he has been tricked. There is no light of recognition in the soldier's eyes. It is as if he is sleep walking.

They lead him out. The sound of the large gates closing behind them resonates in the stillness of the night.

Again, a lurch forward in Elwah's memories takes me further into the desert and I now stand at the dark gaping opening of the cave of Gibrar. They enter the large cave. One of the soldiers has lit a torch and leads the group deep into the cave. The leader points to a small recess the size of a couch, placing a couple sheep skins on the surface, orders the one who is assisting Elwah, to sit him there.

The initial apprehension of the soldiers begins to ease as they relax, one of them organising to light a small fire. Suddenly half a dozen shadows silently melt out of the darkness of the walls. With little effort and practically no resistance from the soldiers, all the guards are butchered there and then, their bodies lying bleeding where they stood. I sense Elwah's anger and dismay at the sight. One of the Shadows approaches him and applies a rough rag smelling of something foul. Elwah loses consciousness at this point.

I shake my head, attempting to clear my mind of the memories I have just witnessed. I sit unable to move, my body feels heavy, drained of energy. A sadness like a stone sits in my chest at the memory of the brutal demise of the guards.

A palpable hush has descended on the assembly of Elders. Looking around at the Elders, their reaction is similar to mine, they appear to have woken up from a sleep, after having experienced a nightmare.

No one dares to break the silence. The authenticity of the memories we have just witnessed, may be hard to believe or even understand, but they cannot be challenged. Master Ahmad looks as though he has seen a ghost. His features are drawn, his skin is pale, and he stares into the distance, not moving.

"Lord Elwah?" a soft voice, not a whisper but a clear slightly melodious voice, breaks the silence in a gentle way, much like a tender spring breeze.

Elwah turns to face a woman of indeterminate age. Her eyes are sincere, and though the energy in the room is heavy, her voice has the effect of diffusing it. She is one of only three women on the Council of Elders; my godmother being one and another whose name I have not yet learned.

"Mahjira Mitra, yes?"

"Lord Elwah, it may take some time for us all to absorb the significance of these memories."

I lean to Hasan and ask him quietly, "Who is that Elder?"

"Her name is Mahjira Mitra. She is one of the high priestesses. She holds the power over the summoning of Guardians," Hasan whispers back.

'Mahjira, I completely agree with your statement. I would advise the Council to take the time it needs. I understand that no one can come to any conclusion of the memories you have witnessed. I could only give you the facts as accurately and in as much details as they had genuinely occurred." Elwah pauses, then turning to one of the Elders, asks, "Master Vasilis, may I ask you as Master of Visions, that you confirm the authenticity of the memories you all have witnessed?"

Master Vasilis bows briefly, "I can attest that your memories as they appeared were yours and were not manipulated."

Elwah pauses, not looking at anyone in particular, he adds, "it would be unfair to judge someone's actions based solely on the behaviours I observed. I do not know the motives behind any one's actions unless I could speak to them directly, or they speak to me. I therefore urge the Council to deliberate what you have seen with caution and not come to any hasty decision."

Another elder stands, his face looks ancient. Long flowing white hair drops to his shoulders. Deep furrows have been etched over his leather like features. I am certain each line holds a deep and powerful story.

If Master Sahir is *only* one hundred years old, I would not hazard a guess as to his age. He gives a little cough, seemingly to clear his throat and catch Elwah's attention.

"Lord Elwah." The old man begins in a strong but slightly raucous voice.

Elwah bows deeply in obvious deference to this Elder's age.

"Master Sindarin, can I confirm my memory – You are the Keeper of Secrets and Cosmic Magical Keys?"

The old man bows slightly, raising his head, he looks Elwah directly and asks, "Your lordship, we witnessed quite clearly from your encounter with the goddess Ishtar, that you were able to," he hesitates, "absorb the Sacred Sapphire within you. How is it then that you claim it is no longer with you?" As the elder sits down again, I notice to my surprise that although Master Sindarin briefly looks at me, his gaze shifts to Saeed.

"Master Sindarin, as I explained earlier and as Master Ahmad stated, although still under the restraint spell of the sorceress, using a little-known method, I was able to safely pass the stone to Azizi."

A whisper of "What method did he use?" is heard. Elwah waits for the room to fall silent. "As you are also now all aware, once Azizi used the stone to defeat the sorceress, both sapphires were reclaimed by Ishtar, or at least the guardian appointed by her."

Master Ahmad, swiftly regaining a level of confidence, asks, "Could you not have passed it on to someone else, someone better trained and qualified to receive it?" The inference is obvious–he means one of them.

"If I had passed the stone on to someone unprepared, the effect on that individual would be as if they had suddenly been struck by lightning. If they survived the experience, it would have at least utterly destroyed their magical ability."

"Are you saying that Azizi, even at such a young age, had the ability of a trained Mahjir?" Master Ahmad stares, outrage simmering at the audacity that a child was chosen instead of a trained elder.

Elwah allows himself an ironic smile. He looks at me, the elders turn to me with curiosity.

"While reviewing the book of Ancient Prophesies, I experienced a vision. After consulting Master Vasilis, who holds the power of Visions and their interpretations, I believed that a boy would be conceived in the northern Region of Asfaine. This child, although unknown, would have an important role to play in fulfilling one of the prophesies. It was not until Mahjira Aïschah contacted me with the star chart of the son of Haakon and Caelesti, that I confirmed Azizi had the potential to be that person."

I swallow at the sound of my mother's name. I look down at my hands, a longing like a bubble bursting from my heart, fills me with the memory of her picture on my father's desk. My eyes moisten.

Again, Elwah pauses until the room once more falls silent. "Unknown to him and to his godmother, who took him on as an apprentice, I began his training at the age of six." Elwah turns to me, smiles. I can only stare back, suddenly remembering all the occasions, I would see his eyes in the flames, or a voice whispering the answer to a complex Parvus in my mind, or a presence that always felt like a warm blanket of protection. "He has grown into a healer of reputation amongst the Hills People of Asfaine and a Magician of great control and power, as his defeat of the sorceress demonstrates."

The rustle of stares and slow nodding of heads in my direction fills the silence. Elwah is still smiling at me. Ijlal holds my hand and squeezes it gently in a gesture of strength and courage. Saeed is looking at me, blushes modestly and looks down at his feet.

C H A P T E R   F I F T E E N

"I find it strange," Ahmad has recovered most of his confidence, if not his arrogance, "that we have not addressed the presence of the many foreign soldiers in our city, and who have now taken residence under the protection of his excellency Hasan, general of Naasée." The last few words pointedly inferring that Hasan has a personal agenda.

"Master Ahmad," Hasan puts on his most diplomatic and dangerous military commander's tone of voice. Standing up, he addresses the Council, "May I formally present to you all, Prince Ijlal, heir to the throne of Schiraz, eldest son of his Highness the Sultan of Rashãd." Ijlal stands and gives a little bow, "and His Highness Prince Shahulm, recently appointed Regent of the Citadel of Mina, eldest son, and heir to the King of Glesskerel." Shahulm stands in turn and bows.

Hasan continues, cutting off any interjection Ahmad seemed

to be formulating, "If you permit, I will allow Prince Ijlal to speak and clarify the reasons for their presence. I am sure that you will find them most pleasing." His last words spoken directly to Ahmad.

Ijlal gives Hasan a small bow. "Thank you, your excellency. I begin by conveying my father the Sultan's greetings and through me our most sincere gratitude for your kind hospitality." A respectful silence greets Ijlal's words. Taking his time in measuring his speech he goes on, "It was with the aid of the king of Glesskerel's army, that my uncle, general Giafar vanquished the overlord and took control of the Citadel of Mina. This then allowed Hasan, Azizi and the Companions of Schiraz to seek out and defeat the sorceress, which in turn led to the rescue of Prince Elwah and Prince Shahulm. Once the Citadel of Mina was secured with a significant contribution from the soldiers of Naasée, it was expedient to safeguard the well-being of both princes.

Schiraz offered the quickest and safest sanctuary. My father, Sultan Rashãd extended his hospitality to Prince Elwah to recover from his ordeal. Subsequently my father then entreated Prince Elwah to administer his healing skills to my beloved, prince Shahulm who had been abducted by the sorceress and treacherously tortured."

Ijlal pauses for the subtleties to penetrate. I am enjoying the spectacle, admiring Ijlal's brilliant political manoeuvring, complimenting and in the next breath pointedly criticising. Several Elders squirm uncomfortably realising that they were being admonished for not having offered to bring Prince Elwah back themselves.

"The retinue that we chose was to safeguard the return of prince Elwah, and upon the insistence of the King of Glesskerel, to ensure the safety of his only son, Shahulm. However," Ijlal makes a weary gesture, dismissing some imaginary image before him, "it is now all in the past and peace has returned to the kingdoms. As a result, we find ourselves in the fortunate position to be able to extend a proposal of trade agreements between our neighbours. An arrangement, which can be detailed at another time. For the moment, my beloved prince Shahulm and I wish to offer a small gesture of good will." Ijlal waits for Shahulm to stand by his side, "If the Council would permit," both princes move to the door and open it. Faruq marches in, attired in his outfit of royal guard and carrying a large wooden box.

"Elders of Naasée, I present my cousin general Faruq, captain of the royal guards of Schiraz and my personal aide. He will present to you our token of good will."

Faruq places the box in the centre of the room and opens it.

A collective gasp echoes around the chamber.

Faruq, in his deep and resonant voice announces, "There are twelve red gemstones from the Schiraz tree. Their magical powers of healing are prized throughout the four kingdoms. In addition, the King of Glesskerel offers twelve of the largest and most precious pearls from the Ocean of Malkizar." Faruq stands up and takes two steps back. Ijlal once more takes the floor.

"We will of course, in addition, compensate his Excellency Hasan, for his courteous and generous hospitality for housing our soldiers."

Master Suffrah, responsible for rites and ceremonies stands. "Your highnesses, we are deeply grateful for your gifts, which we humbly accept. We thank you for your gracious visit and the offer of trade with your kingdoms. On behalf of the Council of Elders, I sincerely apologise if our internal political debates have in any way distressed you. Rest assured that we will resolve these matters in time. In the meanwhile, on behalf of the Council, I extend our courteous invitation to remain in our city for as long as you wish."

The Elders nod their heads vigorously, there is even a short applause at Master Suffrah's genuine and meticulous words. I am impressed with Master Suffrah's manner and words. A true orator and diplomat.

Princes Ijlal and Shahulm bow and leave the chamber with Faruq.

An uncomfortable silence follows. The attention is squarely back on Master Ahmad and the memories everyone witnessed from Elwah.

Master Suffrah stands once more, addressing Elwah, "Your lordship, this has been a day of events. Please be assured that we are deeply grateful for your safe return. I think, with the Council's permission, we should all retire to our respective dwellings and consider the events that have taken place. We need to carefully reflect on the memories that you have conveyed to us, and more prudently, as you have suggested, to not come to any hasty conclusions. I suggest that we adjourn this meeting until such time as we can debate our next plan of action if any."

A rustle of agreements meets master Suffrah's words. Elwah graciously bows to Master Suffrah, "Thank you, master Suffrah. You have spoken wisely, and I agree. I shall remain with his Excellency, general Hasan until further notice." With those last words, Elwah heads to the door, closely followed by Hasan. Caught a little off guard, I get up quickly, taking Saeed's hand and lead him out following Hasan and Elwah. As I do so, I sense the energy of someone looking at me. On pretence that I am checking on Saeed, my eyes meet Master Sindarin's penetrating gaze. He stands, not breaking eye contact, revealing a symbol on his gown. I immediately search my memories of magical symbols from the time I spent studying them with my godmother. I shiver slightly as I recognise it to be the symbol of the Triple Moon Goddess.

We return to Hasan's residence and climb the stairs to his study, the only sound that of our footsteps on the wooden boards and the soft breathing accompanying my effort to keep up with Hasan's soldier's stride.

We sit or stand in silence, each to his own thoughts of the events that have played out.

There is a soft knock at the door. Hasan goes to open it, he expresses surprise, with a simple gesture motions someone into the room.

Master Sindarin enters. I try to remember his role and remember Elwah greeting him as master of Secrets and Cosmic Magical Keys. He ambles, given his apparent ancient age, it is no surprise, though I am amazed at his ability. He does not look at anyone and makes his way to the couch, where Saeed has been sitting. Saeed upon seeing the old man, suddenly stands up and offers his seat. The old man pauses, seems to rest a moment while considering Saeed's kind gesture.

"Ah, young man, thank you for your kindness." The old man looks into Saeed's eyes, and mutters, "I was right. I think the choice was obvious from the beginning."

With a bit of a grunt, Master Sindarin sits, closes his eyes briefly, then smiling at everyone in the room, nods his head several times.

No one speaks, waiting of this unusual visitor to begin.

"Master Elwah, it is good to see you in good health after your ordeal."

"Master Sindarin, thank you." Elwah is as surprised as the rest of us to see him here. "Is there something that arose from the Council meeting that you wish to discuss?"

"Oh no, young Elwah. No, not that. I think all that needed to be said and conveyed was enough." There is an air of energy that surrounds this old man. If I were to dare to look at his Hala, I am sure that it would be filled with golden fire, the sense of magic is so strong with him. We all wait, almost holding our breath for him to go on.

"I have something much more important to discuss with you."

I look at Elwah and ask him, "Would you like us to leave the room while you have this conversation?"

Before Elwah can answer, the old man raises a hand waving it down, chuckles a little and adds, "No, no. Please stay, young master Azizi. This concerns you and your friend."

I turn to look at Saeed, who suddenly pales.

The old man takes a deep breath and begins. "It is obvious

from your shared memories that you were forewarned of the danger to the Sacred Sapphire. The warning came through your servant Hasan."

Elwah looks at Hasan, not knowing how this will unfold. "Yes, Master Sindarin, it was him who conveyed the urgency. But..." Sindarin holds up a hand, looks directly at Hasan and asks him, "Hasan, tell me," Sindarin eyes suddenly take on a power that I have often seen in my godmother's eyes, one that commands absolute truth. "Tell me Hasan, was it a young woman that conveyed the message?"

Hasan suddenly looks like a schoolboy being questioned by the oldest teacher.

"Yes, Master Sindarin, it was." The old man holds up his hand again.

"Now, let me ask you this, was she alone?"

"No master," before Hasan can go on, the old man stops him once more. He nods his head several times before resuming, "Was it a young boy, who could have been her twin?"

Hasan gapes, astounded.

The old man chuckles, nodding his head several times. "This is as I thought."

Everyone is staring at Master Sindarin. The silence draws on for a long time. Finally Master Sindarin looks up at Elwah. "Elwah, what do you know of the Sacred Tears and their prophesy?"

Elwah looks around, a degree of confusion fills his eyes before he can go on.

"They were the Sacred Sapphires given to King Apphat, to restore the Great Harmony." Elwah pauses his brow creasing slightly perplexed, waiting for the old man who gestures for him to go on, "however, king Apphat, was not able to achieve this in his lifetime. The stones were separated upon his death and given into the keep of separate custodians. Naasée was one of those." Sindarin holds up his hand again, interjecting, "Thank you, yes. I don't mean to belittle what you are saying, I certainly do not need a lesson in history."

My jaw drops slightly at the apparent chastisement and catching myself, I realise that Master Sindarin was probably born a long time before Elwah came into power. The old man goes on, "First tell me what you know or even think of the origin of the Sacred Sapphires?"

Elwah takes a short breath, "They have been referred to as the Tears of Creation."

Sindarin nods, "Yes, that is all very well. But Elwah, who shed those Tears?"

My body suddenly becomes tense, my back straightens, my breath deepens as I sense that a deep revelation is about to be made. Elwah looks at me briefly.

"Elwah, it is fine for him to know." Master Sindarin reassures Elwah.

"The oldest recorded legend states that they were the Tears shed by the goddess Ishtar, upon the creation of the physical world of men."

"Mmm. Yes, yes. Go on Elwah," the old man urges him on.

"The legend also states the tears took on form. They were attributed to her as her children. In the old language the first was named Sorrow for the tribulations of men and her second was named Joy for their ability to overcome difficulties."

The silence and stillness of a cold morning air fills the room.

My skin is crawling with goose bumps.

"Very good Elwah. Now to the prophesy. How were the Sacred Sapphires formed and how were they to be used to establish the Great Harmony?"

"Master Sindarin, even the best of us is unclear about that. Though as far as separating the stone to two different Keepers, has always puzzled me."

Master Sindarin lets out a prolonged sigh, the type of sigh a kind teacher would give in exasperation for his best student's lack of understanding of a simple principle.

"Young Elwah,"

I find myself smiling at that address, compared to me, I think Elwah is ancient, and yet here he is looking like a schoolboy, being instructed by a man possibly three times his age.

"If as you say, the Tears took form, how would they manifest to a mere person – what form would they choose to take, so as not to scare the living life out of them?" Elwah pauses, appearing unsure. "Be confident, Elwah, you have seen them in your visions."

Taking a breath, Elwah speaks softly, "A young girl and a young boy of similar features."

Sindarin smiles and sighs, "Yes, Elwah. You are right." Nodding his head a few more times, he goes on. "Now, we come to the Sacred Sapphires. Do you think that these are actually, the children of the goddess Ishtar or something else? Take your time Elwah, the answer is a lot simpler than it appears."

Elwah pauses for a significant amount of time. I am searching my memories of all the readings I did with my godmother and cannot think of an answer. The revelations of the origin of the Sacred Sapphires are already astounding me.

Elwah's face lights up finally concludes, "They are the Soul energy of the children and given form as Sapphires, gifted by the Sacred Twins to the world to create Harmony."

The old man smiles, satisfied.

"Now perhaps we come to the most important part. One you have expressed concern over. Elwah, why were the stones separated?"

All apprentice magicians know the legend of king Apphat and the revelation he made on a piece of parchment paper upon his deathbed.

"They were deemed too powerful and dangerous for a single individual to hold." Sindarin is looking at Elwah, when suddenly he shifts his gaze to me.

"Young master Azizi, perhaps you can answer this question then. Why were both of the Sacred Sapphires given to King Apphat?"

I swallow hard. I look at Elwah, conscious that I am being asked a question to which only a master magician should know the answer. My heart is beating faster in my chest. Hear rises to my cheeks. My hands are suddenly moist with perspiration, I am about to say that I do not know, when master Sindarin, asks again, "young Azizi, reflect for a moment, do you think that King Apphat was special in any way? Do you think he had the ability to control both stones? And yet, he was never able to achieve what he was destined to do..."

I stand hesitating, now knowing what to say. *Yes and no, perhaps king Apphat had skills we do not know of, and yet why did he not restore the Great Harmony, what was he lacking?"* too many questions crowd my mind.

Master Sindarin chuckles a little, nodding his head. "I can see the questions crowding your mind, young Azizi. They are perfectly reasonable questions. But you are ignoring the answer that you already know."

This feels more like having to open the box that had no key and no keyhole in my early training with my god mother. I relax my mind and begin to look outside the box, in this case outside the question.

"Master Sindarin," I am surprised at the sound of my own voice, and speaking a little more softly, I add, "Master Sindarin, I saw what happened to the sorceress when she held both stones. So, in my view, king Apphat must have been a very special individual to hold both."

The old man nods his approval, "You may be right, young Azizi. He must at least have been pure of heart, with no intention for personal gain. Yes, that would allow him to hold both stones and not be destroyed by greed." Sindarin nods to himself then gives another long sigh, "but then, why was he not able to bring about the Great Harmony?"

My voice is now a whisper, admitting defeat, "Master, I do not know."

The old man smiles, "Do not worry young Azizi, I don't think young Master Elwah knows either."

Why do I feel that my performance is suddenly being compared to an older and more knowledgeable student? The feeling of standing before Delena Tobaha in a classroom of the Temple School of Asfaine is almost strange and a bit comical.

"Tell me, young Azizi, do you remember the words you pronounced as you surrendered the Stone of Elwah into the greedy hands of the sorceress?"

Both Elwah and I speak with one voice,

"The Tears of Joy and Sorrow

Cannot be One without the Other."

Master Sindarin holds up his hand.

A long pause follows. The deep resonant voice of Master Sindarin cuts through the room like a knife.

"Young Elwah and Azizi, you have just revealed the long lost and misunderstood meaning of the prophesy."

We both stand gaping at Master Sindarin.

The old man takes a long breath and softly but with great power pronounces, "The Sacred Stones cannot be separated. But the Stones cannot be One either."

I feel as if I am back again in my godmother's herbarium, at my first lesson as she declares, 'Magic is real.' My head goes into a spin. The old man gives another chuckle and a cough before speaking, "Master Elwah, you have long suspected what I am about to reveal to you."

I am suddenly scared that the old man will die before he finishes his sentence. I am willing with all my will for him to live long enough to deliver his words.

He chuckles again, a joke that none of us are privy to, "It is so simple that the truth lay hidden for a hundred years or more. For the Sacred Stones to deliver the perfect Harmony, they must be together, but not in the hands of a single individual. They must each be held by another, who will work in harmony with the other."

'That made as much sense as – Magic is real' and then the truth of the statement hits me like a mountain.

Two stones. Two individuals. One for Joy, the other for Sorrow, in balance and harmony.
But how and who?

CHAPTER SIXTEEN

"Elwah, you have already known the 'who', perhaps not consciously, but you have made choices that have followed the destiny of the prophesy. However, the 'how'," Master Sindarin chuckles again to a private joke, "the 'how' will be a little more complicated. It will need to involve, my skill as master of Magical Keys, Master Ngaway, for his abilities with incantations and spells, Mater Elim, who has power over the gateways, I think Mahjira Mitra for summoning the Guardians, Master Suffrah, as master of ceremonies and rituals, and of course you, Elwah, as master of magic. Your ability to create spells at will, dictates your role to control the process and see to its successful conclusion."

We stand in awe at that pronouncement. Elwah, clears his throat, his voice comes out a little uncertain, "Master Sindarin, if I am to understand you..." Elwah regains control, "Master Sindarin, are you suggesting that we perform the ritual to call the Sacred Sapphires back?"

The old man looks up, a sparkle in his eyes, "Yes, Elwah. Was it not obvious from the start, that we need to call the sapphires back and work to establish the Great Harmony?" He chuckles again then. I look at him and want to smile, *this man must have such an easy sense of humour.*

Elwah still looks confused, "Master Sindarin, dare I ask who?"

The old man suddenly looks very serious. "Well, definitely *not* master Ahmad."

The statement is spoken so seriously and with such complete lack of malice that we all break into laughter.

"I think you know the answer to that." Elwah stands apparently mute, casting his eyes to the ground and remains that way.

Master Sindarin closes his eyes a moment, then turns. With that unmistakable power in both his words and his eyes, he asks, "Saeed, do you love Azizi?"

My head whips around and I stare at Saeed. He appears rooted to the ground. The terror in his eyes is not the terror I saw when he had been struck by the scorpion in the desert. His terror now seems far beyond mortal terror.

It seems an infinity before the gentle voice of Saeed is heard, "Yes, master. I love Azizi." His cheeks immediately glow the brightest red I have ever seen.

My heart is beating like a drum, threatening to give me away. Tears fill my eyes at his public declaration.

Master Sindarin turns his fierce gaze upon me then, "Young Azizi, should I question your love for Saeed?"

"No, no. I love him." My voice answers in a whisper. And now, how I wish I had shouted it out.

The old man then turns to both Elwah and Hasan. "Your love and care for Azizi have brought him safe and sound to this moment. Without your care for him, he would have suffered defeat at a very young age. Then, the world would have had to wait for another hundred years for the conjunction and alignment of stars to begin again. I say this to you both, Elwah and Hasan, that you may feel wholesome and joyful with your actions – they were the right actions. It does not in any way diminish your love for Azizi."

A gentle breeze suddenly moves through the room, carrying with it the unmistakable fragrance of pine needles and the scent of orange blossoms. I am astonished not at the breeze, nor the fragrance, but the balance with which both of those perfumes support each other. A high note and a deep note singing in harmony.

"Master Sindarin, thank you for those revelations. I do not question your wisdom. There is one detail though, in the prophesy that is unclear. The prophesy spoke of a child born of the Tears of Sorrow, who would appear from the northern regions. That is clear and speaks pointedly of Azizi. Until now I had always thought that one individual would be destined to hold both Sapphires. Have I been mistaken then in my interpretation?"

"No Elwah, based solely on that prediction, you were not mistaken. However, there is another oracle that no one has ever given any attention to. It is contained in a Sacred Parvus of king Apphat. It is certain that Apphat did not entirely trust those around him. He hid the greatest prophesies amongst the Parvus dedicated to the subject of Love." The old man gives another chuckle, looking at me directly he adds, "He did this to bewilder the common students, knowing that most young men would have an aversion to the subject of love. Perhaps we should ask young Azizi to give us some interpretation of the most pertinent of the Parvus on love?" The mischievous smile tells me that somehow, he knows of my school days and the incessant monotone of the students as they attempted to repeat word for word the inflections taught by Delena Tobaha. I can feel my cheeks burning.

"I will cease my taunts young Azizi. The original Apphasian is a complex language that required the study of exact inflection. In their original form the poems were extremely short and very beautiful, conveying complex emotions and meaning in just a few words. The Parvus I refer to, tells of another prophesy." Master Sindarin's voice takes on a resonance that belies his age, "as best as I can translate without losing a lot of the original intent,"

"Where Elwah meets Malkizar
Though they be distant and afar
The desert spring, the snow and ice
The forest moss, the scent of spice,
The lock of stone opens his fire.
The ball of thread,
The key that cuts the brier."

The words weave through the air, resonating in the small chamber. Images spring up in my mind of my beloved forest, only to be replaced with the soft light of sunsets on desert dunes.

"Would you agree young master Elwah, that the mention of Elwah and Malkizar in this case refers to the names of place as well as the seasons. The opposing elements of snow and ice balanced against stone and fire, again I think are obvious. Observe that the lines number seven. This number is associated with intuition and truth. The important thing to note, is not the description of time and place but what is meant in the last three line of the Sacred Parvus."

I am reminded with a sudden feeling of nostalgia, of my 'scholarly' discussions with my god mother about the possible meanings of the legends and various Parvus that hinted at future events.

"These are the lines that place this Parvus in the book on love. It is not only a prophesy, but a statement of love. Does this make sense Elwah, or am I required to detail the meaning of those lines?"

Elwah is pensive. He nods his head. "I understand now, Master Sindarin. There is a hint of something else though, it almost as if it is an instruction."

Master Sindarin nods affirmatively. "Well spotted Master Elwah!"

Elwah waits. The old man's eyes take on a far way look, before going on, "I will need to wait for Masters Elim and Ngaway for their interpretation. You are correct though; I believe it is a set of instructions on the process that both will need to confront and how they will ultimately achieve success."

A knot forms in my stomach, I do not like the sound of those words. They imply a test of some kind, a test that if failed could be dangerous. I look at Saeed, who has remained silent throughout. He is pale, a look of worry is written over his face. His shoulders are tense, he keeps scratching and rubbing his left thumb with his index finger, his right-hand clenches, and releases. I walk over to him and gently place my hand on his shoulder.

"Saeed?" He turns to me; his brows have knitted forming a deep line between his eyes; he takes a sudden breath and releases it quickly. I have not seen Saeed this anxious before. "Saeed, I'm here. You are safe, you are with me." He takes a deep breath and lets it out, finally giving me one of his shy smiles. "Saeed, what worries you?"

He takes another breath, he whispers, "I do not know what is happening Azizi. I do not know what they are talking about, but I feel that I am a part of it." He looks away for a moment at the view through the window, "I do not understand any of this." Turning his face back to me, with tears in his eyes, he leans close to my face and whispers, "Azizi, can we please leave and go to our room?"

I whisper back, "Yes, Saeed. We can." I bow to Master Sindarin and look up at Elwah, "Masters, this has been a long day. Saeed and I will take our leave and rest a while. Master Elwah, be aware that this all new to both of us. Saeed has never had any training in these matters. I think it would be a matter of urgency to ensure some guidance."

"Of course, Azizi. You and Saeed take your time. I will discuss this with Master Sindarin and Master Suffrah."

"Master Sindarin, thank you for your instruction and your trust in giving us those revelations." In the fashion of a student from the Temple School of Asfaine, in a gesture of deep respect for an elder, I bow placing my right fist into my left open palm. Master Sindarin acknowledges me with a nod. Turning to Hasan I bow to him quickly. He looks concerned for me, acknowledges with a gesture indicating to take care of Saeed.

I take Saeed's hand and lead him out of the room into the cool air of the corridor leading to our room. Saeed begins to draw quick breaths, and then suddenly bursts into tears. I understand, the tension has been too much. In between sobs, he apologises, "I'm sorry Azizi, I'm sorry."

Stopping, I hold him in my arms and whisper, "The rain falls from the clouds because it is too heavy. Tears fall because your heart can no longer bear the pain." I hold him, remembering a young boy who once held me tight and begged me not to let him die. "Cry all you want Saeed. I am here. You are safe, I will hold you for as long as you want me to."

His sobs ease, his breathing calms. He looks up, clear pearls of tears still hang onto his long eyelashes. He attempts a smile, and so innocently asks, "Can you repeat what you just said?"

"About holding you?"

"No, about the clouds."

"Oh. Rain falls from the clouds because it is too heavy. Tears fall because your heart could no longer hold the pain."

He looks at me with those wondrous emerald green eyes, still awash with tears. "That is so beautiful Azizi. Thank you." He holds me tight for a while more before releasing me. "Thank you for being with me." Unexpectedly, and to my surprise I am aware of how tall he has grown, his eyes almost meet mine. He gives me one of his most boyish smiles, my heart begins to beat like a drum.

I hold his face between my hands, and before I can reason with my heart, I place a gentle kiss upon his lips.

His eyes widen in astonishment. His face flushes and turns bright red, he smiles, wraps his arms around me, whispers in my ear, "Thank you Azizi. I do love you."

I hold on to his hand as we make our way back to our room. The white wolf is curled up before the fireplaces, briefly looks up and resumes his nap.

It is mid-afternoon "Saeed, what would you like to do? Do you want to take a warm bath or just rest for now?

"I think I will rest for now. I am a little tired."

He takes his shoes off, and without taking his day clothes off, slips between the covers of the bed. I pull the blanket over him and watch him close his eyes. I whisper, "sweet dreams, Saeed. I am here, you are safe." He lets out a sigh and curls up into a tight ball. He must have been exhausted, it is not long before his breathing settles into a regular rhythm, and I know he is asleep.

A soft knock at the door draws my attention.

I open the door. My godmother is standing before me, a twinkle in her eye and a warm smile.

I stand before her, neither embracing her, nor receding from her touch. I am before her, no longer a boy but a man, an initiate and Seer of Apphat. She steps forward and gently brushes my cheek and on pretence, makes to brush my hair from my brow.

"You are grown so tall."

Her hair has grown greyer around her temples; her eyes still hold a mischievous smile. There is a sense of lassitude about her, taking care of the sick, and seeking answers amongst the stars have taken their toll. Still, there is abundant strength and energy radiating from her.

A scene flashes across my mind. The day I came back from the forest, having seen the wild blue star flowers and nursing a black eye from a beating by Knut and his friends. The memory triggers a response and I wrap my arms around her, the fragrance of wild herbs still on her.

"Godmother," is all I can say, and I try to hold back my tears at the flood of memories.

"Azizi," her voice still holds power and melody, a shiver runs up my spine, "for a moment, I thought you had become too much of a man to embrace me."

I laugh light-heartedly, "I am still a boy," reminding her of our discussion on manhood and initiation, "in your eyes godmother, always a boy."

"Oh, my Dear One, how you have grown into your manhood." She smiles a warm smile, "still wise beyond your years."

I hold my finger to my lips, indicating Saeed's sleeping form in the bed, and invite her in. She looks briefly in his direction, nods her head in understanding. We walk quietly and sit on the two comfortable chairs facing the window that overlooks the marketplace.

She motions with her head, the sleeping form of Saeed, "Is he the boy with the wondrous emerald green eyes?"

"Yes. His name is Saeed."

"He seems to hold you in great esteem. Tell me the story of how he came into your life."

I do not know how it is that I can still feel heat rise in my cheeks, when my godmother questions me on matters of love.

I tell her of the incident in the desert, as his parents had brought him to their chief, mourning the inevitable death of their only son, from the sting of a scorpion. How I had sought permission and it had been granted to heal the boy. I told Aïschah how he was instrumental in ensuring the support of the Huda people, when we were pressing to find Shahulm and Elwah. Leaving out most of Saeed's passionate request for me to train him, I relate our voyage to Naasée in the search of a master that would agree to train him. I come to the end of my story. Aïschah acknowledges my words, her smile seems a little sad. Her eyes take on that familiar far away look. A small shiver courses through her body, and she brings back her focus to the room. Turning her head, to me, she sighs, "Azizi, that is a beautiful and compassionate story. It is not surprising that he has taken to you." A moment of silence passes, "I am glad that you contacted me and that I came. The politics of the Council of Elders have become complicated. I was astounded with Elwah's memories. I had always suspected foul play, but this goes a lot deeper." She sighs once more. "Azizi, your goal is not complete. Your destiny to establish the Great Harmony is still not accomplished."

I am silent. I wait upon her words.

"Azizi, I will tell you of a vision that I had some time ago. Before you were born even. I do not know how, and I have not understood until now; but I think that you and Saeed will play a large role in bringing about that destiny."

My skin is crawling with goose bumps. It is only a short while since Master Sindarin alluded to the same thing.

"God mother, how can that be? Saeed is untrained. I love him dearly and would not want any harm to come to him, but he has not instruction in the art of magic."

"My Dear One, as I have so often said to you," she allows herself a small and sad smile, "I do not see everything Azizi. I can only tell you what I know. Whether this makes any sense to you, heed well the words I will tell you, for they contain a wisdom beyond the understanding of most men." Aïschah closes her eyes, focussing on her inner mind, in a soft but clear whisper, she speaks the words of her vision,

"For only he can speak the true name of the King, for the king has two names. They are the names of the incantation that will heal the world. One will guide and protect him to the end of his days, for they were both born of the waters of creation. Though he is born of the Tears of Sorrow, and will suffer for it, another will love him, who will gift him with the Tear of Joy. And yet a third, who will become one with him, though he holds the balance of destiny to heal the world, also holds the power to destroy it. It is only in their unity that the incantation may be sung, and thereby restore the Great Harmony. This is the prophecy. Many have sought to understand it, few have been given the revelation. Guard it and treasure it."

The white wolf has stirred, quietly ambles over during her words and sitting in front of her fixes her with his steel blue eyes.

Aïschah's eyes brim with tears, she smiles and speaks only one word, but that word hits me in the chest and drops into the deepest part of me, "Halim."

It is all I can do not to burst into tears. The white wolf turns his attention to me and places a paw on my knee.

"Azizi, Halim was born under the constellation of the northern star. His birth preceded yours by only a few mahé. The significance of his chart is that he was destined to be the protector and guide. That is exactly what he was. I do not know how it is that his spirit visits this wolf, but even in this guise, he is still protecting you. Halim was the first mentioned in the Oracle I have just given you. I have only just now realised that."

I am still shaken with the mention of his name. A well of tears is threatening to burst forth at the mention of his role as guide and protector. I hold the wolf's face in my hands, I place my forehead to his and I whisper, "Thank you."

My godmother looks on with empathy, and speaks again, "The second is obvious Azizi. He is the one who unbeknown to the world was able to pass on the Sacred Tear of Joy to you. This was stated so clearly in the Sacred Parvus I found:

> *... and in its darkest hour*
> *Elwah will be safeguarded, for*
> *In a moment of bliss and Joy, the Sacred Keeper*
> *Will make his beloved whole,*
> *And his beloved will become the Gateway.*

It has taken me until recently to understand those lines. Even when I suspected that you, in the desert, had already experienced that transfer, and that you were holding the Sacred Tear within you, even then I could not comprehend the enormity of those lines."

I remember how Aïschah had stared at my eyes, only to conclude that the blue light that shone, was my transition into manhood.

"And now Azizi, I come to the third part of the Oracle. The mention of one who will become one with you, and which at first reading, infers one who holds the power of balance. I do not claim to understand that. The final part regarding the sacred incantation I am also uncertain. It holds a mystery beyond my comprehension. I do not know if King Apphat had two names..." Suddenly Aïschah pauses mid-sentence and softly exclaims "Oh...

Oh, is it really that simple?" She shakes her head and lets out a small laugh. I sit dumbfounded. I do not follow her reasoning.

"Godmother, what have you found?"

She looks at me deeply, reaching down to the depths of my soul and then whispers: "Azizi, you hold the knowledge of the Sacred Incantation that will restore the Great Harmony. It may not be obvious to you now, but trust in your destiny for it will come to you when you need it most."

More enigmas! I stare at my godmother. Another box without a keyhole or a key. I let out a laugh of frustration.

"Can you at least give me a clue?"

"Meditate on the King's name, Azizi." She smiles that unfathomable smile at me. And she adds, "But Azizi, please be careful. I do not like the politics or the energy I have encountered today. Be careful who you place your trust in."

I hear a small plaintive sound behind me, turning, I see Saeed waking up, stretching his arms and legs, and raising himself on his elbows. He stares at me and then Aïschah. His mass of red curls completely tousled making me smile. He looks a little embarrassed at first and then decides to get up. He makes his way over to us, looking at Aïschah bows to her, "Mahjira, you must be Azizi's godmother. I am Saeed."

Aïschah smiles her kindest smile, reminding me of the way she had warmly received Halim in her cottage, "Hello Saeed. I am so pleased to have met you." She extends both her hands and takes his. Invariably, Saeed blushes. I will never tire of watching him turn the colour of a ripe peach. "I hope he hasn't been telling you tales of how I turn people into frogs or beasts."

Saeed briefly stares at me, a small look of horror on his face and then he realises the jest and shaking his head, making those curls suddenly come to life, he exclaims, "no, no, and even if he had, I would not have believed him." Spoken with such absolute conviction that it makes us all laugh.

Aïschah is serious again, "I must speak with Elwah before I return to the Asfaine mountains. I will depart in the morning Azizi. Until then, rest and think on the things I have told you." She pauses for a moment. "I will return for the Calling Ritual."

With very little ceremony, my godmother being someone of few words, smiles at Saeed, gives me a final hug and leaves.

Saeed is smiling, just a small gentle smile. "I like your godmother." He softly declares. "She doesn't scare me like the others do." He quickly looks down at his feet, a little embarrassed at his declaration.

Light heartedly I respond, "Believe me, she can be scary for some people, especially if they cross her." Saeed looks a little awed. "She came to my school once because the teachers were not teaching me as well as she thought they should. It only took a short moment talking alone to Delena Tobaha. I don't know what was said. I was scared because I thought my schoolwork was very poor. She came back in a short while; her eyes had a fierce look about them and then she took me away from the school to begin my apprenticeship with her."

CHAPTER SEVENTEEN

The window that overlooks the marketplace is opened. Although the stalls have long closed for the day, a gentle breeze drifts through the room carrying with it the scents of a busy market day, mixed with a hint of the ocean. Warm golden beams of the late afternoon sunlight set the dust in the air floating in a slow dance. My shoulders are tense, the day's events are still crowding my mind. I want to lie down and forget the world for a while. I long for my childhood forest.

"Saeed?" I turn to face him, "Saeed, I will take a bath. My body aches from all that has occurred. Would you like to join me?"

He is thoughtful and decisively answers, "Not straight away. But I will join you in a little while?"

I acknowledge him and leave, seeking out Hasan's aide Sarek and the bathroom. I turn into the corridor in the direction of Sarek's room. A small prickling in the back of my neck makes me turn. Late afternoon shadows fill the corridor. There is no one there. I reason with myself, *I am tense; I see danger where there is none.*

Sarek tells me that in anticipation, he has already begun to fill the bath with warm water. I am very grateful for his attention and his ability to anticipate need. I leave Sarek to his chores. Fresh towels and a fresh change of clothing in hand, I enter the bathroom, marvelling for the second time at its grandeur and beauty; the golden bathtub sitting against an impossibly large window that faces the ocean. The room is filled with steam, small droplets of water condensing on the walls. I take off my clothes, leaving them on the floor to separate them from the clean ones.

Carefully, testing the temperature of the water with one foot first and almost pulling it out with the shock at the heat, I ease my foot back into the water. I follow with the other foot, holding the side of the bathtub for balance. Standing now in the bath, allowing my legs to accommodate to the warm water, I cup one hand around my manhood and ease the rest of my body into the water. The worst of the hot prickling sensation over, I relax, close my eyes, and let out a long satisfying breath.

Tentatively, I turn my head to the spectacle of the ocean below. Bracing myself for the sheer drop of the view to the ocean, instead I focus my attention to the furthest spot from the edge.

A hot ball of light sits over the horizon. The sun is setting in all its glory, spreading its light and turning the waters of Elwah into a fiery tumultuous ocean.

I let the thoughts of the day drift off with the surrounding steam and slipping deeper into the bath, I close my eyes. Invariably the voices of the day chatter in my head, teasing me to give them my attention. I think of clouds and let them drift away.

The water begins to feel somewhat cooler. I have either become accommodated to the heat of the water or I have been soaking for a while and not noticed the darkening sky. In any case, I turn the hot water tap on to replenish it.

The door opens and Saeed steps in.

"The sky has grown dark. Is it too late to join you?

I smile at Saeed, glad to have his company. "No, come in. The water is still hot." Pointing to the table, I add, "I brought a spare towel for you in case you decided to join me."

Saeed carefully places his satchel on the table, holding it for a moment longer than seems usual. He takes off his clothes, walking over to the side of the tub, he tests the water with one hand. Mimicking my previous behaviours, sets one foot into the tub and then the other, gauging his capacity to immerse himself into the hot water. Likewise, protecting with both hands the more sensitive parts of himself, he eases into the water facing me, letting out a sigh of pleasure.

The late afternoon light suddenly winks out, plunging the bathroom into a soft shadowy dusk.

"Oh... how wonderful." Saeed has turned his head to the window. The sun has passed setting, the oranges and reds have dissolved. The sky has turned a light cobalt blue, a large star has just winked into existence. Constellations begin to sparkle into life and crowd the night sky like ambers floating up from a desert fire. I am just as transfixed as he is.

"It feels like we're floating in the sky!" Saeed is smiling broadly, no longer concerned with the height at which the room sits, he is looking at the spectacle unfolding. I look at Saeed enjoying in his delight. His face has relaxed, his youthful fresh appearance has returned, his shoulders are no longer tense.

He stretches his legs releasing more tension. I can feel his feet near my hands. On impulse I take one of his foot and begin to gently massage it. His initial reaction is one of surprise that is quickly replaced with a sigh as he half closes his eyes.

"That feels so nice."

Audaciously, I massage his calf and as I slip my hand near his knee, he bursts into giggles and retracts his foot, calling out, "that tickles!"

I laugh and stop teasing him. I take his other foot and massage that, focussing solely on his foot and trying to keep the growing excitement in my groin under control.

A thought suddenly occurs to me, "Saeed, your naming day is soon, is it not?"

An air of seriousness replaces the previous laughter. "Yes. On the next full moon of Ayshah, I will be eighteen."

I do a quick calculation, the second appearance of the moon Ayshah in the season of Elwah, is due only two lahé away; and then I reflect a moment, Saeed was born at the end of the season of Elwah. I will need to think of a suitable gift. I can ask my godmother to give me the recipe for the honey barley cakes and tease the cook in the kitchen to help me make them. For the gift, I almost wish I was back at home in the Asfaine mountains; I would ask the smith to create a special talisman. My mind wanders, thinking of a suitable piece that could hold a form of magic for him. I look at Saeed's face, that gentle relaxed young man, unaware of his good looks and so open to the possibilities of life.

I want to protect him; I fear for his innocence at the hands of selfish and unconscionable individuals who would use his naïve and generous spirit for their own ends. I do not have the time or means to create a physical talisman, but I can create an etheric one, imbue it with an energy of my intent, that will protect him. Once created, I can place it in his Hala.

"Azizi?" I look up, "Azizi, what are you thinking about?"

I smile at him. "It's a secret."

A look of disappointment momentarily shadows his face.

I smile, relenting, "I was thinking what gift I could possibly give you on your naming day."

"Oh." He smiles timidly. "You don't have to give me anything."

"Tsk, tsk. Of course, I have to. I just need to think of something special. Do you still have the ceremonial scimitar that your father gave you?"

His eyes soften. "Yes, but I left that behind when I set out on my journey."

I am thinking about the things he does, or wears and at once I realise. "Saeed when you were at the markets the other day, you were speaking with the fragrance merchant. You looked disappointed with what he was showing you. What were you looking for?"

He frowns slightly, then "Ah, yes I remember. I am running short of the oil I use on my skin."

"You mean the oil of orange blossoms?"

"Yes. I could not find one that was the same as the one I use. The one the merchant had seemed too weak. It is a skill to distil the right fragrance."

Where could I possibly find such an oil. Perhaps I should

ask Hasan. He might know of a merchant who deals in refined perfume oils.

Saeed is looking down; a little furrow creases his brow.

"Saeed, where do you find such oil. I cannot imagine that orange trees grow in the Huda pass?"

Saeed smiles, his face once more softens. "My mother told me it is because of my Yumma."

"Your Yumma? Oh, you mean your grandmother?"

"Yes. When I was little, she used to nurse me often. Her clan came from a desert tribe, north of the Great Desert near the foothills of Asfaine." My ears prick up at the mention of my mountain home. "There, the weather is warm and the soil rich enough to grow orange trees. My Yumma loved the scent of orange blossoms. She had an oil made from them and wore it often. My mother says that is why I love the same scent, because my Yumma used to nurse me, and I could smell that perfume on her." He adds a little shyly, "I love my Yumma, this scent reminds me of her." His eyes glisten, I can see the love he has for her. "She looked after me, when you and prince Ijlal went looking for the sorceress."

The memories float up in my mind. I am amazed how his memories seem to fit with mine like a complex puzzle. Saeed suddenly looks up, some concern in his eyes. "Oh Azizi, were you thinking of this as a gift? Oh. But you don't need to."

His sudden change of mood puzzles me. "I thought you said that you were running out of it and could not find a suitable replacement?"

Saeed now looks embarrassed.

"Azizi, after you left for your bath, there was a knock at the door and when I opened it, I nearly slammed it shut. I wished then that I had gone with you to the bath."

"What happened Saeed, who was at the door?"

"It was that servant, the man with Master Ahmad."

I sit bolt upright so suddenly that waves of water crash onto the floor.

"What? What did *he* want?"

"It is fine Azizi. I was scared at first, but he said he had come to apologise."

The memory of the prickling in the back of my neck as I left Saeed earlier on comes back to haunt me. *So Tabrass was waiting for me to leave before approaching Saeed on his own. What did he want?*

"What do you mean Saeed? Apologise?"

"I'm sorry Azizi, I do not mean to upset you."

I take a deep breath, try to maintain an outward calm, while my heart is racing; I want to get out of the bath and yell at this man to leave Saeed alone. "Tell me what happened then, Saeed?"

"He said that he wanted to apologise for the way he had handled me. That his master had ordered him to do so. But then he added that his master was also sorry, that he had misunderstood why we were here. He then offered a small vial, it is refined oil of orange blossom, which he says only his master knows the person who makes such quality oils."

The tension in my body has returned. "How did Tabrass know that this is what you were looking for?" I can hear the abruptness in my voice and regret it immediately.

"He asked the perfume merchant I spoke with."

The pieces of the marketplace begin to fall together but why wait until I am out of the room?

"Azizi, you seem angry. Did I do wrong?"

Saeed looks concerned, almost scared. I need to calm down. I imagine that the intensity of my blue eyes could make anyone feel apprehensive.

"No Saeed. You did nothing wrong. I am just questioning the motives that Master Ahmad has in making such a gesture."

"Azizi, is it any more than an apology?" Saeed's voice is meek.

I want to reassure him, but all my senses are now screaming warnings in my head.

"Saeed, I believe you, and I understand that an apology seems appropriate. I just do not trust Master Ahmad's motives. I think he is always after something else."

Saeed looks dejected. I feel that I have disputed his claim. I try to make light of the matter and dissipate the energy of sadness, "Ah well, Saeed, I will have to think of a better gift for you then."

Looking a little reassured, he attempts a half smile.

"Will you at least show me this precious vial of quality oil?" I detect the note of sarcasm in my voice. I only hope that Saeed has not noticed.

Carefully, to not completely flood the floor and making sure we don't slip on the quantity of water I have already spilled, we step out of the bath and dry ourselves.

With a degree of caution and some hesitation, Saeed opens his satchel and pulls out a vial made of the finest alabaster with a small cork in the top. Holding it delicately in his hands he holds it up for me to look at. Respecting the apparent gift, I do not reach out for it.

"It is such a beautiful bottle, Saeed. It is made of fine alabaster that will preserve the perfume oil in the desert heat for a very long time."

Saeed smiles in acknowledgement.

"Are you happy with the scent of it?"

He nods his head and opening the cork stopper, he adds "It is very delicate. It is somewhat different to the one I am used to. I think that is due to a different distilling method. But still, I am glad of it."

He allows me to smell the top of the bottle.

It is definitely the fragrance of orange blossoms. But there is a subtle note under the main one. I am unsure of it and that sets my mind racing. The note is not unpleasant and is masked by the dominant fragrance of the blossoms.

Not wanting to upset or undermine Saeed's excitement, I just make a neutral remark, "It seems a fine oil, Saeed."

My chest tightens a little, my stomach feels a little heavy. I am not sure what to do or think.

Unusually for him, Saeed does not rub any of that oil on him. I am glad of it—something just does not feel right.

We dress. I attempt to clean up some of the mess I am responsible for and we return to our room.

Saeed is subdued; his normal sparkle is missing. Upon reaching our room, Saeed silently undresses, slips into bed, and turns to one side.

I am unsure what to do. There is a small but uneasy discord between us.

The distant roar of a rogue wave crashing against the walls of Naasée echoes in the night air.

I undress. Gently, I slip into bed next to him. I can feel the heat of his body radiating. I desperately want to hold him and reassure him. I lay on my back allowing the images of today's event run through my mind.

"Azizi?" Saeed timidly asks, "Azizi, are you asleep?"

"No Saeed. I'm awake."

"Azizi, do you remember your promise?"

I think for a moment, not wanting to make things worse by not knowing which promise I had made.

"Do you mean about your training, Saeed?"

"Will you be training me?"

I hold back a sigh. He is determined that I be the one to train him.

"I haven't forgotten, Saeed. I will speak with Elwah tomorrow morning. I promise."

I lay awake for a very long time, unable to clear my mind of the emotions and events of the day. I can tell by his soft regular breathing, that Saeed is already fast asleep. Every time I close my eyes, I see darkness and then a sensation of falling. I snap my eyes open, resisting the expected trance. Sleep attempts to creep in unnoticed, my eyes repeatedly flutter shut and open wide.

The darkness dissolves, a red sunset fills my vision, the sun begins to resemble an orange. A hand appears, by a trick of distance, it seems to hold the sun, stopping it from sinking below the horizon. The hand moves towards me and now offers me this large ripe fruit. I look up, Saeed is smiling at me, he looks down, I interpret that he wants me to look at his hand. He is holding a large green emerald. He hesitates a moment, offers it to me then closes his fingers over it. His features have turned to sadness. Small black smoke like tendrils attempt to penetrate between his fingers, unsuccessfully prizing his hand open. He looks at me with a plea in his eyes. My chest expands, energy fills me with a yearning to protect him. I raise my right hand, a blue flame surrounds it, I am about to release an energy to protect Saeed, when I sense a presence behind me. The irksome energy has all the sliminess of the Shadows I encountered in Halim's mind. A dark hand is holding my hand down, preventing me from releasing the blast of protection. A knot forms in my stomach, my heart begins to beat faster I am filled with a nervous energy, unable to move, I try to call out and can only whisper "Saeed, help."

I look up and I see Saeed's face turn to anger, such an anger I had never imagined him capable of. He suddenly raises both hands palm upwards and behind him appears a wave of enormous proportions. Dark green, frothing with anger, streaked with bolts of pure white lightning. The wave rises menacingly, terror fills me, my breathing quickens, and I start to gasp. I think if he releases that wave, I will surely drown. My breath finally finds voice and I call out, "No Saeed, no, wait. Saeed no..."

C H A P T E R   E I G H T E E N

I wake up with a start, sitting bolt upright.

Saeed is staring at me with concern in his eyes.

Tears are falling onto the blanket. Realising they are mine; I quickly wipe my eyes. I take a deep breath reassured that this was a dream, *or was it? It had all the energy of a warning.*

"Azizi, were you having a bad dream? You were calling out my name, and then you woke up."

I take deep long breaths, trying to regain my bearings and my sense of calm.

"Azizi, you sounded scared. You kept saying 'no Saeed, no'. Did I do something wrong in your dream?"

I look at his youthful face, so full of concern, my heart goes out to him.

"Saeed, I am well now. I do not know what the dream means. I will have to think about it."

Saeed's concern remains etched on his features. I understand that he is also concerned for something he might do or something that would place him in danger. I decide to tell him a part of it.

"No Saeed, you did nothing wrong. In my dream I was in danger, and you were trying to protect me." Saeed looks a little awed that he would take on a protector role. "I was worried for you that you might get hurt in trying to protect me."

His brows furrow on that otherwise immaculate face. He obviously wondering how he, without any training, how he could possibly protect someone who is a trained magician as well as one who has defeated the sorceress.

Cautious not let out too many details but wanting to support his self-esteem, I add, "Saeed, in my dream it seems that you were a fully trained magician and that you called forth such a powerful magic to protect me, that it threatened to destroy all those that were around you." Saeed's mouth is gaping, "that is when I called out for you to wait and stop before it was too late."

Elwah's words echo in my mind, '*Young Saeed, it will be necessary for you to ground and master your innate power. If you do not, I dread to see the reality of your guardian. Were your love be challenged, the power that is your guardian would easily engulf half the world.*'

A shudder briefly pulses up my spine.

Saeed looks down. "Saeed, nothing bad happened. As you say, it was just a dream." I don't add that the dream was prompted by my concern for the gift Master Ahmad had made to him.

"Azizi," his voice is almost a whisper, "Azizi, do you think that I should not study to become a magician."

He looks defeated. My heart goes out to him.

"No Saeed, I do not think that." He looks up a little hope returning in his eyes, "I think that when you begin your training you will discover your power, but that you will need to learn to master it so that it remains in your control."

Saeed becomes pensive; to reassure him I give him a gentle hug. He looks up meekly, smiling.

Fully awake, I make my way to a small table near the window that holds a large bowl full of fresh water and some clean towels. I wash my hands, splash some water on my face and dry myself. Dressing myself for the day I turn to him, "Saeed, I will go to see if Elwah is up and ready to speak with me."

Saeed pales a little. "Azizi, please don't leave me. I'm scared to be alone."

On reflection, I think it would be better if he did not remain in the room by himself at the mercy of Tabrass.

Considering the options, I turn to view the markets, which are just beginning to open. A few people have begun to wander around, some already making purchases of food for the coming meals. My attention is drawn to two young men going aimlessly from stall to stall, occasionally stopping to make inquires or stop to purchase a fruit or something else to eat. One of them is amused at something and a light sparkling laugh drifts up to the window. I immediately recognise that laugh.

I turn suddenly to Saeed. "You do not need to be alone. Saeed, dress quickly and come with me."

His hand in mine, I run out the door and make our way down the stairs. I almost jump two steps, still holding on to Saeed's hand, the speed at which we are now descending threatens to bring us both down. He starts to giggle and in between fits of laughter calls out, "Slow down Azizi, I am about to fall."

Upon reaching the markets, I look around, orienting myself to the stall where I saw those two young men. I look up to determine my point of reference from the window. I turn again and at a stall not far from us, I see a young man a little shorter than me, his back to me, dark brown curls almost confirm my suspicion. He then moves, another young man is by his side, tall and slim, a serious look on his face, shaking his head at something his companion has just said. They are about to walk away, their soldier's stride finally betrays them, and I call out, "Rauf! Isamadeen!" The twin companions are here. They must have remained behind after Ijlal and Shahulm left.

They turn at the sound of their names, and their identical faces break into the mischievous smiles I remember so well. They quickly make their way over, and Rauf with his usual assurance, wraps his arms around me, "Azizi, my brother." He stands back and declares, "Your skin is still white, when will you bake it?"

Isamadeen punches him in the shoulder, "Rauf!" Rauf bursts into laughter. Isamadeen approaches and likewise gives me a vice like embrace.

Saeed stands a little apart, not quite knowing what to do.

"Rauf, Isamadeen, this is Saeed."

Saeed bows, blushes a little; Rauf in his inimitable way, takes two steps and embraces Saeed. "Ijlal told us about you, Saeed. You are famous amongst the Companions of Shiraz."

Saeed's cheeks turn a deeper colour of sunset, attempts a smile, and looks at me quizzically.

Isamadeen steps forward, a serious look on his face, nevertheless smiles, taking both Saeed's hands in his and states,

"Saeed, it is good to see you again. Don't mind my twin brother, Rauf. He lacks social manners. If he annoys you, let me know and I will punish him severely."

Rauf's eyes roll upwards in mocking challenge. "Don't listen to him Saeed, I know exactly how to greet a beloved friend of Azizi, and it requires nothing less than a brotherly embrace of welcome."

"Oh," is all Saeed manages to say. The colour of his cheeks has not lessened.

I laugh at the greeting, Saeed's small discomfort and the well-intended remarks of the twins.

"Saeed, you may not remember these two. They are the companions of Ijlal, who came with us in our quest to find Shahulm. You would have met them briefly when we had an audience with your chieftain."

Saeed's eyes light up in recognition. "Oh, I remember. I was much younger then."

Isamadeen mischievously turns to Rauf, "See, I told you that you are starting to look like an old man." Rauf pokes his tongue at his brother, making Saeed smile, which he quickly conceals with his hands, adding, "I'm sorry, I did not mean it that way. Of course, I recognise you, but it was a long time ago." He adds quickly, "I remember thinking that I was about the same age as you, and that you were already a soldier of Shiraz. I wanted to be like you."

"Ah! There you are Isamadeen." Rauf amiably places an arm around Saeed's shoulders and in a conspiratorial tone declares, "I knew my youthful looks remained intact." Turning to his brother, he defiantly adds, "I think I will take Saeed as my twin brother." Turning to me, "Don't you think Azizi? Do we not resemble each other?"

I can't help but laugh out loud at the brothers' antics. Saeed starts to laugh. How I delight in seeing him happy. This is exactly what I was hoping for, to leave Saeed in the care of the twins, and especially gentle Rauf who I knew would immediately take to Saeed; leaving me to talk to Elwah without worry.

I take on a solemn look, considering Rauf's question and in a serious tone of voice, "Yes... why yes Rauf, I can see the resemblance. But you will need to do something about your hair."

Rauf takes a long look at Saeed's red curls, gently touches his hair, which of course sets Saeed's face blushing again. Rauf then declares, "If his hair were a forest or even a garden, I would want to walk through it in bare feet."

It's too much for me and I laugh out loud, adding, "I would hope, Rauf, that you would wash your feet first."

Isamadeen is laughing and shaking his head. It is now Rauf's turn to blush. Saeed does not quite know what to make of Rauf's remark, so I state the obvious, "Saeed, I think what Rauf means is that your hair is so soft and pleasant, that it would be a delight to walk through such fine curls as yours and enjoy the sensation."

"Oh." Saeed looks down, smiles, and whispers, "Thank you."

Rauf turns to me, a small nod of gratitude for getting him out of an awkward moment and states, "Azizi, I really like this young man. I think we will become great friends. Can we keep him?" before I can answer he adds, "Saeed, what do you think, we can teach you all sorts of fun things. We can leave the serious Azizi to his magic and spells and we can go and have fun?"

Saeed looks at me enquiringly.

"Isamadeen, Rauf, I have urgent business that concerns Saeed's training, but I need first to speak with Elwah. I don't want to leave Saeed alone in this town and am hoping that you might have the time to be with him until my business is concluded."

Both Isamadeen and Rauf immediately and in unison agree, "Of course!" Then turning to Saeed, I ask him, "Saeed, are you happy to be with these two clowns for a while until I finish with Elwah?"

He nods his head, smiles at my remark, "Yes Azizi, yes. I will be fine."

I am about to turn and leave as Rauf asks, "Do you know how to ride a horse and swing a sword at your enemy at the same time, Saeed?"

Saeed looks a little embarrassed. "I have never learned to ride a horse. The Huda people mostly know how to run in the desert."

"Oh, then we can teach you how to ride. Our horses are just outside the gate. This is going to be fun."

As I walk away, I turn once more to look at them walking off; Rauf has his arm around Saeed's shoulders, chattering away. I need not have worried, Saeed is taken by Rauf's and Isamadeen's care, his steps are light, his whole body has lost its tension.

～

I MAKE MY WAY back to Hasan's residence, returning to my room first, to let the white wolf out. I open the door and without prompting, the wolf takes one look at me and heads out.

I climb the stairs to the guest room where Elwah has taken current residence.

I knock at his door. Elwah's soft voice answers, "Azizi, come in." I should not be in awe at his ability to know and see, and yet I open the door wondering how he knew.

Morning light is streaming through an open window facing east, giving the room a sense of elegance and airiness. Slightly to one side, there is a large round rug made up of a border of golden yellow, its centre is filled with tightly woven midnight blue wool and bejewelled with countless silver stars. The fine work that has gone into representing the colours of a desert sky is breath taking.

At the far end near the window, at an angle that allows the sitter to face both the door and the window, are a couple of wooden armchairs adorned with cushions echoing the colours of the rug. A small table sits in between the chairs. On the table, a pot of fresh steaming tea sits and two cups of fine glazed clay and painted a soft emerald green awaits my arrival.

Elwah is sitting on one of the chairs, greets me with a warm smile.

"Come Azizi, I have made some fresh tea to energize the senses."

The fragrance of lemon verbena that is drifting from the teapot, reminds me of my godmother's herbarium. Aïschah grew a combination of plants indoors that could not survive in the cold climate of the Asfaine mountains.

I sit opposite him; his presence radiates a sense of peace that I find reassuring.

"I sense that you have released the white wolf."

Again, I am taken by his foreknowledge, but the statement is ambiguous.

"I thought he should not be kept in a room, so I let him to wander outside."

Elwah nods in acknowledgement. "It is possible that he may not come back tonight."

I stare at Elwah, not understanding.

"Perhaps, Azizi, I should tell you the story of how this magical creature came into your life."

I wait. I have been wanting to ask how Halim's spirit came to inhabit this wolf, in complete contradiction to Halim's gentle nature and as a fiercely protective shepherd.

"I was fully aware of your grief at the loss of Halim. It became a grief that if left unresolved could have led you to a life of despair. At the time, I did everything to filter out those energies from your Hala, but they kept re-appearing. Your connection to him was so entwined that it required constant vigilance on my part and some subconscious effort on yours to untangle."

The memories of Halim are still strong, but they seem more distant now. I look at Elwah, waiting for him to go on.

"The decision you made to return to your godmother for further training, was in some ways a good one but an ill-timed one. I could not however stop you as I sensed that it would somehow affect your destiny in a negative way. So, I let you go."

I remember embracing Elwah on my last day in Schiraz. A warm evening, as he was standing on his balcony facing the Asfaine mountains that were a faint outline on the horizon.

"I could also see Halim's spirit appearing around you, responding to your grief. He was constantly attempting to reassure you, to lift the guilt of his passing from you."

My heart is pounding, my throat tightens, tears are welling up.

"Even now, as the white wolf wanders the desert sands outside this city, Halim's spirit is beside you, smiling, projecting his love to you and reassuring you that it was not your fault."

Tears begin to form and roll down my cheeks. I let them be and do not wipe them away. I understand that this will be my final release of the boy I first fell in love with. Elwah's eyes express compassion and lets me be and continues, "It was obvious that Halim also had difficulties in letting go. His desire to protect you was strong. So, I asked Halim what he wanted to do. He simply expressed a desire to protect you and live happily."

I give myself to my sobs, uncaring for the tears that now pour out from me.

"Shortly after you left, I foresaw danger to you. Grave enough that you could have lost your life. I also understood that I could not intervene. You must understand that as one of the Elders, it is forbidden for me use my powers that would result in the death of a being. Your destiny is still unfolding, Azizi. I decided to allow Halim's spirit to inhabit a magical creature of a wild white wolf. It was the easiest way to manifest a guardian for you on the physical plane that would not require magic on your part or mine to protect you."

Elwah pauses, collecting his thoughts, "the wolf's ferocity was its own. Halim was simply satisfied that no harm had come to you. The man who died at the wolf's attack also fulfilled his own fate."

I take a sip of the warm tea; the sharp and sweet flavour soothes my nerves and clears my mind. I sit up, wanting to hear more.

Elwah continues, "It was also necessary to involve another, as he is intrinsically linked to your destiny. This individual had been inspired for some time to seek you out. He simply suited the task of bringing the wolf to you."

I look up. My heart begins to pound in my chest.

"Yes Azizi, I speak of Saeed. The boy you saved in the desert." Elwah smiles a reassuring smile, "but before I answer your questions regarding that, I want to finish by clarifying what I meant earlier on. Halim's spirit is reassured that you are safe. It is now time, and it is essential that Halim is allowed to move on." My throat tightens a little at that news, but I bow to the knowledge that this must be. "Azizi, his spirit will be reincarnated. I do not see what will be of him. My sense is that having fulfilled his tasks lovingly, he will be rewarded and protected."

Elwah pauses before taking another breath, "This is the reason I said earlier on, that the wolf may not return tonight." My chest tightens a little, "but Halim's will to protect you has been so imprinted on the wolf's mind, that the wild beast will sense if there is any danger to you and if it can, will respond accordingly. In that way, Halim's desire to protect you will live on through the wolf." Elwah takes another breath, "But the wolf is wild, it must be allowed to live as such, to hunt and eat and behave as a wild animal should." Elwah momentarily looks out of the window, and adds, "It is possible that in the future, out of a sense of obligation, the wolf may return to you. But be aware that it will be just that – a wild animal with a sense to want to protect you. It will not return to you as a domesticated pet would."

A small breeze blows through the window. The air is clear. A certain peace fills the space around me. My back straightens, my heart is filled with a sense of joy and peace that I have not felt for a very long time.

"Azizi, later tonight, rest a while in your room or somewhere you feel at ease. Think upon everything I have just told you. Take a moment to bless Halim's spirit and with joy in your heart, let him go and wish him well. It is possible that many lifetimes from now, you and he will meet again."

Elwah's eyes are gazing into the space around me, and adds, "Halim seems at peace now. There is a powerful energy of joy radiating from him and his spirit is beginning to glow and disappear."

The moment passes. The beams of sunlight suddenly seem a little dull, as if something bright has left the room.

CHAPTER NINETEEN

"Azizi, now we come to your questions about Saeed."

Elwah pauses, looks at me and nods his head once to signal for me to begin.

"Elwah, thank you. Now I understand what has transpired." I gather my thoughts, seeking the best place to start. I am sure that Elwah, with his ability to perceive most things, will already know much of what I am about to tell him.

"When Saeed came to me in the desert, following the incident, he asked me to train him in magic and healing. I am still an apprentice, barely past my first initiation."

Elwah is silent. He gestures for me to go on.

"Initially, I told him that I didn't think I was either experienced enough or that I would be allowed. I led him here on the promise that I would find a suitable master to train him. I think deep down, he still hopes that I would be approved to train him, despite my lack of experience."

Elwah smiles kindly. "Azizi, you should not doubt your abilities."

"Difficult not to, when all I heard from my tutors at school, was my lack of ability or talent." With a little surprise, I hear the bitter note in my voice.

He shakes his head a little, almost in disbelief. "Azizi, I was truthful when I said that I had begun your training when you were six years old. This was not an exaggeration to bring the Elders on my side. You can let go of what your tutors told you. If only they could have seen who was at your side, they would have run out of the room."

Elwah looks around then back to me. His eyes have taken on a serious look. "Azizi, when your godmother heard that her friend Celeste, your mother, was expecting a child, she immediately mapped out your potential star chart. You may not know this, but your godmother is a leading and most respected master in the casting and interpretation of star maps." His eyes take on that faraway look I have seen in my godmother when she sees something that the rest of us cannot. "I had already sensed your conception and had a vision of things, which at the time I could not interpret. That was when I decided to telepathically press on to your godmother the need for her to take on an apprentice.

As soon as you were born, however, Aïschah came to see me with your birth chart and a vision she experienced that confirmed what we had both suspected. You are a child of magic, gifted with powers beyond most novice magicians.

You have nurtured within you the Sacred Stone of Elwah when it was most vulnerable. You know, that to hold one of the Scared sapphires increases the level of your powers." Elwah shakes his head a little, smiling to himself. "Sure, your tutors lacked, that was deplorable, not completely unforeseen but sad in many ways. So, a decision had to be made. I would continue your training on the ethereal level, and your godmother would take up training you on the physical level." Elwah smiles at me again. "But you already know all this Azizi."

Elwah releases a very long sigh.

"Azizi, in some ways, it was part fate, and part destiny that guided you to Saeed. You may not be aware of this, but fate has a strange and often ironic sense of humour. Saeed's fate was that he should have died in the desert from the sting of the scorpion." My heart sinks a little at this news. "But destiny intervened, and you appeared, and you were able to use your healing powers to bring him back."

Elwah lets out a small laugh, shaking his head "Even Hasan, when he related this to me, found it hard to believe that this young man, just turned eighteen, could have such healing powers and save someone with apparently so little effort. You certainly made an impact on the tribe and his parents." Elwah becomes pensive.

"Saeed actually has natural and very organic magical abilities. Something he is almost completely unaware of. You may have observed some of those abilities and wonder how he could possibly have developed them without any training."

I must have looked dumfounded. And then I remember the dream I just had.

"Azizi, have you not noticed that every time Saeed enters a room that either directly or indirectly connects with the Ocean of Elwah, suddenly monstrous waves rise up and crash against the towers and walls?"

Several instances come back to my mind. *Surely this is just coincidence and only a vague explanation for his fear of heights and the sound of the crashing waves.* Personally, I think this is normal. Elwah nods his head, obviously reading my thoughts.

"Azizi, waves rise and crash, that is their nature. But if the elemental spirits of the ocean sense, even on an unconscious level, the energy of one who is charged with magical power, they take on a different behaviour. After all, water is one the major Elements of nature and it will respond."

"But now? How is he able to do that?"

"Are you not aware of this?" I must have frowned in confusion, "You, Azizi. You are his source of power. You are like a loadstone to him. Because your power seems so limitless, unconsciously, he is attracted to you, and he also draws power from you."

I am not sure what to feel. I don't know whether to be angry about this or pleased. I didn't realise he was doing that to me.

Elwah looks at me concerned. I am sure he has heard every word I spoke in my mind.

"Azizi, I am sure his intent is pure. Fortunately for you, the source of power, as you have come to realise, is neither within you nor outside of you. I do not have to remind you of what your godmother frequently said: that you are an instrument of power, that power flows through you and not always at your command."

Those words are all too familiar.

"Azizi, what you have not yet realised, is that you are connected to your power." I can feel myself frowning, this is starting to sound like a box without a key or a keyhole. Elwah smiles benignly, "You will soon discover, that not only you are connected to that source, but that in fact, as part of this universe, you are the source."

That's it. There's the keyless box. I am confused now.

"Azizi, I do not mean that you are the only source of power in the universe." Elwah lets out a small laugh, "No, I mean that if the universe is responsible for creating you, then you are a part of it and therefore, in a small way, you are It."

The energy in my head is beginning to spin.

"The source of your power then, as it flows through you is limitless. Saeed needs to discover also that he is a part of that origin. For Saeed to draw and enable his magic through you is not ideal. It is as if he does not believe that he has that power. However, that is the reason you and him were chosen to bring back the Sacred Sapphires. You and him, working together, in harmony with each other, can bring balance back. But first, both of you must find your inner balance; you will be sorely tested for it." More questions are arising in my mind. Elwah obviously senses this as he adds: "Azizi, just think back on what your godmother instructed you with the box that had no keys." *Ah the irony of it all. The lesson has come full circle!* Elwah doesn't even blink and goes on, "remember that on some level you understood that you are a part of creation, therefore you are truly creation."

It is obvious to both of us, that my mind is struggling with this concept. Elwah adds, "What I have just told you may not make sense to you now, Azizi, but you will understand the deeper truth of it soon enough."

Elwah pauses a moment, "Saeed, must learn to control his own innate power. It tends to waver to the energy of Chaos; hence the waves of Elwah that either respond to his unconscious call and emotional state or simply Nature's wish to revolt against his will. He must also find the way to control that source of power within himself and not through you. Then, working together, you both will be able to harness and harmonise that power. In part, I think this is what Master Sindarin saw." After a moment's thought, Elwah adds, "Keep an eye on Saeed, I believe a sign will manifest on his body once he has attained the full potential of his magic. Look out for it."

The air is cooling a little, the afternoon wind is shifting and begins to blow from the ocean to the desert. The light is changing, the shadows in the room are taking on a cooler shade. Briefly, I wonder how Saeed is managing with the twins and whether he has successfully learned to ride a horse. Even now, in my mind I want to protect him from harm.

"Elwah, I am struggling a little to clarify my feelings. My love for Saeed stems from a deep desire to protect him. I cannot deny that I find him attractive, but it goes beyond the pure physical. I often experience a brotherly love for him." Not sure how to go on, I wait to see Elwah's reaction. He simply waits for me to go on.

"I am concerned that Saeed is often at the mercy of ill intended persons. His gentle and often naïve nature leaves him vulnerable to the manoeuvrings of others. Elwah, I am concerned with a gift he has received from Tabrass, master Ahmad's servant. Saeed was gifted a vial of scented orange blossom oil, apparently as an apology for roughly handling him some time ago. When he allowed me to smell the oil's fragrance, I detected a subtle note, a kind of addition, that just does not seem right. There is a sense of coercion or manipulation in that fragrance."

Elwah waits for me to go on.

"I raised my concerns with Saeed, telling him that I suspected an ulterior motive with the gift." I sigh remembering the awkward energy that followed when I told Saeed that. "I think Saeed has already succumbed to the influence of the gift. It is a fragrance that has deep emotional roots for him, it reminds him of his Yumma." I hesitate to go on, "Saeed was adamant that the gift is nothing more than an apology; an apology he felt not only was due, but that it was sincere and well-intended and therefore welcomed. I think he became a little angry at my inference of the ill intent of the gift." A little more vehemently I add, "I think the oil has been tampered with, and I am concerned for his well-being."

Elwah looks at me with compassion. "Azizi, you should not be ashamed of your attraction to Saeed. Your intentions have always been untainted. I believe that you have been close to each other in a previous life. That would explain your feelings and need to protect him." Elwah eyes take on that far-away look, before he adds, almost dreamlike, "It would not surprise me, if he and you are twin souls."

That statement penetrates my heart, my chest expands with a warm energy that fills my being. My skin is covered in goose bumps, my heart begins to race, and I recognise a deeper truth in that last remark.

"Elwah, I am not sure what you mean."

"The deep and Sacred knowledge holds that the souls of some individuals were conceived or created at the same moment. That they were only separated after they incarnated into physical bodies. You have witnessed the physical twins, Rauf and Isamadeen, they are inseparable and yet can be complete opposites on some level. The same applies to twin souls. They are both created at the same moment, or as some would believe, that a single soul was somehow split in half. Each will have its own characteristics. In some cases, those individual personalities may be complete opposites."

The world suddenly seems to have gone silent as I wait.

"It explains your love for him and your need to protect him. On some level, Saeed also feels a deep love for you and probably looks up to you and may in fact want to protect you, if not from others, perhaps from yourself." Elwah adds that last remark with a quizzical smile.

Elwah looks up as if shaking off a thought. "As for Master Ahmad, I am still unclear of his motives. I cannot say whether he is prompted with a sense of duty towards protecting the Sacred Sapphires or whether he is tempted by the power that they offer. Perhaps, he is also in a state of confusion about his role in all this."

"In terms of the oil that you say has been tampered with, without confronting Master Ahmad, which I do not think will resolve anything, I can only wait and see what will transpire."

I must have looked concerned, he then adds, "Be assured Azizi that I will keep a watch as much as you will. As far as protecting Saeed, Azizi, we each have a particular strength within our magic. Other than the ability to create any spell at will, my strongest ability has always been to be able to look into the deep future; to be able to peer into the destiny and look at a multiple of potential outcomes." In answer to my unspoken question he adds, "some things however are hidden from me and not every outcome is predetermined. This ability comes with a 'curse' if I can word it that way – it cautions me where and if I am able to intervene to alter an outcome. There have been many instances where I am forbidden to interfere as to do so would have catastrophic consequences." Pausing for a moment, Elwah turns his soul-searching stare at me. "Apart from your obvious abilities with magic, your visions and channelling the voice of the Spirit, Azizi, have you even wondered what your special strength is?"

No one has ever said those things to me or asked me that question. I have always considered my abilities as at least average. In many ways I consider myself still on the path of an apprentice.

Elwah makes a small, amused noise, "Hmmm, Azizi, still now you undermine yourself."

"Other than the power of visualization my godmother taught me when I was young, I think my greater strength then would be her art with healing herbs, which she says I learnt much faster than she expected."

Elwah continues to look at me, smiling that enigmatic smile both he and my godmother are so good that. An amusing thought occurs to me, *how long will it be before I can say that I have acquired that slightly condescending expression?* Elwah gestures, encouraging me to delve further.

A series of images float up from my subconscious. An image of Halim's mother and my intervention in healing her. Healing Halim from the deadly poison of the Shadow's knife. The healing of Saeed from a scorpion sting in the great desert. The creation of a sacred talisman to protect Ijlal and Shahulm and enhance their love. Finally, it hits me:

"Healing."

Elwah's face transforms with a warm victorious smile. "Yes, Azizi. You are a healer of hereto unknown power. Your ability to seek and obtain permission from the Spirit Source and then channel that healing power is unheard of in our history."

He then adds, "Contained within the power of healing, is an empathy and deep understanding of pain. You are able to connect with that pain, soothe it, and dissolve it. That is a wondrous magical ability – the ability to bring back the natural balance of health and well-being in its original creative form." As an afterthought he adds, "Just as I am sometimes forbidden to intervene in some matters, you may find that there will be occasions when permission to heal may not be granted." His eyes re-focus on me and he shakes his head a little, "even a disease can come with a lesson."

I decide to consider that statement for another time and press for a more personal need.

"What can I do to protect Saeed?"

"You already know the answer to that. Azizi, the other side of your power is your imagination. You even formulated the 'cure' not so long ago, as you mused on how best to protect him without his conscious knowledge."

I must look a little dazed if not confused. And then I remember, when we were taking a bath, my wish to give him a special gift for his eighteenth naming day. I initially thought of creating a sacred talisman, like the one I had the silversmith make for Ijlal and Shahulm. I do not have access to a silversmith, so thought that I could create an etheric talisman of protection, and simply place it in Saeed's energy field.

Elwah continues, "The sign that will appear on Saeed, will be a manifestation of the full potential of his power. You will simply add to it – by doing so, it will not diminish in any way his power, it will simply add a component to it – it will empower it with the energy of protection for himself as well as for others he cares so much about. That is the quintessence of your magical strength; your ability to imagine and create an etheric artifact of immense healing and protective power, using the simplest and least demanding concept. Your idea is so simple, so powerful and so effective. It will completely baffle even the most powerful magician, unable to detect or even understand."

Even I am a little awed at the idea. Elwah smiles.

"Azizi, your imagination that drives your powers is truly remarkable."

I can feel heat rise in my cheeks, thinking that I must resemble Saeed now. I urge my mind to remain humble and say nothing more. Looking at Elwah, I simply smile.

"For now, Azizi, it would be of great benefit to both of you if you were to guide him in simple techniques that would allow him to explore his potential. The sanction of the Council of Elders to appoint someone to train or not, is not necessary. If you have the abilities that you wish to transmit to someone else, and you believe you have the skills to communicate those, then you should."

Elwah looks at me smiling. "The appointment of an apprentice is the choice of the master, not some far away group of old men." He adds, "The student is at liberty to refuse the training." Reading my unspoken question, he finishes "The final test of initiation, of course is left to another master to ensure continuity of excellence; but that is the only requirement." Elwah smiles enigmatically, "and that requirement is not always necessary either."

A wave of energy rises from the pit of my being. Elwah in his way is giving me permission to train someone else. Suddenly, I am both excited and anxious at the thought of taking on Saeed as an apprentice.

Elwah sighs a little, "You may encounter objections from some, but that should not deter you from doing so. Trust your instincts for they have always proven true." Those last words, echoing my godmother's advice during my training. He smiles his most loving smile, "and Azizi, I am always here to listen and if I can, guide you along that path."

Elwah stands and goes to the window. He turns to me, "Now go to him and share his joy."

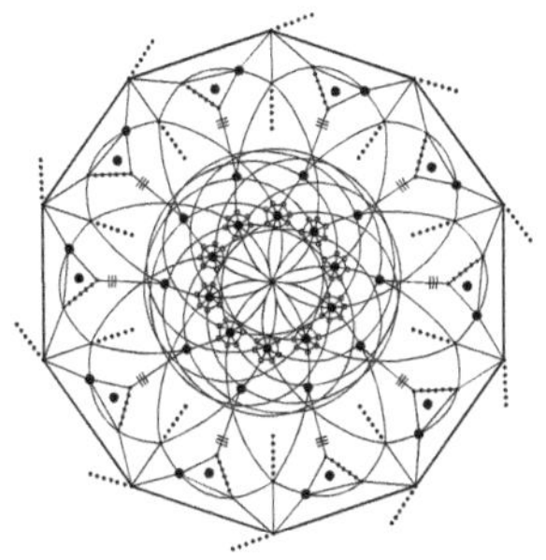

C H A P T E R   T W E N T Y

The sun is setting over the desert dunes. I reach the encampment of the soldiers from Schiraz on the outskirts of Naasée. There is activity where the horses are stabled. The dust raised by the commotion highlights the last rays of the sun. Several attendants are taking care of the horses that have just returned with their riders, Saeed is among them. Perhaps he senses my presence, he turns to me, seeing me, runs to me beaming a most glorious smile, all the while calling out my name, "Azizi! Azizi, I did it! Azizi it was amazing." He finally reaches me out of breath, his face flushed with excitement.

"Oh Azizi, it felt as I was the wind itself. I was flying over sand dunes, the air rushing towards me. It was, it was..." he is searching for the words that best describe his joy and sense of achievement, "it was so much fun!"

His exuberance is infectious, I find myself smiling.

Rauf and Isamadeen approach grinning.

Rauf speaks first, "Azizi, have you been secretly teaching Saeed magic spells?"

Saeed's jaw drops and he stares at me blushing a little.

"He took to riding as if he had done it all his life. How is that possible? I gave him a horse that is gentle but also, how should I say it—a little lazy? We had a race and he won it outright! I swear that he speaks to his horse and his mount listens to him."

Isamadeen, smiling and looking at Saeed with admiration nods in agreement. Saeed is beaming, says nothing and looks at me.

"Truly Rauf, it does not surprise me if he knows how to speak to a horse. I have seen Saeed make a dangerous desert snake move away from him."

Rauf for a moment loses his smile, instead his jaw gaping, he stares at Saeed. I expect at any moment, a change in the colour of his face, but Saeed smiles and coyly looks down.

Rauf places both hands on Saeed's shoulder, in a sincere and respectful tone of voice declares, "Saeed, promise me that we will always be friends."

That did it—Saeed blushes but smiles at Rauf, not quite sure how to respond, he replies in his typical gentle and generous manner, "Yes, of course. Yes Rauf, we will."

Rauf does what he is superbly good at: he wraps his arms around Saeed and holds him in an embrace. "Thank you, Saeed, thank you." Very gradually, Saeed responds, and his arms gently wrap around Rauf.

Isamadeen looks on bemused for a moment and then joins the two in the embrace, "Me too, Saeed, me too." It's a touching moment and a little comical as well, I can't help myself and in overly dramatic tone, I pronounce, "I think, I should immortalise this moment. I will cast a spell and change you all into a loving intertwined old tree and leave you here for the world to admire: *"THE LEGEND OF THE THREE BROTHERS."* They look up and with a loud "Aww", they come to me and just about suffocate me with their embrace. The fragrance of orange blossoms with a mixture of desert spice envelops me.

A little awkwardly, the huddle comes apart. Nevertheless, there is a sense of deep kinship. The light in Rauf's eyes for his newfound friend is reflected in Saeed's eyes. He must have been alone a lot of the time in the Huda pass. Saeed straightens, a look of pride fills his features, I am surprised how tall he appears, he is almost taller than me, his whole being radiates energy.

"Isamadeen, Rauf, thank you. This has been a wonderful day."

The twins smile at him. Rauf reaches out with both hands to hold Saeed's right hand, "Saeed, it is good to know you. Make sure you come and see us in Schiraz."

I turn to Isamadeen and ask, "When do you return?"

"Our horses are being made ready. We leave tonight, and travel until morning. We hasten to the Desert City of Ahvasar to catch up with Faruq, Ijlal and Shahulm. They will have stopped for trade dialogue with their chieftain."

Isamadeen turns to leave, notices that his brother is still looking at Saeed. Reaching out, he wraps an arm around Rauf, playfully tousles his hair, "Come Rauf, you will see each other again. Who knows, by then Saeed may be an important magician."

Rauf turns to Isamadeen, I am surprised to see tears welling up in Rauf's eyes. He smiles weakly at his twin, "I hope to see him before that happens." Rauf turns to me, "Azizi, please take care of him, and bring him with you when you next come to Schiraz."

Saeed has gone quiet, "Rest assured Rauf, Saeed is in my care. Anyone who dares hurt him will be turned to dust." Rauf pales at the mention of dust, remembering no doubt how the sorceress perished. With a final effort on Isamadeen's part, the twins turn and leave, occasionally looking back to wave at Saeed who is obviously touched by the emotion of parting.

I understand the feeling of seeing someone you care about walk away from you. We remain watching as the twins mount their horses and unhurriedly make their way south. A memory surfaces of Halim, who had spent the night in my room the first day I had met him. How, in the morning I discovered he had left early to tend his sheep, and the way my heart felt, knowing that a newfound friend was not there.

The last rays of sunlight wink out. To the southwest, the sky darkens to a cerulean blue; like a thin gash across the sky, a long cloud turns a soft pink.

Gently, I place my arm around his shoulders, drawing him into me. Letting out a long sigh, his voice a whisper, he asks, "Azizi, why does it hurt so in my heart?"

Sensing that he is not ready to go back to the room, I turn to him. "Saeed, shall we just walk into the desert for a while?"

He nods his head in agreement. We walk off silently and a little aimlessly.

"Today, you have made two new friends. They are a part of your heart now."

Moist green emerald eyes look up at me.

"The love you have for them pulls at your heart when they are not physically present." Saeed nods, "Your heart reminds you that you already miss them. It also tells you that they are important to you."

We walk silently for a while. "Saeed? Can I ask you about your childhood?"

He nods and whispers, "yes."

"Did you make many friends while you were living with your Yumma?"

He is quiet for a moment. "No. The other boys would spend much of their time with their fathers hunting. The girls would spend time learning skills from their mothers and their Yumma."

"What about your father?"

Saeed is reflective before answering in a small voice that holds a little bitterness. "My father belonged to another tribe. He would spend much of his time with them."

A long heavy silence, filled with hurtful memories of his father's absence sits uncomfortably between us.

"How did you learn your skills as a desert dweller then?"

"My mother taught me some basic skills of survival. My Yumma told me stories of how to find my way in the desert and be guided by the stars. When I was older and before I came of age, an elder showed me some ways of dealing with animals." He looks up at me, "especially how to make a snake go its way without harming it." He adds, "I also remember having dreams at night, someone telling me how to do things. Although I could not see who, there was a man who would always show me how to do certain things, such as finding water; naming things that I had not seen before. Sometimes, this person would also tell me of things that would happen before they did."

I wonder if Elwah was also preparing him for his destiny.

A thought gradually forms in my head. *I should test his ability with a simple technique; lighting a fire should be simple enough.* There are plenty of small dry shrubs that grow among the dunes that would be suitable for a small fire.

"Saeed, help me collect some of these. We will sit somewhere and light a fire."

Saeed gives me a puzzled look but starts to collect brambles that have already broken off the main bush, being careful of some of the thornier ones.

One of the dunes not far, has formed a hollow rising on three sides affording some protection from the night breeze that may pick up later. We drop our individual bundles on a spot that seems best protected.

Saeed sits on the ground, looks at the mass of dry sticks, raises his head to me with a puzzled look, a 'what now?' question in his eyes. I sit next to him, my skin begins to warm and cool alternately, butterflies take flight in the pit of my being and fill my chest in anticipation of what I am about to ask Saeed to do.

Taking a deep breath, without taking my eyes off the small mound of sticks, I ask, "Saeed, can you start the fire?" I do not use the command voice and wait for his response. I turn and look at him, a confused look on his face,

"Azizi, I do not have the fire stones to light this fire. I thought you had them."

I smile, taking another breath to settle the buzz in my body. *I cannot do this for him. He needs to uncover his magic.* With an inward smile I add, *I wonder, did my godmother also think that at first, when she began to train me?*

I turn to him, raising the power within me so that it fills my eyes, demanding nothing but compliance, I say to him, "Saeed, it is time for you to use your own magic."

A look of absolute astonishment, quickly followed with awe and a hint of doubt fills his features.

Quickly, before his doubt begins to take hold, I add, "Saeed, I will show you how, but the magic must come from you."

He swallows hard, slowly nods his head, and stares first at the pile of sticks, then turns his eyes to me. A look of naïve resolve to submit to my instruction.

"Saeed, you will allow the power to flow through you. Believe in your own power, it is waiting to manifest. First take a deep breath and allow yourself to focus only on the sound of my voice while looking at the bundle of firewood."

Saeed obeys. Briefly looking at his Hala, I am aware that he has unconsciously formed a link with me. I see it clearly as a multicoloured cord, fluctuating between gold and silver, speckled with hints of green, blue, and pink. As tenderly as possible I visualise tying a red cord around the link and securing it to stop any energy travelling through it. I will not cut that cord, until I see that he is ready to access his own power. Almost immediately, Saeed senses the subtle change and says, "Azizi, I am not sure I can do this. I have never been taught any magic."

"Saeed, I believe in you. This is only the start of your training in magic."

His eyes wide open, he stares at me. In my mind I hear his wordless questions: *Has permission been granted to train me? But you said nothing. Are you taking a risk training me without permission? Did you speak of this to prince Elwah? What did he say? But this is too sudden, I don't know if I am ready.*

I smile, empathy for his doubts; after all who would not react this way, being told that you have the power to practice magic?

"Saeed, this is a simple technique. Trust me and follow my instructions."

He takes a deep breath and lets it out slowly.

"Now, just for a little while, close your eyes and focus on your heart. Don't let anything else intrude in your mind. Believe, really believe that you can do this."

His body relaxes, his shoulders slump slightly, his steadies his breathing.

"Saeed, the next breath you take, imagine that it rises from the earth and through the very base of your spine. Let it rise into your heart."

I watch his Hala and I am immediately surprised how quickly he is able to achieve this. His heart is glowing with positive Earth Energy.

"That is very good Saeed. Now, in your mind, I want you to picture a small fire. Look at it, and even feel its warmth."

It only takes a moment, and I can see his mental image. It is accurate and lively.

"Now Saeed, even though this fire appears to be real in your mind, I want you to know that it cannot harm you. First place your hand in it, and just feel its warmth."

Saeed moves his hand, as if the fire is in front of him. A smile breaks across his face. I feel his surprise and delight.

He whispers, "Oh, it is warm, and it tickles a little."

Now, I empower my voice with a moderate amount of energy. This will take a leap of imagination for him.

"Saeed, while you can feel the flames dancing around your

hand, imagine how it would feel if you were the fire; how your body would feel, how powerful it is, how warm it can be and to continuously dance."

Looking again at his Hala and the link he had previously formed; I now gently reinforce the knot to stop any energy flowing between us.

Saeed has fallen into a light trance, his features are relaxed, his whole face is smiling. He is obviously enjoying the exhilaration of the fire.

"Saeed, I will now tell you the secret name of the fire. Remember it because in a moment, I will ask you to speak it out loud. Keep your eyes closed for now. The name of the fire is *Narum.*"

This is the moment. He has gathered his energy; it is flowing in a constant current. With one quick movement in my mind, I cut the cord between us.

"Saeed, move your hand once more through the fire and close it, as if you were capturing one of its flames."

Saeed gently waves his hand in front of him and quickly snatches something.

"Now open your eyes, point your hand at the sticks in front of you and speak the name of the fire."

"Narum!" A burst of light erupts from his outstretched hand, a flame at once appears in the middle of the brambles catching them alight.

Saeed quickly withdraws his hand. His jaw is agape, he stares in absolute wonder and astonishment at the fire that now quickly engulfs the sticks in front of us. He rubs his eyes in disbelief, eyes wide open he turns to me staring back and forth between the fire and me.

I just smile at him.

"Did, did I do that?" He looks back at the fire. "You must have helped... I have never done that!"

I laugh light heartedly at his doubt.

"Saeed, I clearly saw the fire come from your hand and ignite those branches."

Again, he stares at me, caught between disbelief and the blazing fire. He looks at his hands, turning them over and stretching his fingers in and out.

"Azizi, how is that possible? I have never been trained."

"Saeed, you did this, not me. I wanted you to experience this. I want you to understand and believe that you have power. You do not need to rely on me for that source. It is within you also."

Saeed now looks at his hands with a new wonder and understanding. He places them over his heart, and tears of joy and excitement begin to roll down that soft and gentle face.

"Saeed, let me ask you a question."

He is looking at me with absolute devotion. He nods his head, unable to speak.

"Saeed, will you allow me to train you?"

A gust of wind whispers over one of the dunes. Saeed looks at me, eyes bright with tears of joy.

"Saeed, Elwah has granted permission. That is the surprise I have been holding back."

Saeed is speechless. At once, he moves to me and takes hold of my hands. He looks as though he is about to fall to his knees, I hold him up immediately.

"Azizi, truly?"

I smile back and nod my head, "Yes, Saeed."

Tears are rolling down his face. He whispers at first, "Yes." Then almost a shout, "yes Azizi. I will work very hard to follow your instructions."

My heart is bursting with joy to see him so happy. I embrace him and he quickly holds me tight.

I give a small chuckle, "I do not know if this is completely appropriate between student and master."

He releases me quickly with a "Oh." And then shyly, "Master Azizi."

"Saeed, I will be more comfortable if you call me Azizi. I will instruct you to the best of my ability. You and I are closer than master and student, even closer than friends. There is a bond between us, and Saeed, I treasure your love for me."

Gently, he wraps his arms around me and whispers, "Azizi, thank you. I love you."

I hold him a while, releasing him, "Saeed we will need to work hard, both of us. I think it is the Elders' wish that you and I carry out the ceremony to manifest the Sacred Stones." Seriousness mixed with a little anxiety has returned to his face.

He looks at me and says nothing. I know how quickly the doubts could creep back, so I add, "Saeed, I will prepare you for that and we also have Elwah to assist us both."

CHAPTER TWENTY-ONE

We head back to the main gate of the city. Saeed is aglow with confidence and joy. I look at his face repeatedly, more precisely, without making too much of it, I stare at his eyes. I understand now, what others saw in my face when the power had flowed through me. Saeed's emerald green eyes could light the way, they are so bright. The power is manifesting so intensely, it is difficult to ignore.

We reach the main gate. Two soldiers are at their posts. One is about to signal us to stop, when looking at Saeed, promptly steps back his jaw gaping. The other soldier, seeing his colleague's reaction, initially sees me and bows, then looking at Saeed, literally stays rooted to the spot. Saeed, in his innocence does not realise what has just happened and steps through casually.

Saeed leans in and whispers, "I am glad they finally recognise you as the magician you are." I am not sure if the words were audible enough for the soldiers to hear, I smile looking for a way to explain.

A small fountain is nearby, water murmuring into the basin.

"Come, Saeed, let me show you why they have let us through so easily."

Taking his hand, I take him to the fountain's edge. "Look at the surface of the water Saeed. Tell me who do you see?"

Saeed gives me a puzzled look, "Azizi, I will see myself." He begins to laugh, adding, "Is this a test?"

He turns and stares briefly at the water. He suddenly steps back and looks at me, his eyes wide with shock.

"Azizi, what is happening?" He swallows hard, "Is this really me?"

I reach out, placing one hand on his shoulder. "Saeed, there is nothing to fear. I will explain this. I wish someone had explained it to me when the power first manifested through me."

I take a deep breath and think of way to say this that will not frighten him or inflate a sense of self-importance.

"Saeed, you have beautiful green eyes. They attract a lot of attention, because most people believe that it is a sign of strong magic. The power that you experienced and flowed through you, emphasises the colour of your eyes." He briefly looks back toward the fountain, shakes his head and looks back at me.

"Azizi, will that not frighten people?"

I smile, a little melancholy settling around my heart. I know now that I can finally share the torment of power.

"Saeed, when the power first flowed through me, people were scared because they could see how intensely blue my eyes became." Memories float into my mind. The way Halim called me

'Master'. The way the Companions had bowed to me calling me 'Mahjir', even the way Hasan had dropped to his knees, openly weeping saying that he was not worthy to look into my eyes.

"Saeed, that made me sad. I felt very lonely because people no longer saw me as Azizi the boy, instead they saw me as an instrument of power. Someone to be revered. I never wanted anyone to admire me. When I was younger, I desperately wanted a friend. Someone who would see me just as Azizi. Not a master, or a magician. Just someone who wants to laugh, eat, and play with others. The power that sometimes flows through me isolates me from everyone else." A hush fills the space around us, even the fountain seems muted.

Saeed stares at me; tears are welling up in his eyes. All at once he steps to me and folds me in his arms.

"Azizi." He whispers, holding me tight.

A wave of release rushes through my body; a shudder that liberates years of loneliness and isolation as the instrument of the Great Guardian Spirit. I hold him.

For the first time, feeling that someone else sees me as I am, not afraid, not awed but just another person who loves to be held. Sobs rise from the deepest part of me at the sense of release. I let them flow and I cry on Saeed's shoulder, feeling that someone truly understands me. He holds me tighter and whispers, "Rain falls because it is too heavy for the clouds, let your tears flow because your heart can no longer hold the pain. Azizi, I love you."

I begin to laugh in between my sobs at the words he has memorised and now repeats. How the roles have been reversed. The student now consoles the master – I smile at the irony.

I release him, half laughing and sobbing, "Oh Saeed, thank you.

I am so glad that I met you." I wipe my tears and stepping to the fountain, splash cool water over my face. I manage a smile. His look of concern for me is tender.

"I will be fine, Saeed. Thank you for understanding."

We walk back to the main residence in silence, each to our thoughts.

"Azizi?"

"Yes, Saeed?"

"Will my eyes go back to the way they were before, or will they stay like this?"

I laugh light heartedly. "They will go back to the way they were, Saeed." As an afterthought, "But every time the power flows through you, your eyes will take on that intensity."

"Oh." Saeed, carefully keeps his eyes down, feigning to mind where he places his feet.

"It is nothing to be ashamed of Saeed." I stop and wait for him to turn and look directly at him, "You have the most wondrous eyes." Invariably, even by the light of the stars, I can guess that he is blushing.

~

WE CLIMB THE STAIRS to our room; the corridors are dark making it difficult to see our way. I stop and quietly call to him, "Saeed, wait a moment."

He turns and without question stands beside me. Focussing on my source, experiencing the thrill of energy rising from the centre of my being, I extend a hand and whispering into the palm of my hand, I pronounce, "Noor." Immediately, a blue tinged elf light manifests itself, floating in mid-air, throwing a silvery radiance around us.

Saeed stares in wonder. Looking at me, he sees my eyes become intensely blue. He involuntary steps back but then reaching out, he holds my hand. He says nothing. There is a deep moment of communion between us that transcends words.

We tread on soundlessly, our shadows shifting along the walls in silvery outline; everyone would be asleep.

"Azizi?"

"Yes, Saeed?"

"Is 'Noor' the name for the light?"

I whisper back, "Yes, Saeed. For that light, it is. There are many other names depending on the kind of light I would want to conjure up."

He nods his head pensively.

"I will teach you all of them in time."

He again gives me such a devoted look that it melts my heart.

We enter our room. Something is different. There is something out of place, and then I realise—the white wolf is not here. Saeed looks around, aware also of its absence.

"Where has it gone?"

Elwah's earlier words surface. A sinking feeling fills my chest, I don't move.

"Azizi? What is it?"

I dismiss the image of Halim from my mind. Instead, I picture the white wolf hunting for prey among the desert dunes. I hesitate, turning away from Saeed and his question, as steadily as possible I reply, "It is probably hunting in the desert."

Saeed doesn't answer. A desert dweller would understand

the nature and instinct of a wild animal. He has undressed and already lays in bed.

I take my day clothes off and slip next to him. He turns to me, rests an arm across my waist and nestles his head onto my chest. Wavering a little, I place my hand on his shoulder. *Thank you, Halim. Be joyful. I hope we will meet again in another life.* Saeed's breathing eases, his chest rises and falls smoothly; *and thank you for him that you have sent to console me. I am grateful for his company and his love.*

My throat tightens a little, I let out a sigh, a sound like the whispering wind of my mountain, *"Halim."*

～

LIGHT FILTERS THROUGH MY half open eyelids. My arm is still outstretched that supported Saeed's head and shoulder. The sheet is cool; pins and needles prickle my arm and hand; I clench my fist in and out to regain sensation. I turn my head to the window; Saeed is standing looking over the marketplace. He has obviously finished his ablutions and has dressed for the day. A vague fragrance of orange blossoms drifts across the room, mixed with something else. I suddenly sit upright, realising that Saeed has used the oil given to him by Master Ahmad.

"Saeed!" I realise that I almost shouted out his name. Saeed turns and gives me a puzzled look. "Oh, Sorry. I didn't mean to call out your name so loudly."

"Azizi? Were you having a dream?"

"No. uhm, I was just surprised to see you dressed already."

I dress hurriedly. *What can I say to him that will not hurt his feelings?*

"Saeed?" He looks up from the table, having re-packed his satchel. "You are wearing the oil given to you." I realise it's not a question. Saeed gives me an odd look then nods.

"Can you tell how different it is from your usual oil? It just does not feel the same." *Why did I used the word feel instead of smell?* Saeed's look does not change, if anything his brow furrows. He says nothing, his eyes are focussed on his satchel, his hands pull on the leather straps.

My stomach tightens a little.

"I know you don't like Master Ahmad." His tone is reproachful and a little icy.

The space between us becomes aloof.

"Saeed, it is not a matter of liking or not. I am just cautious of his motives."

He looks up briefly. His eyes wander around the room and to the window. His back is almost turned to me, "Do you not trust me?" he whispers.

I want to wrap him in my arms. "I trust you, Saeed." *But do you trust me?*

I leave that question unspoken. There will be a time for that trust to be tested.

He meets my eyes finally. Picking up his satchel, he moves to the door, pauses and turning, adds, "I am going out to look for the white wolf. He has not come back this morning."

I am about to call him back, and I think better of it. I drift to the window, hoping to see him. A few moments later, he emerges making his way through the main gate and out into the marketplace. I watch a while, a little dejected at having created this tension between us again. *All over a simple vial of perfumed oil.* Annoyance boils inside me, *no! Not just a simple oil. A tampered oil to make him obedient!* I slam my fist against the wooden windowsill, wincing at the useless pain.

I see him, his red hair like a wandering flame, people making way for him. He meanders through the market, his shoulders hunched a little, his head down. He takes the main street; I lose sight of him as he walks down to the city gate.

I pace aimlessly around the room, looking for something to do, someone to talk to. *Why does it hurt so much here?* My hand reaches for my heart.

I need some distraction from the thoughts that keep running around in my head. I dress hurriedly.

I stride out of the room intending to go to the markets. At least I can lose myself in the crowd. Making my way down the stairs, taking each reluctant step at a time, questioning my motive, I reach the front door to the residence. My hand rests against the door, pushing my thoughts aside, picturing where I will go, I hear a sound outside the door and step away from it. My heart rises to my throat thinking that Saeed has come back early. The door opens and Sarek walks in, surprised to see me he stops.

"Ah, master Azizi, I was about to come looking for you."

"Sarek, is Elwah in his rooms?"

'No, master Azizi. Prince Elwah has gone out and won't be available until he returns later tonight."

"Master Azizi, I'm not sure how to make this request." Sarek looks embarrassed.

"What is it Sarek?"

He hesitates, then taking a breath, "There are individuals at the front gate insisting on seeing you for remedies." I must have looked astonished, he quickly adds, "I do not know how it is that they heard of you. They claim that only an initiate healer of Apphat can attend to them." He looks down briefly, "I have explained that you are a guest of his Excellency and that there are other masters here who could attend to their needs."

I dither, a part of me wants to lose myself in something other than my thoughts of Saeed, another part rebels at the thought at having to listen to other people's health problems.

"How many are seeking remedies?"

Sarek looks uncomfortable, "There were about six or so. I fear however, that once word gets out, a lot more will come."

Several thoughts run through my head, *this is an opportunity to pay my way and not rely on Hasan's generosity. I carry my journal of remedies and notes that I had compiled while studying with Aïschah, but I do not have any herbs with me.*

"Shall I fetch one of the other masters?"

"No Sarek. That's fine." I add decisively, "Sarek, how do the people here pay for their remedies or is it the same way as in my village, they barter with goods?"

Sarek seems relieved at my decision. "The poorer ones will offer to barter with goods. Most will pay with coin."

"Sarek, would you or someone else take the coins or goods as my way of repaying Hasan's hospitality? I will also need to know if there is an herbalist in the market that specialises in herbal remedies. I can then write out the herbs that would need to be purchased to make certain healing potions." Sarek nods, "I will also need someone to assist me in preparing some potions, and in keeping some order with those seeking help." As an afterthought,

I ask, "Sarek, is there a place for me to treat these people with consideration for their privacy, and also a table to prepare some potions that I could administer straight away?"

Grateful for my decision, Sarek is quick to answer, "There is a small room that is often used by the night guards for respite. It is part of the main gatehouse, not far where the people have gathered. Would Saeed be of help to you in the preparation of remedies?"

Unconsciously I wince at his name. "Saeed has gone out for the day. I do not know when he will return. Is there someone who can follow directions?"

Sarek considers my request, "I'll ask the cook if she can spare one of the kitchen boys. This one is brighter than the rest and follows instructions well. As for the herbs, there is a merchant who has a stall in the markets. You may have seen his wares. He specialises in dried herbs, mostly for food preparation, though he is reputed to also sell some herbs for common ailments."

"Thank you Sarek. I need to first fetch my journal of remedies from my room. I will meet you by the front gate, can you then take me to this room you spoke of?"

"Yes, master Azizi. While you are preparing yourself, I will ask one of the junior soldiers to join you to prepare the room. He will also assist with keeping order and to collect and record any payments made."

Relieved with Sarek's organisation skills, my previous anxiety is slowly melting away. Possible ailments and their remedies run around in my head in anticipation. I take a deep breath secretly pleased to have my healing skills called upon. Grateful also to be able to earn my keep, a smile broadens on my face, I stride purposefully to fetch my notes.

As I emerge from the main residence, I see Sarek is waiting for me by the gate with a young soldier in uniform and a boy of about sixteen, dressed simply still wearing a kitchen apron around his waist.

Sarek introduces me, "Master Azizi, this is Aqueel. He has only recently joined our ranks and is already proving to be a worthy and reliable soldier." Aqueel acknowledges his introduction and makes a small but sincere bow of his head to me.

"And to help you with the herbs, Luam. He can read and write and follows instructions well. I had a hard time convincing the cook to let him go." The young man blushes slightly at the compliment and smiles calmly.

Sarek indicates to head out of the main gate and leads us out. "The room has some basic furniture, master Azizi, will you require anything other than a table and chairs?"

Turning to the young kitchen hand, I ask, "Is there a mortar and pestle that I could borrow from the kitchen? And a pot to boil water in? Sarek, not knowing what ailments these people will present, I may need some towels and perhaps even some bandages. Is the room equipped with a wood stove to boil water?"

"I will fetch some towels and bandages. There is a small wood stove and a stock of dry wood. There are some utensils including a few pots. As for the mortar and pestle, if I understand you, master Azizi, there is a stone pot and stone pestle, which have been used by the soldiers to grind their coffee beans. Will that be suitable?"

I had forgotten that the desert tribes are fond of their coffee. Fresh green beans are roasted over a fire, allowed to cool, and then ground to a fine powder before mixing with hot water and cardamon.

"It will be perfectly fine, thank you Sarek. I will clean it first, so that no coffee powder mix with any remedial herbs."

Luam, the kitchen hand seems relieved that he does not have to negotiate a valuable implement from the cook.

Sarek bows and returns to collect towels and bandages. Aqueel gestures to invite me to follow him.

Stepping through the main gate, a group of about twelve women, some with young children and a few men look up and start to call out to be seen for their ailments. Two of the children look pale and weak. Sarek holds up his hand for quiet and calmly instructs them to follow in an orderly fashion.

Aqueel leads the way along the base of the city wall. A short distance later, we come to an extension of the wall itself, made up of the same stones and covered with a thatch roof. There is only one door and no windows. The crowd has gathered behind us and follows quietly.

Entering the 'gatehouse', I am not surprised to see how austere it is. Two large cots are placed on either side with basic bedding and two folded blankets on each, a small wooden table and four stools dominate the centre of the room. A small wood stove and a stack of dry wood sit just to one side of the entrance. Along the back wall, which ostensibly is part the defensive wall of the city, sits a simple shelf with a few pots, cups and plates and the mortar and stone for grinding coffee. The air still holds a slight fragrance of roasted coffee mixed with the smell of burning tallow from several candles, the only source of light in the room. My first thought is that it would be better to set the table outside, but that would not give any privacy for the individuals being assessed or the remedy I would prescribe.

Aqueel, having been instructed by Sarek and as always, having anticipated my needs, opens a satchel he is carrying with him and takes out a large amount of parchment sheets, some inks, two feather quills that have been sharpened to a point. He places these to one side. He then pulls out a larger version of my journal. It is made up of many parchment sheets all equal size and leatherbound. As he opens it, I can see that it is a neatly ruled ledger.

Placing my journal on the table, I take the stool that faces the door. Luam unsure of what he needs to do, stands in the background. Turning to him I smile and indicate the stool to my left, "Luam, come sit here. I will ask you to write out any herbs that need to be purchased as well as instructions for the patient on how to prepare and take the remedies." I take the parchments and inks and place them in front of him. He looks a little nervous.

"Luam, have you recorded recipes for the cook?"

Nodding his head, "Yes, master Azizi. I have."

"This is similar. Write the names of the herbs first and then the instructions as I give them to you."

He smiles and relaxes.

"Sarek, I am ready to see our first customer."

Aqueel goes to the door, opens it wide to let fresh air and light into the room. Several of the candles on the table flutter with the sudden shift of air. I notice that the people have formed a line of their own. A young woman is at the head of the line, Aqueel indicates for her to go in and stands just outside the door, his ledger in hand. She hesitates a moment and then walks in, her eyes a little downcast.

I invite her to sit opposite me. Her face is drained of energy. She looks up at me, then Luam and quickly casts her eyes down. She is tense and fidgety, one of her hands clenches the material of her robe above her stomach. I am almost certain I know what the cause of her discomfort is, but I wait for her find the strength to tell me herself. She half rises as if leaving, then looks at me with pleading eyes. If my diagnosis is correct, I understand that regardless of who I am, she must feel uncomfortable to speak to a young man.

"You seem to be in a lot of pain."

She looks up at me, tears welling up in her eyes, she lets out a sigh, her faces winces, "Yes. I am"

"Are you at the height of your cycle?"

Her eyes widen in astonishment. "Yes, I am."

I nod. Turning to Luam who is slightly gaping at me, catches himself and looks down at his parchment sheet.

"Luam write the following ingredients: ginger, honey, sweet potatoes."

Luam picks up his quill, I notice that he uses his left hand. He turns the page at an angle so that his writing hand will not smudge the ink as he writes. He dips the quill in the ink and writes down what I have just told him. I am astonished at the elegance of his writing, reminding me of my godmother's.

"Luam, add the following instructions." I turn back to the young woman who seems to have relaxed a little. "Boil the ginger to make a tea. Add a good spoonful of honey and drink it warm at least once a day, especially in the morning."

I wait for Luam to finish writing marvelling at the grace of the letters he forms.

Looking directly at the young woman, I add, "During your cycle, you must stay away from rich foods and spices, they will only worsen the pain. Eat instead such things as sweet potato, nuts, green vegetables, and fish. Do you drink coffee?"

She shakes her head.

"Good. Coffee would only increase your pain." I can see that she is astonished at my knowledge, so I add, "There are many women in my village. My godmother has taught me my healing craft."

I turn to Luam who has stopped writing and is looking at me with respect.

"Luam, also add, broth made from the bones of chickens." Turning to the young woman, I add, "Eat warm foods and stay warm. But for your immediate pain," I turn to Luam to signal to also add what I am about to tell her, "Do you know the plant called 'Mother herb'?" She frowns slightly. "It is also called mid-Elwah daisy, it has little white flowers with yellow centres?" She nods, "they sometimes grow wild, but I am sure you could find some at the markets. Just use the leaves and make a tea with them. This will relieve your pain."

I take the sheet that Luam has written, making sure that the ink has dried, I fold it and hand it to the woman. "You can purchase those ingredients from the markets. If you do not know how to make the broth, Luam here works in the kitchen at the palace, I am sure that he can give you instructions on how to make it. She looks at him, gives him a shy smile, then turning to me, "Thank you master Azizi." She stands, hesitates, bows to me, and walks out.

I turn to Luam who is staring at a blank parchment sheet and is blushing slightly.

"Luam, you have beautiful handwriting." The colour of his cheeks does not diminish, he gives me a smile that reminds me of Saeed, and murmurs, "Thank you, master Azizi."

C H A P T E R T W E N T Y - T W O

The queue is long. Eventually as the sun rises to its highest point, only a few persons remain. As I look up to see who is next, Saeed appears, a look of defeat on his face, which changes to curiosity at the line-up. He sees me and I gesture for him to come in. His green eyes allowing him passage as the few remaining people part to let him through; Aqueel looks up from his register and recognising him steps back.

"Azizi, what is happening?"

A slight look of astonishment registers on Luam's face at the familiarity of calling me by my given name, without the honorific of 'master'.

"This morning, Sarek told me that there were a few people wanting remedies for various ailments. They insisted on having me attend to their needs. So, we have set up a visiting room and I can dispense herbal remedies. Saeed, this is Luam, who works in the kitchen; he is helping me write out the herbal remedies."

Luam smiles coyly and bows to Saeed who whispers, "Hello."

Saeed hesitates, making up his mind he turns to me, "Azizi, can I stay and listen?"

"Yes, of course Saeed. Here pull up a stool."

A small buzz of excited whispers breaks out in the remaining queue at having two apparent healers.

The rest of the day is filled with ailments ranging from headaches, skin irritations, mild burns, insect bites. A few, who complained of very small ailments, I suspect came out of curiosity, probably wanting to see 'this new healer of Apphat' and openly stare at Saeed with the emerald green eyes. One person addresses his ailments directly at Saeed, who blushes and hurriedly states, "Oh, no! I have not been trained."

Some older men and women complained of arthritis. For those, in addition to the pain relief herbs, I told them that I would make an ointment for them and to come back in one lahé. It has been a tiring morning, and I am desperate to stretch my muscles.

We did not have time to prepare any remedies, reflecting on my earlier determination to supply people with remedies in the form of teas, tinctures, compress or ointments, I feel a little naïve and foolish. I determine to be better prepared next time and have some remedies already made on hand.

Saeed, throughout the rest of the afternoon, remains silent and attentive to everything I say and prescribe. The last person is a man still in his prime but looking pale and worn-down. Unsure at first, looking from Saeed back to me, finally, captivated by his green eye, addresses Saeed, "Young master, I am unwell, but I am unsure of the reason."

Saeed blushes, looks at me with a look of mild panic, turns back to the man, and with an open-handed gesture invites him to speak to me, "Oh. No, I am still untrained. Please, address master Azizi."

"Ah. Master Azizi." The man looks to me. His eyes are pleading to find a cure for his condition. There is a sense of urgency in his voice. Like a heavy blanket settling over my shoulders, I sense a disease less common and more virulent that most. His skin is pale and damp with perspiration, his breath come in short gasps. His eyes are filled with a dark despair. Reaching out, I hold his hand, "Please close your eyes for a moment."

The man closes his eyes, takes a deep breath, and lets it out slowly. Taking that brief opportunity, using the second sight, I look at his Hala. Energy is seeping out from the stomach and a dark spot appears. The memory of Halim's mother in her cottage surfaces and with it my godmother's words to 'always ask your source for permission.'

I ease my breathing, connecting with my source, silently I ask for permission.

A deep silence follows. It is as if I am in a room facing a door and having knocked, no one answers. Elwah's words, like a breeze over calm water whisper in my mind, *"...there will be occasions when permission to heal may not be granted. Even a disease can come with a lesson."*

I open my eyes, the man has also opened his, looking at me with a silent plea.

"This illness has been with you for some time." It's not a question, the man nods, not surprised at my ability waits for me to continue. "It is draining your energy. Can you do without eating meat for a while?" Frowning, he quickly replies, "yes, of course."

I turn to Luam and gesture for him to write notes, "I will prescribe for you herbs to relieve your pain. You need to focus on eating more vegetables." I notice that Luam has already written the mid-Elwah herb, and I nod in agreement. "Eat more soup made from fresh vegetables. I would like you to come back and see me in one or two lahé if that is convenient. You will not need to pay." Luam folds the paper and hands it to the man, who stands, bows, and leaves.

Both Saeed and Luam are staring at me. In answer to their silent question, and with a heavy heart I tell them, "Not all diseases have a cure. He has not long to live and is in constant pain." Saeed opens his mouth both in bewilderment and protest. "The best I can do for him is make his life as comfortable as possible and allow him to live the rest of his days with purpose and dignity."

In silence, I surrender myself and my will to the Great Spirit whose way is unknown and unfathomable. Luam is reflective, quill still in hand. Saeed keeps looking at me but now with compassion. His concern eases my sense of futility at not channelling the healing power.

I close my journal; Saeed briefly stares at it. Aqueel enters the room smiling.

"There is no one else Master Azizi. I have recorded the gifts of goods and payments made. Should I give you those directly?"

"That will not be necessary, thank you, Aqueel. Please see that they go directly to Sarek with your records."

Aqueel nods, I add, "and Aqueel, thank you for your assistance." He looks at me a little surprised, softly spoken he replies, "It is my duty, master Azizi."

As we leave, Luam turns to me, "Master Azizi, I should hurry back to the kitchen, the cook will be needing me to help with the dinner preparations." He looks up at me, admiration clearly written on his face, "Thank you. I will treasure the advice you have given to those who sought your help."

I smile, "Luam, working in the kitchen is valuable, and now you are armed with additional information on how herbs and food can be a healing force for people. Remember this and always prepare food with love and care."

Luam hurries off. I am conscious that Saeed is looking at me. As I turn to him, he looks down.

"Azizi, I am sorry that I was not there to help you."

"Saeed, you were not to know that I would be required in this manner."

I understand his dilemma. He also feels that Luam has benefited from some of my knowledge; knowledge which I had promised to train him into. "Saeed, I was not training Luam, he was there mostly to write the remedies for those who required them. His skill in writing and recording was welcome. His knowledge of herbs from having worked in the kitchen was helpful, but I doubt that he knew even half of the healing powers of those herbs."

Some tension disappears from Saeed's face.

"I have promised to train you in the healing arts. This I will do in greater depth than merely asking you to record remedies." A thought occurs to me, "Here, Saeed. Take this, it is my personal journal, a record of healing herbs and preparations that I have compiled while studying with my godmother. Read it and begin to learn some of the healing techniques contained therein."

Saeed takes the journal, holding it with reverence. "Thank you Azizi. I will."

I am happy to see him smile. I want him to understand that he is special to me. I would not give this journal to just anyone, regardless of their credentials.

"Azizi?"

"Yes, Saeed?"

"Is it permitted to ask you about the man who came in last?"

I close my eyes, my chest tightens a little, my stomach feels empty.

"Yes."

"Azizi, could you not use the way you healed me in the desert when I was young?"

I stop and wait for Saeed to turn. I look deeply into his eyes.

"Saeed, I am not the one that heals." He looks astonished and then confused. "Saeed, it is the power of the Great Spirit that flows through me, that heals. Sometimes it flows by itself without me doing anything. On other occasions, for it to flow, I must ask permission from my Source. Only when permission is granted, can I then ask for the healing energy to flow through and direct it at the person."

Saeed stares, I can see that he looked upon me as that source. In answer to the question in his mind, I add, "Yes, Saeed. Permission to heal you from the sting of that scorpion was given even before I asked. That is how I knew you would be well and was able to reassure your parents."

Saeed visibly pales. I affirm for him, "Yes, Saeed. The Great Spirit wants you to fulfill your purpose. To that end, the Source of healing chose to flow without being invoked."

Saeed's eyes soften, a little unfocussed. His thoughts are as loud as if he had spoken them, *"What is my purpose then? Why was I healed when everyone thought I would die?"*

"Saeed, there are many questions that cannot be answered. I do not know the answers to all things. I do not know why some are healed and other are not." Pausing a little, I add, "I sought permission to heal that man, but no answer came." I let out a sigh. "I knew then that permission was not granted. The Great Spirit does not always give me a reason."

The expression on Saeed's face tells me that he once thought a 'healer' could just heal anyone that came to them.

"I am sad that this man is in pain and that the disease will continue to drain his life away." Taking a deep breath, I let it out slowly, "I can at least give him some comfort by easing his pain. I have asked him to come back and see me. I can make sure that he is comfortable. It is possible that permission may be granted in the future, or not. I cannot say." As a way of making sure that Saeed does not raise me on a pedestal, I add, "Saeed, I am an instrument through which the power of the Great Spirit flows. I do not always know when or how it will flow. I am merely Its servant."

Those last words have the effect that I sought. Saeed looks at me, still with the same level of devotion, but now he sees me with a deeper understanding, he sees my humanity and despite my apparent power, I can only ask.

For a while, we walk in silence.

"Saeed, did you find the wolf?"

The earlier look of defeat shadows his face. His tone is subdued.

"Yes. I am sure of it. I recognised him by the fine line on his neck." Saeed walks on broodingly.

"I called out to him, but I was surprised." Saeed stops and looks at me. "The wolf growled at me, as if it did not know me. It looked familiar and yet it was different. I do not understand."

I invite him to sit next to me on a bench under one of the trees in the courtyard.

"Saeed, do you remember the guardian spirit that possessed the white wolf was my friend the shepherd boy, Halim?"

"Yes, I remember."

"Saeed, not long ago, I had a dream. Halim was smiling at me, and I understood that he was happy that I am safe. I understood also that having fulfilled his need to protect me when I was in danger, he expressed the desire to reincarnate into another life. Halim made the conscious decision to release the wolf to its own nature."

Saeed's brow creases in concern, "But who will look after you if you are again in danger?"

"I know that Halim is happy to see you next to me. After all, it was he through the wolf that brought you to me. In his way, he indicates that you have become my protector."

Saeed's face registers astonishment, then confusion. His eyes eventually cast down, he whispers, "I don't know if I have the ability or power to protect you Azizi."

"You have more power than you can even imagine, Saeed."

He looks up at me once, looks back to the ground. We stand and walk side by side, each absorbed in his own thoughts. Entering Hasan's residence, the light on the walls have taken a cool tone, the ceiling has begun to darken, corners are filled with shadows.

Saeed stops, I turn to him, "Azizi, may I have your permission to light the way?"

I am taken aback and immediately delighted with his diligence, "Yes, of course, Saeed."

Saeed stands very still; I watch as he focusses his whole attention inwardly. His emerald green eyes begin to glow. He raises his right hand to his mouth and whispers, "Noor." Immediately an elf light appears and floats in mid-air before him.

He stares momentarily at the result, turns to me beaming a glorious smile.

I smile back, butterflies take flight in the pit of my stomach and fill my chest. I am in awe and a little envious at the ease with which he has achieved this.

"Are you still convinced that you lack power? You did very well Saeed!"

"I remembered your instructions with the fire," he replies meekly. "I remembered the name of the light and the way you used it the other day."

"That is the sign of a good student, Saeed. I think you learn quickly."

A thought suddenly occurs to me, *I wonder if he is developing, or has already acquired second sight?*

"Azizi?" I stop and turn to him. "Azizi, where does the light come from?"

"It already exists as energy. You simply call it into existence with your will and your mind. You then feed that thought with the power that flows through you from the Great Spirit."

Saeed looks at me in wonder and I suspect with a little apprehension.

"Yes Saeed, although the power appears to come from you, it

comes from your Source and flows through you. That Source, is the power of the Great Spirit that resides within you." Saeed frowns, reflecting deeply on what I have just told him. I add, "You understand now, that when the healing power flows through me, it is the Source that flows, I simply direct it to the individual."

Saeed nods his head slowly, comprehension dawning, "Azizi, I remember in the desert, when you were healing me from the scorpion's poison, I could hear your voice in my head, telling me that I would be well. I could sense your mind helping me know where the poison was and how to reverse it. How do you see this or know where to direct your attention?"

Saeed's lessons will be like this, informal. I think it is best for both of us if he acquires his skills in an unstructured way. I smile to myself, remembering the boring lessons in the small Temple School of Asfaine, and the punishing cane. *There will be no punishments, only encouragement, like the lessons with my godmother.* "Saeed, I love your questions, they always surprise me."

He smiles, and of course, he blushes, *there may come a time when he will no longer be embarrassed with compliments. I hope, though that he will always retain his childlike humility and wonderment.*

We reach our room, "Let's go inside and I will try and explain that to you."

He walks in, decisively aims for a chair at the table, sits and waits eagerly. The elf light follows him in and floats in the middle of the room, casting a soft silver dancing light on the walls.

I smile inwardly at his enthusiasm. Taking a seat opposite him and making sure he can see my entire body, I begin, "Saeed, I want you to allow your body to relax, but keep your eyes open." Saeed is fully attentive. "Allow your mind to relax also; what I mean by that, is to allow your mind to be clear of unnecessary concerns. Do not focus on any thoughts. If a thought comes to you, look at it and then as if it were a cloud, let it drift away."

Allowing myself to slip into comfortable state, focusing my mind on the source of my energy, I raise a flow of energy from my inner being and let it flow through my arms and into my hands. I raise my arms to waist level; the palms of my hands facing each other and focus my attention on the space between.

"Saeed, as if you are just curious, look at my hands and tell me what you see."

He casually looks at my hands, looks up at me and says, "your hands are facing each other." He looks at me a little perplexed and I say nothing.

He looks back at my hands, taking a breath, he releases it slowly and at once exclaims, "Oh!" His eyes are fixed on the space between my hands. His body becomes still, and I can see that he makes a special effort to remain calm and focussed.

"Tell me Saeed, what do you see?"

Dreamlike and without taking his attention away from my hands, he answers, "The air between your hands has turned gold, it looks like a fine smoke. It moves between your hands."

I consciously withdraw the flow of energy to my hands, "and now Saeed what do you see?"

"Oh, the smoke is no longer there. There is nothing there at all." I smile thinking, *well, there is something there, at least air,* but I understand what he means.

I let my hands drop to my lap.

"Saeed, being able to see things that others cannot see, in the language of my people, is called the sight or second sight."

He swallows visibly, a little unsettled. "What you just saw was simply energy that I was manifesting between my hands. Have you ever seen something like that in the past?"

His brow creases in concentration and in a low voice, "No." His face suddenly lights up then, remembering something, "oh, when I was much younger, sometimes I would see lights in the dark, as if someone was holding a candle and walking away. But these would always disappear quickly. I could never focus on them."

"Saeed, you have second sight. It is not fully developed but you have that gift."

He is looking at me, his eyes wide open, his chin drops slightly. I can see he does not know what to say.

"To answer you earlier question then, I use my second sight to look for the cause of an illness. Sometimes, I see it as a dark spot inside the person's body. In your case, I could see it as a small yellow stream that was moving slowly in your body."

Saeed looks at me, questions forming in his head faster that he can think them up.

"Azizi, will that happen to me also, will I be able to see that?"

I sigh in acknowledgement, "Yes, Saeed. You will and other things beside."

"Oh," is all he responds. He looks back at his hands. We sit there in silence, an occasional sound drifting up through the windows.

"I will train you to use your second sight, so that you can call on it when you feel you need it."

He looks up at me then, gives me one of his shy smiles. His eyes then drift and settle on his leather satchel. A look of resolve washes over him, he turns and meets my eyes. "Azizi, is it what you see that makes you cautious of Master Ahmad's gift?"

The question throws me. *What should I say? It is not so much what I see. I did not use my second sight, but to my senses, the fragrance is not right, the feeling is wrong. I don't want to repeat this morning's set of events,* so calmly I ask, "I am not sure what you mean Saeed."

He looks back at the satchel and then back at me. "Azizi, when you first told me that the oil was not the same, I was angry, because I thought you disliked the gift. But then, I looked at it the next day, and I could see a strange colour around the jar."

It is my turn to stare. *So even then, without any training, he was experiencing second sight.* Maintaining my calm, I ask, "What did you see Saeed?"

"It is difficult to describe Azizi. At first, I thought I was imagining things. I thought that the fragrance was giving off a kind of visible perfume, like steam from hot water."

Saeed pauses, I hold my breath waiting for him to continue.

"But then I could see that the colour seemed to move and change. It was a dark orange, which at first, I thought was normal since it was orange blossom oil. As the colours moved, I could see a fine black thread that wove around it." Saeed takes another breath, looks away for a moment, then looks back at me.

"I remembered though that orange flowers are white. I knew something was strange. I wanted to know how it would behave on my body. So, this morning I used some, just as you woke up. When you called out my name, I was startled. I thought I had done something wrong." Saeed pauses, his eyes a little downcast. "Immediately, I felt an urge not to listen to you. I thought it strange, but the fragrance only became stronger. It was as if I was in a dream and for some reason, I had to get away from you. I could not understand my sudden change of mood."

I can only stare at him. I am at a loss for words.

"Azizi, after I left, I thought about all that happened and the warnings you were trying to give me. But a part of me wanted to know exactly what Master Ahmad was trying to do. I remember how aggressive he was with you when we first arrived. I thought that if you were to challenge Master Ahmad, you may be in some danger."

He blushes a little, looks up at me. His eyes are tearing up a little. "I am sorry Azizi, that is why I was angry, and asked you to trust me. That was rude of me."

Elwah's earlier words come back to me: *Saeed also feels a deep love for you and probably looks up to you and may in fact want to protect you, if not from others, perhaps from yourself.*

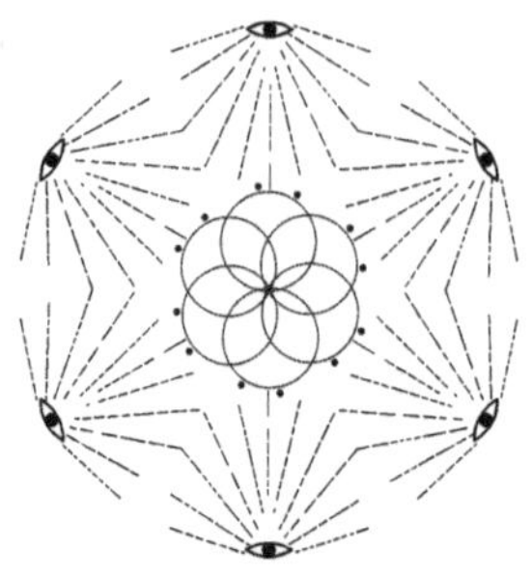

CHAPTER TWENTY-THREE

The elf light is burning steadily, gilding the walls and furniture with its silvery light. A cool breeze from the ocean billows the curtain at the window. The sky has turned a deep cerulean blue, stars are visible.

I am overwhelmed with what Saeed has just told me, and specifically his knowledge that his 'gift' of oil may have been tampered with.

I take my time, tenderly I take his hands in mine. "Saeed, thank you for telling me all of this. It must have taken courage to say what you have just told me. Thank you for trusting me." I look into those wondrous green eyes, adding, "I trust you Saeed, I just did not know that you already suspected the oil had been tampered with."

My heart is pounding in my chest. Moments like these, I realise how much I care for him.

I stand up and walk to the window, taking the view of the waxing crescent moon of Camlac rising above the ocean waves, creating a double headed axe of pale-yellow light. I take a deep breath of ocean air, not caring for the scent of salt; I collect my thoughts, *if we are to work together, we must trust each other. He has just shown me his own trust.*

I turn to him, "Saeed, Prince Elwah agrees with you." Saeed looks up, an astonished look on his face. "I have already told him that I thought Master Ahmad had other motives for the gift. Elwah also said that to challenge Ahmad was both futile and dangerous. He would probably deny the accusation."

"Azizi, do you know what Master Ahmad has done to the oil and what its purpose is?"

"I suspect that the oil worn regularly, would bend your will to his and render you obedient to his suggestions or even instructions. It is almost as if he has imbued it with *vox Imperii.* I do not know how he did that."

Hearing the name of the mind-bending spell, Saeed visibly pales.

He looks at his hands and then his chest where presumably he rubbed some of the oil this morning. Saeed stands, consciously holds his hands away from himself, as if he considers them sticky and dirty. There is look of disgust as he realises that he applied the oil over his body this morning. The subtle fragrance still hangs about him. He stares at me concern in his eyes. Stumbling over his words, he pleads with me, "I..., Azizi, I do not know what to do."

Concerned for his predicament and his realisation of the complexity of the situation, I reassure him, "Saeed, I do not think that the oil has taken full effect. The best thing to do for now would be to wash it off you."

He nods in agreement, a look of resignation on his face. "Azizi, will you come with me?"

"Yes, come Saeed. Let us wash the worries of today away. We will take a warm bath and put on fresh clothes."

~

We are returning from our bath, when along the corridor a figure stands in our way. As we draw near, the elf light reveals the features of Elwah. He seems to have been waiting for us.

Elwah's gaze drifts from us and significantly looks up at the elf light. Turning to Saeed, he states, "Saeed your powers are rising. I think it is time to test them that you may understand the extent of them."

Elwah pauses before adding, "Azizi, Saeed, follow me."

He turns and leads us through doors I have seen but never opened. One such door opens onto a set of stairs that descend. The elf light precedes us, allowing us to see the darkened passage that lay before us. Sometime later, we reach a large room, the far end of which, is open to the elements and extends to a tiled terrace facing the ocean.

Stepping out onto the terrace, Elwah turns to Saeed and asks him, "What Ocean faces you, do you know its name?"

Saeed considers unsure, wondering whether this is a test. Hesitating a little, he answers, "It is the ocean of Elwah."

"Yes, Saeed. It is."

Where we stand, the vastness of the ocean extends uninterrupted to a clear horizon. The sky has darkened to a light midnight blue filled with stars. The dark turquoise waters gently lap at the rocky edge not far from us.

Elwah turns to me and using his mind, he instructs, *"Prepare yourself Azizi. This will take you by surprise. Do not be afraid, I will safeguard you both."*

Elwah gazes deeply into Saeed's eyes and altering the tone of his voice ever so slightly, almost casually asks, "Saeed, I want you to extend your right hand toward the ocean here and then I want you to call the ocean of Malkizar to you."

Saeed stares perplexed, but Elwah's voice is imbued with power. He cannot resist the order.

Saeed extends his hand toward the ocean of Elwah and dream like pronounces, "Näcken Malkizar, beto!"

My skin is suddenly crawling with goose bumps. An oppressive silence stifles me as if all the air has abruptly been sucked out from around us.

Saeed's emerald eyes take on an unearthly green glow.

The air returns with an audible smack. I am at once overcome with terror as a colossal body of water rises on the horizon and rushes towards us.

Elwah's commanding voice, unmistakably rich with power, pronounces, "Égétor Péh Elwah!"

The waters of the ocean Elwah suddenly part and swallow the giant wave into itself.

I look at Saeed who is overcome with terror. His eyes have lost the previous light of power. His arms hang limply to his side, his right hand visibly shaking. A slight film of perspiration covers his pale face. My attention is drawn however to the light shirt he is wearing. A soft green glow appears to be pulsating under his shirt.

Elwah calmly looks at Saeed, nodding his head slightly.

"Young Saeed, it appears that you have come into your full power."

Saeed is staring at Elwah.

"Master Elwah, I do not know how... I have never... I do not know how that happened. Did you...?"

"No young Saeed. My only doing was to command the Ocean of Elwah to calm the chaos."

Both Saeed and I are in shock with what has just transpired. For me, the monstrous wave that responded to Saeed's command almost pales in comparison to his innate and unconscious ability to have summoned it.

Elwah turns to me, "Azizi, as a way to confirm this, would you ask Saeed to remove his shirt, please?"

My body is unable to move. I am still astonished with what has just happened. Elwah is still looking at me, smiling with a gentle but firm command in his eyes.

As if released from a daydream, I take a breath, "Yes. Yes, Master Elwah."

Elwah smiles at the sudden honorific. Stepping to Saeed, gently I ask, "Saeed, could you please remove your shirt?"

As if in a trance, his eyes fixed on mine, Saeed nods and slowly removes his shirt.

There, on his chest just above his heart, clearly etched, a green tattoo, still glowing has appeared. It is in the shape of an inverted crescent moon:

I immediately identify the significance of the design. It is the tidal moon. With a sense of awe, I realise that this is Saeed's power and guardian spirit – power over the tides, the ability to call Nācken, the sacred spirit guardian of the ocean. There is a question in the back of my mind; something that makes me feel uneasy. *Why did Elwah ask him to call Malkizar and the energy of chaos?*

Elwah turns to Saeed and in a voice of utter kindness addresses him, "Saeed, now do you understand the answer I gave you, when once you asked me who your guardian spirit was?"

Saeed, his jaw still hanging loose, the look of terror no less diminished in his eyes, nods slowly and whispers, "I did not know."

Elwah smiles and adds, "Of course you did not. That power lay dormant within you for a very long time."

Turning to me, answering my unspoken question, Elwah continues, "From the moment Saeed arrived, I sensed the energy of the Ocean of Elwah rebel against his, I realised that his energy and power dwell in chaos. That in itself is not a bad thing. It is just that Saeed needs to understand his power and be able to control it."

An uneasy brooding silence fills the space around us. Elwah is serious and addresses us both.

"It was necessary Saeed, for you to experience this and for you Azizi to witness it. Both of you will need to work together in calling the Sacred Sapphires. Azizi, now that you know the level of power that is at his call, it will be your task to teach him how to control it and not let it rule his emotions. In some way, Azizi, it will also be necessary for you to know how to balance that power with yours. Saeed, let your love for Azizi guide you. Trust him, he has a lot to teach you and he will do so with great diligence. Do not be afraid of your power, rather respect it as it is yours to control."

Saeed and I look at each other. A wave of emotion fills me, stepping closer, I wrap my arms around him and gently hold him. I sense his being give way, the tension dissolves, and he lets out a long sigh resting his head against my shoulder.

Elwah smiles and adds, "as for the oil that Master Ahmad has gifted you, Saeed, I will let the both of you decide what to do. However, if Saeed decides to allow the will of master Ahmad to prevail and test his resilience, then Azizi you have already designed the protection."

And with those words Elwah disappears, literally. He was in front of us one moment and gone the next.

Saeed is fixed to the spot, his eyes alternately looking at the ocean, back to his right hand and then to the mark on his chest. Finally, he looks at me. I see the shock and fear in his eyes. Raising fire and a small elf light is nothing in comparison to calling the guardian spirit of the ocean and bidding him to raise a wave that could easily swallow the town of Naasée.

"Azizi," "Saeed," we both speak at once.

"You first, Saeed."

"Azizi," beseechingly he looks at me, "Azizi, this," he holds his hands out to me, "this, this power, it scares me. Can I refuse to use it?"

Mixed emotions conflict within me. I am puzzled how the power came to him so readily and without training. A part of me wants him to refuse it, as soon as that thought formulates in my head, with a sinking feeling of shame my eyes drop to the ground, my breath shortens, heat rises to my cheeks. *I do not have the right to tell him to refuse it. Power came to me unbidden in my youth and with little or no training either.*

"Saeed, your power is a gift. What you do with it is your decision. However, to refuse it could be dangerous."

"If I don't use it, how could it be dangerous?"

"As Elwah said, the gift you have is within you, it lay dormant for a long time. It is not a gift that can be removed. You might be able to refuse to use the power of the gift, however, it responds to your emotions." Saeed frowns. "If you feel threatened or if someone you love is threatened, the power will flow of its own accord to protect. When that happens, you may not have control over it."

Saeed pales. "Azizi, was that the dream you had?"

The question puzzles me and then I remember the dream, when at my call for help, he had used his power and summoned a giant wave of angry energy. I had pleaded for him to stop.

"Yes, Saeed. It was a premonition that was triggered by the fragrance of the oil. In the dream you were trying to protect me from some dark force and your power just flowed with such intensity that I was scared."

With a look of shame and regret, he drops his head down. Whispering, "I'm sorry Azizi."

"Saeed, you were not to know. It may have been a premonition, or simply a warning. Even then I did not know the extent of your power or the nature of your guardian spirit. The dream tells me what you are capable of, and it also tells me that it can be triggered by strong emotions such as anger or fear."

Saeed's face is pale, his body listless. *I need to reassure him. It is not his fault.* "Saeed, now do you at least understand how Halim thought you are my protector?"

He lifts his head, some hope returning to his eyes.

"Saeed, there were many times during my training when the power of the guardian spirit would flow through me, it would overpower me, and I would lose consciousness. The energy was too much for my body to withstand." I smile, mimicking losing consciousness; that makes him laugh a little. "My godmother, then trained me so that the power would remain in my control. I had to learn to receive information from the spirit world without allowing it to overwhelm me."

His eyes ask for more confirmation. "The first time I managed to remain conscious was on the occasion that we were expecting important visitors. I remember my godmother had prepared a meal. The fire in the hearth sent me into a trance, but fortunately my godmother was able to calm me and prompt me to remain focused. That was fortunate because I had sensed grave danger for the visitors. I was able to tell her the details of the danger so that she could act to protect them.

There was another occasion when prince Ijlal was walking with me in the forest, and we were attacked by one of the Shadows. My first reaction of protection was to call the power. I don't know if it was a warning from my godmother, or my instincts but I stopped in time as it would have placed both of us in danger." My throat tightens at the next memory, "Halim, who had secretly been watching over me, burst out of the forest and with nothing more than his shepherd's staff attacked the Shadow."

I pause, my throat is tight and dry, my heart is pounding. I allow the memory to subside.

"Saeed, I have promised to train you, and even Elwah has urged me to continue to teach you. Together we will work on your ability, not to bury it but for you to call it when you need it and for you to control it."

Saeed gives me one of his most endearing boyish smiles, nods his agreement, "Thank you Azizi. I promise to learn well."

We make our way back and are about to reach our room when I notice Tabrass, master Ahmad's servant hurrying towards us, he looks up notices us but does not seem to have time to stop. As he passes by, his eyes wander to Saeed. Tabrass' step faulters as he stares at the green mark on Saeed's chest. He looks at me and quickly drops his head down and continues at his hasty pace down the corridor.

Initial confusion is replaced with a sense of futility, I feel so stupid. Saeed is still carrying his shirt. I should have told him to put it back on. Letting out a sigh of frustration, thoughts crowd my mind, *I am sure Tabrass will immediately report to his master what he has seen. Although Tabrass would not have a clue as to the significance of the mark, Ahmad certainly will. Anger boils in me. Well, let him know. Let him be afraid of Saeed's newly found power. And then it hits me. This is a power that Ahmad would desire. This is power he might hope to bend to his will.* My hand tightens into a fist. *It is now more important than ever to design the protection talisman for Saeed.*

"Azizi, I think he saw the mark on my chest."

"Yes, I think he did. He may not know what it means."

"Azizi, do you know what the mark means and how it came about?"

"Let's reach our room first and I will explain."

CHAPTER TWENTY-FOUR

The elf light follows us and floats in the centre of the room. I am surprised that it has not extinguished. Saeed's subconscious will must be very strong.

Saeed, without pausing casually walks up to and sits on one of the two comfortable chairs and fixing me with a look of anticipation, waits for me to start.

I smile, pointing at the floating light, "Saeed do you wonder what energy is required for the elf light to keep burning like this?"

Saeed's momentary puzzled expression makes me smile even more.

"Uh, no. I thought that... no. I have no idea."

"Saeed, because you called it into existence, using your thought, your voice and energy, it is continuously drawing vitality from you to stay alight."

The confusion and conflict of realisation on Saeed's face makes me want to laugh out loud.

"Oh. I didn't think..."

"Saeed do you not feel tired? This light has been drawing energy from you all evening."

His mouth is gaping now. He swallows hard. "How, how should I extinguish it?"

"Let us light one of the more conventional lamps first, and then just see it extinguished in your mind."

The elf light goes out and the silvery hues around the room are replaced with the golden glow of the oil lamp. Shadows on the walls dance lightly mimicking the movement of the flame.

The simplicity of the technique makes Saeed smile with satisfaction, his shoulders straighten, his face relaxes and now he looks at me in eagerness.

I sit opposite him and gather my thoughts.

"A mark on the body of a magician or healer is usually something that has been made to signify that an apprentice has reached proficiency and is initiated into the elite group of healers or magicians. It marks one who has demonstrated the ability to manipulate certain techniques."

Saeed frowns, I can sense his question.

"But Azizi, I am untrained."

I nod in agreement. "I will try to explain as best as I can. This is a mystery to me as well and I can only speak from my knowledge that I have gained during my training. I also rely on my instincts."

Taking a breath and hoping that my instincts are correct and the knowledge I rely on is accurate, I begin, "First, the meaning. The mark that you now have is a symbol of the tidal moon. It is an old, sacred and powerful magical symbol, which means you have been marked as one who has control over the tides of the ocean." I can see that my words are having a dramatic impact on Saeed. "It is sacred, because it is also in part associated with the Universal Mother, the One who brings forth life."

The goose bumps that suddenly cover my arms, inform me that the knowledge flowing through me is correct. Although it is not a full trance, I sense that another is beginning to speak through me.

"The colour of your mark is also important. Green, not only reflects your innate power, which is obvious with your emerald green eyes, itself a sign of powerful magic. It is also associated with new life and the birth of nature."

I pause. Saeed is staring at me, his eyes wide with bewilderment. He drops his eyes to his chest and raising a hand places it over the tattoo. As he looks back at me, his face briefly transforms into that of a pure young boy, which astonishes and dazzles me. I am briefly unable to speak.

Breaking the silence, Saeed asks, "But Azizi, how is that possible?"

"There are a number of possibilities." Saeed waits for me to continue while I desperately dive into my memories of ancient texts, and the discussions with my godmother on the nature of Guardian Spirits.

"I think Elwah knew that the power over the ocean was already within you and decided to test that theory by bidding you to call the ocean of Malkizar." Saeed frowns and is about to query, "I do not know why he asked you to call Malkizar. All I know is that Prince Elwah identified that since your arrival, the waves of the ocean of Elwah came crashing against the tower more often and with greater force than usual. He surmised that the spirit of Elwah was somehow hostile against your will and that of the power of chaos. And so, he concluded that it was the ocean of Malkizar that would respond."

Those last words have little effect to reassure Saeed of his desire to wield that power.

"The words of the spell that you pronounced came to you without any effort on your part. That alone, for me was astonishing. It means that you already have knowledge buried deep within you and the knowledge rose on Elwah's command."

Saeed is a shade of pale I have never seen in my life. His natural white skin is almost translucent.

"Once the words pronounced, the Nācken of Malkizar, having recognised the call, responded immediately. It identified itself as your Guardian Spirit. As a result, having acknowledged you, the power of the Nācken branded you with his sign, that of the Tidal Moon."

The delicate fluttering sound of a moth attracted by the flame of the oil lamp, the only sound filling the silence.

Saeed sits in utter stillness, eyes softly focused staring into an unseen future.

I silently contemplate what has been uttered. Awed at the power that Saeed has manifested, I am suddenly gripped with uncertainty as to what if anything I can contribute to his training. Sensing that if I don't assist Saeed, he will feel abandoned – a reawakening of the loss of his father in his life.

Turmoil sets my emotions in conflict. A coldness fills my chest and slowly seeps down to my stomach, sluggishly tightening it into a knot. Thoughts race and clash in my mind; I eventually fall back on my constant source of stability and decide to contact my godmother.

"Azizi?" his whispered voice startles me back into the moment. I give him what I hope is a reassuring smile.

"Saeed?"

"Azizi, will this mark remain, or will it also fade like my eyes, once the power has been spent?"

There is a concern within his question. His emerald green eyes already identify him as a being of magic, he would not want that mark to be visible and further confirm his uniqueness.

"Saeed, much like your eyes, I think the mark will only glow if you exercise power. The mark itself will be a permanent sign of your ability." he takes a short breath, "Saeed, it is something to value and protect, so make sure that you wear a shirt that conceals the mark. Much in the same manner, my god mother advised me to wear either long sleeves or gloves once I had been initiated with the tattoo identifying me as a healer of Apphat."

"Azizi, will you still train me?" The fear of being abandoned in his voice is like a knife. If wielded, it would leave a scar upon my heart.

"Yes Saeed. I have promise to do so." Relief fills his features. Nevertheless, I add, "I will need to consult with my godmother and Prince Elwah on how best to fulfill your training. Your power is already active, as such does not necessarily require further development. I suspect it is one that most magician would deal with great caution and respect." His features droop slightly. "I think to begin with, I will show you exercises that will be effective in training your mind to control your emotions." His face still holds some doubt so I remind him, "These are techniques I taught Prince Ijlal when his grief for Shahulm would provoke the Great Bird transformation. He quickly managed to control himself and is still now able to change into the Great Bird at will."

A hint of admiration sparkles in his eyes. Smiling inwardly, I cannot say if it is for the fact that I taught Ijlal the technique to achieve this, or if he wants to be like Ijlal – able to shift his appearance.

I break the silence, "Saeed, there is still the question of Master Ahmad and the oil that he gave you."

Concern and a little fear return, his shoulders slump slightly; and then decisively, Saeed straightens, and his eyes take on a serious and determined look.

"Azizi, I want to know what master Ahmad is planning. I want to know how far he will go with this, this potion." I can't help but be astonished by his determination. "Do you think that his servant will tell him of the mark on my chest? And will master Ahmad know what it means?"

"Saeed, I am certain that Tabrass will tell his master what he has seen. He may not have seen enough to know the detail."

I pause not sure how this will affect Saeed's determination. "As far as master Ahmad, yes, he will know what it means. I suspect that he will want to know more, and he will most likely covet the power that the sign holds." Saeed gives me a puzzled look. "He will want to control you and in turn control the power that you have."

Saeed lets out a long and deliberate sigh.

"Azizi, if I don't use the oil, won't he grow suspicious?"

"Yes Saeed, I think he would."

"Azizi, what can I do to prevent him from controlling me and still wear the oil to avoid distrust?"

Again, I am astonished with his resolve to carry out this dangerous plan.

"The mark left by the Nācken is like a talisman, it is sacred. Its function is not only to identify you as the one that holds the power, but it also acts as vessel through which the power flows."

Slowly at first and then like a rush of wind, my consciousness expands. It is as if my body no longer exists, time and space vanish, I am aware of where I am, but my mind opens to the sky.

My sight opens to great distances. I see the ocean from above, the city of Naasée nestled along its shore. The ground underneath me rushes by, I see my mountains, snow-capped, the creatures within it busy with their necessities, the Star flowers growing in their secret places. My god mother's cottage rushes towards me and dissolves as I find myself in the heart of the forest. Silence weighs all around, I express my thought: "Do I have the authority to change this talisman?"

A voice like the whispering of the wind in the pine trees answers, "The sign cannot be withdrawn, it cannot be sealed nor altered, but you may add to it that it also serves as protection." As the words fade, I hear a soft song playing, sacred words whispered, a vague memory of a kiss in sunlight surfaces and dissolves like mist.

The echoes of my thoughts resonate in the air. I realise that I spoke the words out loud. It was not the voice that I heard in my youth, the grave and authoritative voice that could not be mistaken. This is a voice that came from deep within the earth, tinged with the wisdom of ancient trees, the sound reassuring and commanding.

As if the light of the world itself is suddenly dimmed, I find myself back in the room, facing solid walls, shadows dancing with the flickering light of the oil lamp. Saeed is staring at me. No doubt my eyes have taken on the energy of power.

"Azizi?" his voice is a whisper.

Silence fills the room like a blanket of snow. A shiver runs through me.

"Saeed." I notice that I answer in a murmur. I momentarily close my eyes, regaining my sense of location.

"Azizi, what do those words mean?" Opening my eyes, the expression of Saeed's initial astonishment is replaced by calmness, it tells me that the power in my eyes has abated.

"There is a way for me to help." Saeed waits in anticipation. "I have thought about this for some time, but I was unsure how to create a talisman that could at once be incorporeal and a powerful protection against dark energy." Taking a long breath I add, "now I know what to do. As I said the sign on your chest cannot be altered, it is the mark of the Nācken, as such it is sacred. It cannot be removed, nor can its power be hindered. However, I have permission to add to it and create another talisman that will work with your mark, not prevent it from working as it should but offer protection for you so that the power cannot be used by someone else."

"Azizi, was that the Great Guardian Spirit that spoke?"

"I do not think so Saeed. When it spoke, I found myself in the heart of my forest. I think it is an ancient spirit of nature, it has the energy and wisdom of ancient trees."

Saeed stares in amazement and nods slowly.

"How will you ... do this?" Saeed frowns and adds, "will it hurt?"

A cloud of softness fills my heart, smiling with what I hope is reassurance, "I have never done this before, I am not quite sure of the process myself. I don't think it will hurt since I am not making a physical mark. However, I do not know if your existing mark will change as a result."

He waits, concern mixed with the surrender of love in his eyes.

"Because your mark concerns the tides, my instinct is that I will need water to form the talisman." Pausing to gather my thoughts and delving deeply into my consciousness, I add, "Your mark commands the spirit of Malkizar, to balance this and create a talisman of protection that will not interfere with your power, I will use the water of the ocean of Elwah."

Having just uttered those words, I am unsure where the wisdom of that process comes from. The text of an ancient parchment on the creation of our world and the two oceans appears in my mind. *Of course! Water has memory – the waters of the Ocean of Elwah have mingled with the waters of the ocean of Malkizar at the passage of conflict. Each has a memory of the other.*

"Saeed, do you think we can find our way back to the terrace facing the ocean of Elwah?"

Saeed reflects, "Yes. Yes, I think I can remember the way we took." Then realising the import, "will you do this now?" Saeed stares at me with a solemn look.

"I think it would be best to do it sooner rather than wait for the oil to take a stronger hold on your will."

He nods and stands resolutely. Before we leave the room, I take on the responsibility to call an elf light into existence and extinguish the oil lamps.

THE LONG DARK CORRIDOR looks even more mysterious in the silvery light, throwing our shadows along the walls. We are about to pass by an ordinary door, when I notice the very top corner is carved with an ancient symbol of water:

Opening the door, I immediately recognise the stone stairs that descend. A current of cool air charged with the unmistakable scent of salt confirms that this is the correct passage. I sense Saeed's nervousness as he slips his hand into mine and we go down slowly taking care with each step, the stone slabs shining with moisture are edged with dark green moss. The muted roar of the ocean begins to resonate around us.

Sometime later, we reach the open terrace that faces the ocean of Elwah. The water is lapping at the gently sloping tiled surface that reaches into the water. The ocean is calm. The sky a dark midnight blue, is filled with countless stars. A memory of a sky filled with stars, like the dark blue veil of the Tassili women, floats into my mind. I recall the first vision I experienced as a twelve-year-old of my destiny to seek out the Sacred Sapphires. The memory catches me by surprise, I release it with a deep breath.

Saeed is still holding my hand.

"Azizi? What is it? Are you seeing something?"

The memory must have activated a flow of power into my eyes, charging them with blue energy.

Reassuring him, I smile, "No, I just remembered a dream I had many years ago. This sky reminded me of it."

His hand squeezes mine: I turn to look at him. He looks tense, a worried look on his face.

"What is it, Saeed?"

"I'm afraid Azizi. I don't want to call the Nācken." He is standing still, unwilling to go closer to the edge of the water.

"We won't call the spirit of Malkizar, Saeed. I am only going to create a talisman of protection for you. The only thing I will do is simply to scoop some water from the ocean of Elwah to achieve this."

He stares at the ocean and back to me, "Azizi, will I have to go into the water?"

"Only your feet, Saeed. The ocean needs to recognise you to apply the protection."

Taking a deep breath, Saeed releases it slowly, willing himself to relax. He warily takes a few steps to the waters edge. Taking off his footwear, he tentatively places one foot into the water, waits, looking at the horizon and then a little more confidently, places the other foot in the water. He holds his breath, then letting out, turns to me and smiles.

I step close to him, "Saeed, would you remove your shirt? I will simply place a little water over the current mark and then speak the incantation of protection."

Saeed nods, removes his shirt, and throws it some distance onto the dry terrace.

I look down at the water and immediately notice that the waters appear to boil around his feet and seem to want to withdraw from him. His power of Malkizar being so potent, the ocean of Elwah is reluctant.

I utter the words that I heard Elwah pronounce: "Égétor Péh Elwah!" The effect is immediate, the water becomes placid and clear. Scooping a little water in my hand, I raise it and apply it gently to the mark on his chest. Saeed draws a short breath, responding to the cold water. His eyes meet mine with such surrender and devotion, my chest fills with a warm current that draws from my heart and into the waters. The current is suddenly reversed, the desire to protect and love this young man almost overwhelms me as I stagger slightly with the power of the emotion.

The sacred words surface again in my mind, and softy I pronounce them to a faint tune I hear:

Alsafinat Almuqadasat
Astaqbal Hubiy
Qum bi'iiwa Habi

A strong current flows from my heart to my hand and I feel the power flow into his chest. Saeed shudders a little, takes another quick breath, all the while looking at me. He smiles again. My hand is over his heart, I can feel it beating strongly and by some strange coincidence, I notice my heart responds to the same rhythm.

A brief gust of wind blows over the ocean of Elwah, reaching us, followed by a small ripple of water that laps at Saeed's ankles almost in a caressing way.

Removing my hand, I look at his chest and I am almost disappointed that nothing of the mark has changed.

"It is done Saeed. We just have to wait for it to take effect."

He looks at his chest, "How long will it take Azizi?"

"I am not sure."

Picking up his shirt I turn to hand it to him. Saeed seems frozen into place, the waters lapping at his ankles break into small waves that nevertheless seem to rise to just below his knees. He is holding his hand over his heart, and for a moment seems lost in thought and then at once calls out, "Oh, Azizi. I can feel something warm in my chest."

He moves his hand, and I stare at the talisman I have just created.

A mark in the shape of a drop of water has appeared over the crescent moon. I recognise immediately the combination of water and protection, working in harmony with the Tidal Moon. The whole tattoo is glowing. His emerald green eyes sparkle vividly.

I let out a sigh of relief and smile broadly at Saeed. "It has appeared Saeed. The sign of protection is in harmony with the tidal moon."

Saeed stares at his chest, caresses the mark and looking back at me smiling broadly whispers, "It is beautiful Azizi. Thank you."

CHAPTER TWENTY-FIVE

The bedroom is filled with a soft blue light. Mist-like strands of light flow in all directions, finally settling into a large pool in the centre, it hovers there and then everything goes dark. I can see the room in all its details, my body is paralysed, I am aware of a presence, but try as hard as I can, I cannot move my head and look at the person I know is there. I am sure that my eyes are half opened, and yet a part of me is convinced that I am still asleep.

The light dissolves and I find myself in a large dark cavern, runic symbols are carved into the rock. Shadows of men are standing around the cavern, all hooded and head bowed in silence. A sombre voice speaks and echoes off the dim walls: "There is no mercy here. Chaos wants to dominate. Darkness and Light, do you know what they are? You can feel them both."

As the last word echoes in the chamber, I sit bolt upright. No sooner do I open my eyes, when a weariness comes over me and I fall back onto the pillow, knowing somehow that I am back asleep.

I step through a cloud of fine mist. A memory of my childhood mountains fills me, I see myself as a twelve-year-old, delighting in the first days of the snow season. A voice gently calls my name. I turn, nothing but mist fills my vision. The voice calls out again, this time I recognise my godmother's voice tinged with the tones of the Lady of the Forest.

"Azizi, Azizi my godson, my beloved godson, I am sending you this dream like a gentle arrow, for the stars have fallen silent. Learn to sing the song from deep within, the song of water, let its sound turn greed and harm into tears of Joy and Healing."

I wake up with a start, soft music still whispering in my heart, so beautiful the tune that it brings tears to my eyes. Again, a strange weariness overcomes me, and I drift back to sleep. My godmother's voice speaks softly, each word clear as the purest water.

"Azizi, here are the words you will need to speak to each other: 'May my heart and days of light embrace you. May that love inside of you fly with wings. Magic exists within you both, let it flow into and from you.'

Azizi, Saeed, if there is a stormy sea, make your soul sing. Seek peace inside yourself. Find your inner calm, seek your inner core. Be a bell that is waiting to be rung. Let your love burst out and flow.

Azizi, when all appears lost, at the moment of apparent defeat, speak the words of balance. Speak both names of the King. Speak them clearly and with power!"

I am sitting bolt upright, my eyes wide open, those words still ringing in my head.

Soft strands of pink light break up the pale light of dawn outside the window. Saeed has just stirred awake, stretching like a large and cute animal. Suddenly he sits up and stares first at the room and then at me.

"Azizi, I had the strangest dream." I wait for him to speak, "It was my Yumma, but she had the voice of your godmother."

Saeed's eyes take on soft and faraway look as he concentrates on remembering his dream.

"I was a young child; my Yumma was nursing me. We were sitting by an oasis, the water was very clear and calm, and she was singing a song to me. I could not understand the words, but it was very beautiful and gentle. Then I saw the water in the oasis turn a murky green, dark clouds gathered in the sky and turned the oasis into night. I started to cry; the water began to move angrily. I saw the giant wave that I had summoned with prince Elwah start to rise. I became frightened. My Yumma then said some words I had to repeat. Everything became dark. I was scared. Suddenly, you were standing beside me, and you shouted two words. I do not know what words they were, but then the sun began to shine, and everything was calm. My Yumma was smiling at me, and I woke up."

I stare at Saeed, my mind reels at the similarity of our dreams. It seems that Aïschah, to not frighten Saeed, has somehow used the persona of his grandmother to communicate the same message. I begin to pace, *where to begin? Neither of us knows what the process of calling the Sacred Sapphires will be, nor of the certainty of outcome.*

Saeed is studying my reaction.

"Saeed, do you remember any details, do you remember the

words your Yumma asked you to repeat?"

Saeed frowns, absorbed in trying to recall. Some time passes, and he looks up.

"I don't remember the words so much as a feeling."

"Tell me Saeed, what was the feeling you felt?"

"Whenever I cried as a little boy, my Yumma would hold me but then she would place a hand on my heart and say, 'what is in here Saeed, what do you feel?'" I wait for him to continue. "Everything would be quiet. Nothing could hurt me then. That is how I felt." Tears well up in his eyes at the memory. "Even when I grew up and my Yumma wasn't around, if something went wrong or I got hurt, I would just place my hand on my heart and remember her love for me and my world would be at peace again. The hurt would dissolve." His cheeks blush a little, eyes downcast, "that is all I remember."

"Saeed, that is a wonderful thing to remember. Treasure that feeling. I think that this is the meaning of the words your Yumma told you to repeat."

Saeed smiles timidly.

A soft knock at the door brings our attention to it. Saeed turns his head quizzically back to me. Hurrying to put on our day clothes, I shrug my shoulders walking toward the door; I have no idea who that could be.

Elwah is standing there a knowing smile floating across his lips. Bowing in acknowledgement, I gesture for him to come in.

He immediately strides to one of the chairs below the window and invites us to join him. I take the other comfortable chair, and Saeed moves one from the table and places it near me.

"If my senses are correct, I think both of you are ready for the

Ritual of the Calling."

My stomach twists, my body sinks into the seat as if I am filled with stones. I look at Saeed, his skin has paled, anxiety fills his eyes. A fleeting thought crosses my mind, *we could just make a run for it and disappear among the sand dunes.* Looking at Saeed, I think a similar thought has occurred to him.

Taking a deep breath, steadying my voice as best as I can, I look into Elwah's eyes, "Elwah, I am still not clear, why have we been chosen for this ritual?"

Before Elwah answers, I add, "I understand my original purpose of finding one of the Tears of Apphat and defeating the sorceress. I thought that once achieved, I would return home in my mountains, continue to study with my godmother and live a quiet and fruitful life."

Elwah smiles compassionately, nodding his head.

"Those who have been called to great things, have always desired a simple life."

"Elwah, you were the original Haafiz. Why can't you call and hold the Tear of Apphat again?"

His eyes take on a soft and faraway look. He smiles almost sadly.

"Azizi, I held the Sacred Sapphire of Elwah for a hundred years. I am happy if not relieved to relinquish it." Adding with a weary expression, "and perhaps, find a simple and quiet life to lead."

He is about to speak, when again I interrupt him, "All prophesies aside Elwah, can someone else not take my place?"

Elwah releases a long-drawn-out sigh. "If it were that simple Azizi..."

A tinge of resentment begins to form deep in my gut. It rises slowly, my mind forever the arguer is now finding cause for all the injustices that have led me to this moment. *The other kids at school made such fun of me and my abilities. My teachers were constantly telling me that I would amount to nothing. I lost Halim, my best friend, brutally murdered. And for what? A blue stone...one that disappeared without a trace. And now, they – they expect me to retrieve it from Apphat knows where."* A part of me is shocked at that last blasphemy.

Elwah is silent. Saeed is fidgeting a little, looking at me with a hint of compassion in his eyes.

Finally, Elwah speaks, a gentle but firm tone in his voice. "Prophesies are nothing more than a record of a promise or an agreement made many lifetimes before they are due." I must be frowning as Elwah adds, "I understand your confusion and the hurt you are feeling." I clench my teeth resolute not to move from my mental position.

"Azizi, do you remember your life before your birth?"

I can feel myself gaping at Elwah. A part of me wants to explode, another, a quiet voice is whispering, *yes, we made that pact.*

"Some agreements are mundane. For instance, those that are made between couples, to live a life of harmony or one of struggle to resolve long held issues. Then there are agreements made because the Universe has asked for someone to take responsibility for a greater task. To be instrumental in bringing harmony between nations and people. When those agreements are made, because the task is so huge, so demanding, that many will offer to join your cause. Usually those with whom you have had close or intimate relations with. Their love propels them to want to support you."

I suddenly remember our conversation on Star Souls. That

Saeed is such a one.

"Are you saying...?"

"Yes, Azizi, you made such an agreement. My agreement with you was to guide and train you in your abilities. Your godmother's was to love, support and direct your training." And then with much kindness, he adds, "Your mother was simply to bring you into this world. And then there is Saeed..." I turn to Saeed whose turn it is to gape at Elwah. "His agreement, if he survived the harsh desert conditions and the family he chose to be with, was to love you and be the twin you were meant to have. Part of that agreement also involved taking on power that he had developed in a previous life. He agreed he would use that power to bring back one of the Sacred Sapphires and with you restore the Great Harmony."

A tense silence follows.

"You and all those with you, were each given the choice to refuse." Perhaps sensing my obvious question, he adds, "But when the Great Spirit asks with all the love of the Universe, that love is never refused."

Overwhelmed, I stare out of the window into the limitless sky. Saeed's hand slips into mine. I look at him with all the love in my heart. If he offered to help, at the risk of his life, how can I refuse?

A long stillness fills the space between us. *What now?*

"My role now, Azizi and Saeed, is to prepare both of you for the ritual of the Calling. It is my task to ensure your preparedness and your ultimate safety."

Even that last statement although comforting to a point, alludes to a degree of danger and risk.

"Others will assist taking on roles of guidance and protection.

In addition to the Elemental Guardian Spirit that you will call for your protection, others around you will be tasked to protect the external world." With a sidelong look, he adds, "There is always the possibility that temptation may insinuate itself and greed manifest in the desire to take the power of one or both Sacred Sapphires. If that were to occur, Master Elim, Keeper of the Gateways and Master Suffrah, in charge of the Ritual, will be responsible for closing the procedure. I will also assist with the other Elders to take over and close off the energies. We would need to ensure the safety of you both as well as contain any energy that could escape into the world."

If I were nervous before, my body is now beginning to shake, nausea is twisting at my gut with a sense of panic.

"It will be important therefore that both of you find harmony with each other. I believe that Aïschah has already hinted to you both on how to achieve that. And then Azizi, you will be tasked with calling out the incantation that will restore the Great Harmony – I must be honest with you Azizi, I do not know what that is." He raises his eyes back to me, "however, I have a feeling that you already have that knowledge."

Like sunlight shimmering on still water, the energy in the room is palpable.

A knock at the door, this one a little firmer. Both Saeed and I remain seated, transfixed with the knowledge of what we have been told.

"Azizi, will you permit me to see who is at your door?"

I nod and remain seated, looking at Saeed, attempting a smile of comfort to ease his apprehension.

Elwah makes his way back to the seat, followed by the

benevolent old master Sindarin, keeper of secrets and cosmic magical keys, Mahjira Mitra the high priestess and summoner of the Guardians, and surprisingly Master Ahmad in charge of divination and spells. Saeed visibly tenses at the sight of Ahmad, the man who gifted the oil.

They all stand staring at us both. Ahmad looks at me, manages a smile, which quickly falls away like a slightly cracked mask.

Master Sindarin clears his throat in his usual fashion, then in a voice that belies his age addresses Elwah, occasionally turning to Saeed and me, declares, "Your lordship, the conjunctions of energies and the stars have aligned, we can no longer delay the ritual. It must be done in the next two dahé."

A moment of silence follows.

Elwah turns to the other Elders, "are you all in agreement?" They all nod.

Several of them then depart, leaving Ahmad, Mitra, the high priestess and Elwah. Mahjira Mitra is staring at Saeed, her grey eyes are almost silver in the early light, her face is slender, her youthful looks contradicting her probable age. A long thick strand of pure white hair contrasts her otherwise stark black hair. She approaches and crouching down to face Saeed, compassion gilding the edge of her voice, she addresses him directly, "We will be there with you Saeed. We will watch for your safety and that of Azizi and if this eases your worry, we will be able to speak to your mind to direct you along the process. All you need to do is to call your guardian and let the Nācken protect you."

Her words and her obvious compassion have the appropriate effect. Saeed visibly relaxes and gives her a timid smile.

She turns to me then, "Azizi, this will be no more difficult than your first initiation. You have deep knowledge that is accessible when you most need it. Your power of imagination is potent and will guide you into the process. Every ritual is different depending on the one who leads it. Have confidence in your ability and ours to guide and protect you."

I swallow hard. She has just told me that in fact, I will be in charge. A wave of cold runs down my body and makes me shiver. It is as well that I have not eaten, or my breakfast would now be spread across the floor.

With a small nod, Mahjira Mitra gracefully leaves, leaving Ahmad studying Saeed and occasionally peering at me.

Master Ahmad is muttering, one phrase clearer than the rest brings my head up to look at him: "Something is not right."

Elwah turns to him, amusement touching the edges of his voice, "What do you mean master Ahmad? Do you feel something is wrong?"

Ahmad frowns, shakes his head. Ignoring Elwah addresses Saeed, "Was the oil of orange blossoms to your satisfaction?"

Without blinking once, Saeed replies, "I wear it everyday Master Ahmad. Thank you for asking."

Ahmad's expression turns to almost a scowl. He turns to me then and quite blatantly asks, "Have you been training Saeed in magic? You are not of an age or qualified to be his master."

"Only simple techniques Master Ahmad, such as calling light or fire. Nothing of great importance at this point."

"Azizi has my permission to train Saeed. It is his task to prepare him for the Calling Ritual, master Ahmad. You will agree with me, that having protected the Tear of Joy on my behalf, Azizi is more than qualified to train Saeed."

Ahmad gives a small grunt of acknowledgement and in his typical fashion turns and leaves without another word.

Elwah is biting his lip holding his laughter in.

"Saeed, even I can sense the protection. May I see the mark as it is now?"

Saeed casually takes off his shirt and displays the new mark.

Elwah makes a small whistling noise of appreciation. "Young Azizi, your powers of imagination and creation of protective talismans is astounding. So simple, so pure and highly effective."

I can feel my cheeks burn slightly.

Elwah considers the mark a while longer, "and it will work so well with the Calling Ritual, combining protection with the element of water. Azizi, this is genius."

Saeed is beaming at me. My cheeks burn a little more.

"Azizi is blushing." Saeed declares with a laugh.

Elwah smiles then at once becomes serious. He sits opposite us, extends both of his hands to ours and holds one hand each.

"Azizi, Saeed, do I have your permission to call for preparation of the Ritual of calling?"

I look at Saeed who looks at me with pure loyalty and trust. *Putting it off will not change anything.* I am sure he just heard my thoughts in his mind, he nods once and smiles.

In unison, we address Elwah, "Yes, master Elwah. Yes."

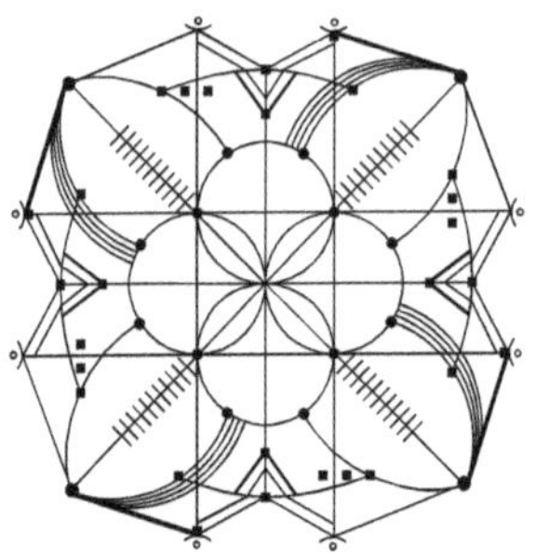

C H A P T E R T W E N T Y - S I X

The Cave of the Gateway - The Ritual of the Calling

The room for the ritual of the Calling is deep beneath the city of Naasée. The entrance, a fiercely guarded secret, lies in the smallest of the golden temples, behind one of the altars. The stone stairs that descend beneath the altar into the bowels of the city, go on endlessly.

Finally, we reach a small semicircular flat edge, overlooking the main chamber for the ritual. At one end, a set of stairs carved out of the rock, descend further into a cave so enormous that it could easily hold the small temple school of Asfaine. The roof is so high it is impossible to distinguish the detail of its surface. Light somehow permeates the space, a series of natural chimney like holes in the roof, allows natural light into the chamber. The light bounces off the damp walls that are covered with tiny crystals, sending rays of blue light in all directions. I am immediately overwhelmed with a sense of a vision hovering on the edge of my consciousness. I steel myself against the onslaught and regain my balance.

A distant, continuous roar echoes through the chamber; the sound reminding me of a fierce wind through the top of the trees of my mountain forest; it is punctuated by regular loud crashes. We must be at the level of the ocean Elwah; waves endlessly collapsing against the outer walls of the city and penetrating the far reaches of the sea cave. A shudder runs through me at the thought of being so close to that immense body of water.

Looking away from the roof of the cavern to the floor below, I am intimidated at the sight of a round flat stone of immense proportions that almost fills the entire ground. The stone is mostly dark with specks of white through it, looking like night when the sky is black as ink. I have stopped walking and can only stare at it. The stone has a brooding presence.

My eyes are adjusting to the sombre atmosphere; I can see that the surface of the stone is carved with patterns and lines that glisten with moisture. Some patterns I recognise as ancient runes of magic; the lines seem to intersect and connect them in precise movements. There are two distinct small circles at equal opposite ends of the stone linked by a deep channel.

One circle is distinctly marked with the symbol for Joy, a straight line with a small sphere above it, its opposite is likewise engraved with a straight line and small sphere below it, identifying it as the symbol of Sorrow.

I am suddenly very nervous, my stomach has turned heavy, the muscles around it, coiling and uncoiling. Saeed's hand slips into mine. I turn, my eyes meet his. We remain locked in this position.

In an attempt to calm us both, I smile at him. With a nod of my head, I encourage him to imitate me as I take deep slow breaths. He begins to breathe in rhythm with me. A powerful energy courses through us both, I can sense his inner being. I am awed at the light within him. A powerful pulse of energy emanates from him and fills my heart with his love for me.

Elwah and the elders have taken their positions on the perimeter of the large stone. Elwah stands on a raised portion of the cave. Suffrah as Master of Rites and Ceremonies, takes position to his left. Ngaway, Master of Incantation and Spells, takes his place to the right of Elwah.

On the other side of the circle and directly opposite them, Mahjira Mitra, High Priestess and summoner of the Guardians, stands on the outer circle nearest the symbol of Joy. Master Sindarin, keeper of secrets and cosmic magical keys, stands to her right and Master Elim, Keeper of the Gateways stands to her left.

This leaves – Master Ahmad, Master Vasilis, Master Sahir, and Mahjira Aïschah. They take neutral positions, two to each side of the circle. Elwah had explained that their role is to protect the summoners if something were to get out of hand. No guarantee has been given, Elwah made it clear to me, that if the power were to suddenly swing into chaos, the Elders could do very little other than to close the Gateways that have opened. It would be up to the protectors to minimise the impact and seal off the ritual. Injury or possible death is a possible consequence.

As such, my godmother Aïschah and Master Vasilis as master of visions take position nearest me and assume responsibility for my welfare. With a note of apprehension, I realise then that

Master Ahmad has taken position closest to Saeed. I am reassured when I see Master Sahir, as the Mage of Names and Potions for the Huda people, also take position for the protection of Saeed.

Moving cautiously onto the large circular stone, Saeed and I take our place opposite each other. On instinct, I have moved to the smaller circle marked with the symbol of Sorrow. Saeed, looking uncertain, stands on the circle marked with the symbol of Joy. The power emanating from the stone platform is palpable. It sends a current of energy through my being. Saeed looks down at his feet, then nervousness in his eyes, looks around before once more locking eyes with me.

Elwah raises his hands, together with Master Ngaway, in a calm resonant voice they command:

ᛁᚾᚢᛟ<ᛟ ᛊᛈᛁᚱᛁᛏᚢᛊ ᛏᛖᚱᚱᛖ ᛖᛏ ᚨ<ᚢᛇ.

ᛚᚨᛈᛁᛊ ᛖᛏ ᛁᚷᚾᛁᛊ.

ᛞᚢᛟ ᛊᚢᚾᛏ ᚢᚾᚢᛗ.

<ᚢᛊᛏᛟᛞᛖᛊ ᛚᚨ<ᚺᚱᛁᛗᚨᚱᚢᛗ ᚢᛟ<ᚨᛗᚢᛊ!

I recognise some of the words, they are using the ancient language of runes. They have just invoked the Guardians of Earth and Water, Stone and Fire. Mahjira Mitra in a light, yet powerful voice repeats the incantation, finishing by imbuing the last words with great power:

"Custodes lachrymarum vocamus!"
"I invoke the Sacred Tears of Apphat."

Then in unison, and by contrast speaking softly, Masters Elim and Sindarin pronounce the following words:

Elwah and Malkizar
Though they be two yet one
Desert spring, snow and ice
Forest moss and scent of spice
Lock of stone open his fire
Ball of thread
Key cuts the brier!

Clearly, with his usual deep voice, Master Suffrah proclaims, "Elders, Protect the Summoners! Azizi, Saeed, summon your Guardians!"

The Elders begin by emitting a deep hum, that initially resembles the notes of a song. The Calling Stone responds at first with a vibration of its own, matching the pitch of the voices and then suddenly, dropping its note so low it is almost inaudible. Slowly the vibration of the stone increases, the air around us begins to shimmer. All at once a deep resonant gong reverberates in the chamber coming from deep within the earth. Energy fills me in waves, transporting me into a state of mind unlike I have ever experienced. The cave around shimmers and for a moment dissolves into nothing. A night sky surrounds me.

I have never consciously summoned my Guardian. A small panic suddenly seizes my heart, *what if I am unable to summon my guardian? But Elwah told me that my guardian spirit is made up of all the elements of nature. Which one do I call?*

Clear as a bell I hear my godmother, Aïschah's voice in my head, "focus on that which has always inspired you." Intense colour blue accompanies her words and fills my entire being. I merely pronounce one word: "Elwah!" I wait, nervously for my guardian to manifest.

Opposite me, Saeed's tattoo glows an impossible emerald green. His eyes take on a power I had not imagined, his voice full of confidence calls out, "Näcken Malkizar, beto!"

The sound of a raging torrent fills the chamber. Small waves suddenly lap at my feet. A colossal tower of angry, dark green water rises around us, completely sealing the outer world from us. I sense more than hear, the gasp of the Elders as they witness the power of the Näcken of Malkizar, at Saeed's call. At some level, I also sense fear and I identify a small but significant emotion of greed. I am certain of its origin.

The tower of dark green water starts to swirl in one direction. Anyone hoping to enter or leave through that wall would be immediately taken and drowned.

Doubt and fear begin to creep into my subconscious. The power of the Näcken unsettles me. My guardian has not manifested. I am unsure. Then a voice, laden with silky smoothness, tinted with the scent of orange blossoms, whispers, "You are not worthy to hold the Sacred Tear of Apphat." Involuntarily, I look down at my hands, and question their power. Small strands of black silk appear to weave around my fingers, and suddenly I am afraid. I look up and stare at Saeed's eyes ablaze with power,

I call out to him in my mind, *Help Saeed, help.*

He extends a hand toward mine; a green emerald appears and rests there, glowing with the same intensity as his eyes. A jade stone cut and bevelled to a sharp edge, in the shape of a crescent moon appears and ferociously cuts through the strands of black silk. I sense more than hear, Master Ahmad's mind collapse into silence. I look up, Saeed has closed his eyes. I sense that he is unsure of his own strength to sustain this power.

A current of clear water that reminds me of my mountain streams, emerges and rising, encircles me. Some of my confidence returns.

Elwah's voice is urgent, speaking directly to my mind: *In his hurry to manifest the power of the Nācken, Saeed has injured the core of his power.*

As Saeed experiences that loss, fear begins to steal his resolve, and the tower of water becomes unsteady, threatening at once to collapse. If he does not overcome his fear, all will be lost, and he and I may perish in the aftermath.

Azizi you must go to his aid! Re-establish the balance of his core.

My own fear is affecting the guardian I have called. Ice crystals begin to form and start to fly about, tearing at our flesh. His life is precious to me. At the risk of injury to myself, I summon another guardian, the element of fire. A terrifying tunnel of flames opens in front of me. I have no time to hesitate. I see the fear in Saeed's eyes and rushing forward with it, protecting myself from the ice crystals, I reach him and surround his body with a golden ball of energy. His breathing steadies. There is palpable relief among the Elders.

I realise suddenly that my action has now cost me my own energy and focus. Elwah made it clear to me, that if the power were to suddenly swing into chaos, the Elders could do very little other than to close the Gateways that have opened.

Insidious thoughts begin to filtrate through the protective barrier of energy, attacking me at random, like a giant bird pecking at its prey. A distant voice resembling the accusatory tones of Delena Tobaha, repeats: *"you have no talent!"*. The annoying voice of Knut stating, *"the witch's brat is having a vision!"*. A chorus of mocking laughter echoes around me. The face of Halim appears before me, smiling at first, then as a treacherous knife slices across his throat the horror in his eyes seem to accuse me. *You caused Halim's death.* The dark Shadows that came one night in my village in Asfaine suddenly appear around me. Their inarticulate gurgling sounds mocking me, gnawing at my resolve to stay focussed. A cold stab at my side reminds me of the mind meld with Halim. I hear myself scream as I fall deep into an icy pool of dark water. Ijlal looks at me as Shahulm is taken, desperate grief in his eyes suddenly turning to anger, *why could you not protect him? That was your purpose! The Talisman failed us! Now Saeed will die. Your talismans of power and protection are useless!* Mocking laughter echoes endlessly ringing in my ears.

I feel tired, I want to lay down and sleep.

A silver blade, with the mark of a full moon appears and flies angrily around me. Thoughts are mercilessly cut and dissolved. A voice, an ice-cold voice cuts through pronouncing, "I will protect my godson even with my life. Let him be!"

A heavy sadness overwhelms me. The weight of responsibility to protect, to heal and now to call a Sacred Sapphire to re-establish a meaningless harmony seems so futile. I feel weak and powerless.

The dark tower of angry water is now streaked with bolts of lightning. The water slows down, begins to stagger in mid-air threatening to collapse. I am overwhelmed with fear of drowning.

Faintly at first, I hear Saeed's voice calling out to me. He is pleading with me, affirming his love for me and then in a tone of desperation, he at once pronounces: "Égétor Péh Elwah!"

A gasp of astonished disbelief goes through the assembled Elders. Saeed has just summoned the Nācken of Elwah to protect me. An opposing current of clear water now surrounds me and has mingled with the current I have summoned, creating a sense of stillness around me.

The impact of opposing forces, the fury of Malkizar and the calm water of Elwah do little to restore any balance. I sense more than hear Master Ahmad's dark thoughts, directed at Saeed, *foolish boy! Destroy him if you must, but you do not have the power to hold those opposing forces. Let me assist you!"*

Saeed's quiet voice replies, "Master Ahmad, never again challenge my love for Azizi!"

With that declaration, the colossal wall of water that Saeed has summoned threatens to burst outwards and flood the world. I hear myself call out, "No, Saeed, wait."

"Azizi," Saeed's voice is pleading, "Azizi, I cannot hold this, the conflict is too much for me. Please Azizi take hold of the waters of Elwah."

The world has gone eerily quiet. Both currents of water come to a standstill, shimmering.

My godmother's voice whispers, "Azizi, let us deal with the outer world. Focus on your energy and your task. You are safe, you have always been safe."

The blue of the sky fills my sight, the blue of the ocean fills my being, the taste of salt and the blue of his eyes fills my heart. Sadness trembles on the edges, and then a voice, the familiar voice of my youth, speaking from beyond the silence of the stars, finally speaks directly to my heart:

"Sorrow is the gift of the shadow cast by the Light.

You were born of the waters of Malkizar, that you would experience sorrow. You were gifted with Elwah that you could understand its opposite. It is now your task to find the balance within yourself.

Though you may think 'that one cannot without the other be', and that both will be experienced forever; know that the time comes when you will only experience Joy."

Suddenly the space within the wall of angry water is filled with the blue light of the sky. A current of air first starts to circulate around us, then the cool waters of my mountain streams begin to flow and spin in the opposite direction.

Amid the tumultuous storm, the angry spiralling wall of water that Saeed has manifested, surrounds us both, excluding all of them. Each one of us afraid and unsure. The realisation that both of us is willing to sacrifice ourselves to protect the other, a memory flashes before my eyes. I step across the stone and stand before him.

I place my hand on his heart, I take his hand and place it on mine, and I ask him, "Saeed what is in here, what do you feel?" At once he opens his eyes wide. The uncertainty leaves him.

We both intone each with our own voice,

"May my heart and days of light embrace you. May that love inside of you fly with wings. Magic is within you, let it flow into and from you."

The wind in the chamber suddenly roars with the rage of a thousand beasts, the waters around us tear at us, some drops so sharp that they cut deep into our flesh. Droplets of blood mix with the water, all appears to be lost. We are not separate, we are one! With all my might, calling on all the power within me, I pronounce:

"Ap! Phat!"

The world suddenly stands still. The waters freeze in place. Two lights of the purest blue manifest between us. Two voices in unison command, "Joy and Sorrow cannot one with the other be. Choose!"

The End

Book 1

The Tears of Apphat. Immortal Beloved

Book 2

Silence of the Stars

Chronicles of Azizi, Seer of Apphat. Immortal Beloved

Book 3

Apphat — The Names of the King

Chronicles of Azizi, Seer of Apphat. Immortal Beloved

Chapter One

The sheer power and authority in my voice is unmistakable. With the command of the Sacred words of Incantation pronounced, the world holds its breath.

The simplicity of the Incantation, the power behind it, has left all the Elders bewildered; except for my godmother, who is beaming with pride. *Yes! The King has two names!*

D I C T I O N A R Y   O F
N A M E S   A N D   T E R M S

Aldrik Azizi's child's name. Made up of two parts: ALD/ADAL Norse for 'noble' or 'kind'; and RIK, Old Germanic for 'mighty'. Born on the second hour of the second day of the second month of Winter—A Child of Stardust. Pale, slight of build. Ice blue eyes. Holder of magic. Often misconstrued as 'distant', 'aloof...'

Ahl-Cassim The breath of God, the precursor to the great desert sandstorms the Cassim.

Apphat (pronounced *ap-fat*). Apphat the Wise. Ancient king of Naassee who founded a philosophy based on androgyny. His philosophy was that the duality of creation existed in both men and women. The Apphatians were known for its fierce, honoured, respected and feared soldiers. The Royal guards in particular who were all homosexual, had vowed total allegiance to their King. These soldiers were not allowed into battle unless they had taken a lover. They would fight side by side and could only be defeated in death.

The Apphatian soldiers began the practice of 'Damna': a sacred initiation of boys that have come of age (around 17 years), into the secrets of love making. It was considered an honour to have one's boy thus initiated.

The kingdom of Apphat was destroyed in the great cataclysm and its people disappeared. Many hundreds of years later, a strange people emerged from the Caves of Gibrar wearing arm bands and amulets that the Apphatians had been known to wear. This people settled in the east of the land and became known as the Naasseenes. They practiced the rites of Apphat. (Refer to 'Apphat The Wise').

Aïschah (pronounced *a-ee-sha*) In the Ancient tongue means 'Silver Moon' (see also Ayshah). Godmother of Dear One. Seeress Magician, Teacher and Healer. Mahjira or female master of the seventh rite. She lives in the Asfaine mountains and honoured friend and guardian of the Hills People.

Aqueel Young soldier of Naasée. His name means knowledgeable.

Ayshah (pronounced *a-ee-shü-ha*) The second moon of this world is smaller and has a silvery appearance. According to legend, this moon can overpower the ill omen of Camlac especially if it eclipses the latter during the season of Malkizar.

Ahl-Cassim Literally translated to mean "The Breath of God". A dangerous wind that blows unpredictably through the Huda pass. It can shred a man or beast to pieces.

Azizi Name of power given to Aldrik (Dear One), by his god mother. It means beloved. Named Aldrik, he was born on the second hour of the second day of the second month of Winter—the season of Malkizar, the coldest season of the Asfaine calendar. Also associated with sorrow, the tempestuous ocean that is most fierce by the same name. One of the Sacred Sapphires is also named Malkizar.

Brouille Group of islands in the northern seas. Said to be haunted, constantly enveloped in mist. Tradition has it that for many years it was the secret meeting place of the early Black Witches.

Camlac Name of the first moon of this world. It usually appears first in the cycle of moons, and is usually a pale yellow in appearance. Depending on the season, it usually is taken as a bad omen. It was named after the demi-god its name meaning 'chaos'.

Cârem A desert expression, meaning the hottest part of the day when travellers will rest, take refreshment and possibly sleep until the sun sets and then travel at night.

Cassim A great desert sand storm.

Damna Apphasian for "Sacred Initiation"

Delena Tobaha One of the senior female teachers at the Temple School of Asfaine.

Duna Equivalent to one day, or the time that it takes for the wind to re-sculpt a sand dune in the great desert.

Duwae Equivalent to a year.

Elwah The season of Joy, associated with re-birth and reincarnation. Also the name of the Prince Guardian of the Sacred sapphire by the same name. In our culture Spring.

Elwah Tahir Official title of the prince: Lord Elwah, Custodian Elwah Prince of Naasée Haafiz (Sacred Keeper) of the Sacred Tear of Apphat for the People of Naasée.
Addressing the Prince of Elwah: Most High Custodian of Naasée, or Your highness / Lord Elwah, Custodian Elwah of Naasée, Hafiz of the Sacred Tear of Apphat. OR Lord Elwah, Custodian of Naasée

Errai The constellation Cepheus has a binary system called Gamma Cephei which created the name Errai meaning "shepherd" in Arabic.

Fanak Albino desert wolf. Striking blue eyes and pointy ears able to detect the faintest sound in the desert.

Fariqa Meaning 'Woman Companion.' Mother of Saeed, tribeswoman of the Huda People.

Faruq (pronounced fa-rook) Meaning 'one who distinguishes truth from falsehood'. Cousin to Ijlal, son of Giafar. A year older than Ijlal, aged 23.

Fatin One of the Companions, his name means 'Clever, bright.'

Glesskerel Kingdom of the Northern Region and country

of origin of Shahulm. The nation is situated far north of the Asfaine Mountains and is separated from the Asfaine on its southern most border by a large glacial wilderness.

Gaisha Title of respect meaning "Great Mother/Father" (depending on gender).

Giafar Younger brother of the Sultan Rashãd of Schiraz, his most trusted general, advisor and uncle to Ijlal.

Gibrar Foreboding and desolate cave legendary place thought to be the last stand of Princess Baltazar and her lover. Renowned for the strange beasts that inhabit the surrounding lands. Used as test of bravery by early Apphat soldiers, also thought to be the place of origin of the Naasséenes.

Haafiz Sacred Keeper

Haakon Aldrik's father. His name in old Norse means high son or descendant.

Hadid One of the twelve ancient guardian spirits. Hadid is the guardian of the air taking the form of a great bird; he is also the messenger of the sun god.

Hala Aura or energy field. Visible to those with the Sight.

Halim Meaning 'gentle'. Shepherd boy of the Hills People. Destined to befriend Azizi.

Haroun-al-Rashid Seer and magician at the Court of the Great Sultan Maltizar, ruler of Shiraz.

Hasan Meaning 'handsome'. Naasseene soldier, Captain of the Royal Guard and personal protector of Elwah, regent prince of the Naasséenes. His official title in Naasée is 'Excellency'. His role encompasses the administration of the city in the absence of Elwah.

Habud A small whirlwind of sand in the desert of Keyab. The precursor to a khamsin a smaller version of the large desert storm, Ahl Cassim.

Huda Literally meaning conduit, interpreted as Great Mouth. This pass acts as a channel for fierce winds, known as the Ahl-Cassim

Husam Meaning 'sword edge'. One of the companions.

Ijlal Heir and prince to the Kingdom of Schiraz. The leader of the Band of desert youths, trusted for his courage and fierce fighting skills.

Isamadeen (pronounced isa-ma-deen) Twin brother to Rauf. His name means 'to guard'. Always at attention, ready to pounce. Aged 17. He is the eldest of the twins, only by minutes, but he never lets Rauf forget this.

Ismuth of Mina The narrow strip of land extending from the

Great Marshes to the old Citadel, ruled by the Overlord before his demise.

Jamal Meaning 'kind'. One of the companions.

Jörmungandr In Norse mythology, Jörmungandr, also known as the Midgard Serpent or World Serpent, is an unfathomably large sea serpent who dwells in the world sea, encircling the Earth and biting his own tail, an example of an ouroboros. As a result of it surrounding Midgard it is referred to as the World Serpent

Kershel Measure of distance approximately equivalent to a metre and a half.

Knut Aldrik's bully and nemesis in the village. The name means knot.

Dahé Equivalent to a day

Lahé Equivalent to a week.

Mahé Equivalent to one month

Luam Young kitchen hand in Naasée. His name means 'calm'.

Mahjir (pronounced *ma-here*) for a man; **Mahjira** (pronounced *ma-heera*) for a woman. Term of great respect, literally means 'Master' and is given to one who has mastered the arts of magic and seership.

Mahjir (male) **Mahjira** (female)

Mina Ahmad Master of Divination and Symbols, elder of Naasée. Nasty man. Divination means that he is responsible for interpreting prophesies and signs. He should technically be an expert in astrology and runic symbols.

Mahjir Ngaway Master of Incantations and Spells. His name means 'powerful speech'.

Mahjir Suffrah One of the revered Elders and Magician. Mater of Rites and Ceremonies. He is the master who initiates Azizi into the First Order of Apphat the Healer.

Malkizar The coldest and most turbulent season of the Country. The season of Malkizar sees the Asfaine region covered in snow and cut off from the rest of the country for about 3 to 4 months. In our culture—it would be known as the winter of the long night.

Mina The 3 stone pillars. The isthmus of Mina that leads to the stronghold of the Over lord—the great citadel.

Naasée A strange and enigmatic country built on the cliffs overlooking the Great Ocean of Elwah, its people known as both the Naasséenes as well as the old Apphatians. According to legend the people of Naasée emerged from a deep cave following the great cataclysm that destroyed the kingdom of Apphat. They wore the same clothes and talismans as the traditional Apphatians. They are ruled by priests of immense magical power and their leader is one known as Prince Elwah. It is said that he is a reincarnation of unbroken lineage of such individual and is identified by the priests as one of fair skin and blue eyes. Naasée is also known for its fearsome army of unconquered ruthless soldiers, who also follow the ancient rites and lore of Apphat.

Nakhla Name of the native tree that grows in the desert around an oasis.

Nar (pronounced '*narun*') Fire.

Noor Light. The name for light is invoked to create an elf like light.

Parvus Sacred rhyming verse written in groups of five lines, mostly used for epic poems and sacred text.

Rauf (pronounced ra-oof) Gentle and kind, twin brother to Isamadeen, born a few minutes later. Aged 17.

Saeed Meaning 'Happy; Lucky'. Son of Fariqa.

Sahir Young magician (at least 100 years old) on the Council of Elders. His specialty—names and potions. One of the few masters from the Great Desert of Keyab. Identified by his heavy facial tattoos.

Sarab Mirage—an common phenomenon that occurred at certain times of the day as the heat from the land played with images of caravans of water that were a long way away and made appear to be close.

Sarek Personal Aide to General Hasan.

Shahulm Named after the Guardian of the Night, meaning Lord of Dreams/Hope.

Shemagh A triangular piece of cloth that is used to wrap around the head and face to protect it from the harsh desert heat as well as cover and protect the mouth from dust and sand.

Tabrass Servant to Master Ahmad. His name signifies 'untrustworthy' or 'liar' in some desert dialect.

Tekbiek Predatory bird rarely seen. Dark in plumage it is adept at camouflage. Amongst the simple folk it is associated with the dark spirits that are said to roam the forest at night.

The Giant's Footsteps A group of large stone pillars so called as they appear to be steps. Thought to be remnants of formations like the Huda, which have disintegrated over hundreds of years. They are found from the southernmost tip of the Asfaine Mountains extending across to the coastline southeast of Glesskerel.

The King Apphat He has two names: Ap and Phat. It is an esoteric name; it is rooted in old Sanskrit. it is an incantation as a healing energy which instructs the subconscious to release any emotions, beliefs or programming that has caused the feeling of separation from God (The All that Is, Spirit etc).

EXPRESSIONS OF TIME

Duna Equivalent to one day, or the time that it takes for the wind to re-sculpt a sand dune in the great desert.

Dahé Equivalent to a day

Lahé Equivalent to a week.

Mahé Equivalent to one month

Duwae Equivalent to a year.

Varye Sacred moral duties/codes that bind the magician to using certain powers or techniques only under specific circumstances.

Xan Trusted soldier and one of the Royals Guards to Hasan.

THE COMPANIONS

Ijlal (pronounced *eej-lal*)

Prince of Shiraz. Same age as Azizi— 22. Eldest son of the Sultan.

Faruq (pronounced *fa-rook*)

Meaning 'one who distinguishes truth from falsehood'. Cousin to Ijlal, son of Giafar. A year older than Ijlal, aged 23.

Husam (pronounced *hoo-sa-m*)

Meaning 'sword edge'. Will not suffer fools and can express opinion with brutal honesty. Aged 17.

Fatin (pronounced *fa-teen*)

Intelligent and perceptive. Aged 17.

Isamadeen (pronounced *isa-ma-deen*)

Twin brother to Rauf. His name means 'to guard'. Always at attention, ready to pounce. Aged 15. He is the eldest of the twins, only by minutes, but he never lets Rauf forget this.

Rauf (pronounced *ra-oof*)

Gentle and kind, twin brother to Isamadeen, born a few minutes later. Aged 15.

Jamal (pronounced *ja-māl*)

Means 'kind'. Similar personality to Rauf and just as mischievous. Just turned 15.

THE COUNCIL OF ELDERS OF NAASÉE

Elwah Tahir Prince Elwah Tahir Sacred Haafiz. Master of Magic. He can create spells at will. Rumoured to be over one hundred years old, but looks no older than thirty.

Mina Ahmad Master of Divinations and Symbols.

Suffrah Master of Rites and Ceremonies.

Ngaway Master of incantations and spells.

Vasilis Master of Visions.

Sahir Master of Names and Potions. Mage for the Huda people. One hundred years old.

Mahjira Mitra One of two women on the Council. High Priestess, power over the summoning of Guardians.

Mahjira Aïschah One of two women on the Council. Star Charts Diviner, Plant magic and Healer.

Sindarin Keeper of secrets and cosmic magical keys. His age is unknown, but he is older than Elwah.

Elim Master of the gateways—ability to open a gate into another dimension.

SACRED SYMBOLS

Triple Moon Goddess

Symbolises all phases of Womanhood.

Symbol of the Nācken of Malkizar

It is a sacred symbol signifying the tidal
moon and power over the tides.

Symbol signifying water

Waves / ocean.

The final symbol tattoo that appears on Saeed.

Azizi has created a balance between the tidal moon and
a drop of water that signifies working in harmony with
the ocean. The combination assures protection.

Alain Louis Camus

CYCLES OF THE MOONS

The Moons of Ayshah & Camlac

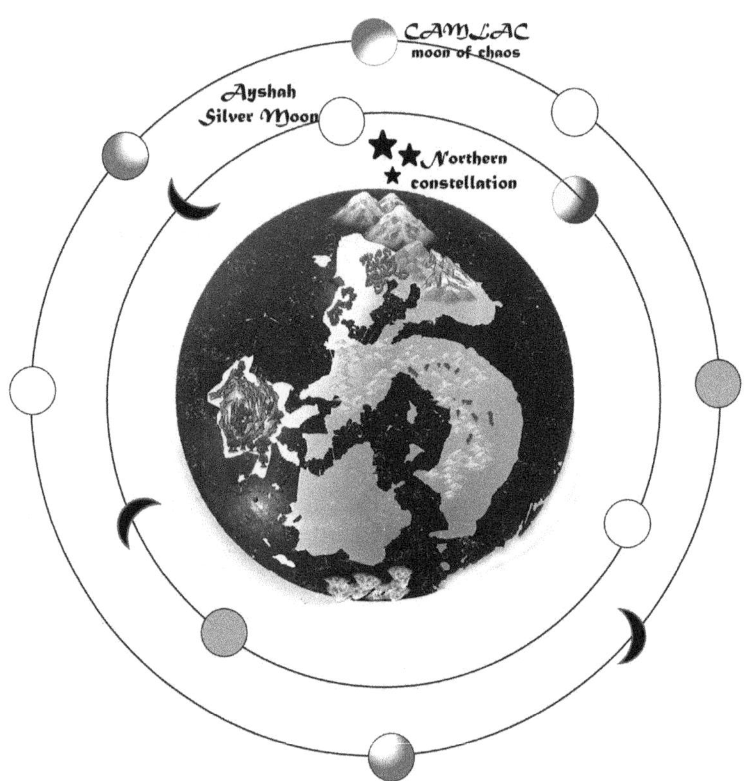

Celestial Map drawn by Mahjir Anatol
First reign of Apphat the Wise

Dredgemarsh

Fire and Water

Dermot McCabe

Published in 2025 by
Forty Foot Press
Sandycove, Dún Laoghaire, County Dublin, Ireland
Website: www.fortyfootpress.ie
Email: fortyfootpresseditor@gmail.com
Copyright © Dermot McCabe 2019

ISBN. 978-0-9553597-4-3

Cover Image and Maps © Dermot McCabe
Character portraits illustrations © Conall McCabe 2025
Typeset: Body Text Garamond
Cover Design & Typesetting © Dermot McCabe 2025

Acknowledgements

I have been fortunate to share my work with so many fellow writers from Abraxas Writers. With courtesy and refreshing honesty they have critiqued my efforts over the years, never failing to hunt down the errors, inconsistencies and mistakes that hide in clear sight from the author.

At the risk of one or all of them accusing me of stooping to the most mundane of clichéd expressions, I could not have done it without them.

In particular I would like to thank Anne Fitzgerald, Rita Canavan, Michael Gordon and Shane Harrison for their detailed scrutiny of, what I initially thought, was the final manuscript.

A very special thank-you to my son Conall McCabe for his unique illustrations.

"Do there exist many worlds, or is there but a single world? This is one of the most noble and exalted questions in the study of Nature." ~ **Albertus Magnus**, a 13th-century Dominican friar and scientist

For

Una McCabe

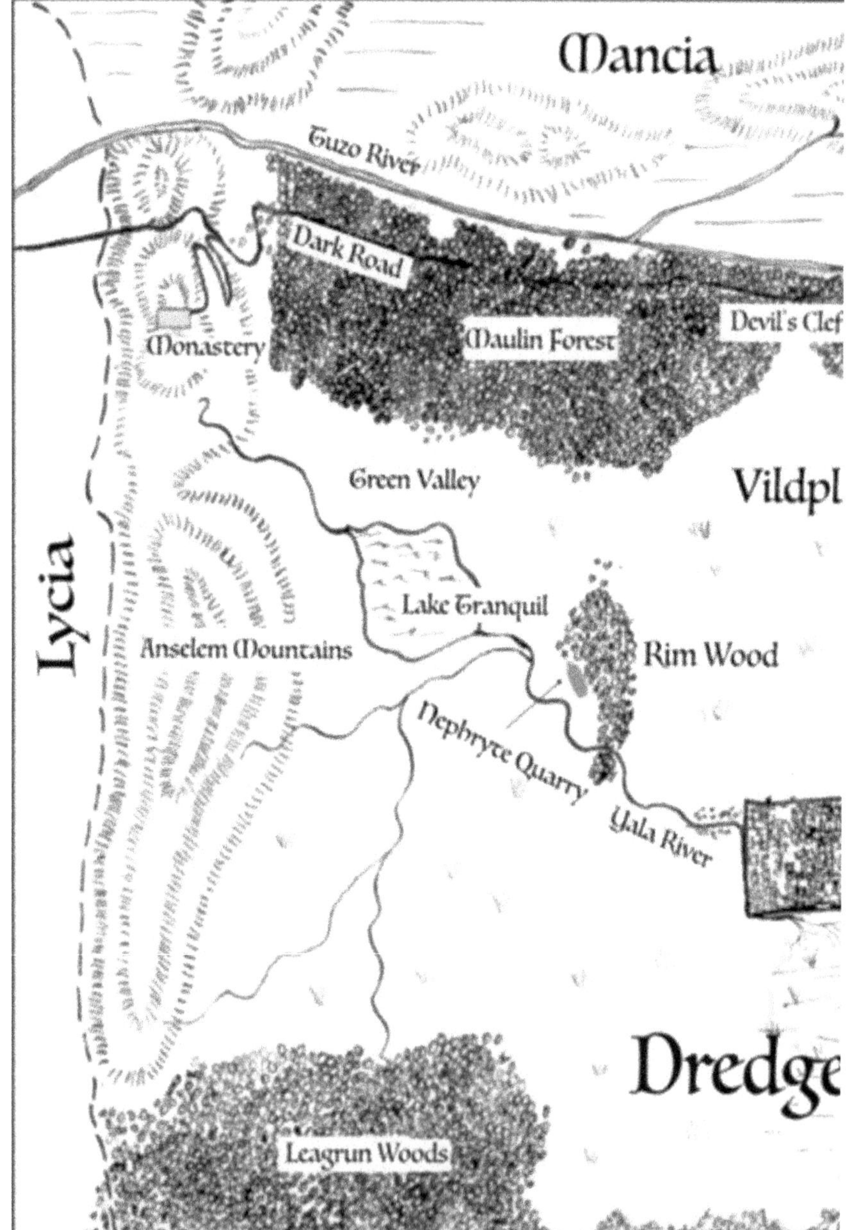

Mancia
Tuzo River
Dark Road
Monastery
Maulin Forest
Devil's Clef
Green Valley
Vildpl
Lycia
Lake Tranquil
Rim Wood
Anselem Mountains
Nephryte Quarry
Yala River
Dredge
Leagrun Woods

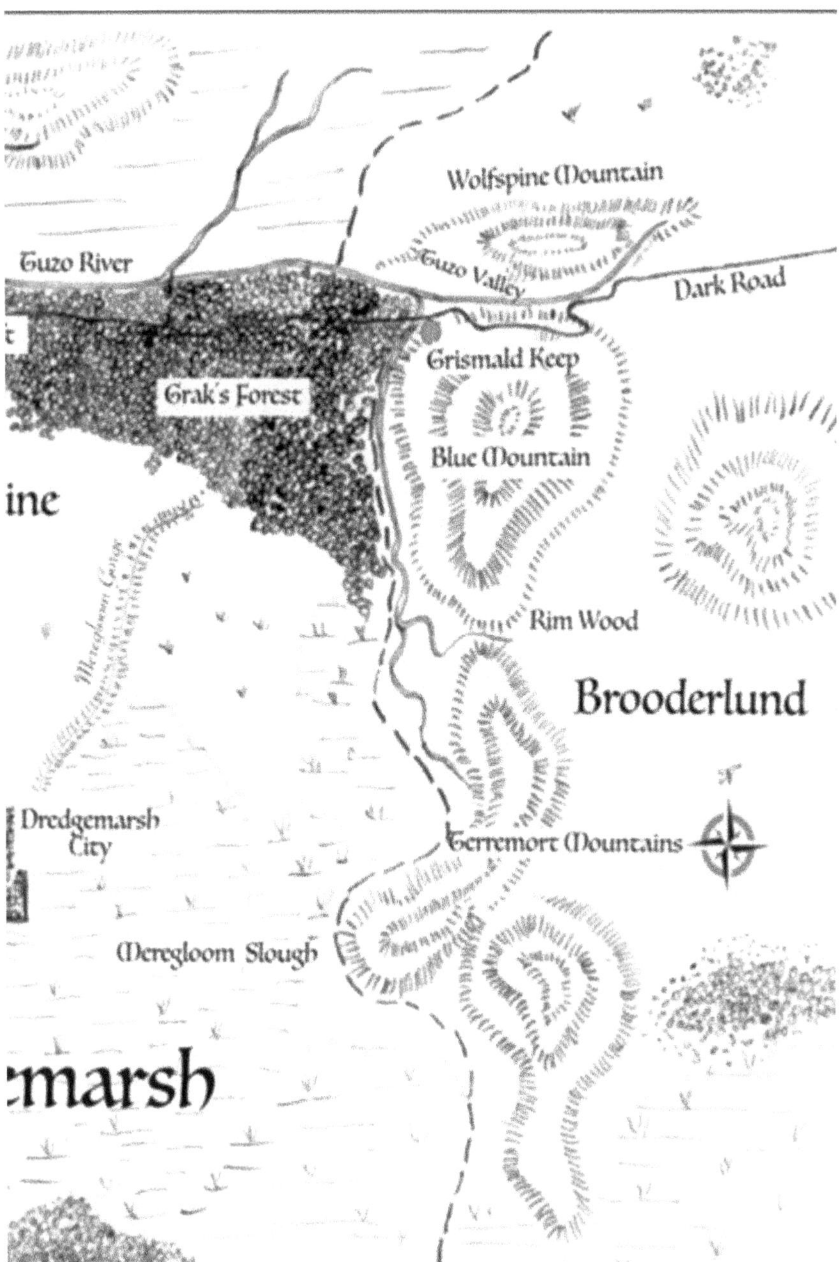

Wolfspine Mountain
Guzo River
Guzo Valley
Dark Road
Grismald Keep
Grak's Forest
Blue Mountain
ine
Rim Wood
Brooderlund
Dredgemarsh City
Terremort Mountains
Meregloom Slough
marsh

Harry Fairgame

Chapter 1

The masons huddled around the hearth in their customary alcove of the Slaughtered Horse. They were already on their third tankard of braggot, when the topic of Harry Fairgame came up, which was inevitable, given recent extraordinary events surrounding the new Prince. They winked knowingly at each other and shook their heads in exaggerated dismay.

'Shoveller Fairgame was no more a grandfather to that boy than you or I,' one of the masons said. 'It's a blessing that the old bastard died. And pray Christ it was a painful death.'

'You never spoke a truer word, Ralf Hardhand,' said one of his fellow drinkers. 'He worked the boy, night and day, summer and winter.'

'Like a dog. And, a grander lad you never met.' Ralf took a deep draught from his tankard and smacked his lips. 'But, by God, he was as good as any canal man and him just a boy. The smartest lad in the whole of Dredgemarsh be it lord or varlet. I'll tell you what, my friends, when he recovers from the torture they put him through and comes out of the infirmary, he'll face up to his new life as a Prince, and no better lad to do it.' Ralf slammed his tankard onto the table 'No better lad to do it and that's a fact,' another echoed.

'If he lasts that long,' said a small twisted man whom life overlooked when disbursing even the average quota of looks and bearing.

Ralf looked askance at the little man, opened his gullet and took another long draught of braggot. 'Didn't he defy death and the executioner at the last moment? It was a miracle. Nothing will harm him now.'

'And they about to relieve him of his head for a murder he didn't do. Evil pig fukkers,' another said.

'And anyway, what would you know about that, you little runt.' Ralf slammed his empty tankard onto the table.

'They tried to murder him again. That's a fact,' the runt said.

'A fact, a fact. You dreamed it when stealing one of your sly little sleeps or stroking your spindle in the granite shed.' The circle of masons burst into laughter.

'Gentlemen, gentlemen, I bring you nectar of the Gods.' Frambert Fullfare, proprietor of The Slaughtered Horse, descended on Ralf and his companions with two frothy jugs of braggot. 'Ralf, fling more timber on the fire there. It's a bitch of a cold day.'

'Never felt it so cold, Frambert,' Ralf said. 'We're in for more foul weather. I can feel it in me bones.'

'This'll help.' Frambert replenished their tankards from the foaming jugs. 'And, trenchers of the finest boar and mustard is on its way, men.'

'Ah', sighed Ralf, 'the smell is tickling me vitals already.' He rubbed his ample tummy. 'By the way, Frambert, do you know what's happening. The runt here,' Ralf thumbed the air in the direction of the little man, 'says someone tried to murder Harry Fairgame, or should I say, our new Prince, and him still in his sick bed.'

Frambert lowered himself onto a low stool that groaned under him. He leaned forward into the circle of masons. 'He's not wrong.'

'What?'

'Poison,' Frambert whispered. 'Someone poisoned his food. And would you believe it,' the masons were open mouthed, 'didn't the kitchen lad, Squint … know who I mean? The sly little weasel with—'

'Yeh, yeh, go on. What happened, Frambert.' Ralph spun his finger in a rapid circular rotation.

'Squint pilfered a sneaky little taste of Harry's breakfast when he was delivering it to the Infirmary. And didn't the little clotpole fall down and vomit up his innards just as he got inside the main door.'

'Bravo Squint, but what about Harry?'

'Fine, but not safe anymore. There's some of Fabian's dogs hiding amongst us still. And, as long as that imposter's alive, wherever he is, they'll try to murder Harry. They want Fabian back. They are nothing without him.'

A grim silence settled over the gathering. In a far corner a rebec player struck up a lively jig. Ralf, roused by the music, spat into the blazing fire.

'That traitor will never return, no matter what. Harry's the true prince. Even if we never guessed it, and him slaving away amongst us.'

'I can tell you a few—' Frambert began.

'Frambert Fullfare! Have you nothing better to do than gossip and drink. Our customers are famished and parched waiting for you.' Hiltrude, Frambert's beloved wife and companion stood over him with hands on hips and as stern a glower as she could muster.

'Duty calls, gentlemen.' Frambert stood to attention, put his arm around Hiltrudes waist and squeezed her close to him.

'Keep your great paws to yourself, Frambert Fullfare. There's a roast hog to be carved; use them for that. And you lot.' Hiltrude shook her finger at the drinkers. 'Stop leading him astray.' They assumed various contrite expressions which was difficult because Frambert standing behind her and a full head taller, though she was a woman of fulsome proportions, was winking and grinning at them.

The discovery that Harry Fairgame, a canal cleaner, was the real heir to the Dredgemarsh throne was not a topic confined to the habitués of the Slaughtered Horse. It was the only topic being discussed in every crumbling corner of Dredgemarsh. The astonishing news spread like a fever throughout the city. Everyone told a different story about how Harry, condemned to death for a murder he didn't commit, escaped the executioner's axe at the last moment.

'The archangel Michael saved him,' some swore.

'The executioner dropped dead the moment he raised the axe,' others said.

'Writing appeared in blood on the walls of the court chamber where he was tried.' The further the story travelled the more fantastic it grew.

Mistress of the Dredgemarsh kitchens, Bella Crumble-Ratchet, consort of Cook Maester, Leopold Ratchet, was preening herself because she always nurtured a soft spot for Harry and always gave him special treatment from the time he commenced studying and working with Professor Quickstrain. That was the time when he and the professor, now deceased, murdered in fact, used to visit her buttery for their mid-day meals. The gossip at the time was that they were building some strange war engine and Harry the erstwhile canal lad displayed such an uncanny aptitude for science that the Professor insisted on taking him on as his understudy.

'No surprise to me,' Bella said repeatedly to anyone who might be close enough to listen. 'No surprise at all. As for that … that horrid impostor Fabian … on the loose with his wretched companions. I never liked him. Didn't I say so many a time, Chef Ratchett.'

'Yes, we all said so.'

'And, to think,' she would continue, 'what the real prince, the little mite I once held in my arms, had to go through … the years he soiled his blessed hands in those horrid canals.' She would become teary-eyed and have to sit down.

'There, there, my dear,' her husband would respond in a weary voice, 'we were not to know.'

'But we should have. We just should have. I should have,' she would reply and the tears would flow.

'That's all in the past.' There was an ever-increasing wistful tone in Leopold's well-practiced response. But despite all of these bland attempts, he could not curtail Bella's tearful outbursts.

'That fiend Fabian,' she would cry out at random moments, 'is still alive somewhere. Him and his disgusting friends wish the poor boy dead. Scoundrels, thieves and murderers the lot of them. Only for that sneaky little Squint … bless him … the poor boy would be … Oh it's too awful to think about.'

'There is not much we can do about it now, Bella.' Chef Ratchet chopped through a chicken neck with unaccustomed ferocity.

'Not much we can do about it! Is that all you can say?' Bella slammed her sizzling frying pan unto the stove, removed her apron and kitchen cap and commenced putting on her "going out" cloak and pattens. 'Well,' she declared in a loud voice, 'we'll see about that.'

'Why are you … Where are you … breakfast is only … Bella.' Ratchet threw his hands up in the air.

The door was already shut behind her.

Lia Celeste

Chapter 2

In the Infirmary, Harry, the object of Bella's distress, was recuperating from the injuries inflicted during his incarceration and brutal interrogation by Fabian's henchmen. He was not told about the most recent attempt on his life.

'The poor boy has enough to be dealing with,' Judith, matron of Santa Philipe Infirmary, insisted.

The one and only possible clue to the identity of the poisoner was a vague recollection by a skullery maid of giving food and water to an old mendicant begging outside the Dredgemarsh kitchens.

On being interrogated by Captain Dante Severino, Chief Marshall of Dredgemarsh, the terrified scullery maid said, 'I pitied him, sir and allowed him to warm himself in the drying room. He was old and blind in one eye and his poor face was grey with the cold.'

Severino despaired of finding the old mendicant or any other possible assassin in that vast and dilapidated city. Abandoned houses, shops, stables, cavernous halls, chapels, towers, ruined mansions and a warren of subterranean canals offered endless hiding places for anyone who wanted to evade capture. He decided that the best option was to increase the number of those guarding Harry.

A permanent watch of eight sentries from Captain Paine's field army were stationed day and night outside Harry's private room in the infirmary. Visitation, apart from Matron Judith Engar and Maester Aidan, was restricted to Chancellor Grunkite, General Hawksfoot, Captain Severino, Captain Paine and Potens a close friend and once mentor during Harry's inauspicious and brief career as a lowly trooper in the Dredgemarsh army.

Judith fretted over Harry as if he was new born. She gave stern warnings to all visitors not to overtax him. In a way, Harry was new born. Though his body was recovering, his mind was not. He was not ready to grapple with the enormity of his new position. The grandees of Dredgemarsh came to pay their respects. It's a dream, he thought. He was Harry Fairgame, and he was just a spectator. This person, this Prince of Dredgemarsh they deferred to was someone else, someone he did not know or recognise.

In those first few weeks of his convalescence, he found solace in abandoning himself, mind and body, to Matron Judith's care. Subsequent to the attempt to poison his food, Bella Crumble cooked all of Harry's meals in the infirmary kitchen and tasted everything before delivering it to Harry with her own two hands.

'Would it not be easier for you, Bella, to cook in the royal kitchen; this is so small,' Judith asked after the first week of Bella's invasion of the Infirmary kitchen.

'This is perfect, Judith. But thank you for your concern.'

For Harry, the days and weeks passed in a dreamlike state where the only signs of activity outside his cocoon of isolation was the low whisperings of the changing guards, the odd laughter of the men and sometimes the voice of Judith or Bella chastising them for making too much noise. Every day the campanile bell rang out the hours and the great bell of St. Johannes Cathedral joined in at Prime, Tierce, Sext and Nones. Further away the multitudes of Prayer Houses and Chapels all responded to St Johannes.

Ragged hosts of crows filled the dawn skies with their discord as they flapped their way over the windy towers of Dredgemarsh. They came from Graks Forest on their way to Meregloom swamp to feed. At dusk the tumult would pass overhead once again on their return to their nests in the forest.

From his sick bed he observed the clouds of early spring through the oriel window of his room. They tumbled across the sky from dawn to dusk flinging down their sleety protests against the glass.

Part of him, that part so long bereft of love and affection, wanted to stay in the little room to be ministered to by Judith and Bella. But with his strength returning, his mind began to reconstruct all the events of his life. His mother; he still thought of Maisie Fairgame as his mother; where was she now? He recalled her frequent bouts of sadness, and how she would say she wished she could give him what, by right, he deserved. He began to understand what she meant. The vicious treatment and humiliations visited on him by his grandfather, no, not his real grandfather, made sense now. He picked over every tiny detail of his life, a life of hardship and drudgery until he, despite his grandfather's opposition, was compelled by law to attend school. That law, that wise law saved him. Learning became the focus, the love of his life, a balm to counter every hardship.

'King Cesare, where is King Cesare?' Harry asked Judith one morning.

'Your father is in Lycia, I believe.'

My father. My father. Harry repeated the words in his head and somehow the idea, a simple statement of fact, induced turmoil in his mind. He had not allowed himself to dwell on such matters. He could not let go of the actuality of his old life. He was a boy canal cleaner turned student and for a short period a lowley soldier. How harsh that life was, but it was real. It was his life. It defined him. But now, in its place was nothing, a void, a terrifying void. The mention of the King, that austere ruler, being his father was beyond his grasp. The idea unhinged him. Who am I? Who was my mother? How could I have ended up working on the canals? My mother was Maisie Fairgame. No, that can't be, can't be if King Cesare is my father.

'Are you well, my lord?' Judith touched his forehead
'What?'
'You look unwell, my lord.'
'Don't call me that. I'm not your lord or anybody's lord.'
'But you are the true—'
'I'm Harry Fairgame. I'm tired. Let me sleep. I want to sleep.'

And he did sleep. He slept for the best part of seven days, barely waking for a few morsels of food, toilet and a tisane of henbane, mint and verbena prepared by Maester Aidan. All visits were cancelled.

On the seventh day, he was sitting on the side of the bed when Judith and Bella bustled into the room with his breakfast.

'Ah, you are awake.' Judith hesitated and then said, 'My lord.' He did not react. Bella laid the breakfast before him on a small table. He devoured it. 'I'll bring you more, my Lord.' He nodded. She rushed off and in a short time pushed her way backwards into the room with a trolley on which an even more sumptuous breakfast was laid out. Harry ate like a famished child after which Bella left with an empty breakfast trolly and a smile as if she had just vanquished the hated Brooderstalt army.

'Can I get you anything else … my lord?' There was a slight edge to Judith's voice as she looked askance at the departing Bella. She set about inspecting his injuries. 'Amazing,' she said, 'it must be all that sleep.'

'I wish to talk to Chancellor Grunkite and Professor Quickstrain, matron.'

'Are you quite—'

'I am ready. I want to see them.'

'As you wish, my lord.'

'And, matron, I will need some clothes.' Harry with his thumb and forefinger shook a loose fold of the hospital surplice he was wearing.

'But of course, Sire.'

Harry felt a tiny quiver of dread rippling somewhere deep inside when Chancellor Grunkite arrived without his old mentor Professor Quickstrain.

'You've come alone, Chancellor,' he said, just above a whisper.

'You don't remember, sire? The trial. You were accused of his murder.' Grunkite was vigorously massaging his chin and staring at the floor.

'Murdered? Is Professor Quickstrain dead? And I was … I don't remember.'

Grunkite looked away and stared at a chart showing bloodletting points on the human body with complex arrays of zodiac symbols.

'He was killed by Fabian's assassins. There was a trial. They produced witnesses — vermin of the worst type — swore you murdered the Professor.' Harry covered his face with both hands. He was quiet for some time. Grunkite waited.

'I can't remember.' Harry looked up at Grunkite, tears rolling down his face.

'Listen to me young man … Sire. I should not have burdened you with all of this. My fault. Rest, you need more rest. You will remember in time. I'll send the matron to you before I go.'

'Wait.' Harry said. 'There are some things I am beginning to recall.'

'Things?' Grunkite said.

'Yes, before the trial. The Brooderstalt? Were they preparing to attack us?

'Yes, they were, and there is already some activity on our borders.'

'Firedrake; what about Firedrake?'

'Hah. Firedrake. Our only hope. Or was our only hope. But alas, it's unfinished. Professor Quickstrain is dead and the King, your father is in Lycia.'

Harry was silent again. He began to massage his temples.

'Sire, rest. I will talk to you anon.'

'No, no, chancellor. It's not rest I need. You forget I was the Professor's assistant. I do know about Firedrake. Maybe, I could finish building it. I know the Professor would want me to try.'

'Sire, it's too much. You are barely recovered and—'

'I must do something, Chancellor. Maybe I won't succeed.' Harry lay back on the pillow. 'But I have to try.' He looked exhausted. 'I would like my writing desk and all drawings and documents relating to Firedrake brought here. The book I brought back from Anselem, the one the King entrusted to me, I will need that. I also need to talk to Gawan the armourer and Pietr Smallhand.'

'If you insist, Sire.'

'I do,' Harry said. 'And Chancellor, I wish you would call me Harry instead of Sire.'

'Sire, it is hard for an old administrator like me to be so familiar with those I serve … but perhaps if you wish it, I could address you so in private … for now. But in public, I must insist, you will be addressed formally.'

Harry nodded.

'I will leave you now ... Harry. Your writing desk and the rest will be sent straight away.'

'The general's daughter, Lia, how is she?' Harry said as Grunkite walked away.

'The young lady was most distressed at your trial, but she is well now. You remember her?' Grunkite half turned towards Harry. There was a hint of mischief in his voice and a coy tilt of the head. Harry did not respond but a slight blush on the deathly pale cheeks was evident to even Grunkite's old eyes.

'Shall I ask her to …'

'No. Not … maybe later when I am …'

'Rest, Sire … Harry.'

The Chancellor pursed his lips, raised a bemused right eyebrow and departed.

'I don't understand you.' Rebecca stood with her hands on her hips in front of her mistress, Lia Celeste, who sat on an unmade bed hugging her knees. The campanile bell was ringing out midday.

'Oh stop, Rebecca, I have already told you I cannot go.'

'Why? Tell me again because I can't make any sense of what you're saying. You could not wait to see him when he was just a common soldier, student or canal cleaner. Now that he is the Prince of Dredgemarsh, you don't want to see him.'

'That's just it. He is now the Prince of Dredgemarsh and I can't just … just throw myself at him.' She scrambled off the bed and plonked herself in front of her dressing table. 'Brush my hair Rebecca. We are not going to say another word about this. That is final.'

'You're not going to speak about it again?' Rebecca arched one eyebrow, a smile playing across her lips.

'Yes, I was happy to be of assistance to someone I thought needed help. That's done with and now … well … he is the prince and he has no need of my help anymore.'

'Still,' Rebecca said and started brushing Lia's hair.

After a long silence Lia said in a subdued voice, 'Still. You said still, Rebecca. What do you mean?'

'Nothing.'

'Rebecca, you are so irritating; now tell me what you meant.'

'You told me we were not going to talk about … him … any more.'

'Oh I could horse whip you.' Lia jumped up, grabbed a pillow from her bed and threw it at Rebecca who caught it and flung it back causing Lia to tumble sideways. She rolled onto her stomach, buried her face in the cool silk of her sheets and moaned. 'What am I to do, Rebecca, what am I to do?'

'I have already told you. Pay him a visit.'

'Oh, I can't.'

'Well, I can't help you if you are not willing to do anything about it. Go back to bed. I'm busy.' Rebecca left Lia in her rumpled dismay.

Chapter 3

General Albrecht Pentrojan threw his head back and drained the goblet of hot clarrey. He was sitting astride a wall-eyed cob facing a vast army of Brooderstalt foot soldiers and cavalry. The fury of the snow storms had dwindled into a frozen white silence that loomed out of the dawn shadows. Pentrojan flung the goblet aside and one of his ever-anxious pageboys scrambled to retrieve it from the slush of snow and mud that covered the ground of the Brooderstalt camp. The general grunted in satisfaction. He surveyed the great host before him, and, pulling his capuchon back off his head, revealed the once jet-black hair now streaked with grey.

He stood in the stirrups and raised a clenched fist in the air. 'For Cawdrult. For Brooderlund,' His voice boomed across the valley and echoed back and forth between Wolfspine Mountains to the north and Blue Mountain to the South. As if in answer to his call the serenade of the Blue Mountain wolves floated down from the hostile peaks above them, a song of desolation. Even the most hardened of warriors felt a shiver of apprehension on hearing the ominous chorus.

A random voice repeated Pentrojan's words: 'For Cawdrult. For Brooderlund.' Then in a louder voice, 'For Pentrojan. Death to Dredgemarsh.' Another and then another took up the cry. They began to beat their swords against their shields until the valley trembled with the fury of twenty thousand men at arms. The battle horns blasted and the war drums began to pound louder and louder. The musk oxen hitched to the supply wagons and the giant-wheeled war engines of the Manchians, bawled out their fright in great vaporous clouds. The mighty destriers whinnied and stomped the ground into a grey mush. The ice-filled air roiled into a frenzy of sound that raged across the valley, swelled and filled all space between the frozen ground and grey mass of cloud that hung unmoving above them.

A bleak smile flickered across Pentrojan's lips and he whispered to himself, 'This time there will be no mistakes.' He jerked the wall-eyed cob around and led the way out of the Tuzo Valley. The army, like a single creature groaned into motion and followed him: foot soldiers, cavalry, supply wagons and the ponderous war engines. Twelve of these monstrosities were being pulled on wagons by teams of musk oxen. Bringing up the rear of this great army, a ragtag mob of camp followers trudged along in disarray. As the climb became more laboured, the blasting of horns and beating of drums began to diminish and give way to the thunderous rumble and noise of a host of men and beasts on the move. The army snaked it's way upwards from the basin of the Tuzo towards the Iron Road that snaked around the side of Blue Mountain.

Late into the morning, Pentrojan and the forward troops reached the road and turned west into a biting wind. Snow and sometimes sleet fell in scattered flurries. The dense clouds began to break up. Visibility was good. The soldiers marching six abreast along the Iron Road began to relax and become more talkative after the climb from the valley floor.

'The General doesn't look happy,' one young soldier remarked to his companion.

'I'm not surprised,' an older veterans butted in, 'old Iron Foot hasn't happy memories of Dredgemarsh.'

'What do you mean?'

'I mean he was there before and it ended in disaster.'

'When?'

'You weren't even in your mother's belly, lad. He was the only person to survive. They sent him back, barefoot. He walked from Dredgemarsh to Brooderlund in the middle of winter … no boots … should've died.'

'So that's where he got his— '

'Yes, Iron Foot, but, if you value your life, don't let him hear you speak that name.'

At that moment Pentrojan turned in his saddle and looked directly at them. Although they knew it would have been impossible for him to hear what they were saying, they cast frightened eyes downwards and tried to maneuver themselves behind some of their comrades out of the fearful gaze of the general. Their guilty demeanour was proof enough in Pentrojan's mind that they were talking about him and about the one dreadful humiliation that dominated his whole life. Every success, every triumph, and there were many, was tarnished by the memory of his ignominious ejection from Dredgemarsh some twenty years previously. He could not forget the derision and jeers of the lowliest serfs of that hateful kingdom as he was marched through the streets and then dragged through the main gates and cast out without boots, weapon or winter clothing. How many times he wished for death on that dreadful journey back to Brooderlund.

Every day, every minute of his life since then was tainted by the shame of being the one survivor from that failed attempt to conquer Dredgemarsh. Even now, twenty years on from those blighted days, his own men were still whispering about the greatest failure of his life. Rage began to well up in him and instead of two cowed and frightened Brooderstalt foot soldiers he saw the taunting faces of Dredgemarsh peasants. His hand reached for the falchion on his belt and to the consternation of those who had been talking about him, he reined in his cob and allowed them to draw closer.

'We're done for, lad,' the old veteran whispered as they drew ever nearer to Pentrojan who was still glaring at them and licking his lips. But then, a shout from the road in front of them and the sound of galloping horses diverted Pentrojan's attention. It was Captain Agobard Luparellus.

'General,' he shouted, hauling his mount to a slithering halt, 'the Grismald Keep was retaken. All our men are dead and the Keep has been abandoned.' For an instant a feeling of dread gripped Pentrojan. Could it be that he would once again be thwarted by this insignificant little kingdom. The moment passed. No, this time there was no possibility of failure. The Brooderstalt army outnumbered Dredgemarsh by ten to one. Moreover the Manchian war engines with their enormous firing distance meant he could stay well out of range of any Dredgemarsh weaponry and pound the accursed fortress city and every one in it to dust. The thought brought a flicker of joy to his heart. The total destruction of Dredgemarsh and all its inhabitants was the balm that would release him from over twenty years of brooding.

'It is no matter, Captain Luparellus, a pinprick of desperation from Dredgemarsh. What of the ford? Is it still passable?' Pentrojan forgot about the whispering foot soldiers and spurred his cob forward beckoning the captain to fall in with him.

'The ford is passable general. The Manchians are constructing a pontoon for the War Engines. They should be ready by tomorrow mid day.'

'And the enemy, captain.'

'No trace. Left days ago. They've scuttled back to Dredgemarsh by now.'

'Let them shiver in their crumbling city. We will pitch tent at Grismald Keep tonight. Once we are across the river there is no need to hurry.'

'Yes General. The Keep is prepared for your arrival.' Pentrojan dismissed Luparellus with a casual salute. The two foot soldiers who almost fell foul of Pentrojan dropped back and well out of sight of their general.

Fabian

Chapter 4

The army lumbered towards Grismald Keep, the most remote Dredgemarsh fortification on the eastern edge of Grak's Forest.

At the same time, four men slinked into the forest through the Devil's Cleft on its western perimeter. They decoupled a team of Bear Dogs from a sledge, abandoned the sledge, but kept the dogs in harness. Their provisions were strapped onto three of the bulkiest of the dogs. They slipped into the dark and silent interior of the forest and set out towards Blue Mountain and, unknown to them, the approaching Brooderstalt army.

'Move you brute,' Fabian, the ersatz prince of Dredgemarsh, lashed out with his boot at the lead dog that stood motionless and, with ears flattened against its skull, sniffed the air. The dog responded with a rumbling growl. Fabian moved back. But it was not the futile kick that raised the animal's hackles.

'He senses danger, Sire,' Baldo, one of Fabian's companions, whispered.

'Shut up, Baldo, and move them forward. We may yet have trackers following us from Dredgemarsh.'

Baldo moved to the head of the dog team. He grasped the lead dog's harness and stumbled his way into the sombre heart of Grak's forest. His companion Slevic held onto the traces to the rest of the dog team. Fabian and Grumbolt followed behind.

'Sire,' Grumbolt said and waited for permission to speak.

'I hope, Grumbolt, you are not going to mention my fukking father again.'

'But Sire, surely he will take your part. I still think we should go west to Anselem and find him.'

Fabian spun round and faced Grumbolt.

'My father will never help me.'

'But Sire ... the Brooderstalt ... why would they want to help us ... you I mean? We know they are about to invade Dredgemarsh and this way,' he pointed in the direction they were traveling, 'will take us into Brooderlund. They will kill us. Surely your own father would—'

'Would do nothing.' Fabian snarled. 'My own father is deranged. He despises me for no reason.

'That can't be, Sire. If you—'

'He will listen to traitors like Grunkite before me. He will choose to believe their lies that a canal scavenger is his real son.' There were tears in Fabian's eyes and his voice faltered.

If ever, in his whole life, Fabian had come close to revealing anything of his inner self to another it was at that moment.

'I'm sorry, Sire,' Grumbolt said, and it was clear that the self-seeking sycophant was, for once, genuine. Fabian stared at Grumbolt as if he was about to reveal something else. But the look of vulnerability slowly hardened to the more habitual scowl of distrust. He averted his gaze.

'No we'll find no comfort there. But neither will my accursed father find comfort when he returns.'

'What do you mean, Sire?'

'The canal bastard will be dead. Mordant Skaldar will see to it.'

'Is Skaldar still alive and in Dredgemarsh?' Grumbolt's mouth stood agape.

'This fukking cold. Move Baldo,' Fabian shouted. There was no more talking. As the day wore on, they fell into a rhythm of exertion that masked their pain and fears. Fabian took the lead. His subordinates wondered at the unexpected stamina of their ungraceful prince and his shuffling gait that favoured the left leg. But hour after relentless hour he ran on.

The indolent Grumbolt, always fond of food and drink, began to fall further and further behind till he could no longer see his companions. Fear seeped into his mind and, worse still, began to affect his body. His legs became leaden and the harder he tried to speed up the slower he became. Fear gave way to panic and he started to sense that someone was running after him. He stopped and listened. Nothing. He plodded forward and was aware, once again, that someone or something was stalking him. He stopped but could hear nothing except his own rasping breath and pounding heart. He tried to focus his mind in an attempt to dispel the terror. It's my own footsteps, he thought.

'That's it. What a fool I am.' He laughed and staggered on through the deepening shadows. Each time he rounded a bend in the path, he hoped he would see them in the distance and each time his hopes were dashed. The fierce pain in his chest and legs had, in a strange way, not diminished but distanced itself as if it were no longer a part of him. It felt as if someone else was doing the running, someone else feeling the raking pain of lungs gasping for air. He scanned the gloomy pathways of the ancient forest, seeking out some clues as to the whereabouts of his vanished comrades. He did not see the ghost-like shadows that appeared to flow through the underbrush each side of the path. He did not see the dark ferns sway and whisper and the passage of lean bodies that began to converge on him, silent as the dark shadows.

Then he gave a little gasp of joy. The light of a fire flickered somewhere ahead of him. 'Praise all the saints above,' he gasped. The light vanished and reappeared intermittently as he moved ahead. He cried out, 'I am ... here ... my ... lord…ha…I am…here.' He was near enough now to make out the silhouette of someone crossing in front of the welcoming flame.

Fabian, Baldo and Slevic stood still and listened.

'Sluggard.' Fabian spat into the fire and the other two forced a laugh. After a few more moments they heard, 'Sire, Sire' and they laughed again at the trembling relief in the voice.

'Here Grumbolt, here,' shouted Baldo as he struggled to hold back the dogs that were now straining on their leases, and snarling at the approach of the desperate Grumbolt.

'Back, back you curs.' Baldo shouted, striking out at the lead dog with his short staff. The dog ignored him and stood bristling on the edge of the small clearing that was their camp site.

Then they all heard a sound that made the hair bristle on the back of their necks and their insides churn. The General started to call out again, 'I'm almost ...' A pause and then 'oh no.' And the word 'no' elongated into a sobbing scream. Then the forest exploded into a snarling chorus of a wolf pack tearing its prey asunder. Baldo and Slevic looked in horror at Fabian.

'What shall we do,' Slevic said.

Fabian scanned Slevic's face with black fathomless eyes. 'Secure the dogs. Gather more firewood. Lots of it.'

The terrified Slevic and Baldo with two of the bear dogs on short leashes began to gather what timber they could find without venturing more than a few ells into the surrounding forest. Fabian remained seated as close to the fire as he could get with the remainder of the dogs around him.

They snatched fitful moments of sleep that night. Baldo and Slevic took turns to replenish the fire. The bear dogs were restless throughout the long dark hours and every now and again one or two of them would rise and stare into the pitch-blackness, hair prickling on their backs and low rumbling growls disturbing what little sleep their masters got.

Deep relief settled over the three men when the first hint of a new day was heralded by the natter and cluck of the snow ptarmigan. They relaxed into much needed, though still uneasy, slumber and later, much later, when the first dim rays of the morning began to filter through the dense snow-covered canopy above them, Baldo and Slevic set about preparing a breakfast of pottage and botargo made from the salted roe of the river mullet. This was accompanied by braggot fortified with brandy. They served Fabian first and then ate themselves. Baldo cut chunks of dried chiterlings for the dogs, which they gulped down, eyeing each other and snarling to protect their ration of food.

They set off again. Fabian ordered Baldo to go in front with the lead dog while he followed with four dogs and Slevic took up the rear with a further four. Their progress was sluggish until the stiffness departed from their freezing limbs. Though there were no sightings of the wolves, they were conscious of their presence throughout the day and the odd snap of a breaking twig or swish of disturbed undergrowth kept them fearful and alert. Towards midday they stopped in a coomb just off the main pathway. Exhausted from their exertions, they surrounded themselves with the bear dogs and slept. It was not to last long. Baldo was the first to wake and discoverd water trickling down his kneck. He leaped to his feet. The ground underneath was soaked.

'Fukk,' he shouted. Fabian and Slevic woke instantly.

'What's happening?' Fabian stood up and brushed water from his cloak. He looked up towards the dark overhang of the forest. Small drizzles of water were seeping through, like leaks in the roof of a lofty cathedral.

'The thaw has started. Damn!'

Fabian scrambled up the side of the coomb to the main path followed by Baldo and Slevic with the dogs. They set off at once. This time Fabian set out, at a fast pace, in front of his companions with the lead bear dog on a leash. From above, the melting snow fell in clusters of slush and icy droplets drenching their clothes and covering the ground in a treacherous sludge. Yet somehow the tribulations that beset them spurred Fabian on. He tumbled to the ground several times and his companions, expecting an explosion of anger, exchanged puzzled looks when he scrambled to his feet and plunged forward again without complaint.

The spoilt, former prince of Dredgemarsh, was exulting in his adversity. He no longer felt fearful. For the first time in his whole life, he had no privileged position or title to protect him. He was on his own, like any other man, struggling to survive and, for him, this was strangely thrilling.

He focused his mind on the simple act of moving forward as fast as possible. Every moment he was calculating where he would place his feet, whether he would jump over, run through or around the next large pool on the path. All day, he ran. Baldo and Slevic struggled to keep up. The bear dogs loped along with ease and somewhere out of sight the Blue Mountain wolves slid like smoke through the shadows.

'Sire,' Baldo shouted, 'we can't keep this up.' Fabian as if waking from a dream slowed to a stop and looked around at his two companions. Baldo was bent over, one hand clasped to his chest and Slevic was on his knees and retching. Despite their extreme discomfort they hung on with grim determination to the traces of the bear dogs. Evening was approaching. The forest rain from the melting snow from above was no longer falling and the ground puddles were beginning to ice over.

'We must find shelter and light a fire.' Fabian set off once more but now at a slow walk, all the while scanning the path each side of him. How long they walked they could not tell but relief, at last, came when they found a forester's hut with half a roof.

There was plenty of wood lying about which they hauled into a great pile within the hut and then built a fire below where the roof was torn off. They tied the dogs in front of the open door and under the shelter of the half roof they lay down and slept.

They were too tired to eat or even think about the dangers they were facing.

Chapter 5

Less than two leagues from where the exhausted travellers slept, the freezing night sky above Grismald Keep was illuminated by huge bonfires set up on both sides of the Tuso River. The Keep itself and all the surrounding land up to the perimeter of the forest was also awash with light from the countless smaller fires around which the Brooderstalt soldiers ate, slept and cursed the cold. Icy winds swept down with ever increasing ferocity along the Tuzo Valley from between the dark peaks of Blue Mountain and Wolfspine.

There was constant activity as work parties hauled timber from the forest to feed the great bonfires on the banks of the river. There the Manchian engineers were working feverishly to extend a huge pontoon to carry their war engines across the river. The sudden thaw had caused the Grismald to rise rapidly, turning a typical military task into a difficult race against time.

The hulking war engines stood like brooding giants on the far bank of the river awaiting the completion of the pontoon.

Albrecht Pentrojan paced the watchtower of the keep and every now and then stopped to stare morosely at the frantic work of the Manchians as they screamed out their orders to the grim-faced Brooderstalt soldiers.

'General, you should eat,' Captain Luparellus said as he stepped up onto the watchtower. He proffered a steaming bowl of fish broth and a chunk of wastel bread to his commander.

'Eat?' Pentrojan glared at the captain 'Eat? How can anyone eat? We were supposed to have them across by mid-day. That's what you told me.' He struck the bowl from the captain's hands.

'Sir, the thaw… we did not expect it so soon.'

'Bah,' Pentrojan pounded his clenched fist onto the balustrade of the watchtower.

'This…' he continued pointing down towards the river where the frenzied work was in full swing, 'this is incompetence. We have spent a year, Luparellus, a full year, assembling this army and hiring these Manchian bastards with their war engines and now … we cannot get them across a small fukking river.' His face quivered in fury as he spat out each word like a curse. 'Well Captain, have we nothing to say? Are we to return to Brooderlund, a laughing stock, the great army that failed to take this miserable little shithole of a kingdom?' A white spittle gathered at the corners of his mouth.

'Sir, we'll get them across but even without the Manchian war engines we can easily defeat Dredgemarsh.' Luparellus stammered out the words and kneaded his hands together. A mirthless smile spread across Pentrojan's face.

'Defeat Dredgemarsh you say, defeat ... I don't want to defeat this stinking little kingdom, I want to pound it out of existence. I want to flatten it so that no one will know it ever existed. I want to plough every last stone, every last man, every last woman and every last child into the mud.' Pentrojan's voice was rising with each word uttered. Then he was quiet for a moment, reached out with one hand and grabbed the collar of the captain's brigandine and in a hoarse whisper said, 'If we ... you ... do not get these infernal engines across, then you and every last man of you will pull down Dredgemarsh stone by stone, brick by brick with your bare hands; every last brick with your bare hands. Now get out of my sight.' Just as Luparellus prepared to leave a great shout went up from those working on the Pontoon.

'General, I think they've done it, I think they've done it.'

'Pray that they have Captain ... and Captain I want you and an advance party to move out now. I will follow at first light. Make sure there are no more unexpected problems.'

Lingering on the Keep watchtower he gave a low grunt of satisfaction when he observed Captain Luparellus at the head of twenty fully armed Brooderstalt horsemen gallop across the bailey of the Keep, through the main gate and then westwards.

He glanced once more at the pontoon bridge, which he could see at last spanned the full width of the swollen river. Already he could discern in the flickering light of the bonfires that the first of the giant trebuchets was being inched towards the bridge. He spun around and left the watchtower shouting as he descended the steps into the keep, 'Pyment, hot as hell.'

Luparellus and his horsemen galloped across the surrounding snow-covered sward festooned with camp fires and tents. They slowed to a walk when they entered Grak's forest. In the impenetrable darkness the riders relied on the horses' instincts to guide them along the Dark Road. Every now and then a small break or thinness in the forest canopy above them provide a meagre but welcome illumination from the night sky by which they could reassure themselves that they were still on the right path. In truth, Luparellus was not concerned about the prospect of attack from the enemy but more about the likelihood of natural obstacles to the passage of the war engines through the forest. He was determined that there would not be a repeat of the general's violent outburst. Whenever he felt there might be a serious narrowing of the road or low overhanging boughs he stopped and made a fire to inspect the area and if necessary mark it for the attention of the Manchian team of military engineers who would precede the main army. They made slow but steady headway and after about midday Luparellus sent two riders back to the main camp to report on their progress while he and the remaining men move steadily westwards.

For a few moments the awakening Fabian hovered between a dream of battle, where he rallied his troops against grotesque demons on the battlements of Dredgemarsh, and the reality of the biting cold of the half demolished cabin. He lifted himself unto his elbows. The fire had subsided to a few embers that glowed fitfully in the wind that whistled through the ragged gap of the doorway. But the sounds of battle continued to assail his ears in contradiction to the evidence of his eyes. He winced at the stiffness in his limbs as he raised himself to his feet instinctively drawing his falchion. What he had imagined or dreamed were the sounds of men at war segued into fiendish wailing of wolf and dog in mortal combat. He lashed out with his boot at the slumbering figures of Baldo and Slevic.

'You sons of whores, get up … get up … the fire, get the fire going, you useless cullions.' He ran to the gaping doorway. In the insipid light of dawn, with the bitter wind blasting in his face, all he could see was a writhing mass of shadows. The howls, human-like, of dying creatures being rent asunder unhinged him. He could smell hot blood. He knew it well. It transported him, in that moment, to the night of madness in the Red Tower when he plumbed the depths of depravity and murdered his own mother. He stood transfixed.

From amongst the snarling pack before him a wolf hurtled himself at Fabian's throat.

'Sire.' Baldo screamed, rushed forward and shoved the mesmerised Fabian sideways. They heard the snap of the wolfs jaws and, even in that instant of turmoil, smelt the stench of the animal as is soared just inches from their faces and crashed into the wall behind them. Before the dazed animal could recover Slevic drove his falchion through its famished torso and the animal fell lifeless to the ground. Fabian and Baldo scrambled to their feet and with Slevic moved so that the fire, which was beginning to flicker into flame once more was between them and the entrance to the hut. They piled every scrap of timber they could find onto it while outside the fierce battle continued. The Bear dogs renowned for their strength and courage, though completely outnumbered, stood their ground against the famished Blue Mountain wolves. But the starving marauders were too many and one by one the dogs began to falter and fall under the onslaught 'til the last one standing was the lead dog, Brute. Bloodied and torn he backed into the crumbling doorway of the hut and there held the crazed wolves at bay.

Fabian grabbed a flaming branch from the revived flames, rushed forward and flung it over the head of Brute into the midst of the wolves. The pack were not deterred. 'More, more!' Fabian, pointing at the fire, screamed at Baldo and Slevic. Startled into action they grabbed two more flaming brands and handed them to Fabian. This time he picked his targets and a couple of wolves yelping with pain backed out of the melee. He continued to shout for more firebrands and inch by inch the wolves moved back from the fiery embers that now littered the ground in front of the hut. But they did not go away. They sat or lay in a semicircle disquietingly casual as they waited with an eerie certainty that their quarry would soon succumb. The valiant Brute stood defiant in the hut entrance.

'We have no more wood for the fire,' Slevic could not hide the trembling in his voice.

'The roof. Pull it down.' Fabian barked out the order. Slevic and Baldo set about the task immediately. The low wattle roof, or what remained of it, was poor firing apart from a few crossbeams of rough oak that once supported it.

'If we can hold out 'til daylight,' they may leave and we can get out of this trap' Fabian said.

'We can't go out there, I'm sorry Sire but we can't,' Baldo said.

'Fool, we'll not last another night if we stay here. Grismald Keep is not far. We will be safe there.'

Baldo was not reassured by his master's words. He looked at Slevic seeking support but Slevic shrugged his shoulders and fixed his gaze on the fire. As the morning approached, beams of light from a bright morning sky pierced the forest canopy above the hut. They could see clearly the wolf pack sitting or lying with unnerving nonchalance blocking all avenues of flight. And the encircling pack was beginning to creep towards them despite hesitating now and then when they flung more blazing embers that spat and hissed in the hard packed snow. But the fire was burning low and as it diminished the wall of grey death tightened around the forester's hut. Brute the lone Bear Dog that had lain down when it was clear no attack was imminent now rose stiffly to his feet and faced the implacable enemy. This was the clearest of signals to the men that another attack was about to take place and as one, they drew their falchions and prepared for the final battle.

'Come forward you devils,' Fabian shouted.

The hopelessness and inevitability of his destruction banished fear from his mind. Once again that feeling of elation that had sustained him in his exhausting journey on the previous day suffused every part of his body. His only emotion now was a fierce anger and he braced himself behind the snarling Brute as the wolf pack slithered forward for the kill. The sheer relentless ferocity of the advancing pack drove both Brute and Fabian backwards. The wolves began to pour like grey ghosts through the broken doorway. Slevic the most fearful of the three was the first to fall, his face frozen in a soundless scream of terror as a trio of wolves began to disembowel him before life faded from his eyes.

Fabian was dragged to his knees under the weight of a wolf that fastened itself onto his left side. His brigandine prevented the wolf from piercing his skin but he could feel the vice-like grip of the fierce jaws. He slashed wildly at the animal and in doing so tumbled forward onto the ground. This was it, the end. He was surprised at how calm he felt. The sounds of the savage struggle around him receded. He waited for death.

Death did not come. As if in a dream the wolves melted away. It took some time for Fabian to realise that the battle was over. He struggled to a sitting position and with shaking hands felt for the rear wall of the hut and leaned back against it with a long shuddering sigh. The calm which descended on him, moments before, when he expected to die, vanished and, in its place, shock took hold and he felt warm piss spreading across his thighs.

Before him stood a tall Brooderstalt warrior, a discharged crossbow in his hands and a dead wolf at his feet. Fabian stared at the apparition in front of him. Was this real? Was he dreaming? Was he dead?

'Well now, who do we have here?' Captain Luparellus leaned in towards Fabian, paying particular attention to the finely wrought leather of his brigandine and the jewelled belt and scabbard. Two Brooderstalt soldiers moved in behind

Luparellus, swords at the ready. Baldo cowered in the corner of the hut. Fabian gazed around him as if in a dream.

'Answer the Captain, pig,' one of the Brooderstalts strode forward and kicked viciously at Fabian's extended foot.

'What?' Fabian said, blinking up at the soldier who now stood over him ready to strike again.

'Who are you?' Luparellus said waving the soldier away.

'I am Fabian, Prince of Dredgemarsh.'

'And I am Cawdrult King of Brooderslund,' Luparellus said. His men laughed.

'I'm not lying.' Fabian rose shakily to his feet and faced Luparellus.

'He is not lying,' Baldo said in a hoarse whisper

Luparellus tilted his head sideways and stared at Fabian. 'And why pray,' he said 'would the Prince of Dredgemarsh be in this god forsaken forest in the depths of winter with a few dogs and this pair,' he pointed disdainfully at Baldo and the disemboweled Slevic.

'It's a long story but I have come to talk to King Cawdrult or whoever leads the Brooderstalt army into Dredgemarsh.'

'You will talk to me.'

'Yes, yes, of course. Whatever you—'

'Take that one out,' Luparellus pointed to Baldo. The soldiers beckoned with their swords for Baldo to move out of the hut, which he did, white-faced, casting fearful glances in the direction of Fabian who ignored him. 'And you, Prince of Dredgemarsh,' Luparellus's lips curled in derision, 'stay here. Kill him if he moves.' He addressed another of his men and left the hut. The lacerated Bear dog, Brute, lay mute by the dying fire. Slevic's body lay beside him, eyes open in a face eerily calm and undamaged amidst the bloody mess that remained of his body. Fabian could hear Luparellus shouting orders outside in the harsh guttural dialect of the Brooderstalt.

By mid-day Pentrojan, at the head of the main army, reached a clearing close to the ruined forest hut where Fabian was now held by Luparellus. They halted briefly to eat and rest the animals. Like his soldiers, Pentrojan ate standing by his mount. It was standard marching rations: bread and cheese and a beaker of fortified braggot and honey. He was amongst a small group of officers when Captain Luparellus approached.

'Ah, Captain Luparellus, this is more like it. We will be clear of this forest in another couple of days.'

'General, we captured a couple of men.'

'Natives?'

'Yes Sir, but—' Pentrojan cut him short.

'If they were natives, I presume they are either dead by now or your men are having some sport with them.' The small group of officers that were gathered around Pentrojan laughed loudly.

'No sir.'

'What!' Despite his much-weathered features Pentrojan began to visibly redden.

'One of them claims he is Prince of Dredgemarsh.'

'All the more reason to be dead,' one of the officers said and there was another burst of laughter.

Pentrojan smiled wryly at Luparellus. 'I hope, Captain, you are not becoming squeamish.' More laughter from the group.

Luparellus glared at them. 'I think when you hear him you may change your mind, General.'

'Why should I hear this impostor.'

'I don't think he is an impostor, General.'

'Damn it, Luparellus, bring your Dredgemarsh Prince here. We will deal with him now. Prepare to move out,' Pentrojan shouted, drained his beaker of braggot and flung it back over his shoulder where his alert squire caught it in mid-air and packed it away in the pannier of one of the General's sumpters. Pentrojan mounted and waited impatiently for Luparellus to return. The war engines, which had stopped briefly on the road, began to rumble forward again with shouting and cracking of whips over the heads of the straining musk ox teams. 'Hurry man,' he called out above the horrendous din as Luparellus dragged Fabian into the presence of the general. 'You,' he pointed his finger at Fabian, 'you have one minute to explain who you are and why you should live.'

'I can help you.'

'Help? Who needs help. Look around you, oaf. Your little kingdom will be crushed like an insect.' Pentrojan pointed at the Mancian War Engines trundling by. Fabian hesitated. 'Well, what else, what else, your time is running out.' Pentrojan's horse was becoming restless as if sensing its master's impatience.

Fabian, with the calmness of one who has nothing to lose, stared defiantly at Pentrojan. 'General, you and your whole army will be annihilated.'

'Enough, enough of this buffoonery.' Pentrojan jerked at the reins. 'Move out,' he ordered the officers around him. 'And you sir,' he glared at Luparellus, 'finish him here and follow immediately.'

'You will fail just like you did before, General,' Fabian called out. The words flew through the air like a dagger and all those within hearing experienced a strange feeling of time being suspended. The noise and mayhem of the army rumbling along the dark road seemed to fade into the distance and they were pinioned by an intangible yet powerful sense of foreboding.

'Move out,' Pentrojan's snarled and the spell was broken. The officers looked at each other as if to confirm that they all heard and experienced the same feeling of impending disaster. 'Move out,' he shouted and wheeled his horse back towards Fabian, his right hand grasping for his falchion.

Luparellus stepped forward in front of Fabian. 'General, we must listen.'

'How dare you. Out of my way, Captain,' Pentrojan drew his weapon.

'Sir, they have their own war engine; they call it Firedrake. He swears it will destroy us.'

Pentrojan urged his mount forward pushing Luparellus sideways.

'General, please listen. What have we to lose.' The captain stumbled sideways and Pentrojan raised his falchion to strike Fabian.

'I am the only one who can save you from another defeat.' Fabian, the spoilt and petulant false prince of Dredgemarsh, had an uncanny ability to sense another's weakness. He homed in on the one event in Pentrojan's career that haunted him: his ignominious defeat and expulsion from Dredgemarsh three decades ago. Even the mention of defeat now, no matter how improbable, triggered a tiny ripple of panic deep in Pentrojan's gut. He withheld the blow and with forced calmness addressed Luparellus.

'So be it, Captain. We have nothing to lose. Your prince lives … for now. I will question him later.'

Chapter 6

I s he well enough?' It sounded more like a challenge than a question from Chancellor Grunkite.

'The Prince is strong, recovering fast, but Chancellor, you look unwell. You need rest. You need to eat.' Maester Aidan looked askance at the untouched breakfast pushed to one side of Grunkite's cluttered writing desk .

'No time for that. We do have need of him now. Much as I would wish to give him more time, Dredgemarsh needs its Prince.' Grunkite stood with his back to the blazing fire. Despite the heavy surcoat of broadcloth and a bulky vair-lined mantle, he looked cold with that hollowed out look that signals the first onslaught of age. 'Get him prepared, Maester Aidan. Captain Severino will go with you. He's outside. Bring the Prince back here.

'If that is your wish, Chancellor.'

'Wish. It's not my wish. None of it is my wish, Maester Aidan.'

'I didn't mean—'

'My wish is that the Brooderstalt were not marching through Grak's Forest right now with an army, the size of which, we've never encountered before and with some monstrous war engines that we've never faced before.'

'I'm simply concerned,' Maester Aidan said. 'The Prince has not quite grasped the enormity of his new position and if— '

'Has anyone?' Grunkite glared at Maester Aidan. 'I will wait for him here.' He lowered himself painfully into the sprawling chair beside the fireplace.

Maester Aidan left the Chancellor's room and found Captain Severino in the outer vestibule in deep discussion with a group of officers. The tension was palpable: a tingling in the air that presaged some horror about to descend on them. But with that grim presentiment or because of it, there was a powerful bond of solidarity between them. They listened with unaccustomed attention to what Maester Aidan said to Captain Severino. It was as if they sought some shard of hope, no matter how small, in what anyone had to say.

'Gentlemen,' Severino nodded to two of the officers, 'come along with me. The rest stay here. We'll be back shortly.' Those remaining settled into their seats and waited.

'The old man has something up his sleeve,' one said nodding towards the door of Grunkite's rooms.

'You can be sure of that. That old devil knows a thing or two about surviving,' another responded. They all laughed.

'He can't stop the Yayla River from rising. I've never seen it rise so quickly and the thaw has only started,' a gloomier voice said.

'That's cheerful,' another said, 'even if we fight off the Brooders, we'll drown.' They all laughed again, laughed too loudly, too long.

'You can laugh all you like, but remember last time … stinking water … sickness,' the gloomy one said. No one responded; they were all too well aware of the ominous forces of both nature and the accursed Brooderstalt that, like some unholy conspiracy, filled them with dread. To add to their dark ruminations the snow-filled wind outside began to rise. It moaned like a living creature through the spires and the decayed windows of the turrets above them. They sat in silence after that, each man with his own drear thoughts. Later they were roused by the return of Captain Severino and his two officers in the company of Harry and Maester Aidan.

The gaunt young man, the erstwhile canal boy, looked different to them: taller or nobler or was it simply the knowledge that he really was the Prince of Dredgemarsh. Whatever it was, they nodded in quiet deference.

The door of the Chancellor's room opened to admit Harry and his escorts. Before closing it, Captain Severino addressed his men, 'bear with us gentlemen. We will call on you presently.' So they settled themselves to wait once more, their sporadic attempts at banter a thin veneer over the anxiety that infected their spirits. The only distraction, some moments later, was the arrival of General Hawksfoot and Captain Paine who were ushered into the Chancellor's room.

'The lad's petrified,' The gloomy one piped up again.

A fellow officer jumped to his feet and faced the sepulchral one. 'A turd in your teeth, Egbert. He has more than proved his courage. He survived capture by the Brooderstalt.

'Leave him be, Stigmar. You know what he's like. He's not worth it,' another called out

'Killed more of them than you ever will.' Stigmar continued. 'Survived that murderer, Fabian. Curse him and you.'

'Stigmar, enough.' an older officers put a restraining hand on Stigmar's shoulder. He shrugged it off.

'Queynt.' He spat the word in Egbert's face and sat down, all the while glaring at the morous target of his rage.

But, Egbert was not entirely wrong about the Prince. There was fear in Harry's heart; fear that he could not be what these eminent men wished him to be. He was still Harry Fairgame, brave and confident in his previous constrained world of impoverished canal cleaner turned scholar and trusted assistant to the now dead Professor Quickstrain. Within the bounds of that small world he thrived and knew his worth.

Also, the life-threatening tribulations when forced to serve as a foot soldier and being accused of murder, before the startling revelations of his true identity, left no doubt about his physical and mental courage. But that was of no comfort to Harry now. Absurd as it was, even to Harry himself, he had not managed to shake off the self-doubt that the ridicule and belittling tirades of his impostor grandfather, Shoveler Fairgame, imprinted on his young mind. Was he good enough?

When he stepped into the Chancellor's rooms, he was invited to take his place at the head of a table. All present stood until he was seated. His stomach heaved. He had no experience, no reference point to anchor himself. What was he supposed to say or do. He responded to the brief introductions with a stiff nod. General Hawksfoot and Captain Paine arrived. More awkward introductions from these former superiors of his. Harry didn't notice that the General and the Captain looked just as uncomfortable as himself. No doubt they were remembering their indifferent and even harsh treatment of him when he was no more than just another low-bred and impoverished recruit. They sat at the table to the left of Harry. To Harry's right Grunkite and Captain Severino were already seated. The two officers that Captain Severino nominated to accompany and protect Harry sat in the background with Maester Aidan.

The storm outside intensified. No one spoke. Harry shifted and fidgeted in his seat. Were they expecting him to say something? He could not quell the anxiety on his face when he looked to Grunkite who was reading a missive passed to him by Captain Paine. Grunkite's ever vigilant deputy, Dante Severino leaned in to Grunkite and whispered into his ear.

'Yes, yes, of course.' Grunkite pushed his chair back, leaned on the table and hoisted himself up with a groan. 'Sire, thank you for coming,' he nodded to Harry. 'Gentlemen, I called you here because we face the biggest crisis ever in our history.' He hesitated, looked around to where Maester Aidan and Harry's two guards sat. 'You understand,' he addressed them, 'that not a word said here goes outside that door.'

'These men are trustworthy, Sir. I would vouch for them with my life,' Captain Severino interjected.

Grunkite picked up the missive of Captain Paine and waved it in the air. 'They're here. The cursed Brooderstalt are here. Captain Paine, you have the latest information.' Grunkite eased himself back into his seat.

Captain Paine unfurled a vellum map of Dredgemarsh onto the table. He unsheathed his Seax and, with it, weighed down the curling lower edge and held the top end flat with his left hand; a hand scarred and weathered with half his index finger missing. 'They're here.' He pointed to the crossing at Grismald Keep.' Those around the table leaned forward to see. 'Twenty thousand at least,' he said. There was an audible intake of breath. 'We have two thousand fighting men.'

'That's enough to hold Dredgemarsh against any army,' Captain Severino said, 'no matter how big, they can only attack from the north. Meregloom swamp and the Yayla River protect our flanks and rear.'

'Two thousand might have been enough in the past.' Captain Paine removed his left hand from the map and it curled into a tube. 'But what I saw of their war engines changes everything. They can fire boulders twice as big and twice as far as anything I have ever seen. And with deadly accuracy.'

'You've seen this?'

'With my own eyes.'

'So,' Severino said, kneading his temples with the tips of his fingers, 'they can sit well out of range of our ballistae and mangonels and—'

'Pound us to dust.' Captain Paine thumped the table with his closed fist.

'How long do we have before they attack,' Hawksfoot said.

'Our scouts are watching them,' Captain Paine said. 'They are making their way along the Dark Road. But they are slow. The war engine carts are ponderous. They should reach Devil's Cleft in about two days. From there they will move onto the Vildpline and it will be only a matter of hours before the first assault begins.'

'They are not concerned about our knowing where they are,' Hawksfoot said.

'They have no reason to fear us, General.'

'Damn them to hell?' Grunkite muttered. They lapsed into silence and listened to the doleful gale moaning over Dredgemarsh. Other sounds like the crackling of logs in the fireplace, the murmur of the men outside, the distant rattle of iron wheels on cobbles and the odd slammed door echoing from faraway corridors were poignant reminders of the ordinary life proceeding unheedful of the looming disaster.

'What about Firedrake?' Severino said.

'What is this Firedrake? Paine asked.

'During those long dark years of King Cesare's great silence, he, unknown to any of us, poured out his grief in the study of light.' Grunkite paused to gather his thoughts. 'I don't understand any of this, but it's something to do with the storage and release of light. Professor Quickstrain understood it and using King Cesare's manuscript and papers, began to build a war engine that creates lightning bolts. It was named Firedrake.'

'And do we have this Firedrake?'

'The Professor was murdered before it was finished—'

'So, what's the point of talking about it.' Captain Paine stood, upending the chair he sat on. He paused, combed tense fingers through his tangled blond hair. 'Pardon me gentlemen, Sire, Chancellor but we have no time for this. The Brooderstalt will not be stopped by an imaginary—'

'Captain Paine, you forget yourself, Sir. Be seated.' Grunkite half rose from his seat.

The captain righted his chair, apologised again and sat.

'Our Prince,' Grunkite nodded towards Harry, 'long before anyone discovered his real identity, fools that we all were, was Professor Quickstrain's chosen scholar and confidante in the design and building of Firedrake. Yes, you may well look surprised, Captain Paine, but our Prince, if you'll pardon me Sire, inherited his father's brilliant mind.'

General Hawksfoot cleared his throat.

The uncomfortable memory of the harsh treatment he had meted out to the boy foot-soldier, now prince and heir to the Dredgemarsh throne, was, no doubt, to the forefront of his mind. 'Sire,' he addressed Harry, 'you are the only one who can tell us if there is any hope for the completion of Firedrake.'

All turned towards Harry. Severino, Hawksfoot, Paine and Grunkite; experienced and courageous men, dared not look at each other lest the incipient despair in their hearts, once manifest, would engulf them. Instead, they fixed their eyes on the young prince, in the desperate hope that he could somehow dispel the gloom, could offer them hope. And each one of them felt guilty that they should place such a burden on the young and inexperienced prince.

Maester Aidan stood up. 'Chancellor, gentlemen, this is too much of a—'

'Quiet, Maester Aidan.' Grunkite stretched his hand out, palm towards the physician but did not divert his gaze from Harry. 'Sire,' he prompted, 'can we even hope that Firedrake will be part of our defense.'

In the breathless hiatus that followed, Harry realised that, far from being non-essential in this gathering of the most powerful men in Dredgemarsh, he was, in fact, the only one person that could offer a glimmer of hope. For him it was an epiphany, terrifying but life changing. The confusion that confounded him during his recuperation was put aside. Harry Fairgame, the supposed grandson of a canal cleaner, was no more. In his place was Harry Greyfell, son of Cesare Greyfell and heir to the kingdom of Dredgemarsh.

That momentous internal mental shift, through some inexplicable alchemy, entered the consciousness of those around the table. Was it some physical manifestation, some spiritual resonance that heralded this change in Harry? Was it the way he looked into their eyes, each in turn, some inchoate majesty in his blood made manifest? But they knew with unexpected certainty that they could dispense with the guilt of burdening a callow youth, for here before them was a prince. Even before he spoke, they felt the tenebrous fog of despair shifting.

'We can complete the construction of Firedrake within four days,' Harry said.

'Hah,' Grunkite struck the table with his open palm, 'I knew it, I knew it.' He was beaming at his companions.

'We can build it,' Harry continued, 'but that is just part and a small part of what needs to be done to make it effective.'

'Captain Severino, all officers should hear this. Show them in,' Grunkite said.

There were twelve officers in all representing the field army and the Royal Guard waiting in the outer chamber.

'Be seated wherever you can gentlemen,' Grunkite said as Captain Severino ushered them into the room. 'It's vital that you understand in detail how we plan to repulse and defeat the Brooderstalt horde. Listen carefully. At your pleasure, Sire, continue.'

'We'll complete the construction of Firedrake in four days and have it mounted on the firing rampart facing unto the Vildpline,' Harry said. The officers looked confused.

'Sire, we heard rumours about this Firedrake. What is it?' Stigmar asked the question that was on all their minds.

'Firedrake is unlike any war engine you have ever seen. It fires bolts of lightning.'

'Sorcery,' someone whispered.

'Scientia,' Harry said.

'Allow his majesty to speak without interruption,' Grunkite slapped the table with his open palm again.

With calm deliberation Harry set out a plan for completing the construction of Firedrake and mounting it on the firing rampart by the main gate. He explained that, before Firedrake could work, they would need six quintals of black nephryte crystals for Firedrake and as many wagon loads as possible of golden nephryte boulders. They would have to transport them from the nephryte mines below Rim Wood. He explained in detail how they would lay the golden nephryte boulders on the Vildpline in the path of the approaching Brooderstalt army, not as physical barriers, but as targets for Firedrake to unleash its lightning bolts. The more Harry talked and explained the more animated and confident the officers became.

Grunkite marvelled at the natural ease and authority of this transformed Harry, and, despite the incredible dangers facing them, he felt, for the first time in many months, that there was hope. For a brief few moments, his thoughts drifted away from their discussion and he observed Harry with a kind of wonder and joy in his heart. Harry was facing him now and was saying something.

'Chancellor, Chancellor,' Harry reached out and placed his hand on the old man's arm, 'are you unwell?' Grunkite covered Harry's hand with his swollen arthritic fingers.

'I've never been better … Harry,' he whispered the word Harry 'never been better.' The other men exchanged bemused glances. Grunkite glared at them, cleared his throat and said, 'Well, gentlemen what are we all staring at? Let's get on with it.' Captains Paine and Severino exchanged wry smiles.

'Sire, Chancellor, may I ask a question?' one of the officers stepped forward.

'Speak.'

'What of the King. Will he be returning soon.'

'The King,' Grunkite said, 'along with the Knights of Anselem could still be in Lycia defending it against Manchia, or he may be returning already. We don't know.'

Captain Paine interjected. 'We must assume we are on our own. That is all that—' his words were cut short by wild ringing of the campanile bell.

'Brooderstalt!' one of the officers whispered.

'Brooderstalt!' another officer said and the word spread throughout the room.

'Stop.' Captain Paine held up his hand. It can't be the Brooderstalt. It's impossible. You,' he pointed to one of his sergeants, 'Stigmar, go and see what's happening.'

'In the meantime, gentlemen,' Grunkite said, 'we will continue where we left off.'. 'The King knew Cawdrult's Brooderstalt would march on us at the same time as Luther's Manchians attacked Lycia. We can allow neither of these tyrants to succeed. What's happening or has happened in Lycia, we don't know. We can only hope the King returns soon. For now, Sire, can you continue with what needs to be done to have Firedrake ready.'

The Campanile bell was still flinging out its discords against the roaring gale. Harry finished his explanation of Firedrake to the distracted officers and what might be achieved by this strange weapon. When he finished the campanile bell went silent and Harry repeated the salient points of the required preparations.

'Now would be a good time to break from our discourse.' Grunkite said. 'Captain Severino, send word to the kitchens that we wish to eat. They're awaiting our call.'

Quietness descended on the room. A strange sense of the surreal, of something dreamlike and intangible enveloped them. Death was on the march, seeking them out, a wondrous war engine that could mimic the thunder and lightning of the heavens just might protect them if and only if the boy Prince, once an anonymous canal urchin, could somehow transform into something beyond their imagining. They sat together in the heart of Dredgemarsh, the elements howling about them and they waited for food. That most mundane act, eating, would be an act of defiance, a repudiation of death and for many a distraction from the inevitable horrors of war. The food came quick and hot.

Bella Crumble, mistress of the kitchens, with her assistants erected two trestle tables, set out trenchers of brown bread and filled them from a steaming vat with a thick stew of meats: pork, chicken, venison, wild fowl and slices of bartago. They ladled in chopped cabbage, turnip, potatoes and peas. A wooden spoon and a beaker of braggot was placed next to each trencher. Great wedges of cheese and wastel bread were laid out in the centre of the trestle tables and on a small side table sweet doucettes and fruit were piled up for later.

'Eat hearty, men,' Grunkite said. And they did. For the briefest of periods the assembled officers, though not forgetting, choose to relegate their fears to some mental holding place that permitted them to imagine that all was under control. They ate, drank, chatted and argued. By mutual unspoken consent they avoided discussing the horrors that would soon engulf their world. But the spell was sundered when Stigmar walked into their midst with a one-armed man. A shroud of silence settled over the assembly.

'Sire, Chancellor,' a wide-eyed Stigmar, snow in his hair and the folds of his capuchon, picked out Harry and Grunkite in the melee of bodies scattered around the room eating and drinking, 'it was a flood warning.' The Yayla is now above the level of the aquaducts and still rising.'

'I told you. Didn't I tell you?' a voice said.

'Shut up Egbert,' several voices responded.

'Stigmar,' Harry was the first to respond, 'what about the run-offs and drainage chambers.'

'I don't understand these things, Sire, but Eudo the Water Bailiff does.' He beckoned his one-armed companion to step forward.

'We know each other. Eudo, what is happening?'

Eudo swallowed hard and began in a trembling voice. 'The run offs are all under water … Sire and ...' His voice wobbled out of control.

'The past is forgotten, Eudo. Just answer the questions.'

Eudo, once Harry's overseer on the canals resumed. 'Thank you, Si, — '

'What about the drainage chambers?'

'We are opening as many as possible. The real problem, Sire, is the sluices on the aqueducts. They are jambed with ice and we need to open them wider but nothing's working. If they collapse under the pressure, we will have to abandon our efforts to control the flooding.'

Once again, all heads turned to focus on Harry and he along with everyone else realised for the second time how his previous life of drudgery on the canals fitted him for this new challenge. 'How long have we got?'

'A day at most, Sire.'

'We'll find a way, Eudo. Stay, eat and you also, Stigmar.' Two officers made space for them at one of the trestle tables.

Chancellor Grunkite rose to his feet. 'Gentlemen.' his voice was hoarse and low. The older men shushed their loquacious comrades. 'Gentlemen,' he repeated, 'enough of talk. We know what faces us. We know what has to be done. Finish eating. Go to your quarters and find what sleep you can. There will be no rest after that. When the campanile bell rings again, assemble with your men on the Grand Plaza.'

Chapter 7

The pretence was over. Death was creeping across the land towards Dredgemarsh like an obscene reptile. It was not that the citizens were unaware of the threat before them, but they chose to believe that somehow it would just go away or would be handled by those in charge. Someone would take care of it. But fear, infectious and terrifying insinuated itself through the snow-covered narrow streets and laneways of the old city. Before that, the butchers, bakers, street hawkers, jongleurs, tavern men and women, the guilds, the canal men, the old and the young immersed themselves in their work and play with single-minded vigour as if such diversion could put a stay on the inexorable approach of the Brooderstalt.

By mid-day the grand plaza was reverberating with the clamour of women, children, the sick and the old. They streamed in from every corner of the city. Snow was still falling, gently now, a soft dreamlike backdrop to the turmoil of the frightened citizens. Captain Severino's officers and soldiers were directing them onto every conceivable class of horse drawn conveyance. There were the long six-horse transporters used by the army, the massive mine drays, turf carts drawn by oxen, tiny market traps and private carts of all types sequestered by the army that morning. Covered wagons of food, water, blankets and medical supplies were already packed and ready for departure. The pristine white carpet of morning snow turned into a brown slush of steaming dung and horse piss. The oxen bawled out their protests. The horses stamped and nickered their anxiety into the freezing air. At first the children laughed and whooped in excitement. The young mothers tried to be cheerful for their sake and the old women and men sat grim-faced in their allotted places. But, as the crowd swelled, the fear grew. The children stopped their play and huddled close to their mothers whose faces were filled with dread. Overhead brooding clouds rolled and furled in the dark sky.

'I am not going and that is that.' Lia threw her hairbrush onto the dressing table, knocking over a bottle of lavender water.

'What have you done now?' Rebecca whipped away the towel which she had just placed across Lia's shoulders for her morning toilet and began to mop up the spilt liquid. 'And,' Rebecca continued, wiping the dressing table with unnecessary force, 'there is no question of us remaining behind. You heard your father; it's far too dangerous.'

'Why should we have to go?' Lia grabbed the brush and attacked the golden tangles of her hair.

'You know quite well, Lia. What do you think would happen to us if we were caught by the Brooderstalt?'

'We won't be caught. And anyway, I would kill myself before allowing them to get their filthy hands on me.'

'Give me patience. You've no say in this,' Rebecca prized the hairbrush from Lia's hand and resumed a gentler brushing. 'And your father, the council, the prince himself will insist you leave for your own safety.'

'Why would he care?'

'Why would your own father care? Now you're being silly beyond belief.'

'No, not my father.'

'Ah … ah … now I see. The Prince.' Rebecca said, hands clamped on hips. 'I told you he is far too busy for personal things. You must know that.'

'It's not that at all. I just don't like being ordered around by … by ….'

'The Prince,' Rebecca finished the sentence, a sardonic grin on her lips.

The door was flung open. General Hawksfoot swept into the room.

'Ye Gods! Are you not ready yet, girl?'

'Father, this is my private room, you should knock before—'

'No time for this nonsense. Rebecca, get her and yourself ready now. Two of my men are outside to escort you to your carriage directly.'

Lia stood and faced the general. 'Father what is to become of us?' All the feigned petulance was gone from her voice. Hawksfoot stepped forward and folded his arms around his only child. 'Please be safe, father.'

'Try not to worry, dear daughter. When this is all over, and it will be soon, I will come for you in Anselem.' He released her from his embrace. 'Rebecca,' there were tears in his eyes, 'I … I …'

'I know what to do, General,' she said and patted his arm. With a grateful nod he left his daughter and her companion. For some time after he departed there was silence until Lia spoke.

'Rebecca, my hunting clothes. We will ride, leave the carriages for the children and our elder folk.' Rebecca was not surprised by the change of tone in her young oft-times volatile mistress. Those childish outbursts of Lia's were a way of relieving the frustrations of a keen mind constrained and frustrated by the customs and expectations of the ruling class.

Without fuss they prepared themselves for the long arduous journey to Anselem and within the half-hour were riding through the narrow streets towards the grand plaza. Heads turned to gaze at the beautiful young woman with the silver fox fur montero and cloak riding a jet black palfrey, and many a mind was buoyed by the illogical thought that nothing bad could happen with such beauty in their midst. The two soldiers assigned to escort the young women guided them through the narrow streets and alleyways avoiding as best they could the ever-growing throng that was converging on the Grand Plaza. They reached the end of Baker's Alley where it opened onto the North Parade. They could hear a deafening roar of voices chanting and shouting with excitement.

'Wait here, my lady,' one of the escorts said and galloped to the end of the alley.

'Well what is it?' Lia asked when the breathless escort returned.

'I'm not sure. The new prince is there. It's like a parade or something.' A loud hurrah and clapping boomed out.

'We can avoid the crowd if we go back and circle round through the market square.' The escort shouted to make himself heard.

'No, move forward, move forward.' Lia coaxed her palfrey into a trot and reached the end of the alleyway to witness an astonishing sight.

Harry was approaching on foot along the centre of the North Parade, flanked by a couple of nervous officers of the Royal Guard. They were striding along at the head of a long procession of canal men, three abreast, leading their ponies and drays like proud charioteers going into battle. Crowds along each side of the street cheered them on.

'What's happening?' one of Lia's escort asked an onlooker. The man just shrugged his shoulders.

Lia focused on Harry alone. The noise and chaos around her began to recede and all that was left was the image, the bright luminous image of Harry, Prince of Dredgemarsh. A fierce desire made her gasp aloud. Passing by the junction where she sat astride her palfrey, for no apparent reason, he turned and looked straight at her. This was not a time for coyness. Lia did not divert her eyes. They held each other's gaze. There was no pretence, no game. Words were unnecessary. She knew then, as she had always known, deep in her heart, that the bond between them was irrevocable no matter what happened. He slowed to a halt in those few moments but the canal men began to bunch up behind him.

Harry faced forwards once more and resumed his march. She watched him go and the incredible elation she felt dissolved and in its place grew an awful dread that they might never meet again.

'Be safe, dearest Harry,' she whispered to herself, 'be safe.' As if he heard her, Harry looked over his shoulder and raised his hand in salute, a confirmation of what had just passed between them. She smiled and nodded to him and resolved that no matter what happened she would see him again.

Chapter 8

The oak stairway, hidden in the shadows of the armoury, groaned under the weight of General Hawksfoot and Chancellor Grunkite. They left their wet footprints and scatterings of snow on each worn step as they ascended.

'Here we are, Chancellor. Ideal for our command centre, don't you think?' said Hawksfoot. His voice echoed in the empty room at the head of the open stairway. 'Housed one hundred and fifty armoury apprentices, squires and stable lads at one time.'

Grunkite heaved himself up the final step and nodded his head in approval. 'Good, good.' He gasped for breath.

The hollow sound of their footsteps on the dust covered floor was amplified and bounced to and fro off the bare walls and high ceiling. Grunkite approached a window, pushed aside a curtain of cobwebs and stared out at the cavalcade of carriages, walkers and riders trailing through the freezing sludge across the plaza and out through the main gate of Dredgemarsh. Children wailed and old women keened as the endless procession trundled by. *Anselem is a long way*, Grunkite thought. *Are we too late?*

'Maps, and tables are on their way,' said Hawksfoot. There was no response from Grunkite. Hawksfoot moved closer. 'Chancellor, I was saying that the maps—'

Grunkite raised his hand and without turning said, 'I know, I know General; they are on their way, but what about some heat. I can't feel my hands and feet in this blasted cold.'

'We'll have that lighting in no time,' Hawksfoot pointed to a massive iron stove in the middle of the room.

'I presume Captain Severino's already left.' Grunkite continued to stare through the window.

'As planned. With thirteen mining wagons.'

'When is the Prince due back?'

'When the canal men know what he wants of them. Hopefully they can avert the flooding or at least control it. The Yayla is still rising fast.'

'Can we trust these canal men, General?'

'From what I have seen, Chanceller, they'll do anything for their new Prince We need have no fears on that count. They trust him. Ah! At last.' There was a loud commotion and some swearing from the stairwell.

'Hold it, hold it, Hawksfoot will have your balls if you drop it. Lift it up . If it was Gretina's skirt you'd be quick enough.

'Blast you and Hawksfoot,' another voice bellowed.

Bemused, Hawksfoot and Grunkite watched a man staggering backwards from the stairs, carrying one end of a large table As he struggled into the room another head, grimacing with the effort of carrying the other end of the table, appeared above the stairwell. This carrier spotted Grunkite and Hawksfoot.

His companion, still unaware of his audience behind him, said, 'You're right. Fukk Hawksfoot. The old bastard should try carrying this himself.' His companion's red face already a mask of agony turned to a rictus of horror.

'What's wrong with you now,' the first carrier said, dropped his end of the table on the dusty boards and leaned forward on the shiny surface. His cheeks were blowing like a small bellows. His companion dropped the other end of the table and, as surreptitiously as he could, nodded in the direction of Hawksfoot. His companion, still blowing hard, glanced over his shoulder. He froze.

'Over here, by the window, gentlemen,' Hawksfoot said in an exaggerated polite tone and exchanged a wry smile with the chancellor. The men, now demure, silent and with panic etched on their faces did as directed and tip-toed to the stairwell at which point they scurried away at speed. A quietness settled over the room accentuated by the fast fading sound of their retreat. Grunkite and Hawksfoot smiled, looked at each other and erupted into uncontrolled laughter.

'Oh, I enjoyed that, General,' Grunkite said as the laughter died down. 'That was good,' and both men roared laughing again. But, despite their attempts to sustain the mood, the grim reality of the disaster facing them began to reassert itself and the laughter grew brittle.

It was not long before the gloomy silence was broken once again by another visitor.

'Chancellor, General.' Captain Paine greeted them in his usual brusque manner. He unfurled a large map of Dredgemarsh on the table. The two older men joined him.

'We think they are here, about two days away from Devil's Cleft.' The captain pointed out the position on the map.

Hawksfoot groaned. 'If they reach Devil's cleft in two days we are doomed. Captain Severino will be too late to lay out the Nephryte boulders across the Vildpline. Without them in place, Firedrake is useless, and without Firedrake there is no hope.'

'We may as well leave for Anselem with them.' Grunkite pointed through the window towards the Plaza and the tail end of the departing citizens.

'There is no way we can stop the Brooderstalt army,' said Captain Paine.

An uneasy silence settled over the trio for an uncomfortably long time until at last it was broken by Hawksfoot.

We can't stop them, but maybe we can slow them down.,' he said.

'How?' said Grunkite.

'Captain, if you were to take a company of men, foresters mainly, and moved as fast and as far as you can into Grak's Forest,' Hawksfoot ran his finger along the Dark Road on the map, 'and felled as many trees as possible across their intended path, then— '

'Yes, yes,' Grunkite was nodding his head, 'that would slow the bastards down.'

'They cannot take their war engines on any other route, other than the Dark Road.' Captain Paine rappeded his closed fist on the map. It could work, by God.'

Grunkite slapped Hawksfoot on the back.

'Don't delay another moment, Captain,' Hawksfoot said, 'Go now, and may the saints and martyrs be with you.' The Captain saluted the two elders and left.

Grunkite turned back towards the window. The plaza viewed through the veil of snow looked so tranquil and empty now. Two subdued table carriers returned, carrying maps and a slate board. The General was talking to them and pointing to the stove.

Grunkite was thinking of his old friend, Professor Quickstrain, and wondering if he would soon follow him to his eternal rest. It would be a happy release from the pain of watching Pentrojan and his Brooderstalt demolish his beloved Dredgemarsh. He watched the main gates of the city closing behind the last few stragglers. Now all that were left were soldiers and able-bodied civilians, who volunteered to stay and help to defend their city in whatever way they could.

Below the window where he stood, a giant low-slung dray was being maneuvered in close to the ramp that was used for loading heavy equipment from the armory forges. The Marshal At-Arms bellowed orders at the labourers who were hauling Firedrake out, section by section, and strapping it, with the utmost care, onto the dray. When it was loaded, a carter leading a team of six cobs hauled the precious cargo across the grand plaza towards the gate towers where it would be hoisted onto the firing rampart and assembled. Not for the first time Grunkite wondered if their reliance on this strange weapon, without Professor Quickstrain, was foolish and misguided,

'Too much. Harry's too young, it's unfair to expect this of him. But what else can we do?' Without realising it, Grunkite was speaking out loud.

'Chancellor?' Hawksfoot looked alarmed 'What do you mean, Chancellor?'

'What? … oh never mind, General.' Grunkite shook his head like one emerging from a dream. 'Tell me again. The Prince, is he is coming back here to the armoury?'

Hawksfoot shrugged his shoulders.

'Time, if we had a little more time,' said Grunkite.

'Yes, time is our enemy, but, look here.' Hawksfoot pointed towards the slate board where he had begun to create a list of the tasks that required action. Grunkite showed little enthusiasm at first, but as they began to fill in all the details and make contingency plans, the despondency that beset him earlier began to dissipate. He started to fulminate and call down the wrath of heaven on the Brooderstalt.

'That brute, Pentrojan and his whoremaster of a king, Cawdrult, will be taught another lesson by Dredgemarsh.'

Hawksfoot laughed. 'While you're here, Chancellor, these Brooderstalt are doomed.'

Grunkite stared at the General for a moment and then, punching him on the shoulder, grinned and said 'yes, as long as I'm here.' He glanced towards the windows and his demeanor changed. 'Has it grown dark of a sudden, General, or do my old eyes deceive me.'

Both men approached the sleet-lashed windows.

'Dark as night, Chancellor, and St Johannes has not yet rung nones.

A blinding flash flickered on and off for several seconds illuminating, in its stark light, the drear spectacle before them. A savage rumbling, so loud that the two men clasped their hands over their ears, shook the fabric of the building.

'S'lids,' exclaimed Grunkite. Outside, dense clouds hung low and ominous over the city. The snow cascaded down. In the west the sky bloomed and darkened constantly, each cycle followed by the crash of thunder. 'It will be heavy going for the women and children on Storn Way.'

'My God, they are walking straight into the tempest. This and the Yayla already above flood level.' There was a hint of panic in Hawksfoot's voice.

'Once they get to Anselem they'll be safe. But what about Meregloom, General?'

'It's already like a vast ocean, Chancellor.'

Grunkite turned towards the newly-hung wallmap and after examining it for a few moments pointed to where the vast Meregloom enveloped the full lenght of the eastern and southern city walls of Dredgemarsh, and where the surging Yayla flowed along the full length of the western wall.

'At least there is no possibility of any surprises from the rear or either side. They have no option but to face us and come straight down the Vildpline.'

'Only one way into Dredgemarsh,' replied Hawksfoot.

'And one way out,' said Grunkite, 'if the accursed flood doesn't sweep us all away.'

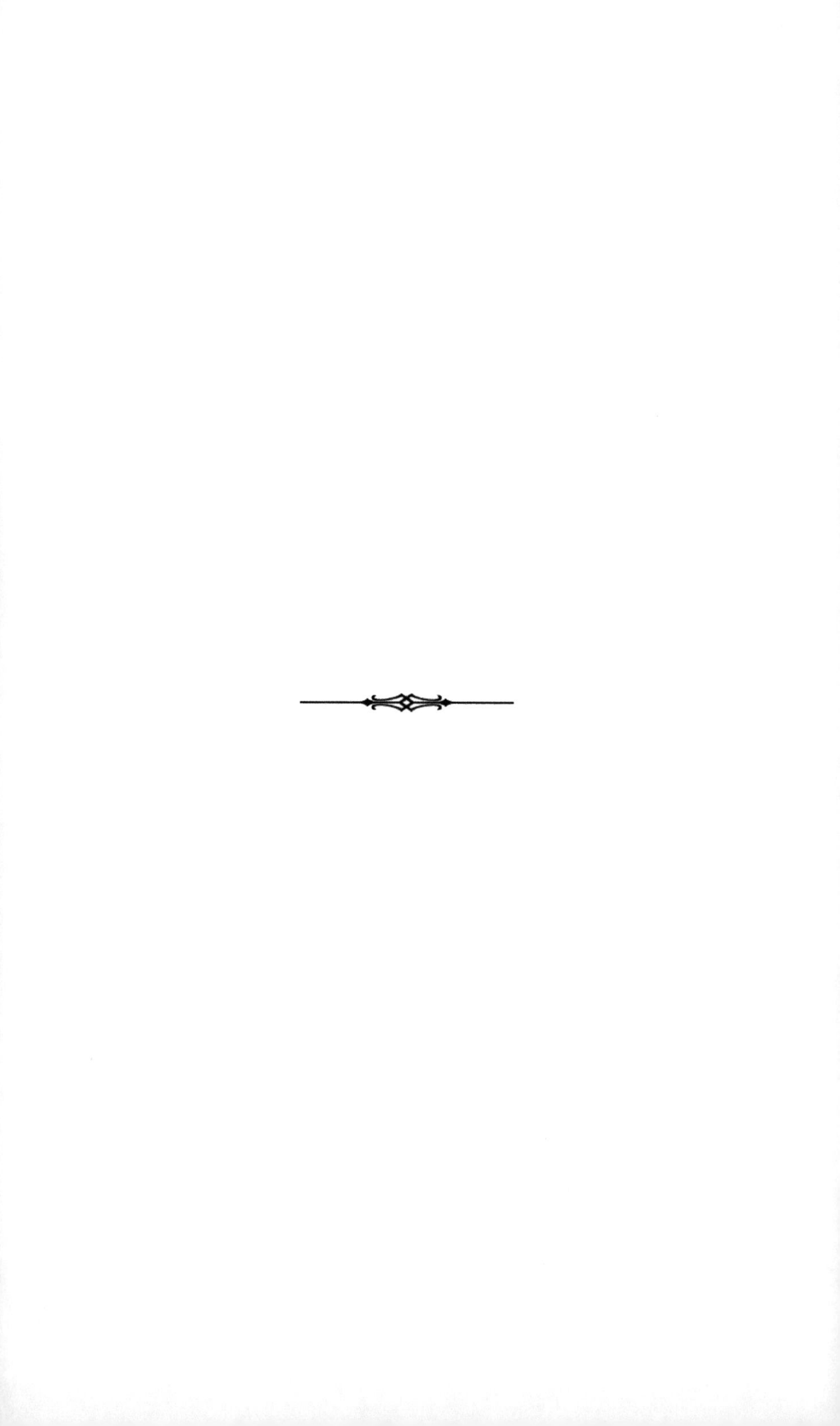

Chapter 9

The source of the Yayla river lay high in the grey wintry peaks of the Anselem Mountains. It tumbled from those distant heights to Green Valley, through Lake Tranquil, past the southern end of Rim Wood, across the western regions of the Vildpline and slammed straight onto the western wall of Dredgemarsh. The great wall, like a colossus, repelled the roaring waters that bucked and spewed against its green algae covered flanks as it had done for centuries. The swirling waters spun southwards and dropped through series of weirs by more than two hundred feet. When it reached the Southern end of the west wall it swept over a fifty foot cliff, a foaming cataract swallowed by Meregloom Swamp, a vast decaying morass that enveloped the southern and eastern regions surrounding Dredgemarsh.

Below the surface of those furious waters racing along the western wall, sluice gates at regular intervals opened into a network of aqueducts and canals. These ran deep below the city streets and like the external river dropped in level through a series of underground weirs as they flowed from west to east under the city and disgorged themselves through another array of sluices on the eastern wall and into the all-embracing Meregloom swamp.

Watermills and turbines harnessed the power of the flowing waters through these canals to grind grain, control airflow to the heating furnaces and air vents that warmed the royal quarters and many of the great public buildings. Hoists, lifts, fullers' pounding-engines and the giant metal-working-engines in the armoury forges all derived their power from the water. It was this reliance on the water that necessitated the endless day after day clearance of these sub-terra canals. It was more than a poetic conceit to say that the waters of the Yayla were the lifeblood of Dredgemarsh and the canal network its arteries.

With the thaw, the Yayla was more than twenty feet above the sluices and still rising. Some of the canals and aquaducts were already overflowing when Harry and his ragged army of canal men descended deep down to the base of the western wall. The roar of the raging torrent from the Yayla through the sluice gates and giant rusting conduits was unbearable and they pulled the flaps of their monteros tight around their ears.

'We have got to reduce the flow,' Harry shouted to one of the more senior canal men. 'There, there' he pointed through the gloom to where their flickering lanterns revealed the contours of a massive iron capstan with its protruding ten-foot levers and circular path for men or beasts that might turn it. As they got closer, they could see that the capstan connected to the first sluice gate was covered in a thin layer of ice. The man nodded to Harry and began to unload timber from his dray.

'You three help him.' Harry directed. They built a fire with a couple of large vats full of water slung over the flames. While they were doing this, Harry dispatched the remaining men in groups of four to the other sluices instructing them to do the same as the first team. When the vats of water were boiling they poured them over the frozen cogs and spindles of the capstans. It took three vats of boiling water before the first engine succumbed to their straining muscles and broke its icy bonds. The men punched the air and shouted in triumph. It sounded small and somehow pathetic against the monstrous yowl of the floodwaters. The Royal guards who accompanied Harry and who, at first, were suspicious and aloof from the lowly canal men were now laughing and shaking hands with everyone around them and, without bidding, joined their rough companions at the capstans. They managed to reduce the flow of the water and set off to the next sluice beyond where the other teams of canal men were working. Harry, left this ragged army doing battle with the Yayla.

'Well Sire?' was all Grunkite could say when Harry entered the room, a pool of water forming around his feet from his sodden clothes.

'The flooding is contained … for now, Chancellor,' said Harry.

'At least that.' Grunkite sighed. 'At least that.'

'Sire let me take your cloak.' Hawksfoot without waiting for a reply peeled the wet cloak from Harry's shoulders and then like a fussy parent took Harry's arm and led him over to the stove. The Chancellor and Hawksfoot explained every details of their plan. Harry listened intently. When they finished, he spoke.

'Gawan is working on the final reflector for Firedrake. I will visit him as soon as we are finished here. It must be completed by tomorrow. After that, we wait for Captain Severino's return with the Nephryte and hope Captain Paine can somehow delay the Brooderstalt.

'Before you go, Sire.' Hawksfoot removed his own cloak and handed it to Harry. Harry nodded his thanks, donned the cloak and left. The thunder rattled overhead and the snow turned to sleet. Grunkite and Hawksfoot stared through the windows that rattled under the howling cataclysm.

'It's like the end of time,' Grunkite said.

Chapter 10

The sleet pounded the steaming backs of the draft horses and oxen as they hauled the wagons and carriages through the snow and mud on Storn Way. Captain Severino's troopers hauled a broken wagon to the side of the roadway and shouted at the malingering passersby to keep moving. It was late afternoon and the evacuees looked weary. Dense clouds above them took on a frightening solidity; inverted mountains spewing lightning and fire from their innards. Thunder ripped through the valley. Children whimpered and clung to their quaking mothers. The snow kept falling. Men tried to hide the fear in their eyes.

'Captain, they can't go on much longer, a sergeant called out.

'Keep them moving. They can rest overnight in the woods by Lake Tranquill.'

Aye, Captain.'

Captain Severino pulled to the side of the road with his sergeant. 'If they get a night's rest and some hot food you should be able to reach Boar's Tusk by this time tomorrow.

Another night's rest and then a nonstop climb with short breaks to Anselem.'

'I understand, Captain, but I would rather go with you. I want to fight the Brooderstalt scum, not run away.'

'I need you to lead our people safely to Anselem, Segeant Bertols. Who knows what dangers lie ahead. Take ten troopers with you.'

A short time later thirteen empty mining wagons peeled off from the dismal procession of Dredgemarsh citizens. Captain Severino and thirty mounted soldiers also turned aside with them. For a few brief moments they looked back at the bedraggled horde streaming past, wet, cold and frightened. There were cries of dismay when some of the them realised that Captain Severino was leaving them. But Segeant Bertols and his ten troopers reassured them and the long caravan moved on.

Had he stayed longer the Captain might have seen two saddled but riderless horses hitched behind one of the smaller carriages on their way to Anselem. One of the horses was a fine-boned black palfrey.

The Captain and the mining wagons set their course north towards the Nephryte quarries. They could see no more than twenty ells ahead of them but they knew that once they kept Rim Wood and its towering cliff face on their right-hand side they would come to their destination. It was well past mid-day before they reached the quarry. Without pausing to rest or eat the wagoners and the soldiers set to work loading the wagons with Nephryte boulders that lay strewn in heaps around the quarry.

'Captain, Captain!' a soldier, who had hauled back the drenched canvas cover from one of the wagons, called out. When Severino looked into the wagon his face reddened and the urbane and controlled Captain glared at the two wet and bedraggled young women who stood up to face him.

'What … what stupidity is this?' he shouted. 'Answer me now.' It was a rare sight to see Severino so angry.

Lia, though wet and begrimed threw her shoulders back and said, 'We have decided to return to Dredgemarsh with you.'

'You. You have decided. You reckless child. You do not decide anything. Your father, the army council, the Prince of Dredgemarsh, they are the ones who decide, not a stupid girl.'

Lia's lips trembled and for an instant she looked unsure and even frightened but she controlled herself. 'I don't care what you think, Captain. We are going back to Dredgemarsh with you.' She returned Severino's furious gaze.

He breathed deep through flared nostrils and turned his face skywards as if to quench his anger in the cascading rain. After a few moments he lowered his gaze.

'Get out.' His voice was cold. 'You two stay out of our way.' He turned his back on Lia and Rebecca as if they did not exist anymore. 'Continue as you were, men,' The young women obeyed without speaking, and searched to find some shelter from the rain and Captain Severino's fury.

Chapter 11

Darkness settled over Dredgemarsh. Rain fell relentlessly. Deep in the bowels of the city the canal men defied aching bones and laboured to open all the run-offs and drainage chambers downstream from the sluices on the west wall that they had partially closed. Even with the restricted flow, the Yayla, still rising to unprecedented levels, was forcing water through at such pressure that the men could barely work fast enough to stay ahead of the cataracts of freezing water that threatened at any moment to engulf them.

'If the head sluices go, and they will, we're all doomed,' a tall ragged canal man said.

'Shut your damn mouth, Shem, and just get on with it,' his companion hissed. 'We fukking know and don't need reminding.'

'Just pointing out what you're all ignoring,' Shem began

'Well don't,' several more of the canal men shouted. Shem grumbled and reached his long arms down under the two-foot of water that covered the chamber floor and hauled open the water vent with a massive heave. The floodwater began to spiral down the conduit behind the vent to the next water table in the ever-descending internal network of weirs. The exhausted men relaxed for a few moments, but, before they could recover from their exertions in that chamber, their foreman was roaring at them

'Next level, next level. Let's show them what canal men can do.'

As they worked their way eastwards under the city, those above ground tried to maintain their spirits by carrying out their normal duties. But it was not a normal situation and everyone knew it. Bella Crumble who refused to leave with the caravan of women and children was insisting that the kitchen lad Squint should clean and polish the buttery tables like any other day. Squint set about the task with little enthusiasm, muttering his complaints to Miss Lowsleg, who also refused to leave Dredgemarsh if Bella Crumble was not leaving.

'Why polish tables for the Brooderstalt,' he said, 'we should just abandon the city.'

'What kind of treacherous talk is that,' Bella Crumble who was closer than he thought was red-faced and bristling.

'You just listen here, you little coward. No Brooderstalt will come into this buttery without my say-so. We thrashed them before. We'll do it again.' She slapped the wet cloth in her hand down onto the table. 'Now do your duty.' She poked him in the chest and the tiny man staggered backwards his lips trembling.

'I don't want to die.' The half century old kitchen lad said in a trembling whisper. The stern look vanished from Bella Crumble's face.

'You're not going to die, you daft little man,' she wrapped her arms around Squint and squeezed him tight to her great bosom. 'No one is going to harm any of Bella Crumbles people. Now, like a good man, clean the tables like you always do.'

'Yes, Mistress Crumble,' Squint sobbed.

'Good!' she said and released him from her arms. She walked back to the cooking area and assumed a stern look once more. 'No more shilly shallying,' she said and Cook Maester Ratchett, her husband and, in theory, her superior in the kitchen, continued in silence to slice the hot moile and lay it out with the trenchers of steaming chitterlings while Miss Lowsleg filled beakers from a great puncheon of braggot and set one beside every trencher.

'Listen. Vespers are being rung in St. Johannes. Those poor young men will be coming off the evening watch. They must be starving,' Bella Crumble spoke to no one in particular. She nodded in satisfaction at the array of steaming trenchers and beakers of beer. The doors of the buttery opened and one of the evening watch crews, four men streaming water from every crease and crevice of their clothing, tumbled in. Their faces were grey, their eyes fearful.

'Come on, come on, sit down.' Bella Crumble beckoned them to the tables closest to the central stove. They hesitated, looking down at the pools of water gathering around their feet.

'Oh forget about that,' Bella said, 'What harm can a bit of water do.' Leopold Ratchett exchanged a disbelieving glance with Miss Lowsleg and then looking back at Bella he noticed with a little shock that her eyes were moist and she was twisting the cloth around and around in her hands. The men sat and began to eat.

'Where's our young Prince?' Bella asked.

'We don't know, Bella,' the sergeant of the watch answered. 'They've finished work on that Firedrake engine some time ago. He was with them then but we haven't seen him since.'

'He's not with Grunkite either,' another said stuffing a large chunk of moile into his mouth.

'Will the Fire … thing save us?' Miss Lowsleg, stared wide-eyed from behind Bella in an uncontrolled warble of anxiety, fully expecting to be rebuked for asking a stupid question. But to her surprise, when no immediate response was forthcoming, Bella said,

'Well, will it?

The sergeant removed a piece of gristle from his mouth. 'Firedrake. We don't know what it can do, Bella, but we do know that if it's to do anything we need Captain Severino to get back from Rim Wood quarry with some special rocks.'

'And that's not very— ' one of the younger men began.

'Hold your tongue.' The sergeant slammed his fist down on the table. Nellie Lowslegg shrieked. 'Pardon me miss. It's this clotpole I was addressing. Now if you'd be so kind, more braggot.' He glared at the young loudmouth.

Harry was alone at the university. There was nothing he could do now but wait. Sleep was impossible. He sauntered around the old laboratory where he had been so happy working and studying under Professor Quickstrain. How

soothing was the familiar deep whirring sound from the shaft of the great anemometer that ran down from the centre of the University Dome and, through the floor of the laboratory rotating as it had done for over half a century. He brushed his finger tips across the embossed spines of the beautiful bound volumes of Peregrinus's studies in light and optiks. He sat at his old maester's desk and stole a few tranquil moments thinking about the past. The tolling bells for vespers jolted him into the present reality and great waves of fear and doubt engulfed him. What if Severino was not back before the Brooderstalt laid their siege. What if they never get a chance to use firedrake? What then? Even if they got the nephryte, would Firedrake work? What then? What then? He cried out, and filled the void around him with sound: words with no meaning, detached, eerie. Was this madness? The thought, even in his state of confusion began to draw him back to reality. He sat and covered his face with both hands. And the word Lia came unbidden to his lips. He was quiet once more.

'At least she will be safe in Anselem, ' he whispered into the shadows, laying his hands flat on the surface of his beloved maester's desk. 'At least that.'

Chapter 12

We'll never get there?' A young Brooderstalt foot soldier scowled and sat down on the root of a giant Shagbark. The Manchian War engine ahead juddered to a halt.

'Patience lad,' a comrade said, 'there's no rush. Once we get through this lot,' he gestured with both hands at the dense forest that surrounded them, 'we'll be onto the Vildpline and straight down to Dredgemarsh where you can blood that shiny falchion.' He pointed at the young soldier's scabbard.

Albrecht Pentrojan's scouts informed him that they were about three leagues from Devil's Cleft where they would turn south onto the Vildpline. There they would have their first sight of the fortress city of Dredgemarsh, and, within half a day, that same city would be within range of their fearsome war engines. Pentrojan could not conceal his excitement. Despite his earlier contention that the element of surprise was of no consequence against the 'gnat' that was Dredgemarsh, he, nevertheless, started to chide his officers over every little delay. So, when a scout returned from the advance party and said that the dark road was blocked by trees that had been deliberately felled and it would take the best part of a day to clear them, the General struck the hapless messenger to the ground and cursed those unlucky enough to be in his immediate company.

'I'm surrounded by imbeciles and laggards.' A foam of white spittle formed at the corners of his mouth. 'Pitch camp. But be warned,' his eyes were wild and bloodshot, 'this is the last time we will stop.' He pointed to each of his officers in turn.

Now that he was so close to Dredgemarsh, he could not suppress that old disquieting anxiety brought on by the memory of his humiliation decades before. And the closer he got, that humiliation became more visceral and present 'til it felt like it happened just days ago. He could still hear the jeers and laughter of the citizens's of Dredgemarsh, feel the spittle on his face, smell the rotten fruit hurled at him as they ejected him barefoot to make his way back to Brooderslund and public humiliation.

'Damn the scum,' he muttered, addressing no one in particular. 'They simply delay their extermination. We will make them pay, they will beg for death, beg for it.' He paced up and down as anxious soldiers made haste to erect his tent. The great blobs of melting snow cascaded down from the canopy above and did nothing to improve his temper.

'General,' it was captain Luparellus, 'our so called prince says he knows why they are trying to delay us.'

'What?'

'He swears he knows; I think you should hear him sir.'

The general stopped pacing, glared at the men erecting his tent and snarled 'Hurry, hurry. And you captain,' he flicked his hand in the direction of Luparellus, 'bring him here.' Luparellus nodded to two of his men. They left and soon returned with the manacled Fabian. The tent was erected by then. A canvas ground sheet and a single chair and table were put in place and even while the men were hammering home the final pegs Pentrojan entered the tent and beckoned Luparellus to follow with the prisoner.

'Well, Prince of Dredgemarsh.' Pentrojan smirked at Fabian, 'Tell me why your accursed subjects think delaying me will achieve anything. They are finished. They know it.'

'General, those who are left in Dredgemarsh are not my subjects; they are traitors. I detest them as much as you do.' Fabian measured out his words with meticulous care. 'We have a common purpose.'

'We? There is no we.' Pentrojan clenched his fists and stepped closer to Fabian. 'Just tell me what you know and pray that it's enough to spare your miserable life.'

'They must get Nephryte from Rim Wood quarry before your army arrives.'

'Nephryte? What is Nephryte?'

'It's a special rock from Rim Wood Quarry and they need it for a war engine called Firedrake.'

'Ye Gods, what is this fool jabbering about?' Pentrojan scowled at Luparellus. 'I have no time for this buffoonery.'

'Sir,' Luparellus said, 'please listen. They are trying to delay us and this may be the reason.'

Pentrojan considered for a moment. 'Go on, get on with it.' He sat at the small table and leaned back, waiting for Fabian to start.

When Luparellus and Fabian emerged from Pentrojan's tent the manacles were gone from Fabian's wrists.

'Sergeant,' Luparellus shouted to one of those waiting outside, 'assemble two hundred armed horse at once. We ride out now. And fit him out.' He pointed at Fabian. A short time later, at the head of what in some cities would constitute a small army, Captain Luparellus accompanied by Fabian galloped from the Brooderstalt camp in the direction of Devils cleft, spraying half-melted snow in great arcs on each side of them.

'Leave some for us,' a footsoldier shouted to one of the passing horsemen who laughed and raised a clenched fist high in the air. They slowed to circle around the felled trees and then, waved on by the party of Brooderstalt soldiers and military engineers who were chopping their way through the great tree trunks, they resumed their headlong gallop towards Devil's Cleft.

Thunder and torrential sleet swept in waves across the Western end of Grak's forest where Anvil Paine and his party of ten foresters and twenty soldiers worked feverishly to fell as many trees across the dark road as possible.

'Every tree felled is a thorn in the bastards' side,' the Captain yelled and buried his axe into the base of huge spruce.

They intensified their efforts under the ever-increasing deluge of melting snow spilling down from the canopy above them.

Despite the all-encompassing pandemonium of pounding axes and growling saws, a more distant and rhythmic sound began to impinge on Anville Paine's ever alert senses.

'Stop, stop!' he shouted.

The pounding of soldiers' axes against the sturdy trees ceased and the forester sawmen gratefully straightened their backs from their exhausting labours.

Now against the whine of the biting wind and swish and patter of falling sleet, a low rumbling sound became more distinct 'til one of Anville Paine's foresters called out, 'lots of riders approaching fast.' He pointed eastwards.

'Quick, to your horses,' Anville Paine commanded. He and his men melted into the forest on the north side of the dark road. That is except for Potens who picked up his axe and continued to slice through the final few inches of the towering oak which he was working on.

Anville Paine doubled back when Potens resume chopping, 'Come. Now.' he hissed the command.

'One more,' Potens shouted and delivered a shuddering blow to the tree trunk. The giant tree tilted slowly, rending timber groaned and the behemoth tumbled across the Dark Road, tearing and smashing everything in its path. Potens backed away and then plunged into the dense underbrush of the forest.

Captain Luparellus, though still some distance away, turned onto a straight stretch of the road that gave him a view of the enormous plume of snow and water that billowed up around the fallen oak. The cavalcade of galloping horses slowed to a canter. Luparellus hauled his mount to a stop in front of the new barrier across the Dark Road. After a few moments talking to his officers, two small contingents of about twenty men each rode into the forest, one group going North and the other South.

'They're close. Take no prisoners,' Luparellus called out to them as he and the main body of riders picked their path around the felled trees and then lashed their steaming mounts into a frenzied gallop westward.

It was well into the afternoon when Luparellus and his men reached Devil's Cleft. They wheeled south onto the Vildpline and rode out onto the great plain, still covered in a white blanket of snow. Despite the sting of sleet sweeping across the white expanse, they descried the outline of Dredgemarsh city in the distance.

'For Brooderland, for Cawdrult,' they shouted into the bitter sky followed by wild ululations.

Luparellus stood in the stirrups and waved his arms. 'Quiet,' he shouted, 'we're here to kill not sing to them. He set out at a steady gallop in the direction of Dredgemarsh.

From the watchtower on the eastern side of the main gate of Dredgemarsh, Luparellus and his large cohort of riders were spotted. The captain of the watch sent for Hawksfoot who arrived breathless and perturbed.

'How many captain?' he asked.

'Hundreds, General,' the captain said without removing his eye from the oculmagnus which was mounted on a heavy iron tripod. 'See for yourself, sir.' he invited Hawksfoot to look through the small lens of the instrument.

'No war engines?' Hawksfoot squinted his eyes against the sleety rain.

'No sir, just riders.'

'I can't make out … ah I see them now, There, there they are,' Hawskfoot exclaimed when a momentary cessation in the sleet revealed the far away riders.

Harry and Grunkite arrived.

'What's afoot.?' Grunkite said.

'Riders coming from Devil's cleft.'

'Reconnaissance?'

'No, too many for that. And they're riding hard.'

'What are they up to.' No one answered.

'It doesn't make sense.' Hawksfoot relinquished the oculmagnus back to the captain of the watch. 'They must use their war engines first. It would be madness to start an attack with mounted troops. No, there's something else happening—'

'Sir. Sir,' the Captain of the watch called out, 'they're turning west above Rim Wood.'

'What?'

'They're heading west.'

The colour drained from Grunkites face. 'It's the quarry. They know. They know about the Nephryte.'

'How could they know, Chancellor, how could they know about Firedrake or Captain Severino's mission. No, it's impossible.' Hawksfoot said.

'Impossible or not, they are heading for Rim Wood Quarry.'

'Get your fastest rider now, General. We're still closer to the quarry than those Brooderstalt. Captain Severino must

be warned of the enemy coming from the north. Do it now.'
Hawksfoot departed.

Harry, who, up to then was resolute and clear as to what needed to be done, looked uncertain. He looked around him as though searching for some solution to their frightening predicament. But there was none. The forlorn figure of Grunkite stood apart, heedless of the freezing sleet, staring out at the ever darkening Vildpline. Harry joined him. They watched in silence as a lone rider galloped from the postern gate onto the castle promenade and wheeled west towards the southern tip of Rim Wood.

'Are we too late?' Grunkite said without diverting his eyes from the rider who was fast vanishing into the distance. Harry could not respond.

Dante Severino

Chapter 13

The Dark Road was cleared of felled trees. The Brooderstalt army lumbered along the water-soaked roadway. But, despite the declining light, Pentrojan would not hear of stopping. Hundreds of lantern bearers lined up each side of the road. In the centre of that channel of light that weaved through the forest, clouds of steam billowed ghost-like from the backs of the bellowing oxen hauling the monstrous trebuchets over the rutted surface. And still the endless rain and sleet dribbled through the leafy colander of the forest roof.

The mood of the soldiers was as vile as the weather. They stumbled through icy potholes and over stones sharp as razors protruding from the washed-out roadway. They cursed Dredgemarsh. They cursed Grak's Forest, the sleet, the rain and most of all they cursed their morose leader, Pentrojan, for his indifference to their suffering.

'General, the men need rest,' a young officer had the temerity to say. Pentrojan, at the head of the army, glared at the him.

'Sorry general, I just meant to … in case … just bring to your …. He trailed off under the malevolent gaze.

'Get him out of my sight,' Pentrojan hissed to the more senior men around him and spat a great gob of phlegm onto the water logged road. They plodded on.

'We will camp on the Vildpline tonight,' said Pentrojan. 'and by mid-day tomorrow, Dredgemarsh will quake in fear.' Above their heads the dark impenetrable canopy glowed and flickered eerily followed instantly by thunder that made the forest tremble.

The Brooderstalt cavalry under the command of Captain Luparellus and guided by the traitor Fabian, were converging on the north tip of Rim Wood. Though Luparellus pushed his troop to make as much progress as possible before total darkness enveloped them, he, unlike his general, was determined to find some form of shelter and respite from the foul weather. So, when they reached the Northern perimeter of Rim Wood, they made camp. The men found what scant cover they could under the trees and managed to light some fires despite the interminable downpour. They ate their rations of dried ling and drank fortified braggot to ward off the cold. As best they could, they rested and waited for the command to move on.

At the the southern tip of Rim Wood, some two leagues from where Luparellus and his troops sheltered, a mud-spattered rider from Dredgemarsh turned northwards off Storn Way. Half way between him and Luparellus was his destination: the nephryte quarry and Captain Severino. He was just about able to make out the tracks of Severino's wagons. He dug his heels into the flanks of his foaming mount, a great dappled Lidian hunter. The frequent flashes of lightning gave him visible confirmation that he was on course but in the main he relied on the instincts of his horse to guide him along the road.

At the Nephryte quarry, Captain Severino staggered through the mud, his hands bleeding and torn from the rough boulders of Nephryte.

'Almost finished,' he gasped as he helped one of his men to heave another rock up and over a wagon tail-board. The man, leaning forward hands on knees and sucking air into his lungs managed to nod his head in response. Thunder, lightning and pelting rain assaulted their minds and their bodies. They were beyond exhaustion and, like creatures bereft of all feeling and thought, they focused on a single task: filling the wagons with Nephryte. It was no wonder then, that not one of them noticed the rider from Dredgemarsh 'til he plunged into their midst as if he had dropped from the cataclysm of fire and sound above their bowed heads.

'Captain Severino,' the rider looked around trying to identify the captain amongst the mud-covered men.

'Here.'

'Captain, my name is Chilperic.'

'I know you.'

'General Hawksfoot sent me give you warning, sir, Brooderstalt. Coming from the north.' Chilperic pointed northwards, 'Hundreds of them.'

'Brooderstalt,' Severino said, 'why would Brooderstalt come to Rim Wood?'

'Sir, I don't know. It's a large troop of cavalry. They were spotted from our watchtower … cutting through the north of Rim Wood and coming in this direction.'

Severino furrowed his brow. 'They couldn't know we are here … or why we are here … how could they?' He was not addressing anyone in particular. In the meantime the word Brooderstalt spread like a fire and the men ceased their labours to gather around their captain and the messenger from Dredgemarsh.

'No, there is no reason they would come in this direction. It makes no sense. Are you absolutely sure?' Severino addressed Chilperic.

Yes sir, there's no doubt. The Chancellor and the Prince himself confirmed it.'

'Captain, what's happening?' It was Lia.

'Brooderstalt … coming from the north. Hundreds of them'

'O merciful God above, Lia! Those demons. We're lost.' Rebecca wailed.

'Quiet,' Severino shouted, 'we'll have none of that. They are flesh, and bone who have fled before Dredgemarsh steel many a time.'

Lia patted Rebecca on the shoulder. 'Shush Rebecca.' She faced the captain once more. 'How could they know we are here, Captain?'.

'They know somehow, but the question is why. Why would they go to the trouble of intercepting us unless they knew what we are about and that's impossible … the only ones who know anything about Firedrake are the council members.'

As soon as he said the words council members, he hesitated for a moment, and then groaned and struck his forehead. 'Fabian, that accursed creature. That foul accursed wretch. There is no other possible answer.' He struck his forehead again with the heel of his hand. 'We have to move out fast.'

The exhausted men found some hidden reserves of energy. The canvases were flung over the wagons and the oxen, bawling in protest, were whipped into motion and lined up for departure. Captain Severino ordered two of his men to ride in one of the wagons and their mounts were given to Lia and Rebecca. He instructed another two men to ride northwards to determine how close the Brooderstalt were. He ordered the wagons to move off. He and his men, Lia and Rebecca followed behind. The going was torturous and slow. The loaded wagons were sinking to their axles on stretches of the road. They reached Giant's Eye: a short section of the roadway hewn through solid rock just wide enough for a wagon to pass through. Once through they picked up some speed.

Severino guessed it was somewhat after midnight, and too soon for his liking, when the riders he sent out to spy on the Brooderstalt returned.

'How far?' he asked.

'Two leagues captain. They were breaking camp when we spotted them. They're riding towards us.'

'Numbers?'

'Hundreds, three or four.'

'How fast are they riding?'

'They ride with caution, Captain, but they'll reach us long before dawn.' Severino turned his face away from them.

'Captain,' one of his officers began' but Severino raised his hand for silence and urged his mount off to the side of the muddy track. There he found some sparse shelter from the flailing torrent. He sat in deep thought. The officers and men including Lia and Rebecca reined in their mounts where they stood. They waited, frequently looking north for any sign of Brooderstalt and south where the wagons grumbled onward. Despite the sluggish progress the wagons were almost out of sight and Captain Severino had still not rejoined them.

'Why are we just sitting here?' one man could not restrain himself.

'Quiet,' an officer hissed. The rain grew heavier. They could just about see their captain through the deluge and all attention was fixed on him. All movement, all thought, even breath itself was suspended.

'I think he's coming.'

'At Last.'

'Good.'

When he reached them, Captain Severino beckoned the officer Alberic aside. They talked for some time. Alberic rejoined the men. His face was a mask of sorrow.

'What, what is it, Alberic?' some of men asked. He did not answer but called out six of them as well as Lia and Rebecca and ordered them to follow him. Before setting off in pursuit of the wagons he saluted Captain Severino. It was just a salute, but, to Alberic's men looking on, there was some intangible finality in it, and their hearts beat faster. Alberic turned and his little band rode after the wagons.

Captain Severino spoke. 'Men of Dredgemarsh, those wagons with their precious cargo of Nephryte must not fall into the hands of the Brooderstalt. The lives of our families, of our wives, sisters, parents, children and the future of Dredgemarsh depends on our courage this day. The enemy approaches in great numbers. We ride to meet them at Giant's Eye.' There was an audible intake of breath from the men. 'Few though we are, they will pay a tribute of many lives before they pass through that stoney tunnel. Tonight, it is certain we will dine with our forefathers in heaven, but our families, friends and generations to come, will sing of our bravery and will remember each one of us forever.' A tremor of elation and fear was palpable. They raised their falchions and shouted, 'Dredgemarsh! Dredgemarsh!' Even above the sound of pounding rain, Alberic and his small group including Lia and Rebecca heard that battle cry, and, looking back, could just make out Severino's small band of men galloping north to meet the fearsome Brooderstalt.

'May God be with them.' Alberic said.

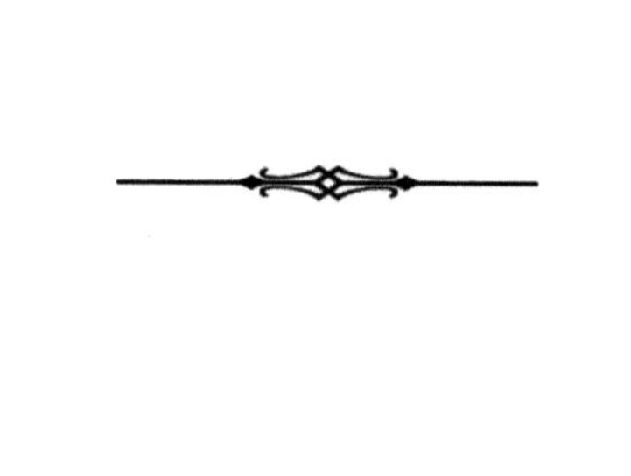

Chapter 14

The scribes, Havelock and Dipslick, sat in the King's library with the castle's journal and a leather-bound book: *Dredgemarsh Annals no. 121* that occupied half of the writing table. Dipslick, despite swollen arthritic fingers, was transcribing from one page of the Journal into the Annals and Havelock was poised, pen in hand over the opposite blank page of the same journal. His lugubrious eyeballs tracked the pacing Chancellor Grunkite.

Havelock's face was blotched and bilious looking; it was too early in the morning for the effects of the previous evening's "tastings" of medovukha and melipsis to have worn off. Dipslick, his colleague and bosom companion who, long ago, abandoned sobriety, was unaffected by the unusual dawn summons to duty. It was cold. Timid flames flickered in the grate. The wind complained in the rafters and rattled the stained glass casements.

Grunkite was ashen faced.

'The enemy is at hand. Brooderstalt!' his voice was cracked and harsh. 'Come on, write it down, write it down.' He glared at Havelock who appeared to have drifted into a semi-comatose stupor.

Grunkite stopped his pacing and thumped the table. 'The enemy is a hand. Brooderstalt.' Havelock's hand, fine boned and smooth in contrast to the wrinkled and mottled other parts of his body began to write. The text flowed gracefully across the smooth vellum. 'We are vastly outnumbered but we will resist to the last man. We cannot use Firedrake without nephryte. There is little hope that Captain Severino and his expedition to the Rim Wood quarries will return now. We believe that he and the nephryte has fallen into enemy hands.'

Grunkite stopped his pacing and, like one about to depart on a long journey, began to scrutinise everything around him. A last lingering goodbye perhaps. Havelock coughed and cleared his throat, an obvious exhortation for Grunkite to continue.

The Chancellor snapped out of his reverie and resumed. 'We pray that our King, Cesare Greyfell, is safe and that he will avenge our destruction … and honour his valiant son, Prince Harry Greyfell.' His voice faltered and he looked with great sadness at Harry, who was seated in the shadows, submerged in his own thoughts. He continued, 'A son whom he has never known who refuses to abandon Dredgemarsh. He has chosen to stand with our troops despite our most earnest entreaties that he should depart.' The last few words were drowned by a savage howl from the gale outside.

'What, what did you say?' Havelock asked.

'Despite all our entreaties … earnest entreaties that he should depart.'

Grunkite's voice trembled but not with anger now. It was the voice of desolation. He turned away from Havelock to compose himself. In the intervening moments, the only sound was the wind outside moaning through the buttresses and high chimneys and in the quiet lulls the scratching of the scribes' pens came to the fore. 'When you are finished, seal them in the tower,' Grunkite said.

'Chancellor!' someone was shouting and approaching with rapid steps to the door of the king's library.

A loud knocking and Grunkite commanded, 'Come in'. A young red-faced soldier opened the door and shook rain from his streaming locks and clothes before entering.

What is it?'.

'Sir, they are here, they are here.' The messenger was gasping for breath.

'Severino?' Grunkite's eyes filled with a sudden gleam of hope. 'Is it Severino?' Harry rose from his seat and joined Grunkite.

'No sir, no. It's the Brooderstalt, they have just moved onto the Vildpline. They are coming.' The brief glimmer of hope was extinguished. Grunkitee stood transfixed, staring with a blank expression at the young soldier in front of him.

Harry took his arm. 'Chancellor, rest.' He led the old man to a soft chair. 'I will keep you informed.' He nodded to the young soldier to follow him, leaving the chancellor and the scribes in the King's Library.

Harry made his way onto the north-facing battlements. It seemed as if every last soldier in Dredgemarsh stood along the walkway. Indifferent to the downpour they focused on the Vildpline. Harry looked through an embrasure and, in those brief intervals when rain abated and the odd break or thinning in the dense clouds occurred, he caught glimpses of a vast Brooderstalt army advancing towards them. The plain was still covered by snow but here and there dark patches of blackened grass were beginning to appear and spread like stains across the landscape.

The men on the walkway managed to light fires that spat and hissed under pitch cauldrons. They were clearing the channels to the gargoyle spouts protruding from the curtain wall and the machiolations on the exterior of the drum towers. At fifty meter intervals along the full length of the allure, ballistae and their three man crews were ready with piles of javelins stacked beside them. Interspersed with the ballistae were mangonels. Between the great ballistae and mangonels and all along the brattice works, lines of arbalesters and longbow men stood waiting and watching.

'Keep those bowstrings and torsion cords dry,' an officer, pacing up and down, was shouting and the men double checked the oiled leather coverings of their weapons. On the firing platform by the main watchtower Firedrake stood forlornly against the turbulent sky, a great metal giant, silent and indifferent to the rain flooding down its ironl flanks.

Then, for the first time, they heard it: the blare of battle horns, a distant threat, rising and falling with the swirling winds. Harry, now joined by General Hawksfoot, could sense the unease of the men. He strode along the ramparts with the General, ostensibly inspecting the men and their weapons.

'Make every one count,' he shouted to the crew of a ballista, tapping the huge javelins stacked in neat piles ready for action.

'Every one, General, every one,' the men replied, laughing away their fear and buoyed by the presence of the young prince who so recently and so miraculously escaped certain death.

'He will be a great king,' one said, as Harry and the General passed on to the next group of men.

'Aye, that he will, an' I mean to serve him for many a long day,' another responded. It was thus all along the rampart; the men finding courage in the thought that such a vibrant and fearless young leader was not destined to die no matter how great the odds against him.

But their courage was tested soon after Harry's arrival. With the Brooderstalt army half a league away and the expectation that it would be another hour or more before battle would commence a distant thunder clap rolled in from the Vildpline. Moments later, a small round boulder whistled though the air and bounced off the curtain wall. Those nearest the impact looked in alarm to discover the source of the missile.

'Where did it come from,' one shouted.

'I can't see,' another said and dozens of men leaned out through the embrasures expecting to see some catapult or trebuchet that had been surreptitiously brought into firing position by an advance party of Brooderstalt. There was nothing to see, nor was there anywhere such war engines could be concealed. Another thunder clap from somewhere over the Vildpline was followed by a second boulder striking the wall. A third and fourth smashed into the brickwork.

'What sorcery is this,' one said and by degrees the unimaginable began to enter their minds. The boulders were being fired by the Brooderstalt from way beyond the range of their largest ballista.

'It's impossible.'

'Not from that distance.'

'It can't be.'

'It must be sorcery.'

Harry hurried back to quell the spreading panic.

'Stand fast. There is no need to be frightened. There's no sorcery, no magic.'

'But Sir,' one of the crew of a ballista spoke, 'the distance sir, what kind of weapon can fire from such a huge distance?'

'I know, but it is not sorcery,' Harry said and the men gathered closer around him. He could see their desperate need for reassurance. What could he say? How could he bolster their flagging spirits? He looked around him. They watched his every move, every gesture. Harry's eyes settled on Firedrake.

'There, look there!' he pointed with outstretched arm, 'if you want magic, there it stands: Firedrake. But it's our magic, the magic of science and nature.' A distant boom was followed moments later by the thud of another boulder striking the outer wall. 'Don't be frightened.' Harry raised his voice, 'those boulders are tiny. They are taunting us. But they will have to come much closer. Then we will confound them,' Harry continued pointing out over the Vildpline 'We will confound them and terrify them when we release our firebolts.' The men laughed, a short and nervous laught.

'Sire, why do we not use it now?' a Ballista crewman asked.

'When our wagons return from the Nephryte Quarry we will be ready.' Harry declared.

'What if …' It was obvious that the man was about to query Harry's assertion that the wagons would return. Harry glared at him.

'… nothing, Sire, it's nothing. A foolish thought.'

Chapter 15

The thirteen mining wagons packed with Nephryte emerged onto Storn Way. They turned eastwards through the lower tip of Rim Wood and headed for Dredgemarsh. After a short while, Alberic, riding ahead of the convoy, signaled them to halt.

'Why are we stopping? This is madness. We must keep moving,' Lia called out and spurred her mount forward to Alberic.

'We cannot outdistance them,' he said with a certainty that clearly frightened her.

'But we must try, we have got to try. Captain Severino has given us a chance and we can't just—'

'My Lady, we will try. You must listen now. Captain Severino knew he could not hold them long enough for all of us to get back to Dredgemarsh.'

'But why—'

'Just listen, my lady. We are not giving up.' The wagoners and soldiers exchanged nervous looks when Alberic took Lia aside and talked to her, gesticulating and pointing southwards off Storn Way. They could hear the odd word but not enough to make sense. Alberic rode back to the lead wagon. 'You're carrying the Black Crystals?' He addressed one of the wagoner.

'Yes sir.'

Alberic lifted the corner of the wagon canvas and checked. 'This wagon will move south, straight through Hazel wood to the Yayla. There is an old mining slipway there. The young ladies and you Brunald,' he pointed to one of his older men, 'will take them there and wait. Stefan and you Cassian; you two will ride as fast as you can to the Lake Village and find Olaf. Tell him that this wagon must get to Dredgemarsh by barge, orders of Captain Severino. Tell him it will be waiting for him by the old mining slipway. Impress upon him that all is lost if this is not done as fast as possible.'

He handed a signet ring to Stefan. 'It's Captain Severino's. Show it to Olaf and say that the captain owes him a fish supper. Olaf will know you speak for the captain. Now go.'

Stefan and Cassian galloped off and, shortly after, the wagon carrying the black nephryte crystals, the old soldier Brunald, Lia and Rebecca turned south off the roadway and headed towards the Yayla while Alberic, with the remaining wagons and soldiers continued on the road to Dredgemarsh.

After some time lumbering along the main roadway, with no sign of Brooderstalt, Alberic was beginning to think the impossible. Could it be that Captain Severino was still, by some miracle, holding back the accursed enemy? When they approached that part of Storn Way that emerged from the trees of Rim Wood and onto the southern end of the

Vildpline with a straight run to Dredgemarsh, Alberic urged the wagoners to speed up. They just might make it.

But that inchoate feeling of optimism was crushed in an instant when he emerged from Rim Wood. His vision took some moments to adjust to the sudden change in light. Before him on the roadway stood a torn and bloodied figure of a man. The face was swollen and distorted. But there was something familiar about this forlorn spectacle. The slashed brigadine and tattered cloak were Dredgemarsh apparel. As Alberic got closer the slow accumulation of tiny details of the undamaged areas of the flayed body and clothes began to register and he whispered, 'Captain? Captain Severino?' He leaped from his saddle and ran to Severino who collapsed into his arms. Alberic knelt down and with great tenderness laid his beloved Captain on the ground. 'What have they done to you.'

Perhaps it was the tears in his eyes, but, it was only when he was grabbed from behind, hauled to his feet and swung around with force that he saw hundreds of Brooderstalt partially hidden by the thinning trees that flanked the two sides of the road where it emerged from Rim Wood. Two Brooderstalt held him fast and forced him to observe the butchery that ensued.

Alberic watched, his face distorted in horror. His men were cut down by the deadly bolts of the Brooderstalt arbalesters. The unarmed wagoners throats were sliced open one by one and their bodies kicked into the mud. One wagoner, the last one alive, was pleading and for some strange reason he was being listened to.

As if waking from the nightmare, Alberic focused on the wagoner's words, 'there is another wagon, another one. I can show you. Please don't kill me. I can help ... I will show you. Please.'

A great fury took hold of Alberic. 'Traitor. Traitor,' he screamed and ripped himself free of his captors. He ran towards the wagoner, drawing his falchion. But before he got to the traitor, he was decapitated by a Brooderstalt long sword.

'Fine swordwork, Barach.' Captain Luparellus rode forward, 'Now, before you clean your blade, finish it. He pointed to the blood soaked body of Captain Severino. Barach raised his sword. 'A pleasure, Captain.' he laughed.

'Wait!' it was Fabian who called out. A bemused Luparaellus signalled the would-be executioner to stay his hand. Fabian whispered some private words in Luparellus's ear.

'Well, well, it seems our prince of Dredgemarsh thinks beheading is too kind a treatment for this man or what remains of him,' said Luparellus. 'Do as he wishes. Then we will escort our savage prince and these wagons back to the General and you, sir,' he pointed to Barach, 'take twenty men. See if this wretch,' he pointed to the wagoner, 'is speaking the truth and ... kill the traitorous dog.'

Barach and his twenty riders entered Hazel Wood in pursuit of Brunald, Lia, Rebecca and the wagon of black nephryte crystals. The captured wagons and the rest of Brooderstalt set out to join General Pentrojan and the main army on the Vildpline. They left death behind them except for one living soul, Severino. His shattered body was suspended from a tree by the wrists. His feet touched the ground just enough to ease the pressure on his arms and prevent asphyxiation.'

'Pray, traitor, that the cold takes you before brother wolf comes to dine,' were the last words that Fabian spat into the dying face of Captain Dante Severino.

Chapter 16

'Sire, wait a few more days. The rains may have stopped by then and the slopes will be easier to descend.' The grand master, Abbot Sigismund, sat opposite Cesare Greyfell in his private dining room above the refectory.

'Nothing would give me greater pleasure.' Cesare leaned back in his chair and sighed.

'You are exhausted, sire. A few more days is all I say … some wholesome food,' Sigismund leaned forward and refilled the king's goblet, 'and good wine.'

'Abbot Sigismund, I thought your business was with men's souls.' Cesare smiled.

'You cannot forget the body, sire. The vessel must be strong and healthy, and you have been through a long and arduous campaign in Lycia.'

Peals of laughter filtered up from the refectory below. 'And your men, sire. Think of them; they need good food and rest.'

'It's not over yet.'

'But Lycia is safe now, thanks to you.'

'And your noble knights,' said Cesare, 'but I fear for my own people and,' he paused for a moment, 'Fabian, a son I have too long neglected.' After another long pause, Cesare drank down the goblet of mulsum and rose stiffly to his feet. 'Luther's ambitions for Lycia may be thwarted, Sigismund, but Cawdrult of Brooderlund will risk everything to smash Dredgemarsh. So my good friend, we must leave now, without further delay.'

'As you wish, Sire. My prayers will go with you. The knights of Anselem will be ready. Shall I inform your officers and men below.'

'I will do that, Sigismund.'

The refectory was packed and loud with banter and laughter. Still in their soiled military uniforms, their bacinets and weapons strewn about in casual disarray on chairs, tables and floor, Cesare's men revelled in the steaming trenchers of chitterlings, dowcettes and cheese and the foaming mazers of strong braggot. The goblets were being replenished from a huge puncheon and served by an attentive team of young Anselem novitiates who listened in awe as stories of danger, terror and courage were recounted time and again by the battle-weary men.

'But the King,' a lean scar-faced trooper from the Dredgemarsh Invinciples was holding forth at one end of the refectory, 'our King,' he raised his goblet and climbed unto a table, 'on the front line, every time. By God, he was magnificent. Those Manchians, those famous fearless fighters …' he smirked and took a mouthful of braggot. His companions leaned forwards grinning, winking to each other, waiting for their comrade to continue. 'Fearless fighters my arse,' he roared. They all shouted, hallooed, slapped each other on the back and pounded the table with their mazers.

'Nobly said, Reef Blackstaff,' a comrade shouted.

Reef raised his hand for silence, 'And when they saw our king … when they saw him,' he lowered his voice and gestured for even more silence, 'his sword and arms red with the blood of their comrades …' He paused and every single person in the refectory was listening now. He continued in a hushed voice, 'they ran.' The grinning listeners remained silent, waiting. 'They outnumbered us ten to one, and they ran. They ran.' The room was spellbound; everyone staring mesmerised as Reef slowly raised a clenched fist into the air. 'The sons of whores ran,' he shouted and the room exploded into a chorus of cheers.

'Well said.' They called out. 'That's true. That's what happened. Long live Cesare Greyfell. Ten to one and the sons of whores ran. Long live Dredgemarsh'.

The novitiates resumed serving the braggot and the talk diminished and scattered into disparate conversations throughout the packed refectory. Cesare, unnoticed at first, entered the room. Then, like ripples on water spreading from a dropped stone, quietness descended. All heads turned towards the king and every man stood to attention.

'We leave for home now,' Cesare said. The men could not hide their disappointed looks and in some cases sighs of fatigue.

'I know you are weary of fighting, but the Brooderstalt, I fear, will have marched on Dredgemarsh by now. We must make haste. Our people need us now,' said Cesare turning to leave.

'Well, what are we waiting for.' Reef Blackstaff jumped to his feet and punched the air. 'Our work is not done. Let's go teach those Brooderstalt curs a lesson in real warfare.'

The refectory was emptied rapidly except for the bemused novitiates who began to clear up after the unruly meal. Before they were finished, the Anselem bells pealed out.

'They're leaving,' a young monk shouted. The excited novitiates, dropped everything and scampered up the narrow stone stairs to the high walkway around the Rotunda. There they could see Cesare and his officers ride out across the cobbled plaza followed by one hundred armed knights of Anselem, two hundred and twenty of the famous Lycian mounted archers, four hundred Dredgemarsh mounted troopers and two hundred and twenty Gliondar Hobelars. There was a longing on the faces of the novitiates as they watched the army vanish down into the driving rain and the mist that enveloped the lower slopes of Anselem. But their ardour soon succumbed to the cold icy wind that blew from the bleak wastelands and upper peaks that had all but discarded their white winter garb. The young men returned to their quiet duties.

Late into the afternoon Cesare and his men were off the lower slopes and galloping along Storn Way towards Lake Tranquil. It stopped raining at last, though the roadway was a quagmire in places. The riders were spattered in mud to such an extent that their outer tunics with their distinctive surcoats of Dredgemarsh, Lycia, Anselem and Gliondar were indistinguishable. They stopped for a brief rest and to water the horses at Sweet Stream, one of the many small tributaries of the Yayla. During that short stop the men ate dried bartago and cheese. In the course of the hurried repast, they heard a series of distant thunder claps north east beyond Rim Wood. But as far as they could see the sky was relatively clear in that direction. When they set out again the ominous thunder was increasing in frequency. Cesare could not quell his growing apprehension. As he neared the Yayla Waterfalls, the apprehension turned to alarm when he rounded a curve in the road and saw trudging towards him a procession, as far as the eye could see, of old men, women and children. These reluctant pilgrims froze in terror when they beheld the army of mud covered horsemen charging down upon them.

'Brooderstalt!' screamed one woman and gathered her young child up in her arms.

'Brooderstalt!' the cry was taken up and passed down along the straggling procession.

An old greybeard at the front drew a short sword from his belt and stepped forward shouting, 'Come on you devils.' But the horsemen slowed to a canter, a walk and then stopped just ells in front of him. The leader of the horsemen dismounted and walked towards him.

'We are not Brooderstalt,' Cesare called out.

'Who are you then?' Greybeard squinted rheumy eyes at the approaching figure but still held his sword poised and ready to strike.

Blood of Grak! it's the King himself, it's the King,' a woman shouted at the top of her voice and the message rippled down through the rest of the travelers changing their wailing to shouts of joy.

'Tell me what has happened,' Cesare addressed the old man who stood open-mouthed, his sword dangling limply by his side.

'Answer your King,' Aubrey of Vilspont, called out.

'Sorry, Sire. It's the Brooderstalt … marching on Dredgemarsh. We were ordered to leave for Anselem.' He pointed back to those behind, some on foot, some mounted on ponies, plough horses, donkeys and mules and others in conveyances of all shapes and sizes drawn by ponies, rouncies and musk oxen. 'The army, the chancellor and the Prince remain to defend Dredgemarsh,' he added.

'You left before the attacks?' Cesare asked.

'Yes sire. The Brooderstalt army was moving onto the Vildpline from Grak's Forest as we were leaving.'

'Continue on to Anselem. You are safe now. I will send for you when this business is done.' Ceasare remounted. 'Make haste,sirs. My son Fabian defends Dredgemarsh.' He signaled his army to move forward.

' Sire,' greybeard called, 'the prince, Sire, your son is not the same—'

'Nor am I, old man.

'But, Sire, you need to know about your …'

'No time now. I will send for you,' Cesare rode by, leading his men single-file along the verge of the narrow road and, as they passed the lines of weary travellers, the women called out blessings on them and held up their children to see the

King and his "great warriors". The old men raised clenched fists in the air and shouted 'Long live Cesare Greyfell, King of Dredgemarsh'. The bedraggled pilgrims faced into their journey to Anselem with renewed vigour.

When he reached clear road again, Cesare called on two of his trusted scouts: Kristoff Surefoot and his son Halbert. 'There is danger ahead Kristoff. You and Halbert ride ahead. We will not be far behind. You know what to do.'

Kristoff nodded. He and Halbert galloped out ahead of the army on their their lithe and swift Gliondar ponies.

'Prepare yourselves for battle,' Cesare addressed his officers, 'It is as I thought, the Brooderstalt are on the Vildpline. Prince Fabian … my son, defends Dredgemarsh.' There was a note of awkward pride in Cesare's voice. They delayed for a short while to give the scouts time to get well ahead of the main party before moving out at a trot.

Kristoff and Halbert stayed off the roadway as much as possible without compromising speed. Within the hour they reached where the side road to the quarry joined Storn Way. Here the ground was like a muddy palimpsest revealing what happened just hours before: hundreds of horses hooves overlaying deep rutted imprints of laden wagons, all headed east towards Dredgemarsh and the Vildpline. They moved forward with stealth through the trees on the north side of the road. They had not progressed more than a few hundred ells when they heard riders moving up through Hazel Wood on the Southern side of the road. They dismounted, moved their ponies further back into Rim Wood and watched. The party of riders coming up from Hazel Wood were not too concerned about concealing their presence. They barged their way through the undergrowth onto Storn Way and rode East.

'Brooderstalt,' Kristoff whispered.

'Yes, and look, look, they have a girl

'Heaven help her, she were better dead.'

'No!'

'What, what is it.'

'The girl; it's Lia, General Hawksfoot's lass and there, look, just behind that is surely not … It could not be.'

'Alas it is. This is a disaster. Prince Fabian in their filthy hands.'

They watched as the band of Brooderstalt with Fabian and Lia galloped out of sight. They retrieved their ponies and followed at a safe distance. When they reached the point where the road and Rim Wood yielded to more open ground, they found bodies strewn in contorted bundles, some faced upwards, staring with blank eyes at the startling sky. Already carrion crows and a lone grizzled wolf, an outcast, were gorging themselves on the unexpected feast.

'Brooderstalt swine. These men were simple wagoners.' Kristoff could barely speak.

'Look, look!' Halbert pointed to what appeared to be a red bedraggled scarecrow hanging by the hands from a tree. They approached with caution.

'He's alive!' Kristoff said.

'No, he couldn't be.'

Their mounts shied away from the ravaged figure. They dismounted to take a closer look.

'By God, he is alive,' Kristoff repeated.

'Leave it … him … or whatever … he's dead. We need to report back.' Halbert said.

'No, son, we can't. He's moved. The poor bastard is still breathing. He's one of ours.' Kristoff approached nearer. The blood-soaked figure whether by accident or volition turned ever so slightly towards him and stared from one eye. Kristoff stopped in fright.

'Help … me.'

'Oh, by the Holy Christ above,' Halbert who was standing well back exclaimed.

'Cap … Captain?' Kristoff stumbled forward recognising from that small undamaged part of Severino's face something of the once handsome features. 'Oh what have they done to you, Captain?' They cut Severino's bonds and carried him with the utmost care to a sheltered place amongst the trees.

They coaxed some water past his blood encrusted lips and bound up what appeared to be the most serious of his wounds with strips of what remained of his own cloak. Severino stayed conscious long enough to whisper to them that the Brooderstalt had taken the Nephryte, 'but not the black … it's gone by water…the black's gone by water.' He grimaced in pain.

'Go back now, Halbert. Tell the King what's happened and exactly what Captain Severino has said. I'll remain here with him.' Kristoff leaned close to Severino's ear. 'You're safe, Captain, you're safe now.'

Chapter 17

Something's amiss,' Aubrey of Vilspont said. He along with the other officers and Jerome the first knight of Anselem halted the army while Cesare rode forward to question the scout Halbert Surefoot who was riding towards them at speed.

'Sire,' Halbert greeted his King. He was out of breath as he hauled his foam-flecked mount to a halt.

'What news, Halbert?'

'Your son, sire, is taken by the Brooderstalt.'

'What? Where?'

'He and Lady Lia. A band of Brooderstalt troopers, about twenty, rode up from the south side of Storn Way and turned east. The Prince and the Lady were prisoners and rode with them.'

Cesare's face paled. He swayed in the saddle as if his strength had leaked away. Halbert looked on in dismay. This proud king, this fearless lion in battle with shaking hands dismounted. Were he not holding unto the saddle of his mount, he would have stumbled to the ground.

Halbert leaped from his mount, but before he reached Cesare, Jerome was already by the King's side.

'Sire, what is it?'

Cesare appeared unable to speak. He pointed a limp finger towards Halbert Surefoot.

'Sir,' Halbert addressed Jerome, 'Prince Fabian and General Hawksfoot's daughter Lia are prisoners of the Brooderstalt. They were riding back towards the Vildpline.'

'You're sure?'

'It was them, Sir.'

'Your father?'

'He is with Captain Severino now. We followed after the troopers and found the captain. He's close to death … tortured and flayed beyond recognition. He could be dead as I speak. There were Dredgemarsh troopers and wagoners also. Butchered.'

By this time all the senior officers had gathered around.

'Sire, what is it.' Andret Longspere spoke for them all. Cesare straightened his shoulders and faced the gathered officers.

'My son, Andret. The Brooderstalt have him—'

'Then we will get him back.'

'Yes,' another spoke up, 'we'll get him back.'

Cesare raised his palm and shook his head. He addressed Halbert. 'You say about twenty Brooderstalt?' his voice was hoarse and constricted.

'Twenty with the prince and girl, sire, but we suspect hundreds passed earlier.

'What girl?' Someone asked.

'Hawksfoot's daughter, Lia.' Kristoff said

'Poor lass,' Dubnar Niells of Gliondar whispered to Ranulf Halfhand. 'It were far better she'd been killed than fall into the hands of those pig fukkers.'

'Sire, there is more,' Halbert said. 'Captain Severino managed to say something. It made no sense to me or father.'

'Speak, Halbert.' Cesare said and all the officers inched closer to hear.

'He said that they captured the nefrit … nef—'

'Nephryte,' Cesare said. 'What else?'

'Yes, Nephryte, Sire. He said, they have the Nephryte.'

'Curse of Grak,, one disaster after another,' Cesare said.

'There was more, Sire. Captain Severino said over and over: "but not the black, not the black; it's gone by water."'

'Not the black. By water.' Cesare massaged his temples, 'It's gone by water. The.. black has gone by … that can only mean the Yayla. It's gone by water. 'Jerome,' he stared at his friend. 'They've transported the black nephryte by barge. It's gone by the Yayla, on one of the old quarry barges.'

'And if they get the Black Nephryte to Dredgemarsh—' Jerome began.

'Yes, you remember, Jerome. The experiments with Professor Quickstrain. The Lightning Thrower.'

'It needs … black—'

'Yes, yes. It needs black nephryte. So, Quickstrain may have his source of power for Firedrake. 'But,' he continued, thinking out loud rather than addressing Jerome directly. 'he needs the golden nephryte boulders to be laid out as targets on the Vildpline.'

'And the Broodestalt have captured the wagons containing them.' Jerome added.

'How did they know about the Nephryte? A spy? A traitor? A traitor at the core of Dredgemarsh?' said Cesare.

'What do we do now, Sire, even if we have this black nephryte, it would appear we are too late if the Brooderstalt are already on the Vildpline and they have the golden nephryte?'

Cesare lapsed into deep thought again. 'Perhaps,' he said after some time, 'they don't understand everything and maybe … what if they bring the wagons of gold nephryte boulders into their midst on the Vildpline? It is a slender hope, Jerome, but—'

'Yes, that's it. We have been given a sign. It is the will of God, Sire.' Jerome smiled, a strange triumphant smile. He took his dagger from his belt and raised it aloft like a cross over their heads. With his other hand he retrieved a small bible from within the breast of his brigadine. It fell open at a page marked by a scarlet ribbon. He read:

> *'He has brought back their wickedness upon them*
> *and will destroy them in their evil;*
> *the Lord our God will destroy them.'*

He repeated the psalm twice more, each time louder than the last.

Those officers who gathered around him could not comprehend the meaning of the psalm but they were buoyed up by Jerome's triumphant tone.

Ceasre regained his composure. 'The professor and the defenders of the city need to know about the gold nephryte. We have got to get word to them fast.'

'I will go, Sire,' Jerome responded without hesitation.

'Take three knights with you.' Cesare said. 'I will send another man down the Yayla, with the same message. It will take longer but,' he hesitated, 'just in case.'

'It's a wise precaution, Sire. I will do everything in my power to bring the message to Dredgemarsh.'

'The rest of us will travel North along the quarry road and through Rim Wood. The enemy will be moving South on the Vildpline to attack the city. We will attack them from the rear.

Cesare spoke with assurance now. 'Sergeant Bernart, Captain Severino is gravely injured. I want you to take him to the Lake Village and see that he is tended to. Halbert will show you where the Captain is.'

He then addressed the Dredgemarsh Invincibles who had now assembled around their king in a tight circle. 'I need a good boatman.'

A young flame-haired man stepped forward. 'I was born on water, Sire.'

'Athelard, always ready.' Cesare smiled at the young warrior. 'Go without delay to the Lake Village. Find a boat and travel as fast as you can down the Yayla to Dredgemarsh. Seek out Professor Quickstrain, General Hawksfoot or Chancellor Grunkite and, if Jerome has not already delivered his message, repeat these words, "the enemy has the golden nephryte. You may yet get your opportunity"' Cesare repeated the words and asked Athelard to recite them twice. 'Tell them also that Prince Fabian and General Hawksfoot's daughter have been captured by the Brooderstalt and that we are at hand. Go now with all speed.'

Jerome picked three Knights of Anselem to accompany him and with a salute to Cesare and Aubrey of Vilspont he set out at a gallop towards Dredgemarsh.

Cesare led the army along the quarry road towards the northern tip of Rim Wood. From there, he knew they would be able to observe, unseen, the Brooderstat hosts marching south on the Vildpline towards Dredgemarsh.

Chapter 18

The fearsome Manchian war engines found their range. They were targeting the most vulnerable parts of the Dredgemarsh defences. The main gate and drum towers shivered and groaned likes sentient creatures under the relentless battering. Small cracks appeared around the openings of loopholes. Brickwork was falling away from overhanging machiolations and brattices. The timber hoards, each side of the main gate, were smashed beyond repair. Grim-faced defenders fired their Ballistae javelins at regular intervals, a defiant but fruitless gesture. Even their most powerful ballista fell well short of the enemy lines. 'Reload, reload.' The commands of the sergeants of the firing crews echoed up and down the ramparts despite the seeming hopeless nature of their defence.

Harry's immediate concern was to protect Firedrake even though it was becoming more likely with each passing hour that it would never be used. But even if that was the case, the task of building a heavy timber stockade around it gave the men something to do and kept up the pretence that Firedrake would come into play later.

'Sire!' it was Grunkite, who, to Harry's obvious surprise, had climbed up to the firing platform where the stockade was being erected around Firedrake. The old man was gasping for breath. His lips were an unhealthy purple.

'Chancellor Grunkite, you should have sent a messenger to fetch me. I would have come down to you.'

'Bugger that. I'd rather die here than sit below in an old man's chair waiting for those bastards. What's happening?'

Harry took Grunkite by the arm and led him out of earshot of the men.

'They just sit out of range of our weapons and pound us at will, Chancellor.' Two ear-shattering thunder claps obliterated Harry's words. Grunkite squinted and looked out over the Vildpline.

'How many of these monstrosities have they got?' he shouted and a boulder screamed just ells over his head and landed with a thud on the plaza below.

'Twelve that I can see,' Harry replied.

'Damage?'

'The walls and gate are holding up well but they will be breached eventually.'

'And meanwhile we can do nothing.' Grunkite sat down with some difficulty on a cast-off timber plank from the stockade. Two more thunderous claps. The stones trembled under their feet as two boulders slammed into the brickwork of the nearest drumtower. 'How long can they keep this up? There must be some end to their supply of rocks and boulders.' Grunkite groaned in exasperation more than fear.

'I'm afraid not Chancellor. The boulders are pink granite.'

'Pink granite?' Grunkite looked confused.

'Pink granite, Chancellor. There's an endless supply at Devil's Cleft.

'Of course, of course' Grunkite said, 'My blasted brain is as decrepit as this' he slapped his own body with both hands. He looked up at the almost completed stockade around Firedrake. 'It's hardly worth the effort, Harry. I wish you would go. Leave this place. A kingdom can always be rebuilt, even if it's reduced to rubble but it needs its kings. Go find your father.'

Harry shook his head from side to side. 'I cannot do that, Chancellor.'

'No, of course not; I didn't think you would — Grak's balls, what's that racket.' Grunkite heaved himself to his feet with a groan. A soldier was running towards them along the wall walk, which was thirty feet below the level of the firing platform where they stood. He was shouting up at Grunkite.

'Damn it, stop babbling man,' Grunkite called out to the soldier. It took the man a few moments to regain his breath.

'Sire, Chancellor, there is a barge on the Yayla. It's Olaf, he has stones for you. That's what he said. We are having difficulty mooring the barge against the castle wall. The flood is unnatural, Chancellor.'

'Stones!' Harry said and looked at Grunkite.

'Yes, stones. That's what he said,' the soldier sounded apologetic.

'Well, what are we waiting for.' Harry was suddenly animated. He ordered some of the stockade builders to follow him and descended to the wall walk and set off running towards the western wall with the bemused men in his wake. 'Follow at your leisure,' he shouted back to Grunkite.

'Damn these useless legs.' Grunkite raged as he shuffled his way along the wall walk in pursuit of Harry. When, at last, he arrived, he was astonished to see Rebecca amongst the gathering. She was in a sad state of dishevelment. Harry and the men with him were frantically operating a makeshift hoist stretching over the wall.

Grunkite leaned out through an embrasure. Not far below was one of the old quarry barges manned by Olaf and his son Roaf. Grunkite gasped. Never in his life had he seen the Yayla so high. It was thirty feet or more above the street level within the castle walls. Like a giant viscous creature it raged along the outer wall. Grunkite stared into the deluge. For a moment it was as if the whole world was swirling around him. Nothing was fixed, nothing stable. The barge, moored front and aft by four ropes tied around the merlons, rose and fell on the flood waters like a toy boat. On the swaying deck Olaf and Roaf were busy loading jet-black crystals from the mine wagon into large leather sacks. The sacks once full were being hoisted by the makeshift pulley.

The Chancellor hauled himself back in from the embrasure. He stood with his back set firm against a Merlon and waited until the world righted itself once more. Everyone, including Harry, was absorbed in the task of hauling up the sacks from the barge; everyone that is except Rebecca and an exhausted looking soldier who appeared to be consoling her. Grunkite staggered towards them.

'You ought to be in Anselem by now.' Her sobbing turned to a wail of anguish. 'And where is your mistress?' Rebecca turned away from him, covered her tear-stained face with both hands and fell to her knees. She was beyond consolation.

'Sir,' the soldier said, 'I am Brunald. The two young ladies were assigned to my care by Captain Severino along with the wagon of black stone. A band of Brooderstalt pursued us and before I could stop her the young mistress galloped off and led them away from us. Otherwise we would not be here. We don't know what happened to her.'

'And Captain Severino?' There was a tone of dread in Grunkite's voice.

'Sir, I don't know. He and about thirty men rode back to delay the Brooderstalt on the quarry road…'

'Thirty men. There were at least three hundred of them.' Grunkite groaned and buried his face in his hands.

'He thought, sir, that he would not be able to delay them long enough for the main wagons to get back here, so that is why he wanted this one wagon to break off from the others and come by barge. But a band of Brooderstalt did follow us and as I said the young lady Lia— ' Rebecca groaned and her sobbing turned to a low wail.

Unaware of the drama, Harry and his men worked with furious intent to unload the Black Nephryte crystals. They were swinging the full sacks up and over the wall walk and emptying them onto the street far below where a team of four men were loading them with shovels and bare hands into a long dray.

'You have done well, Brunald, done well,' Grunkite said. 'See to it that this young lass is taken care of. I will break the news to General Hawksfoot about his daughter.'

'What of Hawksfoot's daughter?' Harry left his place at the hoist.

'We don't know, Sire.' Grunkite took Harry by the elbow and led him aside to relate what Brunald had told him. Harry's face blanched and even when a cry of consternation went up from the men working the hoist he did not respond.

'We need cover! we need cover!' one of the men shouted as a bolt from a crossbow struck the side of an embrasure and rattled onto the ground just feet away from Harry and Grunkite. They rushed to the parapet. To the right where the Yayla waters had risen to unprecedented heights, submerging the steep banks and the lower trees of Hazel Wood, a group of Brooderstalt arbalesters were standing knee-deep in the flood water firing at Olaf and Roaf in the barge and the men working the hoist.

'We need archers here now,' Grunkite shouted.

'They're coming,' A lone Dredgemarsh arbalester shouted from the corner bastion where he was pinned down by some of the those same Brooderstalt bowmen who were raining bolts and arrows on the barge and the men on the hoist. Harry darted from merlon to merlon towards a group of about twenty archers who left their posts on the north wall and were running towards him.

The Brooderstalt bowmen were beginning to find their range. Two of the crew manning the hoist were wounded and both Olaf and Roaf crouched under the prow of the barge unable to move because of the lethal stream of bolts flying over their heads Then arrows from longbows began to pour down upon them from the sky. They tried to protect themselves with the thick leather sacks they were using for the Nephryte.

'Father, they've hit father.' Roaf's cry of despair pierced through the roar of the Yayla.

'They're trying to slice through the moorings. We'll lose the barge, Harry.' Grunkite called out. Harry abandoned all caution and ran full tilt towards the bastion where the west and north wall converged. He arrived unscathed at the same time as the Dredgemarsh archers. He took five with him up the steps of the bastion and ordered them to start rapid fire on the Brooderstalt. The others he ordered to fan out along the western parapet and commence firing also. All the while he felt a mounting panic clawing at his insides. It was not the deadly assault of the Brooderstalt bowmen that so disturbed him but the plight of Lia. Was she dead or hurt? The thought was too dreadful to contemplate, as was the idea that she was now in the hands of the Brooderstalt.

He moved to the parapet to observe the cursed enemy. The lethal deluge of bolts and arrows began to diminished as the Brooderstalt were forced to move back into the cover of Hazel Wood. But they continued their fire concentrating on the barge and the mooring ropes, which were beginning to fray under the continual barrage.

Harry watched as Grunkite attempted to cast a new rope down to the barge. But Roaf was pinned down and could not secure it. One of the two mooring ropes on the bow end of the barge which was facing into the raging torrent snapped and the barge swung out forty five degrees from the wall still held securely by the aft moorings and one frayed bow mooring that looked ready to come asunder at any moment. The new rope cast by Grunkite hung uselessly in the flood.

Harry raced back to Grunkite. Together they hauled in the rope and without a moment's hesitation Harry tied the rope end around his waist and dived into the flood. A stunned Grunkite watched in horror as the rope zipped through the embrasure and it was only when one of the men screamed, 'grab the end!' did the chancellor move with a speed and dexterity that defied his age. The old arthritic hands clamped onto the rope and he spun round wrapping the rope about his body and then braced himself against the nearest merlon. Harry sliced downwards through the mud laden waters and when the rope played out to its full length and Grunkite took the sudden strain, Harry, with lungs on fire, began to curve upwards out of the depths and broke surface downstream from the barge. Grunkite held on with grim determination, every muscle in his body fighting the pull of the Yayla. Two of the men who were operating the hoist grabbed him and the rope. They started to haul Harry back towards the barge. But the Brooderstalt bowmen could see what was being attempted and they concentrated all their fire on the barge so that Harry could not climb aboard and was forced to remain in the water behind the swaying hull to protect himself.

'Sir, what will we do?' one of the rope men looked in wide-eyed despair at Grunkite.

'Just hold it steady at that,' Grunkite shouted, his voice trembling out of control. Harry could not secure the rope onto the barge and the one remaining rope holding the bow was about to snap.

And then the hail of bolts and arrows stopped for no discernible reason.

'Pull, pull,' Harry shouted above the roar of the water and with the help of the rope he scrambled up and over the taffrail of the barge, ran forward and wrapped the rope around a bow cleat.

'By all the Gods, I thought you were dead … last time I saw you,' Roaf was staring at Harry, 'you are the lost prince?'

'Lost and found,' Harry gasped.

You have saved our lives.'

'As you did mine, in this very river, Roaf .' Harry looked over the prow of the boat towards the riverbank. His eyes widened and his mouth fell open.

'What is it, Sire, what is happening?' Roaf scrambled to his knees and followed Harry's gaze. On the upper fringes of Hazel Wood there was turmoil. Knights on horseback were wreaking mayhem on the archers and bowmen.

'Knights of Anselem, that's why they stopped firing on us.' Harry said.

'Father, father,' Roaf called out to Olaf, 'we're safe, it is the Knights of Anselem. We're safe.' The barge was being rapidly pulled in to its original position below the hoist and Grunkite was shouting down to Harry.

'You must be quick, there are just four knights.'

Harry grabbed a leather sack and with Roaf began to fill it as fast as he could. They filled and hoisted twelve sacks. A flurry of arrows began to fly around them once again. Glancing towards the bank Harry saw some riderless horses and a small bunch of archers once again targeting the barge from the shelter of Hazel Wood. And then surging out of the woods one lone knight, Jerome, instantly recognizable from his helmet plume, bore down on the archers and scattered them once more. In the respite from the deadly hail of arrows, Harry and Roaf secured Olaf to the hoist and when he was lifted to safety, they hauled themselves up along the new mooring rope and tumbled through an embrasure to lie panting on the wall walk.

'Jerome, Jerome, go, get away, they're safe.' Grunkite was roaring at the top of his voice. He hobbled along the wall walk bobbing in and out of the embrasures waving his arms in a vain attempt to attract the attention of the lone knight who fought below on the river bank. Harry got to his feet and dashed after Grunkite.

'A horn, we need a horn chancellor,' Harry ran further along the wall walk where he had stationed the Dredgemarsh Archers shouting 'A horn, a horn we need a horn.'

'Here Sire, here,' one of the men shouted.

'Blow for all your worth,' Harry shouted back. The blast from the horn sliced through the confusion and noise like a blade and for an instant in time everything froze in its compass as each and every man, friend or foe, sought the source and meaning of the sound. On the parapet of Dredgemarsh every man focused on the lone knight, sword arm raised and ready to strike at the Brooderstalt who were now encircling him. And all the combatants below looked towards the parapet towering over them and in that fraction of a second they beheld an old man gesticulating madly and shouting something. Jerome was the first to react. He spurred his mount forward and broke through the circle of Brooderstalt, but instead of veering off into Hazel Wood where he might escape he rode straight towards the castle wall, raised his visor and called out to Grunkite.

'What's he saying, what's he saying,' Grunkite was demanding but no one could hear Jerome above the roar of the Yayla.

'Something about wagons,' one of the Dredgemarsh archers said. When Harry heard the word wagons he rushed to the spot on the wall walk that was directly above Jerome. He slid out through an embrasure on his stomach and peered down at the knight and cupped one hand behind his ear. Jerome shouted out once more from below but the words were still lost in the howl of the floodwaters.

'Behind you.' Harry was gesticulating furiously to where the Brooderstalt archers and crossbow men had regrouped and were running along the edge of the Hazel wood towards Jerome. Within moments Jerome was hemmed in but still trying to shout his message to those above.

'Move, go, look out,' the men above, including Harry, were screaming at Jerome who, despite the imminent danger, was still trying to tell them something. A shrill command from the hazel wood, and low flying bolts and arrows hissed through the air, all aimed at Jerome's horse. The wounded animal slumped to its knees and rolled onto its side throwing Jerome onto the flooded bank. The knight rose slowly and once more tried to shout his message, the message he had sworn to deliver, but his words were swallowed by the raging waters. Harry, Grunkite and the Dredgemarsh archers watched aghast as the terrible drama unfold below them. Another command and a second flight of missiles flew from the hazel wood. The force of so many hits, though not piercing Jerome's armour impacted like a sledge hammer and he stumbled into deeper water closer to the submerged edge of the Yayla's banks. He rose again with great effort, the water spilling from every opening and crevice of his armour. A third command and the arrows flew once more. Grunkite turned away unable to bear the sight. Harry watched as Jerome fell for the last time and sank into the heaving swell of the Yayla.

'He was the finest of us all,' Grunkite said. His legs collapsed under him and he slumped down onto the parapet weeping without restraint for his lost friend.

Albrecht Pentrojan

Chapter 19

Pentrojan's officers exchanged glances of disbelief. Their General, who had driven them and the army beyond endurance over the last week, was smiling like a benevolent father. They entered the gaudy coloured Pavilion that the Broodestalt engineers had erected in the centre of the Vildpline. Behind the Pavilion, the vast army waited to move forward. A couple of the Manchian War Engines were postioned in the forward ranks and were firing a continuous barrage of boulders at Dredgemarsh with, it appeared, little intent other than to show that even from that great distance they could reach the walls of the old city.

'Come, come gentlemen, be seated, enjoy yourselves.' Pentrojan spread both hands above a trestle table sagging under a bewildering array of food and drink. They exchanged puzzled glances, but as ordered, took their seats and waited for further instructions.

'Sirs, do you not like delicious victuals and fine wine?' Pentrojan laughed. 'Or have you grown too used to dried bartago and cold braggot.' He raised a goblet in his hand.

'The finest clarrey you will ever drink, gentlemen. A toast to Cawdrult, Brooderlund and the end of Dredgemarsh.'

'To Cawdrult, Brooderlund and the end of Dredgemarsh,' they responded and picked up their goblets. The great war engines boomed in the background.

'Sweet music.' Pentrojan raised his goblet in salute and then drained it. 'But that is just a taster for our friends in Dredgemarsh.' He smacked his lips. 'Captain Xue, move all your war engines forward and into place as we planned.' The Manchian captain bowed to Pentrojan and without a word left the Pavilion.

The officers' anxiety began to dissipate when they tasted the rich spicy clarrey.

'Nectar, by the balls of Grell,' one whispered closing his eyes in mock ecstasy. They surveyed with amazement the food laid out before them: boar's meat in gravey, stuffed ptarmigan, salmon covered in cameline sauce, pies, pates, gelatines, fritters, and the finest wastel bread trenchers.

'Eat gentlemen. Eat.' Pentrojan insisted and the men, discarding all lingering apprehensions, began to gorge themselves. They laughed and joked, congratulating each other and their leader for what was now certain victory. The sound of bellowing oxen hauling the Manchian war engines past the Pavilion into forward positions mingled with and incited further the raucous banter of the officers.

'They await our arrival like a fat capon, all comb and no cock,' one man stood up wielding a capon leg from which he took a bite and moaned with pleasure.

'You can take the capon, Gur, we'll spear the chicken,' a comrade bawled out in response pointing to his groin and thrusting it forwards and back with a lewd grin.

'We'll tup the lot of them; muff or podex, it doesn't matter,' another called out. 'Muff or podex,' they all shouted and raised their goblets.

Pentrojan grinned and gestured to those serving the clarrey who withdrew straight away. As one by one the officer's goblets emptied, they began calling out for the missing servers. Pentrojan rose up from his seat at the head of the table. Like a slow wave, silence spread over the assembled men.

'This,' Pentrojan gestured towards the half-eaten feast before them, 'will recommence this evening and your goblets will be replenished.'

They were puzzled, disappointed by the sudden cessation of feasting. It was a trick. They should have known. After all, when did Pentrojan ever show them any courtesy or respect.

'Within those accursed walls.' Pentrojan pointed towards Dredgemarsh. 'We will continue this celebration in their banqueting hall this very evening.' It took some moments for the message to sink in. A sergeant called Gur stood up with his empty goblet and shouted

'What are we waiting for, let's go piss on the bastards?'

The others all rose in support and began to chant 'Yes, yes, lets piss on them ... no delay ... do it now...'

Pentrojan smirked and placed his still full goblet on the trestle table. 'Now it's the time of reckoning.' He strode out of the pavilion and his officers jostled each other in their attempts to be as close to their leader as possible.

As if it had been choreographed, Captain Luparellus , with two of his officers flanking Fabian, and a manacled Lia rode into the open space to meet Pentrojan as he emerged from the Pavilion.

'Well, well, captain Luparellus, I don't remember asking you to bring back any dainties.' He stared at Lia. The men around him sniggered and though their stomachs were partially satiated, there was now a different kind of hunger in their eyes. They examined every contour of the beautiful young captive. She sat straight and defiant and, without flinching, returned Pentrojan's lacivious stare.

'You have news for me, Captain?' Pentrojan said without diverting his lewd gaze from Lia.

'He was right, General. 'Luparellus tilted his head towards Fabian, 'They were bringing boulders from a quarry back to Dredgemarsh. We have captured all of their wagons except one. But that's being taken care of.'

'Well, Prince of Dredgemarsh or whoever you are,' Pentrojan addressed Fabian, 'it seems you may have saved yourself … for now.'

'He is no prince,' Lia spat out the accusation.

'She speaks. Seems to know you,' Pentrojan continued to address Fabian.

'She is a traitor just like her father, a one-time Cook Maester in my father's kitchens and now parading as a General Hawksfoot.

'A Cook Maester, you say,' Pentrojan's demeanor changed. It was clear that some unwelcome memory from the past unsettled him. The smirking condescension of a few moments before turned to a scowl full of hatred. 'This Cook Maester turned general will have his head roasted on his own spit but not before he watches his bitch spawn impaled on Brooderstalt cock.' He pointed to Lia. 'Tie her up … and him. We will have use for them later.'

'But general—' Fabian began.

Luparellus held up a hand for silence and nodded to the prisoners' escorts who dismounted, hauled Fabian and Lia from their saddles and marched them away.

'So, Captain Luparellus, how many wagons?' Pentrojan directed his gaze towards the first wagon that was just coming into view.

'Twelve General.'

After a few moments, Pentrojan laughed and then said, 'Captain Luparellus, you will just have to give them back to their rightful owners.'

'Give them back?' Luparellus said.

'We can't have you stealing from those good people. We'll return their precious boulders.' He paused and smiled at a bewildered Luparellus. 'Yes, Captain, we will return them … one by one. We may break a few heads in doing so but we'll do the right thing.'

His entourage began to comprehend the joke and started laughing and clapping their appreciation of their clever leader. 'You men, take these wagons, one for each war engine, and deliver these boulders back to their rightful owners. Rip their walls and main gate asunder. Remember we continue our supper in their banquet hall this evening.'

The officers scattered and commenced bawling out orders to those in their command.

Chapter 20

They've stopped,' a boy soldier called out. He and his companions who were packing the black nephryte into the belly of Firedrake looked to Harry. The ominous silence after hours of incessant noise and flying boulders, was disconcerting.

'They are moving in,' Harry said, and, though every man already guessed this to be the case, the spoken words left no room for even the faintest hope that the danger had, by some miracle, melted away. Harry saw the mounting panic in their faces. 'Just what we want,' he said. The men looked confused and doubtful . 'Hurry,' we need to start on the second part of our plan. Pieter Smallhand will take charge here.'

Pieter shouted to his companions, 'You heard. Get a move on.' The moment of paralysing fear passed. The soldiers recommenced loading the black nephryte. Harry left them to finish and descended, two steps at a time, from the firing platform. Pieter watched him mount and gallop across the grand plaza.

Through the desolate streets, strewn with Brooderstalt boulders and destroyed buildings, the pounding hooves of

Harry's mount beat out an eerie tattoo on the cobbles. It amplified an inchoate panic that made his stomach heave. The nausea subsided when he rode onto the Campanile Square and saw Grunkite supervising the loading of golden nephryte blocks into ten remaining wagons in Dredgemarsh. The blocks were being retrieved from the rubble of the collapsed Golden Campanile. Harry alighted from his mount and joined Grunkite.

'What a happy time it was when we built it, Harry,' Grunkite said. 'Built to celebrate your birth. Glorious days. Now we're helping that scum to destroy our own city by pulling it down.' Grunkite rubbed his sleeve across his eyes. 'Damned dust," he said.

'We need the nephryte, Chancellor. We can always rebuild the Golden Campanile.' Harry placed his hand on the old man's shoulder.'

'If we survive. I say it again, Harry. Go find a way out of here. Then there is hope that this city can be rebuilt.' Harry did not respond.

Beside him a soldier carrying one end of a golden nephryte block collapsed under the weight. His companion dropped the other end and staggered backwards. All of the soldiers loading the wagons looked exhausted and were barely able to lift the remaining blocks into the last empty wagon.

'Come on lads, almost there. Remember these are part of a little surprise for the filthy slime that pollute our sacred soil.' The speaker, covered in dust, bent down and hauled a great block of Nephryte up onto his chest, stumbled towards the wagon and heaved it over the edge.

Harry peered intently at the man. 'Sergeant?' he said after a few moments.

'Sire.' Sergeant Blazer stood to attention and saluted Harry. 'We're finished here. We'll have this lot back at the main gate in no time. We'll give them a hot welcome; one they won't forget. Right lads.'

Those nearest shouted their approval and fisted the air.

Harry smiled, returned the salute and faced Grunkite 'Do we have our volunteers?'

Grunkite shrugged his shoulders. 'So you're staying.'

'Yes.'

'Volunteers,' Grunkite called out.

Five of the men stopped working and looked towards Grunkite who beckoned them to join him and Harry.

Harry shook each of their hands. 'Dredgemarsh will honour you after this day.' The soldiers, all young men like Harry, exchanged self-conscious smiles with each other. They looked tense but there was the fire of youth in them.

'We are ready sire.' They spoke as one.

'Good,' said Harry. He unsheathed his sword and began to sketch a rough map in the dust. 'When these wagons are full, take five of them to the main gate here.' He stabbed the sword into the ground. 'When I give the signal the gate will be opened just long enough and wide enough for the wagons to get through. I want you to take the wagons out to the redoubts and place them across the Vildpline like this.' He swept the sword across the dusty ground in an arc. 'Make sure they can be seen from our firing platform but out of view of the approaching Brooderstalt.' They nodded and he nominated each individual in the order in which they would place their wagons. 'When you are in position unhitch the wagons, take the horses and return through the postern gate. We don't have much time before we are under fire again. Good fortune go with you.' Harry saluted them and they rejoined their comrades.

When Harry returned to Firedrake, it was fully loaded with the black nephryte. Pieter Smallhand and Gawan the metal worker, who had constructed some of the more intricate parts of Firedrake, were already making the final adjustments to it. They followed the strict procedures laid down by their dead mentor Professor Quickstrain. Two silver panels made by Gawan were the final pieces that would complete the construction of Firedrake. Gawan handed them to Harry.

'I have done my best, Sire.' He blushed with pride when Harry lifted them up and after careful inspection said, 'Beautiful, beautiful.' The panels interlocked and formed an elliptical pentagram. Harry slotted it into the optical chamber of Firedrake.

'Perfect.' He stood back and surveyed the completed lightning thrower. Now loaded with the Black Nephryte, the louring metal contraption seemed to pulsate with life. It was protected on the front and sides by the heavy stockade and bridged across the top with massive timber beams. On the front of the stockade several of the protecting timbers could be lowered by pulleys and ropes like a small drawbridge revealing the cone shaped nozzle of Firedrake. Harry smiled to see that despite their hopeless plight someone painted the head of a dragon on the cone in such a way that the opening of the nozzle was the dragon's mouth.

'Who is the artist?' Harry asked and Gawan nodded towards Pieter Smallhand who was standing with his back to them and looking towards the main gate.

'They are ready, the wagons are ready,' Pieter shouted.

Harry climbed onto the highest point of the stockade and scanned the Vildpline with a small telescope.

'They're moving in, but we still have time. Give the signal,' he shouted and the sergeant of the tower waved a red flag. The sentries hauled the main gates open, just wide enough to let the wagons pass.

'Wait, wait,' Harry shouted and the sergeant lowered the flag and waved his arms frantically at the main gate sentries to disregard the signal. The gates were closed again.

'Damnation, curse them, curse them,' Harry groaned.

'What is it?' Pieter asked.

'There, there.' Harry pointed to a small stand of hazel trees about three hundred ells away on the western edge of the Vildpline. He handed the telescope to Pieter.

'The devils.' Pieter gasped. 'Brooderstalt troopers. Do they know our every thought? The wagons will never make it to the redoubts.' He looked to Harry. 'What can we do?' This time there was no ready answer. For the first time, Harry looked uncertain. He had no clever words to buoy them up.

'Sire?' one of the officers on the firing platform called out, and that single word, and how he spoke it, expressed the anxiety of every man there. Harry held up one hand, a soundless gesture asking for quiet. He moved away from them and closed his eyes. The men exchanges worried glances but only moments passed before Harry spun round to face them.

'I want the ballistae and the longbows on the north west drum tower to start firing into those trees.' He pointed out the copse of hazels from where the Brooderstalt troopers were observing the castle. 'There's no more than thirty of them. Sergeant,' he addressed the duty sergeant on the firing platform, 'Send two of your fastest men to deliver that message now. When the ballistae and longbows commence we will execute our plan.' All those around Harry, nodded in agreement.

'You heard his lordship, you and you,' the sergeant pointed to two young soldiers, 'go.'

'Yes, sir.' They swung themselves from the platform down onto the lower walkway without using the steps. The older men smiled at their enthusiasm as they bustled and barged each other to see who would be first to deliver the message. It did not take long before the Brooderstalt observers in the hazel copse came under fire. They first retreated out of range of the longbows and then the ballistae until finally they rode out onto the Vildpline and headed back towards the main army. It was clear that they had no intention of losing any men; not when victory was just a matter of time and a short time at that.

On a signal from Harry, five wagons, full of golden nephryte from the demolished Campanile, raced out from the main gate and were set out in an arc below the redoubts. The volunteer drivers unhitched the horses and galloped back to safety through the postern gate.

The retreating Brooderstalt troopers observed this odd maneuver with derisive laughter.

'They are more stupid than we thought,' the leader of the troopers shouted to his men.

'Mad with fear,' one of his men responded.

'We'll let the fools set up their puny defenses,' their leader said and they continued back towards the main army.

The defenders of Dredgemarsh greeted this small victory with cheers of jubilation.

Chapter 21

Albrecht Pentrojan strode out from his tent wearing a finely wrought hauberk with the insignia of the Brooderstalt boar woven into the breast in gold links.

'Are they in place?' His tone was reverential as if some sacred ritual was about to be enacted.

'All our war engines are in place and ready,' said Captain Xue astride a foam flecked Manchian mare he had just ridden from the front line. His hauteur reinforced the mood of gloating satisfaction evident in the Brooderstalt high command.

'And, as you ordered, General, we have assembled a full cohort behind each war engine. There is no escape.' Captain Drago added.

Pentrojan, basked in the smiles, approving nods and the congratulatory words of his officers.

'So gentlemen, the vermin are trapped. Take a last look. Those walls will be pounded to dust and the dust soaked in their blood by the end of this day.' There were loud murmurs of approval. 'Destroyed with their own boulders, that they sweated to dig from their own quarry.' Laughter followed with hand clapping all around. Luparellus snapped his fingers. Two serving men hovering in the rear rushed forward with a chair for the General. He settled himself as if he were seated on a throne. His men gathered behind, jostling and sniggering like schoolboys. They were two hundred ells back from the nearest war engines which were spaced across the full width of the Vildpline at a distance of six hundred ells from the Dredgemarsh curtain wall. The eight cohorts directly behind the war engines formed an inpenetrable wall of infantry, bowmen and mounted troopers. There would be no survivors from Dredgemarsh.

'Look, look.' An officers pointed to where giant javelins from the Dredgemarsh Ballistae fell harmlessly short of their front line.

'They're fukked.'

'And they know it.'

Pentrojan nodded. A war horn blast ripped across the sky and echoed off the walls of Dredgemarsh. Every man on the Vildpline shouted at the top of his voice 'For Cawdrult, for Pentrojan for Brooderlund.' In unison the war engines erupted with such violence that the ground trembled under the feet of the Brooderstalt army. Huge boulders screamed through the cold air towards the old city walls. They crunched into the curtain wall, many of them embedding themselves in the old brickwork. The walls shivered under the onslaught. The main gate rumbled like a giant drum when a boulder smashed into it.

Pentrojan looked over his shoulder to Luparellus who leaned forward. 'I think, Captain, 'this may be quicker than

I thought. Make sure we are ready to go in, and …Captain
… no prisoners.'

'We'll be ready, General.' Luparellus smirked and left.

On the battlements and drum towers of Dredgemarsh
fear was as tangible as the showers of splintered brickwork
raining down on the defenders.

'Stand fast, stand fast,' the officers cried out to their
ballistae and mangonel crews and to the archers and
arbalesters. 'Wait for the enemy to come within range.' Brave
words but not delivered with any conviction. The more
tense the situation grew the more they looked towards the
firing tower where Harry stood staring out at the surging
hosts of Brooderstalt who befouled the sky with their hate-
filled ranting. The second barrage of boulders screamed
towards their targets and the men cowered behind the
merlons. Harry stood where he was despite the appeals from
Pieter Smallhand and Gawan to take shelter. The boulders
struck. Men cried out in fright and the walls and battlements
trembled.

A boulder smashed onto the firing platform just ells from
where Harry stood. A cloud of stone particles and splinters
enveloped him, followed by a piercing scream.

'We are doomed!' a young soldier cried out.

'None of that. Hold fast.' An older voice boomed out.
When the dust and debris settled, Harry was still standing.

'My leg, my leg,' Pieter Smallhand was lying on his back,
blood spilling from a wound in his left thigh. Harry, who up

to then appeared to be strangely indifferent to the mayhem around him, rushed to his stricken friend.

'Let me see,' he prized Pieter's bloodied hands away from his left thigh. A jagged stone splinter protruded from mangled flesh and cloth. Gawan joined Harry who was already removing his belt.

'Gawan, tighten this above the wound.'

The soldiers in command of the firing platform stared at the little tableaux of Harry, Gawan and the stricken Pieter in the midst of the debris. There was a look of frightened bemusement on their faces as if their minds could not or would not accept the disaster that now engulfed them.

'I don't want to die. Please.' The young soldier, already reprimanded, called out in a trembling falsetto. He received a swifter reprimand than before. This time, not in words, but a crunching blow to the side of his head that laid him out cold.

All attention was now focused on Harry. He would know what to do. They watched as he withdrew, as gently as possible, the bloody sliver from Pieter's thigh.

'Move him behind the stockade. Now, now, do it now.' Harry shouted. Two of the men, roused themselves and rushed forward and with Gawan's help carried Pieter to relative safety behind the stockade protecting Firedrake.

Then the strangest thing: Harry, standing exposed on the platform began to wipe away the gore from the sliver of stone and examine it. He shouted something, became animated and ran towards the front of the firing platform. Using the Oculmagnus which was still intact, he scanned across the battle-lines of the Brooderstalt. More thunderous roars from the enemy's war engines were followed by the whistle of the incoming boulders and the crunching impact of stone on stone. The firing platform shuddered under the impact of three strikes and the defenders were showered again with flying shards and dust that stung their eyes and filled their lungs. When it began to clear they could just about see that Harry was still standing in full view on the platform. As their vision cleared, they might have been forgiven for thinking that Harry had gone mad. He was gesticulating to them, grinning and waving the sliver of stone in the air.

'The fools are firing golden nephryte. It's Captain Severino's wagons from the mines. They have our wagons.' Harry was shouting at the top of his voice. The men stared at Harry. Had their young prince, at last, broken under the strain of battle? Harry seeing their confusion beckoned them to gather around him.

'This,' he held up the bloody splinter that he had extracted from Pieter's thigh, 'this is nephryte. They are firing golden nephryte at us. Our wagons, loaded with it, are lined up next to their war engines. We could not have hoped for better placement. Now we will show them a real war engine.' Harry pointed to Firedrake. The men began to smile, and then laugh and punch clenched fists into the air.

'What are we waiting for,' one shouted. Four of them scrambled to the drop-down door in the front of the stockade protecting Firedrake and lowered it.

Harry looked through the siting lens on the light disgorger. 'Left, left,' he called out and Gawan began to spin the horizontal worm drive. 'Stop,' called Harry. 'Up, slowly.'

Gawan switched his attention to the vertical worm drive. 'There, back, stop.'

He reached out his hand. 'Light.' The sergeant of the guard handed him a lighted taper from a brazier beside him. Harry swung open a small hinged door, on the side of Firedrake. Within was mounted the glistening parabolic reflector and at its fulcrum a transparent globe with an opening at the top. Inside the globe a golden liquid exploded into a dazzling light when Harry touched the taper to the opening. He closed and latched the door.

'Look away now,' he shouted. 'Cover your ears.' Gawan and the rest of the men turned their backs on Firedrake. Harry pulled a lever on the initiator. He turned away and clasped his hands over his ears. Even then he could hear, a high pitched pulsating sound building up to a crescendo. The air around them felt sulphurous and alive. An intense light, bright as the sun, enveloped them followed by a sound unlike anything ever heard before. It was as if the air around them and the sky above was being ripped asunder. They fell to their knees.

Pentrojan was leaning back to take another goblet of clarrey being proffered by one of his squires.

'Refill all of them,' he ordered. The officers around him held out their empty goblets like happy schoolchildren being offered an unexpected treat. Then the intense brightening of the sky and a monstrous rending of the air over the Vildpline stunned them into silence. Pentrojan was the first to recover. 'By God these Manchians know how to build—'

Flying shards of stone, dust and metal blossomed from the core of the central war engine and the General, goblet poised to drink, watched in astonishment as a mountain of debris tumbled towards them. They were swallowed by it, flung backwards and blown helplessly along the ground like jetsam in a storm.

'General, General, are you hurt.' An officer crawled to the prostrate body of Pentrojan. Around him men were scattered like discarded rag dolls, one sitting up and staring with a bemused grin at an unbroken goblet in his hand, others groaning and writhing on the ground and still others lying motionless.

'General, are you hurt?'

'What?' Pentrojan's spat and wiped the grime from his lips. 'What happened?'

'One of our war engines … I don't know. It turned into an inferno. Are you all right, General?'

'How could I be all right, you clotpole?' Pentrojan raised himself into a sitting position. He stared at his hands; patted his legs and body, a look of bewilderment on his face. With assistance, he staggered to his feet. 'What did you say happened?'

'The Manchian war engine has rent itself asunder.' The dust was beginning to clear and where, just moments before, they had been observing the giant war engine, there was nothing but a tangle of smouldering metal. Flames and a tower of smoke spiraled upwards from the ruins. All around were blackened corpses, dismembered limbs from men and horses. Bodies with rags of torn skin in place of arms and legs were crying out for death. The sickly stench of burning flesh fouled the air.

'What of the other engines?' Pentrojan was shaking his head from side to side.

'No problem, General. Listen; our Manchians have launched another bombardment.' The distinctive booming sound of the Manchian war engines appeared to calm the incipient fear in Pentrojan's eyes. He brushed the grey ash from his hauberk but to no avail: the instant he brushed it away he was covered in it again. His hands face and garments were besmirched in streaks of grey and black grime.

'Tell me when the walls are breached.' He limped back towards his pavilion most of which hung in tatters around a few of the standing poles that threatened to fall at any moment. A second blinding flash of light was followed by a monstrous roar that made the earth shudder. Pentrojan watched with dread as another scene of desolation unfolded. A second Manchian war engine was wrapped in a dense column of smoke. Bodies, dust and flames blossomed into the heavens. Once again screams of terror from man and beast fleeing from the cataclysm in total panic.

'Horse, my horse, helmet,' he yelled. A white-faced squire tried to lead Pentrojan's terrified mount towards the general. Another ran from the half-demolished pavilion with a helmet, buckler and sword. 'Curse you dogs, hurry, hurry.' The cloud of dust and acrid smoke from the second and more distant eruption rolled in like a fog and Pentrojan's furious cries turned to a spluttering incoherent yowl. Despite the pandemonium, he donned his helmet and buckler, and scramble onto his courser. He burst forth from the smothering cloud and galloped back to the four reserve cohorts of the army some five hundred ells behind his Pavilion.

'To arms, to arms,' he flung out the order to the officers of the reserves who gathered to meet him. The four cohorts waiting for the call lined up in prearranged phalanxes armed and ready to march on Dredgemarsh. The officers and men were anxious for battle and, as yet, unaware of the extent of the carnage around the demolished war engines.

'Now the real work starts.' one giant Brooderstalt in the frontline laughed and swung his flail mace in the air. Those around him followed his example with their swords and war hammers and from them the frenzy for battle grew until the four cohorts were chanting death and destruction on Dredgemarsh and every living creature within its walls. Pentrojan stood in the stirrups in front of his invincible army. He raised his sword towards Heaven. The ominous rhythm of the marching drums echoed back and forth across the Vildpline. Pentrojan swung his sword down and pointed it towards Dredgemarsh. The shrill battle horns sounded the advance. The march was on. Four captains of the cohorts spurred their mounts forward to flank Pentrojan, two on each side. In the distance ahead of them, the war engines pounded away at the old fortress city walls and gate. Moving within sight of the roaring monsters, Pentrojan and his army beheld another eruption of dense smoke and flames. A fourth and fifth followed in quick succession.

Pentrojan halted his army.

'Drago,' he addressed the officer to his immediate left. 'Find out what's happening to those fukking Manchians and their infernal war engines. Now! We'll wait here.' Captain Drago set off at a gallop.

The war drums and battle horns went silent behind the grim leader. The officers on both sides of him ceased talking. The only sound on the Vildplne was the booming from the remaining war engines pounding the walls of Dredgemarsh.

It took longer than expected for Captain Drago to return. As he rode up to Pentrojan, he was shaking his head. 'No one knows what's happening, General. Anyone within two hundred ells of the destroyed war engines has perished. Hundreds are dead or wounded. Some think they saw lightning bolts strike. Others think the war engines are destroying themselves from over-use.'

There was no furious outburst from Pentrojan. He stared straight ahead. Captain Drago shifted out of his line of sight. The other officers exchanged nervous glances. Pentrojan sat silent, immobile except for the slow pulsating muscles of his jaw.

Another giant eruption rocked the Vildplne. Then he spoke. 'Ride back.' His voice was laced in venom. 'Order those Manchian fukkers with their remaining war engines to concentrate bombarding the main gate until it is breached.' Captain Drago lashed his foam-flecked mount into action once more.

'You,' Pentrojan addressed the officer to his immediate right, 'Captain Nazor, move your phalanxes of longbow men and arbalesters forward now. Rain death on their walkways. Not an inch is to remain safe for them. Kill everything that moves.

'At once, general.' Captain Nazor displayed a row of rotting teeth, grinned and rubbed his hands together in joyful anticipation of the work ahead. He swung his mount around to collect his men.

'Leave some for us, Naz,' a fellow officer called out.

In short time, four phalanxes of archers and arbalesters marched forward. The sound of one thousand pairs of feet hammered out a warlike rhythm full of menace. They took up their chanting once more. The war horns screeched and the drums rattled out their discord.

'We wait here.' A begrimed Pentrojan dismounted with obvious discomfort. 'Be ready to march at a moment's notice. We will kill the vermin slowly, one by one 'til they beg for death. His squire ran forward with a leather folding stool for his master.

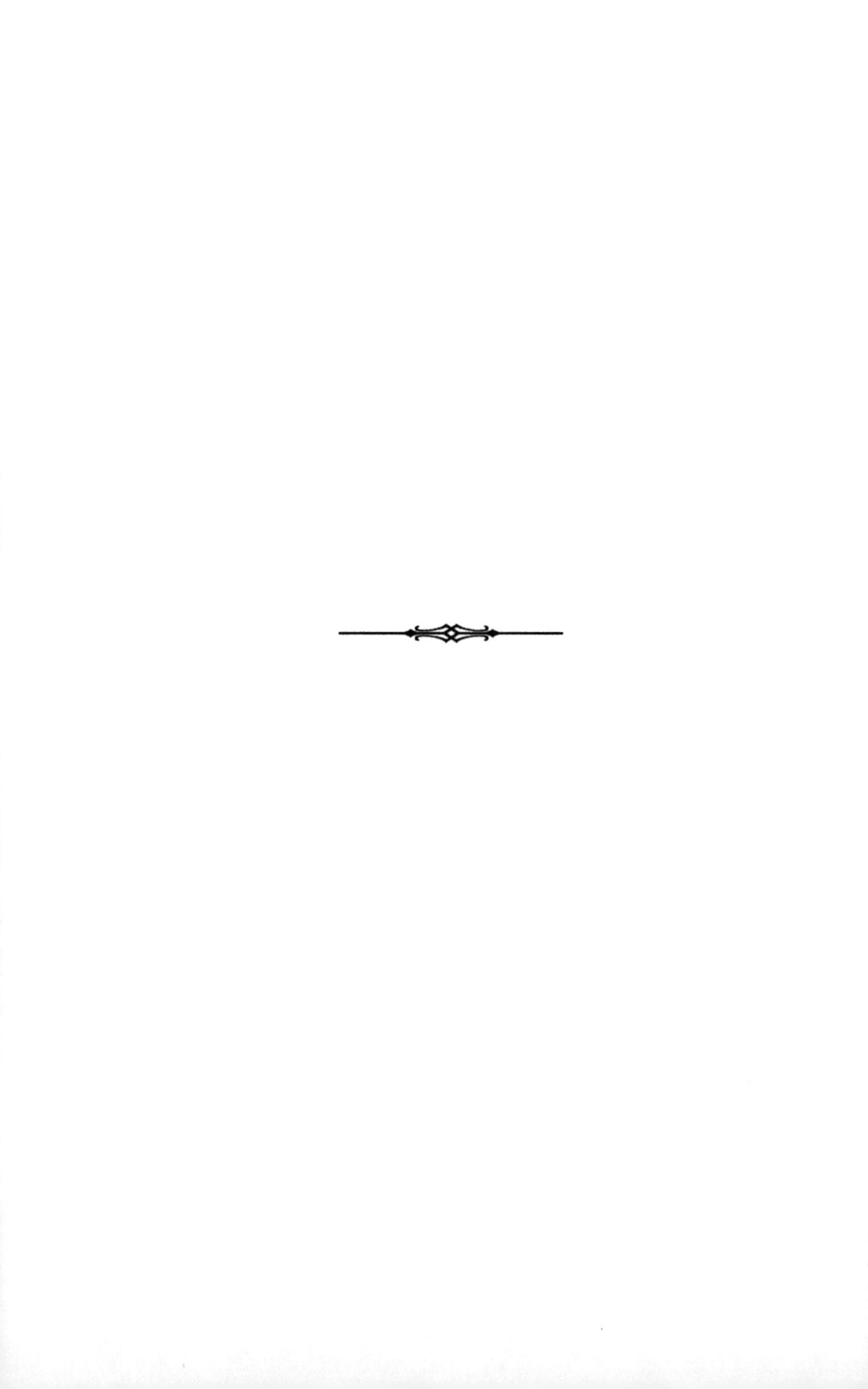

Chapter 22

'uparellus, bring that dungworm friend of yours, that so called lying bladderskate Prince of Dredgemarsh. Bring him here now.' These were the first words from Pentrojan who had lapsed into a disquieting silence for so long that his officers began to fidget and exchange nervous glances and gestures. They were still mounted and the army behind them standing in formation. Out in front of them and still seated on his stool, Pentrojan gazed at the clouds of smoke that marked where the wreckage of six Manchian war engines spewed giant spirals of ash into the crisp morning air.

There was no immediate answer to the General's request. His squires glanced fearfully over their shoulders to where a white faced Luparellus oozed repressed fury.

One of Luparellus's sergeants leaned in close to Luparellus. 'Captain, the General is—'

'I can fukking hear, Sergeant.'

'Luparellus.' Pentrojan turned his head with slow deliberation and stared at the surly captain. 'Are you deaf? Do I need to repeat myself?'

'I'll go now.'

'You'll go now, what?' Pentrojan leaped to his feet.

'I'll go now … General.' Luparellus jerked at the reins of his horse and with something less than urgency trotted back through the ranks towards their base camp.

'He'll pay for this,' a fellow officer whispered.

Pentorjan turned back to observe the carnage before him. Those behind sensed, in a way that they could not explain, a storm of unfathomable rage within their General.

The relentless bombardment of the last four Manchian war engines continued.

Luparellus, emerged from the ranks with a manacled Fabian slung across the withers of his horse. The animal, eyeballs bulging, skittered sideways in an attempt to turn but Luparellus, with all his brute strength, hauled on the reins and raked the animals flanks, forcing it to move forward. He flung Fabian at Pentrojan's feet without uttering a word. Pentojan, as if swatting away an irritating insect, dismissed Lurarellus with an exaggerated sweep of his hand. The Captain re-joined the officers behind Pentrojan, his face contorted in anger. His companions looked askance at him, some indifferent to his humiliation, many others trying but not succeeding to suppress incipient grins of satisfaction. They then turned their attention to the interrogation before them. They could not hear what was being said but it was clear that the prisoner, now on his knees before Pentrojan, was pleading for his life.

'That, that's a Prince of Dredgemarsh? How pathetic.' Captain Drago spat on the ground. 'You should have cut his throat when you had the chance, Luparellus.'

Luparellus did not respond but his hand grasped the hilt of his sword. Drago did likewise and those around them edged away.

'I'm fukking surrounded by fools,' Pentrojan bellowed and spun round to face his officers. The tension between Luparellus and Drago evaporated. 'You fool, clotpole,' he pointed directly at Luparellus. You've brought death into your own camp. You puttock's melt. Those fukking wagons of stones are the cause of all this destruction.'

'I could … how could I have—'

'You should have tortured that piece of shit 'til he puked up everything he knew.' He pointed to Fabian, 'And you might have discovered that those stones are all part of some infernal lightning thrower.' Spittle was gathering on the corners of the General's lip. 'Down, down, out of your saddles, the lot of you,' he screamed 'We stay here until those wagons are moved.'

'What about him?' Drago pointed to the kneeling Fabian.

Pentojan, after a nerve racking delay for the bedraggled Fabian, said, 'Take him back to base camp. He just might be of some use yet … if he is who he claims to be. Luparellus stepped forward to grab Fabian. 'No, no, no. You take him.' He pointed to Captain Drago. 'And you.' He swiveled his pointing arm to Luparellus. 'You have one and only one chance to prove you are not a complete idiot. You will remove the seeds of destruction you have hauled into our midst.'

'But, what do you expect me to —'

'Expect? I don't expect, I command. And you'll do as commanded without question.'

'What do you command, General?'

'Move our forward cohorts, or what's left of them, back from those remaining war engines. Do it now. After that pray that a dark night sets in quickly, because you and your men will remove those wagons of deadly stone.'

'You send us to our death, General.'

'Your duty. I send you to your duty. The rest of you,' he shouted, 'stand down the army. Be ready at any moment to march. And keep those war drums beating till I say stop. Until their last breath, those Dredgemarsh scum will not get a moment's rest.'

Chapter 23

The seventh Manchian war engine demolished part of the main gate of Dredgemarsh moments before it was destroyed by Firedrake. An eerie silence followed.

'What are they at?' Harry scanned the Vildpline with the Oculmagnus. 'Can't see anything.'

'Listen' Grunkite said and from somewhere beyond the clouds of smoke, dust and flames the chanting of a great host followed by the distant beat of the war drums filled the fearful sky. Grunkite peered through the oculmagnus. 'They are not marching forward ... waiting for something.'

'The gate is breached. They know we are too few to defend it,' Hawksfoot joined them on the firing rampart.

'Yes but why not continue firing and weaken us even further before the final attack?' Grunkite made way for Hawksfoot to peer through the oculmagnus.

'Perhaps ...' Harry paused 'Perhaps they think if they stop firing their remaining war engines will not be destroyed. They have never seen the likes of Firedrake.'

'Sire,' Gawan called out, 'we are ready to fire again.'

'Wait,' Harry said. If they start marching, how long before they get here, General.'

Hawksfoot was still scanning the Vildpline through the oculmagnus. 'They've moved all of their troops back from the war engines, Sire. Can't be more than half a league away. But if they were determined to march tonight, they could be on the plaza before St. Johannes rings out Matins.'

'So there is nothing to be gained by destroying their remaining war engines now,' Harry said.

'That's true. They've pulled their troops back from their own war engines,' Hawksfoot replied.

'General, We'll cease firing for now. You decide when we restart. I must leave you for now.'

'Where will you be, Sire?'

Harry appeared not to hear. He was absorbed in scrutinising every facet of the Grand Plaza, North Parade and its surrounding streets below. 'Delay them.' Harry pointed towards the Vildpline. 'They may attack under darkness. Delay them for as long as possible. I need every minute you can give me, General.

'Delay, I'll delay the bastards,' Hawksfoot said. 'They may not attack again until the morning, but, whenever they do, they will wade through their own blood and guts before they reach that gate. Come Gawan, Sergeant, we have work to do.'

Harry started down the stone steps from the firing rampart. 'Chancellor Grunkite, come with me.'

Chapter 24

The canal men, whose heroic labour was preventing the canals from flooding, though puzzled by the order to abandon their struggle, emerged blinking and exhausted with their ponies and drays from the Canal Tunnel. Harry was waiting for them. More than one hundred canal men gathered along Canal Way where he addressed them from the back of a dray. There was no time for detailed explanations, but the incredulous canal men were ordered to seal off every street and laneway leading unto the North Parade and the Grand Plaza to a height of nine feet or more from the western wall to the opening of the Canal Tunnel.

'He's doing what? Did he say he's going to divert the Yayla?'

'Impossible.'

'It's what he said.'

'Never.'

'Bollocks.'

'He want's us to what?'

The older and more senior men were moving through the throng trying to calm things down.

Lift me up, lift me up.' Eudo, the one armed water bailiff, clambered up onto a canal dray next to Harry's. 'Quiet. Quiet.' His voice, long used to shouting out orders in the clamorous subterranean canal networks, boomed out above the din. 'Silence.' He held his fighting club aloft as if about to srike someone.

Harry nodded to Eudo and began again. 'There is no time for explanations now. Trust me, we must build those water barriers now. Use everything and anything you can get. Tear doors off their hinges. Take anything you can find in market square: timber, leather, cloth, stones, clay. Knock down walls, houses if you must. Make the barriers tall and strong enough to hold back the floodwaters of the Yayla. We will divide into teams of twenty. These men,' he pointed to a small group of soldiers, 'will show each team where to build the barriers. Make every second count.'

Eudo stepped forward. 'What are we waiting for? Assemble right here.' He pointed his club in front of the dray he was standing on. We'll set up the teams right now.'

Harry departed for the main gate with Grunkite still following him.

'What's happening, Sire.' Grunkite, looked tired and uncertain when he and Harry arrived at the half demolished main gate. 'What can I do?'

'Start burning that.' Harry pointed at the damaged gate. 'And keep feeding the fire. We need to keep them out for as long as possible.'

'What else, Harry?'

'Keep two wagons of nephryte here, place both at the base of the west tower of the gate. I must be able to see them from the firing platform. Take the remaining four wagons to the western wall. Pile every last nephryte rock onto the battlement exactly where we unloaded the black nephryte. When the time is right, I want your men to erect a tall flagpole with a red flag, tall as you can get. Position it exactly above the nephryte. I must be able to see it also from the firing tower. Everything depends on that.'

'Why are we—'

'Chancellor, I intend to demolish part of the western wall and allow the Yayla flood-waters to flow into Dredgemarsh. We'll discuss the fine detail later'

Grunkite nodded, eyes wide and mouth open.

'Good, good.' Harry placed his hand on the old man's shoulder and turned to go.

'Where will you be, Harry?'

'Firedrake, but first I have to visit an old friend.'

Harry's destination was Canal Way and the small stable at the end of the street. On his way there he visited Bella Crumble in her kitchen and collected two cooked potatoes. As he hurried along, men busy hauling bundle of reeds, timber and sacks of sand from the canal supply yards greeted the young Prince or raised a clenched fist of support in the air.

Canal Way was deserted. An eerie quietness hung over the shabby little houses. And as he passed his old home, its flimsy door smashed and its one small window ajar, Harry was unprepared for the baffling mix of emotions he felt:

nostalgia, contempt but love also. He thought of Maisie, the only mother he ever knew. He thought of her cruel death. Despite her deception, he could not condemn her. Whatever else, she did love him; he knew that for sure, and he loved her.

Those sad thoughts were dispelled on entering the little stable yard and hearing the unmistakable nickering of Pingo, the canal pony who laboured many years with Harry, transporting the detritus of the canals to Meregloom Gorge. Harry embraced the little pony and fed him the two potatoes, his favourite treat. 'I haven't forgotten, Pingo.' Listening to Pingo chewing on the potatoes, Harry allowed himself to imagine he was the simple canal boy once more with no other care but to feed and mind his faithful friend and work companion. Then the vivid memory of Lia's golden laughter, on one of those, too few, stolen moments of youth when he, tongue-tied in her presence, could think of nothing to say except that his pony loved potatoes.

'Come along Pingo. We must see that you are safe.' Harry stroked Pingo's mane and led him away from the stable yard.

Chapter 25

‘Keep it coming men, keep it coming,’ Grunkite shouted through the smoke and flying sparks and then doubled over in a paroxysm of coughing. His face and hands were smudged with ash that gushed upwards from the inferno that was the main gateway. It was falling like snow all around them. Tiny wisps of smoke curled upwards from his clothes where the sparks were burning into the fabric. The Chancellor's eyelids were red rimmed and begrimed. Exhausted men fed the conflagration with timber and any other inflammable material they could scavenge.

'Sir, you are needed. There's a man. Says he has a message for you from the King. Please move back sir, you're too close.' A Royal Guard officer took the Chancellor's arm and began to drag him away from the flames. Grunkite, blinded by the smoke, allowed himself to be led away. 'You men, leave that here,' the officer ordered two men who were carrying a wooden chest towards the fire. 'Sit sir… get your breath,' the officer maneuvered Grunkite onto the chest and beckoned a young man with startling red hair to come forward.

'My name is Athelard, Sir, I have just arrived from—' the young man was silenced by the raised hand of the Chancellor who was bent over gasping for air. Long raking coughs were followed by shuddering inhalations that etched taut strings of pain across his face. The officer and the flame haired arrival watched with dismay as the old man shook with the violence of his coughing.

'Chancellor, can I do anything?' the officer asked, but Grunkite just waved him away. To the relief of everyone the attack subsided and Grunkite raised his raw and streaming eyes to the young man called Athelard.

'Speak.'

'I am Athelard sir. I have come by boat from the Lake Village with word from King Cesare.'

'He's here?' Grunkite heaved himself up from the wooden chest. 'Where, where is the King?'

'He said he will attack the Brooderstalt from the rear. '

'Aha!' Grunkite shouted and clapped his hands together. 'How many, lad, how many with the king.' His grinning lips, combined with his besmirched face, red eyes and rivulets of tears on his cheeks and jowls, created a most alarming and grotesque image.

'About one thousand in all: our own cavalry, Anselem Knights, Lycian Archers and the Glindor Hobelars. The very best sir.' Athelard's red hair glistened in the reflected light of the conflagration at the main gate and Grunkite smiled to see the pride and defiance in the young man's bearing.

'Well said, well said, young sir.' Grunkite clapped him on the arm.

'Sir, I also have a message from his Highness. He told me to tell you that the Brooderstalt captured the neph … nephryte and that you could yet have your opportunity. He said you would know what he meant.'

'We do and we have. You are somewhat late with that news lad but never mind.'

'I'm sorry sir, there were Brooderstalt along the river. I would have been here sooner but—'

'Not your fault young man, I understand.' Grunkite clapped him on the arm again.

'There is something else sir. The Prince and young lady Lia Celeste, daughter of General Hawksfoot, were captured by the Brooderstalt. The King is distraught.'

'The Prince you say?' Grunkite scratched his head. 'The Prince?' He thought for a moment. 'Of course, of course, how would he know. You saw Fabian, not the prince.'

'Yes sir … Prince Fabian,' Athelard articulated the words carefully as if he was under the impression that the Chancellor was confused or slow in comprehending his message.

'No young sir, you don't understand. Strange things have happened here since the King departed and it's essential that he knows about them as soon as possible.'

'Know what, sir?'

'I'll explain but first come with me and tell me about the General's daughter.' Grunkite shuffled his way across the plaza, away from the burning main gate, with the easy striding Athelard by his side. As he went, he shouted back to his officer. 'Find the Prince and General Hawksfoot and tell them to meet me in the command room. Tell them it's urgent.' The officer set off at a run in the direction of the firing rampart.

While waiting in the command room for Harry and Hawksfoot to arrive, Grunkite filled a trencher with hot chitterlings from a large iron cauldron simmering on the wood stove in the centre of the room. 'Sit down and get this inside you, lad.'

Athelard set-to immediately and, as he ate, Grunkite questioned him about every aspect of Cesare's journey from Anselem. Before Athelard was finished eating, Harry and a distraught Hawksfoot barged through the door.

'They've captured my daughter? Is it true? Do you know where they took her? Did they bring her back onto the Vildpline? Was she hurt?' His two hands were stretched out in supplication to Athelard.

'They took her, that's all I know sir. I did not see her myself,' Athelard stood up from the table.

'We have killed her ourselves … if she was anywhere near those …' He slumped onto a chair and looked at Grunkite, his face wild with grief.

'Let's not be hasty General,' said Grunkite, 'they would have taken hostages to their base camp, not the front line. '

'The Chancellor is right, General,' Harry said but he could not conceal the tremor in his voice or the alarm in his eyes.

'Sire, this young man has also brought some good news. King Cesare has arrived with his army. He will attack the Brooderstalt from the rear.'

'What more can you tell us of the general's daughter?' Harry addressed Athelard who was staring at him in disbelief.

'Harry … I mean Sire, am I correct? … I don't understand,' Athelard looked in bewilderment at the chancellor.

'Greet the real Prince of Dredgemarsh. Fabian was, is an impostor. He is not a prisoner of the Brooderstalt, he has joined them.' Athelard stood open-mouthed, staring at Harry.

'What can you tell us?' Harry repeated.

'All I know is our scouts, Kristoff Surefoot and his son Halbert reported that they saw her and the Prin … I mean Fabian being escorted back to the Vildpline by Brooderstalt cavalry.

Hawksfoot groaned. Harry's face was a mask of despair.

'There must be something we can do.' Hawksfoot, head buried in his hands was speaking to no one in particular. Grunkite moved to the general's side and laid a hand on his shoulder.

'Don't despair old friend. The King is out there. He will find her.

'If, if she is still … still…'

'I will find her,' Harry said. Grunkite raised his hand as if about to protest but the tone of Harry's voice and the look on his face made him desist.

'Sire, I will go with you.' Athelard said.

'Yes, good idea,' Grunkite said. 'Sire, the King does not know you or what extraordinary things have taken place. Fabian is still his son and prince regent as far as he is concerned. You will need this young man to explain.'

'So be it,' Harry said. Hawksfoot heaved himself up from his seat.

'I must go with you sire'

'No.'

But, Sire, I must.'

'No, we need you here, General. You must hold them at bay until I get back You are in command of Firedrake. There is no one else. We are all doomed if we cannot delay the Brooderstalt.'

'But, Sire.'

'No General. There is no more to be said. I need to travel fast and on foot. Have no fear; I will bring her back.' Harry patted the old warrior on the forearm.

'Chancellor Grunkite, you know the plan?'

'Of course, Sire. The four wagons of nephryte are on their way to the west wall right now as well as the flagpole and red flag.

Harry grasped both of Grunkites shoulders and stared intently at him. 'When the bells of the Cathedral peal out, raise the flag and not before that.'

'I won't fail.'

'Good luck, Chancellor. I will get back as soon as possible. Come, Athelard.'

'All will be ready, Sire,' Grunkite called out as the two young men departed.

He reached out and grasped the hand of a tearful Hawksfoot. 'Death or glory, General, death or glory,' he said, and the two old warriors stood silent by the dusty window silhouetted against the red glow from the inferno at the main gate. In the backgound the Brooderstalt battle drums beat out their implacable rage and it felt as if the whole world was aflame.

'Death or glory,' Hawksfoot whispered. 'Death or glory.'

Cesare Greyfell

Chapter 26

Cesare's army filtered like smoke through the dim core of Rim Wood. They were no more than half a league from its northern tip. Through a narrow defile Cesare, his senior officers and his squire veered off to a vantage point where they looked down on the Vildpline and the vast Brooderstal army while still remaining hidden by the trees. For hours before, they had listened to the booming of the Manchian War Engines followed by the earth trembling reverberations of Firedrake. Now as they gazed down at the Brooderstalt army preparing for the final assault on Dredgemarsh they could see the smouldering scars on the landscape where Firedrake had turned man, beast and war engines to ash. Even as they watched, Firedrake unleashed another blazing bolt that seared everything in front of it.

'By all the saints,' Aubrey of Vilspont, captain of the Knights of Anselem, exclaimed, 'It's like Lucifer and his legions have been unleashed from hell.'

'Farseer,' Cesare called out. His squire, anticipating the request, extracted a long telescope from a leather pouch.

Cesare dismounted and took the glistening instrument. Unbidden the squire stepped in front of his King and turned his back to him. Cesare rested the telescope on the squire's shoulder and scanned the maelstrom below. He beheld the carnage wrought by Firedrake: unimaginable destruction. The remaining Brooderstalt war engines appeared to be inactive, with just a handful of men crewing each of them. And there, yes, there were the wagons of golden nephryte parked beside them. The fools!

The main army stood a long way back from these silent monsters. Waiting. For what? Despite the devastation wreaked by Firedrake on the forward troops, the army, now poised to march on Dredgemarsh was still vast. It stretched across the full width of the Vildpline. Over twenty cohorts divided into solid square phalanxes of infantry, archers, troopers and knights, creating a dazzling matrix of terror. One man sat out in front of the Brooderstalt host surveying the devastation ahead of him. Albrecht Pentrojan. Even at a distance he was recognisable and even at a distance suppressed fury emanated from that lone figure gesticulating to a rider who galloped off in the direction of the silent Manchian war engines.

Cesare shifted the telescope in the direction of Dredgemarsh. A quick intake of breath through clenched teeth. The great soaring walls of his beloved Dredhemarsh were battered and scarred by the relentless onslaught from the Manchian war engines. The brattice works were in tatters and the machicolations on the walls and drum towers were destroyed. Here and there even the huge merlons were broken or displaced. Worst of all the barbican lay in ruins exposing the main gate which was now a wall of flame.

He repositioned the telescope again to focus on Pentrojan. His heart near stopped. It was Fabian, shackled and thrown to the ground in front of Pentrojan. Cesare's officers saw their King's face turn pale. The telescope slipped from his grasp. His squire caught it. Cesare took the instrument and once more rested it on the squire's shoulder. He took a deep breath and after a moment's hesitation he focused on the scene below. Fabian was kneeling before Pentrojan and it was clear that he was pleading. Pleading in vain, because, with a dismissive wave from Pentrojan's hand, a rider moved forward, leaned down from his mount and dragged Fabian to his feet. He grabbed a rope attached to Fabian's shackles and set out at a trot back towards their base camp. Fabian, ran and stumbled his way in the wake of the rider.

'Take it.' Cesare flung the telescope aside, as if it was an evil thing. Once again, his ever-alert squire caught the instrument. 'We'll attack their base camp without delay. Instruct every single man to watch out for my son, Prince Fabian. No harm must come to him. Move out fast and stay hidden until we are directly in line with their base camp.'

It did not take long to reach that point in Rim Wood that overlooked the base camp. Here at the northern tip, the trees were not as dense and the wood's edge broke onto a vast grassy slope that swept straight down to the camp that lay in a shallow dip in the plain. Cesare gathered his captains around him: Aubrey of Vilspont of the Knights of Anselem, Ranulf Halfhand of the Lycian Archers, Dubnar Niells of the Gliondar Hobelars and the leader of the Dredgemarsh Invincibles: Andret Longspere His instructions were brief and precise.

Ceasre, Aubrey of Vilespont and Andret Longspere, rode out from Rim Wood at the head of the Knights of Anselem and the Dredgemarsh Invincibles. They gathered pace down the slope towards the Brooderstalt camp. They were halfway down before the thunder of their hooves alerted those who remained to guard the camp and also the last two cohorts of infantry at the tail end of the main army. Battle horns blasted and a great howl erupted from the Brooderstalt.

Still hidden in the trees of Rim Wood the Lycian Archers watched the heavily armoured knights cut through the camp like fire racing through a field of dry straw. When they reached the eastern boundary of the Vildpline they wheeled around and came thundering back to wreak even further devastation on the enemy camp. Two cohorts of Brooderstatlt infantry at the tail of the main army wheeled around and began to run in tight formation back towards the camp but, by this time, Cesare's Knights were streaming back up the slopes towards Rim Wood having left a trail of devastation behind them. Their swords, maces and war hammers were bathed in gore.

At the top of the slope Cesare and his knights wheeled around and waited in full view of the two Brooderstalt cohorts who now gathered in close shield-locked formation and started to march towards them in a pincer movement. As they marched, they beat their shields with the flat of their falchions and chanted 'death, death, death.' The knights waited, unflinching. When the Brooderstalt were halfway up the slope, Cesare raised his arm. The Lycian Archers emerged from Rim Wood and almost casually they walked their mounts forward through the ranks of the Knights and fanned out along the embankment in front of the knights. For a moment the chanting from of the Brooderstalt diminished and their forward march slowed a fraction. Then, with the encouragement of their leaders, they began to chant once more. 'Death. Death. Death!'

Death came. It came swift and silent. The Lycian archers unleashed their deadly flights of arrows that pierced the leather shields and jerkins of the enemy. The Brooderstalt front line fell as if a great scythe had swept through it. Those behind trampled over the dead and dying. They had no option but to keep moving forward such was the pressure from the ranks behind them. The chanting died down and faster than they could have imagined another flight of arrows brought death once again to the forward ranks of the Brooderstalt. Their lines began to break up as they staggered over their fallen comrades.

'Charge, charge ' their officers were screaming and the battle horns blared.

The horde ran up the slope and twice more the Lycians rained death down upon them. Still, they came forward and when they were within a hundred ells of their enemy, the Lycian archers split into two separate groups. One rode to the left and the other to the right along the prow of the slope. The Knights of Anselem surged forward again. Cesare at their head raised his sword aloft as they charged in a vee formation. They ploughed a blood-spattered furrow right through the Brooderstalt ranks. At the same time the two groups of Lycian archers rode out and around the sides of the Brooderstalt and, as only they could do, fired their arrows with unerring accuracy from the backs of their speeding mounts. All semblance of order within the ranks of the Brooderstalt vanished. They scattered in every directions to escape the lethal blades of the knights and the terrifying arrows of the Lycians that appeared to come from nowhere with such devastating accuracy.

This destruction of two cohorts at the rear of the army was executed with such speed and efficiency that by the time Pentrojan was made aware of it, the deed was done and Cesare's army under cover in Rim Wood was weaving its way forward through the wood to find another suitable breach in the escarpment overlooking the Vildpline from where they could launch their next surprise attack on the rear of the main army.

Pentrojan ordered Drago and his cavalry back to secure the encampment. When he arrived at the edge of the dip in the land where the base camp lay, Drago stared as if he could not comprehend the carnage of so many dead Brooderstalt soldiers.

'How could this have happened—'

'Captain, Captain, look here!' one of his men emerged from behind a half-demolished tent dragging a blood smeared Fabian behind him.

'He was hiding under the bodies of two of our men.'

'Well Prince,' Drago sneered, 'you have a habit of cheating death.'

'I couldn't fight,' Fabian held up his bound wrists.

'Who did this, you sniviling cur?'.

'Knights. They wore the Anselem colours.'

'And the girl. Did they take the girl?'

'No,' Fabian said and pointed Northwards towards the Devils Cleft. Drago removed his helmet to scan the northern sweep of the Vildpline.

'There, there captain,' one of his officers pointed. Drago caught the movement of a white dress in the distance. Lia was running barefoot towards Grak's forest. Drago's face twisted into a contemptuous smirk.

'Kill her.' Drago said and picked out five troopers.

With whoops and shouts the five horsemen galloped Northwards after their quarry. Drago watched, cold and impassive, as they quickly closed on the distant figure of the girl. The Brooderstalt officers laughed and joked but it was a nervous gaiety that revealed their real fear of the unseen enemy who had wreaked destruction on their fellow soldiers.

The ground trembled.

'Oh please no!' Lia cried to the desolate sky.

The pounding hooves drew closer. The first outcrop of trees on the perimeter of Grak's Forest was no more than half an arrow's flight ahead. It might just as well have been a league. She heard the obscene banter of her pursuers as they closed in on her. Gulping for air, she struggled on, all the time slowing down 'til her strength gave out. With a despairing cry, she sank to her knees. Her executioners bore down on her and in those final moments she thought of Harry. Thought of the first time she ever saw him, a raggedy canal boy with his pony and dray. Then later, her curiosity to see Quickstrain's proclaimed new scholar and her shock at discovering that it was none other than Harry Fairgame. She remembered with perfect clarity how he lay close to death in the infirmary and then the extraordinary revelation of his true identity: Prince Harry Grefell. She recalled every detail of those too few occasions when their eyes met and her young heart overflowed with love.

'Harry.' she spoke his name, a last invocation of the one most precious to her in the world from which she was about to depart.

Though maintaining a grim silence there was a flicker of excitement in the cold blue eyes of Drago. He watched his men with drawn swords racing each other to see who would strike the first blow. But his excitement faded to be replaced by a more quizzical and alarming expression as one of the five was flung backwards from his mount. Then another fell and the three remaining horsemen veered away from the prostrate girl.

'What in the …' Drago stood in the stirrups to get a better view.

'Sir, to the left,' one of his men shouted and pointed. Four or five horsemen galloping from Grak's forest. It was difficult to make out who they were but one thing was clear: the size of the lead horseman. Even from that distance Drago could see that he was a huge man. The remaining three Brooderstalt, just moments away from their victim dragged their mounts to a halt and were now racing back towards the destroyed encampment. Unsure of the strength of this enemy and thinking that they were part of the army that decimated the encampment and two cohorts of infantry, Drago ordered his cavalry into formation.

'Be prepared for an attack!' he drew his sword and waited and watched.

Another of the would-be executioners of Lia fell from his horse and the final two were caught and dispatched with ease by the giant on a great cob wielding a gleaming battle-axe.

Lia shuddered when two hands grasped her shoulders and lifted her from the ground. Was she already dead? Was this what it was like?

'Young lady, have no fear, have no fear,' a deep voice was insisting. She opened her eyes. The voice was that of Captain Paine. She collapsed into his arms and cried like a child.

'Potens!' Captain Paine called out, 'back to the forest. Take the lass.' Potens returned to the captain reached down, scooped Lia up with one arm and placed her in front of him on the cob. Lia and her small band of rescuers retreated back into Grak's forest.

On Rim Wood, Cesare observed all that happened through Farseer: Lia's rescue and his own son Fabian still a shackled captive of the Brooderstalt.

Chapter 27

The eastern wall of Dredgemarsh lunged skywards ninty feet from the foetid waters of Meregloom swamp. All year round a grey miasma hugged it's slimy surface and settled over the vast quagmire beyond. Where this wall and the North wall met, a bartizan with corbelled roof stretched another twenty feet into the freezing air. The two guards occupying it had a view in all directions through sighting slots in the closed shutters on six lancet windows. A narrow door with a peephole led down a half dozen steps unto the north wall walkway.

'Ye Gods,' the taller of the two said, 'we'll die of the poxy cold up here.' He stamped his feet and slapped his arms around himself.

"Twas always like that here; winter and summer, doesn't matter, always cold, freeze the balls off a musk ox,' the shorter one said.

What I wouldn't give for a blazing fire now. I'd rather be at the main gate despite the danger. At least I'd die warm.'

'Not me,' his short companion replied, 'we might be cold but we're a lot safer here. I want to die in me bed. On top of Sal even better.' They laughed out loud.

'We'd all like to die atop o'your Sal, Ingle Swillard.'

'Sal only wants—'

'Listen!' the tall one interrupted, 'someone's coming.' They pressed close together, swords drawn and their backs to the wall facing the entrance to the bartizan.

'Open up,' a voice called out.

The tall guard approached the peep hole. He looked out into the gloomy shadows that that encircled the bartizan.

'Open up.' The voice was more urgent.

'Athelard, is that you,' the tall guard said, 'is that you?'

'Aye it is, and I know your voice, Tam Small. Now open up for your Prince.' The two guards sheathed their swords and Tam Small slid back a heavy bolt and hauled the door open.

'Sire, at your command,' Tam and Ingle said in unison.

'Have you seen many Brooderstalt,' Harry asked

'Not many out this far, Sire. A few patrolling along the edge of the gorge, that's all.' Tam Small pointed out to where Meregloom Gorge ran north along the eastern perimetre of the Vildpline.

'And East?' Harry said.

'Nothing but swamp there, Sire. No one ever goes there.'

'East it is then,' Harry said and pointed to the lancet window overlooking Meregloom swamp. Athelard fixed the end of a long coil of rope, which he was carrying over his shoulder, to a grating in the floor. He opened the shutters on the window and dropped the coil out.

'Watch out for our return,' Harry said to the two guards, 'and pull this rope back up and close the shutters when we are down.' The pair nodded in bewilderment.

'We'll be back before the night is out ... hopefully,' Athelard said. 'And drop the rope out again when you hear the call of a curlew three times.'

Harry and Athelard climbed out through the window and were gone. They lowered themselves onto the spongy ground behind a forty foot wide and six foot high dyke that ran east from the fortress wall into the mists of the quagmire. On the other side of the dyke Meregloom Gorge ran north like an open wound along the eastern edge of the Vildpline. Athelard followed Harry over the dyke and the pair began to descend into the gorge. Harry knew every detail of the place. How many times had he come here with Pingo and a dray piled with the stinking detritus from the canals? He gasped at how intensely and instantly he was transported into that grim past by the putrid effluvium that seeped up from the cracks and crevices of the gorge floor. Athelard groaned in disgust, covered the lower half of his face with the end of his short cloak and stumbled after Harry. Though it was still early in the afternoon there was nevertheless a murkiness in the air accompanied by a smell of burnt metal. Even in the gorge the stench of the offal and waste from below could not mask out that metallic tang in the air. In the deep shadows they moved with caution lest they stumbled and attract the attention of any Brooderstalt patrols along the upper perimeter.

Harry stopped. 'Too slow. This is too slow. We'll have to go up onto the Vildpline.' Without hesitation Athelard nodded in agreement. Picking every step with care the pair made their way up from the shadows. As they climbed higher, they could hear the chanting and clamour of the

Brooderstalt hosts and when at last they peered over the top of the gorge the scene that presented itself made both of them gasp. All over the Vildpline there were great circles of devastation centred on the smoking wreckage of the Manchian war engines. Here the metallic smell was intense.

Charred bodies, whole and dismembered, littered the smouldering landscape. Wounded men and animals on the periphery of the smouldering circles cried out unheeded. The rest of that great host of Brooderstalt spewed their hatred of Dredgemarsh into the ash-filled sky, the war drums goading them into a frenzy as they stamped and beat their swords against their shields waiting for the order to attack. There was no danger of Harry and Athelard being seen by anyone from the ravening tumult of Brooderstalt whose sole focus was the main gate of Dredgemarsh. Harry could see in the distance that the gate was still ablaze and he whispered to himself, 'well done Grunkite, well done.'

At that precise moment Athelard in readjusting his footing dislodged a small rock and it tumbled down the side of the gorge.

'Who goes there?' a voice called out. Harry and Athelard had not noticed the three Brooderstalt patrol guards who were slouched on the ground drinking under one of the few scrawny trees on the edge of the gorge. They were no more than a hundred feet away. They ducked out of sight. 'Damn' Harry said under his breath.

'Who goes there?' demanded one of the Brooderstalt. With drawn sword he tiptoed to the spot where Harry and Athelard waited. His two companions rose to their feet and drew their swords. The Brooderstalt leaned over the edge of the gorge and peered into the gloom. As his eyes adapted to the penumbra below, the first thing that began to reveal itself was Athelard's red locks.

'You, you there!' the guard shouted 'up, get up.' He trust his sword down towards Athelard. But he did not see Harry who reached up from the dark, grabbed the guard's extended arm and flung him headlong into the gorge. Before his scream of terror died his two companions, at first, rushed towards the spot where he had disappeared but as they got closer, they slowed down, stopped and backed away.

'We'll get reinforcements,' one said. They ran back towards their tethered horses. But, before they reached them, Harry and Athelard closed in on the terrified pair and dispatched them with their falchions.

Harry scanned the around them. 'No one has seen us. Quick, take his helmet and cloak.' He undid the cloak of the Brooderstalt he had killed. Athelard followed suit with the other and without delay they were disguised with their casque helmets and brown cloaks. They flung the dead bodies into the gorge, mounted the two patrol horses and galloped northwards along the eastern edge of the Vildpline towards the Brooderstalt base camp.

A momentous roar arose from the Brooderstalt army.

'They're moving forward again,' Harry said, 'pray we can find Lia fast and get back to Dredgemarsh.' A blinding flash of light brightened the whole Vildpline and was followed moments later by the sound of Firedrake searing the heavens. 'That'll slow them.' They lashed their mounts forward towards the camp staying close to the edge of Meregloom Gorge.

Tam Small and Ingle Swillard were startled when, for a second time that day, the door onto the north wall walkway reverberated with incessant pounding.

'Who goes there.' Tam Small approached the door.

'Hurry up. Change of watch.'

'No one told us about a change of watch. Who are you?'

'Damn you to hell. Let us in. Sergeant Blazer wants you at the main gate straight away.'

Tam opened the peephole in the door. He recoiled at the sight of a one–eyed man looking back at him. The blind eye was opaque with a vertical blemish across the eyelid that continued down the left cheek and corner of the mouth to the chin. The skin was a mottled grey.

'Are we to stand here like fools 'til the Brooderstalt slits all our throats. I told you; Sergeant Blazer wants you. Now.' The words were slurred and sibilent with spittle. The left side of the speaker's face and mouth were frozen in a permanent scowl.

'Your name?' Tam Small drew his falchion. Ingle did the same.

There was a moment's hesitation before the response. 'Mordant Skaldar, Royal Guard to Prince Harry.'

'Open it,' said Ingle, 'and let's get back to the main gate. He's welcome to this freezing tomb.'

Tam and Ingle slid the bolts and stepped back to allow Mordant Skaldar to enter.

The sepulchral figure of Skaldar stepped into the tower room. He was followed by a stump of a man, not a single hair on his head and so broad that he was forced to turn sideways to squeeze through the narrow doorway.

'Has the Prince passed through?' Skaldar examined the coiled rope with one end tied to the grating on the floor. 'Which window did he use?'

Ingle pointed to the eastern window with his falchion. 'He'll be back sometime tonight. When he comes, you'll hear the cry of the marsh curlew three times; lower the rope.'

'We'll do just that. Don't you worry. Now, be off.'

Tam and Ingle backed out of the tower room, still with unsheathed falchions.

'Did you see how filthy and ragged their uniforms were?' Tam said as the door slammed behind them.

'They were Royal Guard uniforms though,' Ingle said. 'Weren't they?'

They sheathed their weapons.

'We need to find Sergeant Blazer fast.' Tam set out at a steady trot towards the main gate and the firing rampart.

'Wait for me. Tam. Wait!'

Harry and the Fallen Lia

Chapter 28

Cesare moved the bulk of his army forward under the cover of Rim Wood. A smaller contingent, led by Kristoff Surefoot, were left behind to search for his son, Fabian, and Lia, amidst the ruins of the base camp.

Hidden from view he tracked the main army of Pentrojan, searching for a suitable breach in the Rim Wood escarpment from where he could launch another attack.

He and his senior officers, hidden inside the perimeter of Rim Wood, led their mounts close to the edge of the escarpment. The advanced cohorts of the vast Brooderstalt army were now in full view. They were standing well back from the Mancian war engines, which were reduced to smouldering twisted metal at the centre of black craters encircled by charred bodies, dead or half alive and mutilated.

'I've never seen such monstrous war engines before.' Aubrey of Vilspont whispered aside to Cesare.

As they watched a soldier touched a blazing torch to the rear of one of remaining intact war engines. After a slight delay a cloud of smoke and flames blew back as if from a furnace. This was shortly followed by a thunderous boom. A great claw-like cup on an armature swung up from the base of the engine and flung a huge boulder towards the Dredgemarsh curtain wall. It smashed into the brickwork already laced with cracks from earlier hits and slowly the wall began to collapse. Cesare groaned.

A triumphant howl from the Brooderstalt army followed.

'Sire,' Kristoff Surefoot arrived breathing heavily.

'You've found the Prince?'

'No, Sire … we had to abandon the search.'

'Abandon. You had to … what do you—'

'Sire, a full cohort of Brooderstalt returned to secure the base camp just after you left.'

Cesare turned away from Kristoff to look back at the breached curtain wall. And although the Brooderstalt Army were still cheering they were not moving forward to take advantage.

'What's holding them back?' Aubrey of Villespont mused.

'Firedrake.' Cesare smiled and made a gesture of triump with his clenched fist. 'It's Firedrake they are afraid to move forward.'

'What do you mean, sire, what is this—'

'Not now, Aubrey. Later. We must return immediately to the base camp. Victory would be hollow if my son dies.'

The cohort of Brooderstalt cavalry, now stationed at the base camp under the command of Captain Drago, were lined up and poised for battle. They were facing north towards Grak's forest where they had witnessed the dramatic rescue of Lia. They assumed that the enemy in the forest was the army that had already destroyed their basecamp. But the first flight of arrows from Ranulf Halfhand's Lycian bowmen in Rimwood rained down on them before they realised that they were under attack on their left flank.

With Ranulf at their head, the mounted bowmen swept down from Rimwood at speed. They were standing in their stirrups firing round after round of arrows with unerring accuracy. The Brooderstalt cavalry, well-seasoned fighters, did not panic despite their heavy casualties. They wheeled around in packed formation and faced their attackers presenting a wall of shields bristling with protruding lances.

The first row extended their lances in a horizontal position from behind their shields. The following rows held their lances in a vertical position. In unison and maintaining their tight formation, they began to move forward at a steady canter.

When the Lycian bowmen were about one hundred ells away from the advancing Brooderstalt, they split in two, each half veering with speed to the left and right. As they parted the Knights of Anselem came thundering through the gap on their heavy armoured destriers.

They were in their vee formation. Like a plough slicing through fine loam, they carved a bloody path through the Brooderstalt ranks. At the same time, the Lycian Archers fired their devastating hail of arrows on each side of the Brooderstalt. Men and horses fell like stalks of wheat before a scythe.

The knights bored through Drago's lines and turned to follow up with another attack. Andret Longspere emerged from Rim Wood at the head of the Gliondar Hobelars.

Mounted on their sturdy Storn Hill ponies, they dashed into the fray with their short swords, maces and battle hammers engaging the Brooderstalt in hand-to-hand combat, from horseback and on foot.

Cesare's troops, hardened by their recent campaign in Lycia crushed the Brooderstalt with fierce and unrelenting aggression.

Captain Drago at the head of about twenty troopers broke away from the slaughter and raced northwards towards Grak's Forest. But when they got to within a few hundred ellss of their destination Captain Paine, Potens and a small band of foresters rode out to face them. The Brooderstalt wheeled about rather than face the towering Potens. But there was nowhere to go and one by one they were cut down by the bolts from the forester's arbalests or the arrows of the Lycian archers. Captain Paine and his men then waded into the ever-diminishing battle arena to help quell the last few remaining pockets of resistance.

Drago was the last to die, impaled on Captain Paine's Zwieshander. His face contorted into a mask of pure hatred as life faded. 'Damn your soul to deepest pit of hell, Albrecht Pentrojan. Damn your ….'

'They must be here somewhere, they must be.' For the first time in over a year of brutal campaigning, Cesare's officers heard fear and anxiety in their beloved leader's voice.

'Prince Fabian, Prince Fabian,' the officers called out as they searched through the fallen tents and ruins of the camp. The evening sky was darkening.

Harry and Athelard, still in their Brooderstalt attire finally reached the eastern side of the ruined Brooderstalt camp. They had witnessed, with some amazement, the speed with which the Brooderstalt cavalry were destroyed. And now they were close enough to hear the shouts of the Dredgemarsh officers calling out Prince Fabian's name.

Athelard looked at Harry. 'They still don't know, Sire. They don't know—'

'It's of no consequence just now. It's the Lady Lia—'

'Look, look, Sire.' Athelard pointed towards Graks's Forest. 'That is surely her.'

In the distance, coming from the forest was a young woman on horseback. She wore white. Harry strained to see, not daring to believe it was her but with each passing moment as she got nearer to the demolished camp the most incredible feeling of relief began to suffuse his whole body. How could it be that simple? Here amidst the dead and dying men and horses, against the roar and tumult of battle, the young woman who was the centre of all his thoughts and desires was alive, and from her movement and posture, unhurt. Transfixed he watched her draw nearer and nearer.

'It's her,' he said. Unbidden tears fell. Athelard smiled. But the smiled faded moments later and the look of joy on Harry's face turned to horror. The unmistakable figure of Fabian emerged from a half-demolished Brooderstalt tent not thirty ells from Lia. He ran full tilt towards her. She halted and tried to turn her mount away but that made it easier for Fabian to vault onto the rear of her horse. They struggled but he locked one arm around her throat so tight she could not cry out for help. He grabbed the reins with his free hand, wheeled the horse around and rode back towards Grak's Forest.

Harry cried out, 'No.' He lashed his mount into instant pursuit and drove it forward at speed. Athelard followed him. The officers searching for Fabian heard Harry's cry and looked towards its source. All they could see was a rider and a girl mounted on one horse being pursued by two others in the distinctive helmet and cloak of the Brooderstalt.

'That's them,' one of the officers shouted. 'Sire, Sire, your son.' He pointed to the fleeing Fabian. There was no need for the alert. Cesare was already racing across the Vildpline to intercept the Brooderstalt horsemen chasing after his son and Lia. He unhooked his battle-axe from his saddle and raised it above his head, ready to strike the instant he closed on the lead pursuer. They converged just as Harry reached Fabian. Cesare without hesitation began the stroke that would cleave the hated Brooderstalt helmet and the head under it. In that fraction of a second between thought and action, Harry, unconscious of everything except the plight of Lia, dived forward off his mount and grabbed the fleeing Fabian. Cesare's battle axe sliced through the saddle of Harry's mount and the poor beast fell like a stone, its spine severed. Cesare's mount collided with the fallen horse and it crashed to the ground, its rider rolling away from its threshing hooves. Harry, Fabian and Lia all tumbled onto the hard frosty surface of the Vildpline. The two men, prince and impostor, rose and faced each other with falchions drawn. Lia though stunned tried to stand.

'Lia, move away,' Harry shouted.

'Harry?' she shook her head and stared in disbelief. 'Harry?'

'Move back, Lia,' he pleaded.

Cesare, though slower to rise, assessed the situation in an instant. Harry stood with his back to him poised to attack his son Fabian. Cesare drew his broad sword and closed on Harry. He raised his sword above his head. This time Harry did not move. A loud scream startled Cesare even as he began the down stroke of his broad sword. Lia threw herself between him and Harry. At the same time someone slammed into Cesare's side with force. He toppled sideways, but, in a desperate effort not to hurt Lia, twisted the sword in his hand so that, although it was too late to stop the blow, it struck her with less force and with the flat of the blade. She fell like a stone. Harry looked around when he heard the scream. Lia was lying prostrate on the ground, blood pouring from her scalp.

Athelard, who had dared to barge into Cesare, was instantly surrounded by Cesare's officers with drawn swords. He tore off the Brooderstalt helmet and cloak, revealing his mop of fiery hair and the Dredgemarsh brigandine.

'Athelard,' one of the officers shouted in amazement. Harry dropped his falchion, removed his helmet and was on his knees beside Lia.

Fabian, his face contorted into a mask of pure hatred, glared at Harry. The uncontrollable madness that infected his soul since the night he murdered his real mother. That awful night when she, a peasant woman, revealed his true lineage. Everything, his crown, his life of pleasure, his power was stripped from him.

With a grotesque scream that startled the already amazed assembly, Fabian ran straight for Harry. He never reached his intended victim. He fell face forward without a sound, a bardiche embedded in his spine. The giant Potens strode in amongst them. Cesare who had raised himself on one knee watched in horror.

'Sire!' Athelard cried out and pointed at the mangled corpse still quivering in its death throes, 'That is not your son. Here is your real son.' He pointed to the kneeling Harry. Cesare just stared at Athelard as if he was speaking in some unknown language. His men had now encircled Athelard and Harry with drawn swords

'It's true Sire,' Potens stepped forward but he too was surrounded.

Cesare stared at the body of Fabian. Here was the son he neglected for so many years. Now he could never make amends. This was his beloved Lucretia's child. She died to give that child life and ... and now they had killed him. The traitors killed him without mercy. He knelt by the corpse of Fabian, removed the bardiche with effort and turned the blood-soaked body over. The eyes were open, cold light blue eyes that Cesare had never looked upon. 'My son,' he whispered, 'what have they done? ... What have I done?'

'Kill them all,' Andret Longspear cried out.

'Stop, stay your hands.' Captain Paine barged into the midst of them.

'What is this, Captain Paine. Why are you—'

'Stay the hands of your men, Sire. You will curse yourself forever if you do not.' He leaned down towards Cesare. 'Sire, you have not lost your son. He lives.' He reached down and with an effort raised the stunned King to his feet. 'Sire, listen. This was never your son.' He pointed to the bloody corpse of Fabian. 'On my honour, I tell you the truth.'

'It is true, Sire, it is true,' Athelard called out.

Captain Paine took Cesare aside. All of those watching as the Captain conversed quietly with Cesare beheld a transformation in their King from utter desolation to bewilderment.

Cesare, who, moments before had stumbled like an old man and needed Captain Paine's support, walked back amongst them. 'Sheath your swords,' he said. He looked long at Harry who was cradling Lia in his arms. Her face was pale as death and blood clotted her golden hair.

'Is she … is the girl dead?' he knelt down beside Harry and touched her cheek with the back of his hand. 'Get Brother Eustace now,' he ordered.

Captain Paine and Potens prised Harry's arms from around Lia to allow the monk Eustace, still wearing his hauberk, to examine her.

'She's alive,' Eustace said after a cursory examination. 'We'll take good care of her.'

Harry and Cesare stood and faced each other.

'Jesu Christe, how did we not see the likeness before now?' Potens whispered aside to Captain Paine.

'We weren't looking for it, Potens. Why would we? But you're right; he's carved out of him.'

'I almost killed you,' Cesare said.

'That's of no consequence to me if … if Lia dies … if you have killed her.' Harry's fists were clenched by his side, his whole body tensed as if he was about to strike Cesare.

'Have a care, young man, this is your King—' Andret Longspear, stepped forward.

'No, Andret.' Cesare held his hand up to forestall his captain. 'I have done this young man much harm. Someday I hope—' Another blinding flash and thunderous boom from Firedrake cut short his words.

When the fury of sound abated, Harry, still staring at Cesare, addressed Potens. 'I must return immediately to Dredgemarsh. Potens, I beg you to stay with Lia at all times and see that no further harm comes to her from foe,' he hesitated for a moment, 'or friend.' He spat out the word friend.'

'No, this is too much, Sire.' Andret Longspear stepped forward again to confront Harry.

'Andret, I have told you already. Desist.' Cesare's words were spoken in hushed tones but all the more menacing in that fraught situation. 'Harry, you may hate me now, but that is for another day. There is an enemy to defeat, lives to be saved, including Lia's. I must know what your plans are.' Harry continued to stare in defiance at Cesare and gave no answer.

'Harry,' Captain Paine approached. 'Look at me, look at me.' With reluctance Harry diverted his gaze to Captain Paine. 'This is not the time, Harry. You know that. Tell me. What is happening inside those walls? He pointed towards Dredgemarsh. 'We need to know, Harry.' Behind Captain

Paine and Cesare, both tall men, Potens, a clear head above them was nodding encouragement to Harry.

Harry spoke at last, addressing himself to Captain Paine. 'The Broodserstalt will breach the main gate by morning. Do not attempt under any circumstances to stop them. And do not, I repeat, do not follow them into the city.'

'What! This is madness, horse shite.' Dubnar Nialls of the Gliondar Hobelars flung his war hammer to the ground. 'Stand by and allow the bastards to enter Dredgemarsh?'

Harry faced Cesare once more. 'That is exactly what we need to do.'

Cesare stared into Harry's eyes. They were the eyes of his beloved Lucretia even though they now burned with resentment. There was silence amongst the gathering, 'til at last Cesare spoke.

'So be it. We will continue to attack the Brooderstalt from the rear and will not attempt to prevent them entering Dredgemarsh or pursue them into the city. Is there anything else I should know.'

'Athelard, come. We must get back,' Harry turned away.

'We'll send some men with you,' Cesare said.

'No, they'll be seen. I need a horse.'

'Cesare nodded to Dubnar Nialls who commandeered a horse from one of his own men and passed the reins to Harry. Athelard donned his Brooderstalt helmet and cloak and set out after Harry.

'Sire, is this wise?' Andret Longspear, who was standing by Cesare's shoulder, said quietly.

Cesare turned to him. 'He is my lost son, Andret. I shamefully neglected him and he has suffered greatly because of that.' There were tears trickling down Cesare's cheeks.

'Sire, forgive me. I …'

'There is nothing to forgive, Andret. 'It is I who need forgiveness from my son. I never gave him anything in his whole life … Today … I give him my trust.

Chapter 29

Tam Small, with Ingle his steadfast friend, trailing behind, picked his way along the rubble-strewn walkway. The firing platform, at last, was in view. Their run from the bartizan along the north walkway, or granite mile as it was called, left both gasping for breath. To their immediate right the ten-foot-deep curtain wall with its massive merlons was being bombarded with renewed ferocity by the remaining Manchian war engines.

'Sblood, slow down, Tam Small.' Ingle Swillard sank to his hands and knees.

'We can't stop, Ingle. Must find Blazer. Don't trust that Mordant Skaldar.'

'Damn.' Ingle struggled to his feet and staggered forward behind his friend.

'Saints in heaven, Ingle, you'll—' Tam's voice trailed off in a strangulated cry as his cloak was pulled with vicious force from behind. He managed to turn his head sideways. Ingle on his knees again, swaying over the edge of the walkway, his fall prevented by the hold he had on Tam's cloak. Tam grabbed Ingle's wrist and dragged him back from the brink. They both collapsed onto the stone littered walkway. Tam, his face turning puce, prised Ingle's clenched fist from his cloak.

'We're almost there if you don't kill us first.' his voice was hoarse and constricted. Ingle stared in terror at him. 'Up, up, we must move on,' said Tam. Ingle's legs were shaking as he tottered to his feet.

'Move, move,' a voice screamed from one of the nearby Mangonel crews. Three thunderous strikes from enemy war engines followed in quick succession and the old walls groaned. Great granite blocks moved from their century's old settings. Then slowly, ever so slowly, a section of the upper curtain wall and three merlons in front of Tam and Ingle began to tilt outwards and away from where they stood frozen by what they were seeing. They teetered on the ragged edge of the instant man-made precipice overlooking the Vildpline.

The Brooderstalt cohorts assailed the skies above the Vildpline with howls of triumph and the beating of shields but still they held back from attacking. Then the scene vanished from view as a plume of dust spewed heaven-wards when the curtain wall collapsed onto the batter below.

The voice from the mangonel crew screamed, 'Get out of there, take cover.' Tam looked around as if for a moment he did not understand. The voice screamed out again. 'Now, Now.' Tam grabbed Ingle by the collar and dragged him away from the jagged edge. They fell down behind the nearest intact merlon.

A flash of intense light banished every shadow from dark crevice and corner within their field of view. The shapes and contours of their world segued into an amorphous dazzling glow. An instant an eruption of sound followed and they clasped their palms over their ears to lessen the pain. When the light and sound that assaulted their sight and hearing diminished, they rose and struggled onwards towards the firing platform and main gate. They passed a Ballista crew preparing to launch one of their huge iron javelins at the enemy.

'What just happened,' Tam shouted to one of the men.

'That's what happened,' the dust covered soldier pointed to the firing ramp. 'It's Firedrake. A lightning engine. I know no more than that.' He held his hands out and shrugged his shoulders.

'We're looking for Sergeant Blazer,' Tam said. The soldier shrugged his shoulders again.

'Ingle, you follow as fast as you can. I'm going ahead to find Blazer or someone in command. I have a bad feeling in my gut.'

As Tam began his search for Sergeant Blazer, Harry and Athelard were cantering back towards the bartizan. They dared not gallop lest they attract attention. They were not halfway to their destination when the lethal Manchian war engines mounted their sustained attack on Dredgemarsh with no response from Firedrake.

'They've moved the wagons. They know.' Harry didn't realise he was talking out loud.

'What?' Athelard said.

Harry spurred his mount forward, a little faster but still constrained it to a canter. After trailing behind for a short while, Athelard moved up beside him.'

'Sire, to your right.'

'I see them. Another patrol. How many? Four?'

'At least.'

Harry slowed his mount to a less urgent pace. Athelard bent down as if to adjust his right stirrup and stole a glance in the direction of the patrol. 'They're not coming this way, Sire.'

'Good, we'll have—' The crash of collapsing masonry of the curtain wall onto the wall batter rumbled across the Vildpline accompanied by the howls of triumph from the Brooderstalt army. Harry slowed up and half turned to see the source of the tumult.

'They've widened the breach in the wall,' Athelard cried out. 'I think they're moving forward. We're too late!'

Then an all-encompassing light filled the sky, followed by a sound like the rending of the very fabric of the earth. An gargantuan column of smoke, debris and flames bloomed upwards, swallowing everything around it. The triumphant roar of the Brooderstalt changed intantly into screams.

'It worked. Our wagons in the redoubts caught them. We still have time.' Harry raked his horses' flanks and set off at a furious gallop towards the Bartizan followed by Athelard. They ploughed through the swale draining into Meregloom Gorge and scrambled up its shallow slope unto the castle promenade and then raced for the north-east corner.

'They've spotted us, sire,' Athelard shouted.

When they reached the bartisan, they leaped from their saddles and climbed over the dyke and around by the edge of the east facing wall. They waded through the quagmire until they stood below the shuttered window of the tower eighty feet above their heads. It would be a daunting climb. Athelard cupped his hands over his mouth and made the unmistakable gulp-gulp cry of the marsh curlew. They fixed their eyes on the shutters of the tower window. No response. Athelard made the sound, louder this time. No response.

'Curse you, Tam Small,' Athelard said. Harry moved back to the corner and looked out onto the castle promenade. He swiveled back towards Athelard, gesticulating with his thumb towards the promenade. Athelard nodded, cupped his hands over his mouth again and made the curlew sound louder than before. The shutters were thrown open and banged against the outer wall. 'I'll murder him.' Athelard grimaced. A coil of rope was nudged out over the sill of the window. It began to unfurl and at several points in its descent slowed as if about to bind itself into a tangled knot. The jangle of chain martingales on the Broodestalt horses and the pounding of hooves was getting closer. Then the voices halloing and swearing as if they were closing in on some cornered beast they were hunting. Harry drew his falchion. The end of the rope dropped within reach.

'Sire, you first. Go, go.' Harry hesitated, 'Sire, if you're killed, all is lost. Please go, I beg you.' Harry grabbed the rope and began to climb.

'They're here, we have them!' A Brooderstalt helmet appeared above the dyke. Four troopers climbed onto the top of the dyke. Two of them were arbalesters who commenced loading their weapons. They took aim, one at Harry and one at Athelard. Harry, thirty feet up, kicked himself away from the wall and the lethal bolt missed and he began to climb again. Athelard also evaded the bolt fired at him. The other two troopers slid down the side of the dyke with drawn falchions and began to wade through the mire towards Athelard.

Somewhere above on the castle walkway men were shouting and a loud hammering on the wooden door of the bartizan began. Two Dredgemarsh arbalesters leaned out from embrasures on the east wall. Their weapons were preloaded and they fired immediately at the Brooderstalt on the dyke. One strike was successful. The remaining Broodestalt arbalester took aim at Harry, fired and scrambled for cover. Harry spun himself away from the wall evading the bolt once more. He swung back and slammed into the wall with his right shoulder and slid several feet down the rope before regaining control.

Below Athelard was beginning to flag under the ever more violent assault by the two Brooderstalt swordsmen.

Another rope was flung down from the embrasure right next to the Bartizan. At the same time the great ruddy face of Sergeant Blazer emerged above the rope and bellowed, 'Not that rope. Assassins … in the tower. This one, this one.' He shook the second rope. Harry attempted to swing across but could not reach Blazer's rope.

Athelard lunged forward and slashed the first of the Brooderstalt across the face. The man fell backwards into the murky shallows of the marsh, a perfect target for the Dredgemarsh arbalesters above. As he struggled to rise from the mire a bolt found his heart. For one moment Athelard's stroke left his left side exposed. That was all the second Brooderstalt needed. He leaped forward and plunged his falchion into Athelard. With one final desperate effort, Athelard spun around and sliced through the throat of his killer. They both tumbled into the shallows of the marsh where a cloud of red bloomed around them.

'Athelard, Athelard.' The cry of desolation was that of Tam Small who was watching the unfolding tragedy from another embrasure.

Harry was still trying to swing himself towards the second rope while watching out for the next flying bolt from the Brooderstalt arbalester behind the dyke.

Sergeant Blazer screamed to someone behind him. 'Break down that fukking door.' This was followed by a fierce pounding on wood. 'It's his only chance.' He leaned out through the embrasure once again, tried to swing the rope towards Harry. The attempt failed. He tried to pull the rope sideways to make another attempt. It would not move. Blazer leaned out further to see what snagged it.

Athelard, his face an unnatural white and his lower half bathed in blood had crawled out of the mire and was dragging the rope towards Harry.

'Athelard, forgive me, dear friend.' Tam Small called out from his embrasure.

The rope came within Harry's reach and just as he swung away from the first rope another bolt embedded itself in mortar where Harry was moments before.

Below Athelard fell stumbled backwards into the marsh and sank below its murky surface.

'Pull, pull,' Blazer shouted. Harry was hauled up to the embrasure where the Sergeant helped him to safety. Harry collapsed onto the walkway gulping for air.

'Help Athelard.' He gasped for breath.

'Too late, sire, too late.'

Harry groaned, staggered to his feet and stumbled towards the embrasure through which he had been dragged to safety. 'There must be something we can do.'

'No, Sire, nothing we can do for him now.' The sergeant stood between Harry and the embrasure. 'Too dangerous, Sire. There's an assassin still out there.'

'How did this happen? Why did—'

'It's my fault.' Tam Small stepped up to Harry. 'My fault, sire.'

'You?' Harry pointed to the tower where two of Sergeant Blazer's men were taking turns to assault the door with a bardiche. 'You were supposed to be—'

'Gotcha, you bastard,' one of the soldiers pounding on the door of the bartizan cried out and levered a huge strip of timber onto the ground.

'My fault,' Tam muttered through tears, turned and ran towards the splintered door. He grabbed the bardiche. Blazer's men stood back and watched as the door timbers cracked under Tam's frenzied assault. Each stroke was delivered with an incoherent yowl of fury and then in a cloud of flying splinters Tam barged through the jagged entrance, bardiche in hand.

Sergeant Blazer was the first to follow after Tam. On the floor a bald man of remarkable girth lay on the cold stones, half his face sliced away. He was still alive, the bloody ebb and surge from the ghastly wound subsiding and he gasping for breath through the mangled remains of his face. Tam Small was leaning out through the east facing window. Blazer joined him. Not ten feet below the window, a face scarred, one-eyed and contorted by hate stared up at him.

'Skaldar.' Blazer's smile was grim. He laid a restraining hand on Tam's arm who was slowly cutting through the rope with the edge of the bloodied bardiche. '

'Name your conspirators, Skaldar, and you might just live.'

'Fukk you, Blazer and your peasant Prince.'

Sergeant Blazer removed his hand from Tam's arm. 'Finish it.' He walked away and called out to one of his arbelests who entered the tower with Harry. 'Make sure the bastard is dead when he hits the ground. Retrieve Athelard's body. Sire, we must go now. You are sorely needed.'

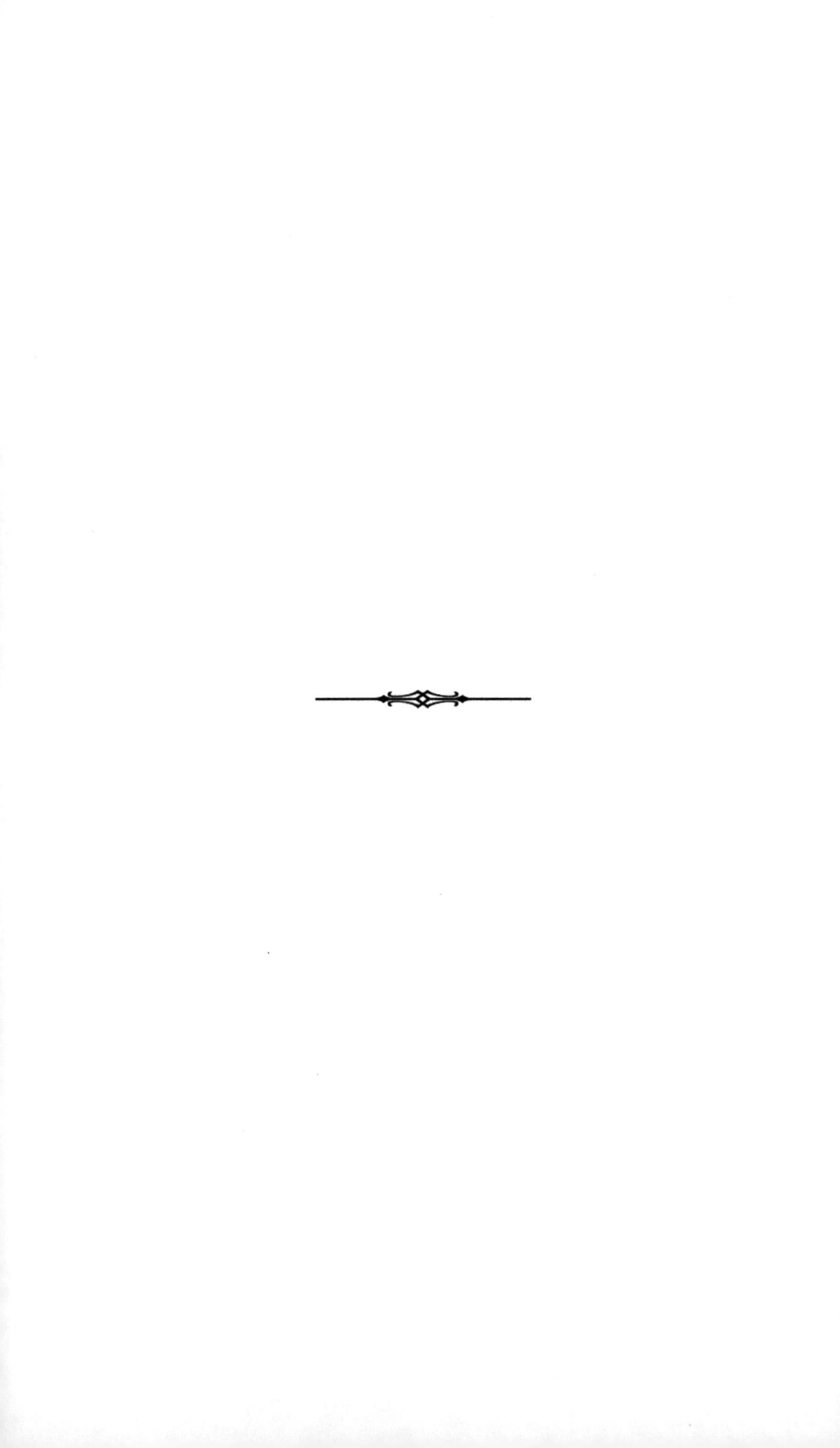

Chapter 30

The sky darkened. Rain came, sharp and freezing on a biting wind. Grunkite wheezed his way up the last few steps of the firing platform. His lips were blue; his soot-besmirched face a mottled grey. He bent over, hands on knees, gasping for air.

'Quick, the Chancellor needs help. Bring him behind the stockade. Get something to sit on. Hurry. Hurry.' General Hawksfoot bellowed out the orders. Another flying boulder smashed into the side of the firing platform. Two soldiers ran forward, grabbed Grunkite and dragged him behind the stockade surrounding Firedrake. They eased him into a sitting position on a dislodged beam. Hawksfoot joined them. 'Give him more room, men, stand back. S'blood, Chancellor, what madness made you come up here?'

'General,' Grunkite was still blowing hard, 'I need to know,' he sucked air into his lungs, 'exactly what's happening.'

'What's happening? You really want to know what's happening?' Another boulder screamed overhead. 'That!' Hawksfoot jabbed his forefinger skywards. 'That's what's happening. They are pounding us to oblivion.'

'How long can we hold them.'

'The Prince, chancellor, where is he? My daughter is—'

'General, General,' the duty sergeant yelled out from his observation position.

'Damn.' Hawksfoot scrambled from the shelter of the stockade and limped across the platform to the embrasure where the sergeant was keeping watch.

'They'r moving the remaining wagons from the redoubts. Just a couple of men and horses on each wagon. The main army has moved back.'

'Jesu Christe, the saints have deserted us.'

'Should we destroy them with Firedrake?'

'And kill a few horses?'

'What is it, General?' Grunkite stumbled across the puddled and rock-strewn platform and stood behind the crouching figures of Hawksfoot and the sergeant.

'Get down,' the sergeant hurled himself at Grunkite slamming him onto the ground as another boulder struck the firing platform and rained rock shards down upon them. The sergeant hauled the chancellor into a sitting position, and rested him against the base of a merlon.

'Sergeant, I'll look after the Chancellor,' Hawksfoot said. 'Get as many ballista and mangonel crews as possible to target the redoubts. Stop those bastards from moving the wagons.'

Grunkite could hear, as if from a distance, Hawksfoot asking him if he was alright. He opened his eyes to a blurred vision of General Hawksfoot looking down on him.

'Stay there, Chancellor. I'll return in a moment.' The voice began to recede and the blear figure of the General faded.

He turned his head towards the eastern wall walk. The ballista crews were loading and firing their iron javelins in a fever of activity. He winched and kneaded his brow. His hand came away covered in blood. The sights in front of him began to dissolve and the clamour of battle fade 'til an airy lightness descended on him. He surrendered to the feeling and gave reign to a memory that suffused his mind like the torrential rain that was now falling. He could see himself and Cesare Greyfell strolling amiably along the walkway. They were discussing the imminent birth of a new prince or princess. Oh, happy times. Another boulder struck the firing platform and reality shattered the fantasy but he could still see the tall figure of Ceasare Greyfell on the walkway. He squeezed his eyes shut for a moment and then opened them wide. The tall figure was still there striding towards the platform.

'Harry?' Grunkite whispered. 'Up, up. God blast this old body. Up.' He rolled onto his hands and knees and with the support of the merlon staggered to his feet. Before he had brushed the grime from his brigadine, Harry was standing in front of him.

'Harry, Sire.' He stumbled forward and embraced Harry whose initial look of concern and shock turned to amused bewilderment.

'Sorry, forgive me, Sire. It's just that—' Grunkite stepped back.

'Sire.' Hawksfoot wedged himself in front of Grunkite. 'My daughter. Did you find her?'

'She is safe. She's with the King.' Harry averted his gaze from Hawksfoot. 'How do things stand here?'

'Is she … is there something you are not telling me? Have the Brooderstalt—'

'They've not harmed her, General. She's safe now.' Harry shouted to be heard over the screech of the sleety gale. The ballista officers were screaming out orders to the crews. Cries of pain and fear swelled and faded with the swirling cataclsm. 'And what's happening here.' Harry addressed Grunkite.

Grunkite pushed himself back in front of Hawksfoot. 'Everything is done. All side streets sealed off and—' Another boulder, as if swept in on the gale, slammed into the firing platform and swallowed his words. 'wagons are in place,' he shouted as the storm subsided for a moment.

'And what about steps to lower walkways and North Parade?' Harry asked.

'Dismantling them now, sire.'

'The western wall?'

'Four wagon loads where you ordered. Red flag ready.' Grunkite was already climbing down the steps from the firing platform.

Harry leaned over the edge of the platform. 'Be careful, Chancellor. Don't forget—'

'I know, I know, sire. After I hear the bells of St. Johannes, I'll raise—' His words flittered away in the wind.

'Turn Firedrake around now, General.' Hary pointed down towards the two wagons of nephryte at the main gate.

'They're on the move. The whole army is on the move' the duty sergeant yelled out.

Chapter 31

Stoney faced, indifferent to the drenching rain, Captain Luparellus fixed his gaze on the slaughter before him. Sixty horses and over two hundred men from his own phalanx were killed by Dredgemarsh defenders while his soldiers were attempting to move the wagons of Nephryte from the redoubts. Their bodies marked out a rain-soaked path of blood and melted snow from the redoubts to Meregloom Gorge into which the survivors flung the hateful stones. When they heaved the last wagon over the precipice, Luparellus rode, stiff-backed, towards the main army.

Four squires struggled to keep the supporting poles of a leather baldachin over the head of General Pentrojan and his mount. Behind him his officers and the Brooderstalt army stood motionless in the ravening storm, their sullen stillness accentuated an inchoate fury waiting to be unleashed. All eyes watched as Luparellus approached Pentrojan.

'It's done,' Luparellus said.

Pentrojan neither looked at nor answered Luparellus.

'I said it's—'

The General dismissed him with flick of his wrist, and called out to his officers, 'Proceed.'

A battle horn sounded once. Every arbalester and archer emerged from his individual cohort and ran forward at a steady pace towards Dredgemarsh.

Two blasts of the battle horn and a siege cat was wheeled out from the midst of one of the cohorts to the head of the infantry. It was drawn by ten oxen. The legs of the crew inside were just visible below the fringe of the cat giving the impression of a giant beetle rather than a cat.

Three blasts of the battle horn. The whole army began to move at walking pace led by Pentrojan still under cover of the baldachin. The squires, battling to keep the poles supporting the leather canopy straight, were joined by four soldiers. The battle drums began to sound. Their hypnotic rhythms spread across the Vildpline dictating all movement of the huge army, a beast of prey stalking the dying carcass of Dredgemarsh.

The bowmen fanned out across the full length of the battered north wall with a heavy concentration around the main gate. When they were within range of Dredgemarsh the longbow men dropped to one knee, heedless of the soaked ground and pelting rain. They removed the oiled leather covers from their bows, spread the covers on the ground and laid their quivers on them.

Four blasts of the battle horn. The assault began. Wave upon wave of arrows swept the ramparts of Dredgemarsh until the already sparse resistance from the Dredgemarsh defenders ceased apart from the odd boulder from a mangonel and the sporadic firing of arbalest bolts from the arrow slits in the drum towers. Even this was quenched when the Brooderstalt arbalesters weaved their way through the longbow men and targeted the last pockets of resistance. Dregemarsh lay helpless before the horde baying for slaughter and death.

Five blasts of the battle horn. Howls of triumph. The siege cat towering above the army rumbled forward past the lines of longbow men and arbalesters. The Oxen pulling it were unleashed and the men inside heaved against the crossbeams moving the monstrous contraption towards the mountain of burning remnants of the main gate, that spat and sputtered in hopeless defiance of the downpour. The men in the cat began to chant. It was taken up by the bowmen and then by the infantry behind them. A great beam swung out from the front of the cat. Back and forth it went. With each swing it emerged a little further. The chanting grew louder. A huge iron claw on the front of the beam ploughed its way into the dying inferno. Steam, smoke and flames belched up from the guts of the charred mound. A mocking ululation replaced the chant. It grew until the sinister chorus filled the whole Vildpline. The iron claw of the cat swept forward and back, forward and back, a beast ripping out the underbelly of its prey. A narrow path was cleared. Dredgemarsh was laid bare.

Six blasts of the battle horn. The cat withdrew. The infantry ran forward converging on the breach. They flowed like an iron river into Dredgemarsh. There was no resistance. Onto the grand plaza they ran and reassembled into their respective units.

Seven blasts of the horn and half of the bowmen and most of the cavalry joined the infantry on the grand plaza where they reformed into individual phalanxes facing north, south, east and west. There was still no response from the Dredgemarsh defenders.

Eight blasts of the battle horn were followed by the blaring of trumpets and sackpipes. As if in answer thunder rumbled overhead and the downpour grew stronger. Into the midst of the Brooderstalt army, Pentrojan rode like an emperor with his officers escorting him on all sides shouting, 'Make way for our great leader, General Pentrojan.' Cheers filled the darkening sky.

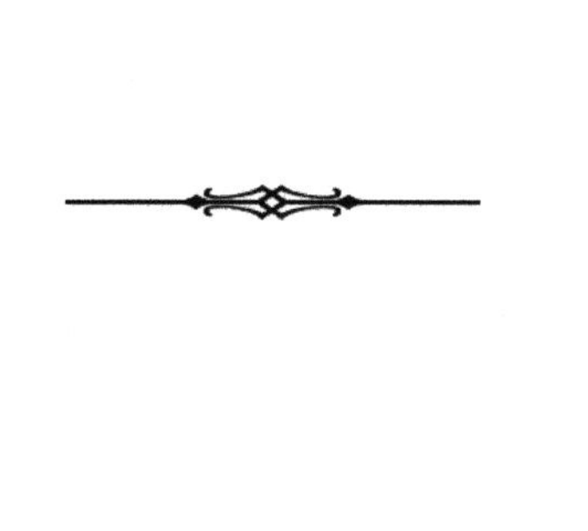

Grunkite

Chapter 32

General Albrecht Pentrojan stood in the stirrups. 'Dredgemarsh is ours!' He punched the air with his fist. The army erupted in a frenzy of cheering. Harry, General Hawksfoot and the last defenders of Dredgemarsh watched the spectacle from on high. They did not attempt to fire on the Brooderstalt but found what cover they could along the upper ramparts behind mangonels, ballistae, and the Firedrake stockade. Pentrojan and his officers dismounted. A space was cleared for them in the centre of the plaza. Already there was an air of ownership in their casual postures and their pointing out the features of the impressive buildings and structures surrounding them with a cursory scan of the curtain wall, its walkways and abandoned weaponry.

'It is time,' Harry said and stepped from behind the firing platform. He began waving a blue banner tied to a spearhead.

Gawan joined him and after a short interval cried out, 'They've seen it, Sire, they've seen it.' He pointed towards the Cupola of St. Johannes Cathedral. There, appearing and disappearing in the swirling curtains of rain, a blue banner waved in response to Harry's signal. Harry and Gawan ducked back behind the firing platform. There was no reaction from the murmuring horde of Brooderstalt on the Plaza.

'Maybe, they didn't see us,' Gawan thumbed back over his shoulder in answer to a question no one asked.

'We're no threat. Probably think most of us are dead,' Hawksfoot responded.

The treble bell sang out from the belfry of the cathedral followed in sequence by the remaining eleven bells down through the scales ending with the tenor bell: The Great Johannes. The sequence with one change began again and then again. The brothers of the Cathedral had commenced a full peal of the bells. It could last for hours.

Harry made some final adjustments to the worm drives on Firedrake. Gawan handed him a glowing taper. He opened the firing gate, touched the taper to the end of the transparent globe filled with oil. It ignited with a flash.

Many Brooderstalt eyes, including those of Pentrojan and his officers, turned towards that tiny flare of light up on the dark firing platform. That and the pealing of the bells though causing no alarm did induce the slightest frisson of bemusement amongst them.

'Look away,' said Harry. Cover your ears.' He pulled the lever on the initiator and the distinctive pulsating sound began to build up 'til even those on the Plaza heard it. Faces stared up at the strange engine on the firing platform silhouetted against the darkening sky.

A blinding flash. A deafening roar. At the bottom of the main gate west tower two carts loaded with Nephryte erupted in flame and smoke. The instant inferno destroyed the base of the tower. The massive structure, over one hundred ells high, tilted and then slowly toppled sideways. Clouds of white ash and burning debris spewed into the sky. When the dust and stones that were once a tower settled into place and the smoke began to clear the dumbfounded onlookers on the plaza realised that the main entrance was no more. In its place was a mountain of rubble sealing off the entrance to Dredgemarsh. It was as if a great door had closed on them.

The unthinkable prospect of possible defeat and ignominy, like he had suffered once before in this hated kingdom, sparked an eruption in Pentrojan's mind. Doubt like a poison coursed through his veins till panic took took hold of his mind. He leaped onto his mount screaming, 'Kill them all, every one of them, kill them now!'. He lashed his horse into a gallop; soldiers leaped out of his path.

'Kill them, kill them, tear it all down.' His horse skittered across the cobbles, the whites of its eyes flashing terror. The Brooderstalt army surged towards the ramparts and firing platform but all the stairways were demolished.

The Dredgemarsh archers, ballistae crews and even the canal men emerged from hiding and rained down missiles of all sorts on the Brooderstalt.

Ignoring their berserk leader the Brooderstalt officers asserted some control over their troops and their arbalesters and bowmen began to assail the Dredgemarsh men with arrows and bolts. This, along with the sustained assault from those still outside the curtain wall, began to overwhelm the Dredgemarsh defenders.

'Hurry, hurry we are being slaughtered,' Hawksfoot bellowed at the sergeant and his men on the firing platform as they heaved Firedrake around to face the western wall.

Harry was scanning the western horizon with the oculus magnus mounted on a small plinth.

'Now, Grunkite, now,' he whispered to himself.

'Can you see it, Sire?' Gawan was beside Harry.

'Not yet, not yet … Wait, yes, I see it.' Harry stood back from the oculus magnus and called to the sergeant and his men. 'Bring it around, sergeant … more.' He twirled his hand clockwise. The men struggled to get Firedrake to shift because of the piles of debris on the firing platform. Gawan and Harry jumped down from the plinth and joined in the effort. They got Firedrake moving.

'Stop. About there.' Harry climbed up on the plinth again and looked through the telescope. He panned it left and right several times. Gawan, the sergeant and his crew, still panting from the exertions of turning Firedrake, fixed their anxious gaze on Harry.

'Sire?' It was General Hawksfoot . 'We can't hold out much longer.'

'It's not there.' Harry put his eye to the telescope again, panned it left and right, and then shook his head. 'It must have fallen or …'

'What now?' the sergeant whispered to Gawan.

'We wait.'

Harry was right. The flagpole had fallen under a barrage of missiles from the Brooderstalt besiegers outside the curtain wall.

Grunkite had done his part when the bells of St. Johannes began to peal. Three of the four guards who accompanied him — the fourth lay dead on the walkway, an arrow protruding from his throat — formed a canopy with their shields and shuffled their way to the flagpole position. Under a blizzard of arrows, bolts and small boulders, they lashed the flagpole to a merlon just above the piles of golden nephryte heaped on the walkway.

They started to retreat. A spinning vireton bolt whistled through an embrasure and pierced the basinet of one of Grunkite's men. Blood poured from beneath the basinet and the man collapsed. Grunkite and the two remaining guards scrambled back to the north wall and from there set out eastwards towards the main gate. They traveled a short distance when they heard cheering from the Brooderstalt.

'Sir, look. It's fallen.' One of the soldiers was looking back to the west walkway.

Grunkite, when he saw, groaned, bent forward and buried his face in his open palms. He rocked back and forward for several moments and then removed his hands from his face and stared once more at the fallen flag. 'No, this cannot be.' He shook his head. His lips were trembling.

'Sir, what should we do? We can't stay here. Was it tears they saw in his old eyes? Hard to tell with the flailing sleet.

'You've done your duty; done it well. Go now as quick as you can.' He turned and walked back towards the west walkway.

'Sir, you can't go back, it's too—'

'I gave you an order. Go,' Grunkites said without turning. His voice was resolute.

The pair set off eastwards, all the time looking back at the chancellor. The Brooderstalt outside the walls appeared to take some respite from their ferocious assault after they had felled the flagpole. Grunkite broke into a shuffling run along the west walkway.

His erstwhile companions watched him stoop to the pole.

'He'll never lift it alone,' one said.

But the pole was raised and Grunkite backed himself against a merlon, grasping it to his chest. Arrows and bolts began to fly again but the old man stood as solid as the granite at his back.

'It's there, it's there,' Harry shouted. He leaped down from the observation post and, with his eye to the sighting lens of Firedrake, spun the wormdrives.

'Sire.' Gawan proffered a flaming taper.

'Not yet. Grunkite needs time to get clear.'

'Sire, there's no time.' Gawan could see that Hawksfoot, the sergeant of the watch and three Dredgemarsh soldiers, already wounded and scarred from battle, were fighting off a party of Brooderstalt that had somehow managed to gain the walkway and were now attempting to climb onto the firing platform. Hawksfoot doubled over, clutched his side and fell. His sword tumbled over the edge of the platform. The Dredgemarsh soldiers moved back. Three Brooderstalt scrambled onto the firing platform. Two jumped to their feet and waited for their tardier companion to rise. Albrecht Pentrojan, Iron Foot, struggled into a standing position, ignoring the helping hands extended by his men. His face was ablaze with fury and focused on one man alone: Harry.

'Greyfell, Cesare Greyfell?' The words Pentrojan spoke were innocuous but the tone was demented and profane. It was as if some demon found the power of speech and befouled the air with its first utterance. All faces turned in alarm and puzzlement towards Pentrojan, even those of his own men. He surged forward, his face a mask of hatred and swept aside the Dredgemarsh soldiers protecting Harry.

Harry grabbed the taper from Gawan, but before he could set the flame to the triggering mechanism of Firedrake, Pentrojan's sword ripped through his shoulder. Harry collapsed and lay spreadeagled on his back. Gawan tumbled sideways, his head striking the side of Firedrake. He lay motionless beside his prince.

Pentrojan stood astride Harry and with two hands prepared to plunge the sword into his hated enemy.

'Damn you to hell, Cesare Greyfell. The instant, before the downward thrust, he hesitated for a moment. Somehow, somewhere within the madness and turmoil that consumed him, a flash of sanity told him that this young man could not be Cesare Greyfell. But the moment passed and he plunged the sword downwards. From nowhere, with the sword just fractions of an inch from Harry's breast, Hawksfoot, blood pouring from his left side, hurled himself on Pentrojan, wrapping man and sword in an iron embrace. His great bulk, moving with such fury, swept them both away from Harry and over the edge of the firing platform onto the Plaza far below.

Harry, with his good arm, grabbed the still lighting taper, and triggered Firedrake. The high-pitched pulsating sound commenced. The air became sulfurous. Light and sound of unimaginable strength engulfed them.

The two soldiers ordered by Grunkite to return to the fray at the main gate looked back and were astonished to see their old leader raise one fist in the air defying the deluge of arrows and bolts that rained down upon him. Then the whole world, it seemed, was illuminated by a blinding light accompanied by a sound that made them wince and clap their hands over their ears. The walkway shuddered under their feet. They fell to their knees. The ear shattering roar subsided but, in its place arose a groaning as if mother earth was being sundered. Their sight adjusted after the blinding flash. Grunkite was no more. That part of the curtain wall where he stood was gone. In its place was a fissure, forty foot wide at the top, through which the raging torrents of the Yayla flood waters screamed. The fissure widened. The massive granite blocks of the curtain wall, more than forty ells deep at the base, began to shift and rupture at the seams.

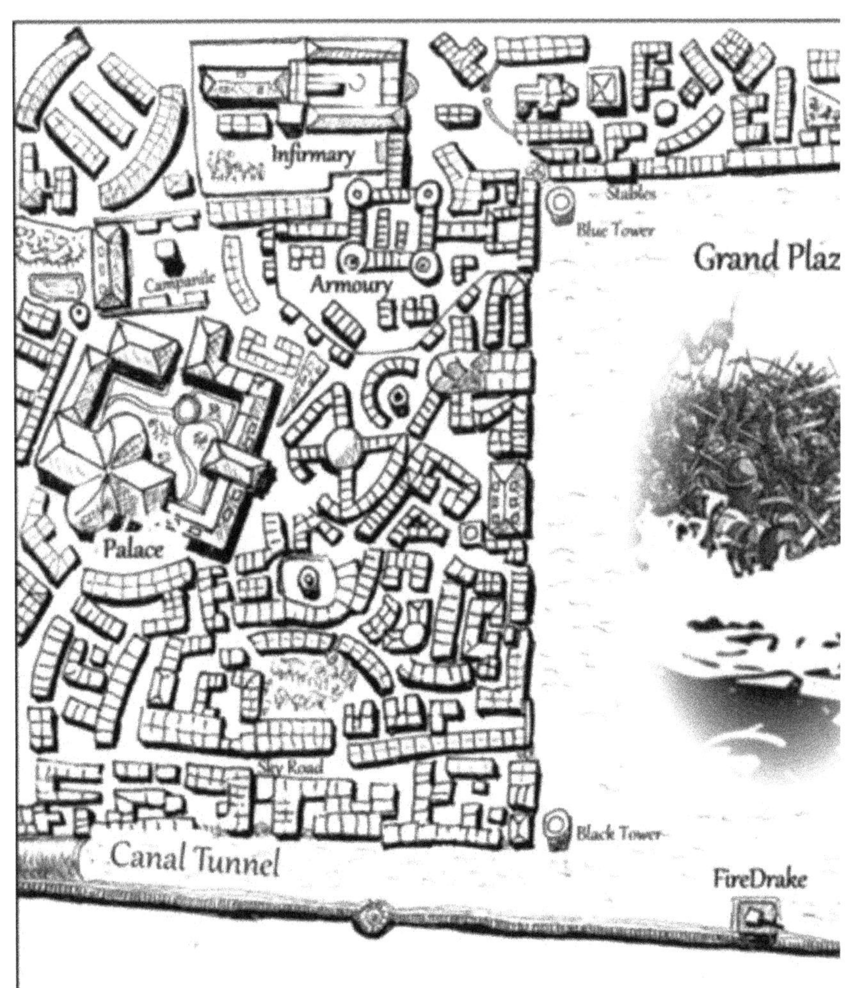

The Drowning of the Brooderstalt Army

In the Grand Plaza

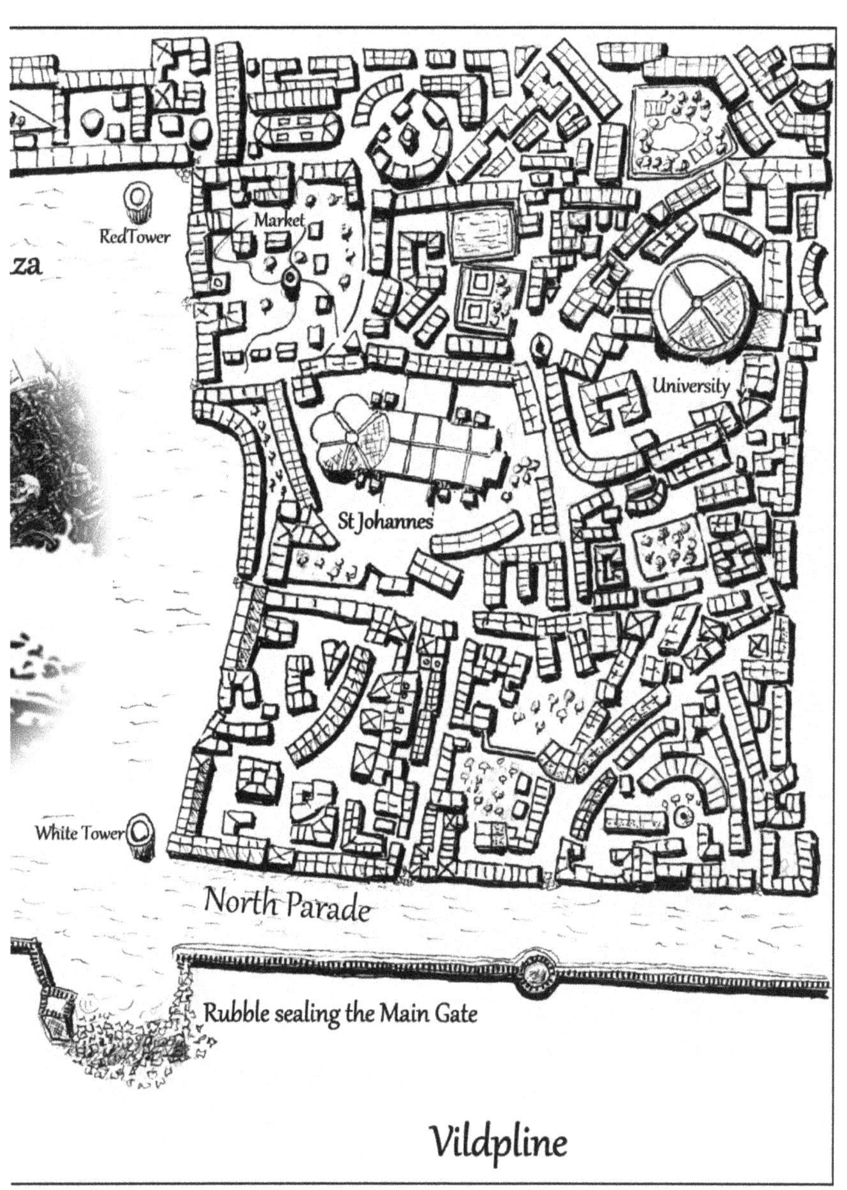

za
RedTower
Market
University
St Johannes
White Tower
North Parade
Rubble sealing the Main Gate
Vildpline

Chapter 33

On the Grand Plaza and its surrounds, every man and every creature was benumbed by the light and sound beyond anything that they had ever experienced. The fighting stopped and all attempts by the Brooderstalt to climb the smashed stairways to the walkways stopped. The ground began to shake. Beyond the spires, walls and buildings enclosing the grand plaza, a murmuring sound grew and grew and a perturbation filled the air with menace.

The remaining men of Dredgemarsh on the upper walkways and the firing platform stared mesmerised towards the west. In the far distance, high buildings, towers and spires collapsed and vanished from view. The rumbling sound got louder like the roar of a gargantuan beast approaching ever closer. The sharp detonations of splintering timbers and masonry and the caterwaul of rampaging water coalesced, immobilising them where they stood.

'It worked, it worked,' cried the sergeant on the firing platform, 'by the blood of the Christ and your genius, Sire, it worked.' Harry appeared not to hear. He sat with his back against Firedrake and stared mutely into the distance.

Panic replaced paralysis amongst the invading horde. They had walked into a trap. All steps to the walkways were ruined and barricaded, the side streets were closed off by the canal men's water barriers and the ominous roar from the West intensified and filled them with terror. A wall of water roared into view, a colossus devouring everything in its path. It swept over the plaza. The level of the water rose at an astonishing rate. The Brooderstalt army was swallowed. Debris, boulders, men and beasts tumbled along in the muddy torrent. The main gate was sealed off. A mountain of debris swept along in the torrent. The plaza became a swirling ocean of mud and destruction spewing forth its horrid contents along the eastern branch of the main thoroughfare. From there to the steep incline of the Canal Tunnel where the melange of muck, wreckage and mangled corpses, dead and dying, mute and screaming were sucked into the vortex of the subterranean labyrinth of canals.

'By the blood of Christ this is hell unleashed.' It was Sergeant Blazer scrambling onto the firing platform who spoke. The duty sergeant on the firing platform and the few men who defended Harry and Firedrake did not answer. They stared open-mouthed at the annihilation of the once fearsome Brooderstalt army expressing neither triumph nor joy. The rain teemed down. Sergeant Blazer stretched out both hands. 'Water, more water.' He raised his face to the sky, 'More damned beautiful water.'

The few Brooderstalt who made their way onto the walkway and firing platform threw their weapons down and knelt with their hands behind their heads. Some were spared, others flung into the flood by enraged Dredgemarsh defenders.

Sergeant Blazer spotted Harry slumped against the side of Firedrake. 'Sire,' he rushed to his side. 'You've done it, Sire, you've done it.' Harry lifted his head. His face was ashen. He stared at Sergeant Blazer and tried to speak. Then like a sleepy child, he closed his eyes and collapsed into Blazer's arms. 'Help, I need some help here,' the sergeant called out.

Despair was etched on every face as they carried Harry, as gently as they could, to the nearest Drumtower. Sergeant Blazer whipped off his cloak and spread it over a stone bench. The sergeant of the Guard made a pillow of his cloak and with the utmost care they laid Harry onto this makeshift bed.

'Go find Maester Aidan. Tell him it's an emergency,' Sergeant Blazer shouted at a young guard. Harry lay unconscious, his breathing shallow. Blood from the wound inflicted by Pentrojan saturated the cloak under him and was beginning to pool on the stone floor beside the bench.

'Take his jerkin off. Remove his tunic.' Gawan shouted out the orders. 'Find some way to heat water on the brazier.'

'We'll wait for Maester Aidan.' The sergeant of the guard, who was kneeling beside Harry, glared at Gawan.

'We're wasting time. The Maester will tell you the same thing.' Gawan was adamant.

'You're an armourer, not a physician?'

Gawan shook his head. 'I've served enough times with Maester Aidan, removing barbed arrows and spearheads while he tended to men's wounds, to know what needs to be done.'

'Do as he says.' Sergeant Blazer pushed the reluctant sergeant to the side. 'The Prince is loosing blood too fast.'

Gawan sliced through Harry's brigadine and undershirt with his knife. 'Put the blade of your seax into the heart of the brazier.'

'Are you sure about—' the now sullen duty sergeant looked alarmed.

'Do it, do it now or he'll die.' Gawan said through clencehed teeth.

With the deft hands of a master armourer, he made a pad and bandage from Harry's undershirt and and bound up the gaping wound on the Prince's shoulder. He tightened the bandage till the blood flow was reduced to a trickle. 'Wine,' Gawan shouted.

'What?'

'Wine, someone must have a wine skin.' Gawan looked around at the perplexed guards. An older man standing at the doorway whipped a leather skin from his belt and threw it to Gwan who uncorked it and poured it's contents over the pad and bandage.

'What now?' said Sergeant Blazer.

'If Maester Aidan does not come, I'll have to use that.' Gawan nodded towards the seax protruding from the brazier.

His limited skills in medicine were not tested further. Maester Aidan arrived, with an enclosed litter and four bearers. He ordered everyone out of the tower room except Gawan. Sergeant Blazer gave the weary soldiers permission to rest and eat what rations they had in their scrips. Most remained standing or sitting just outside the drum tower. The solemn gathering waited for word of their Prince.

When Maester Aidan and Gawan emerged the soldiers surged around them.

'Well?' Sergeant Blazer confronted a haggard Maester Aidann.

'He barely clings to life.'

'He must not, cannot die. Not after all of this.' Sergeant Blazer swept his arms in a wide arc over the foaming waters of the Yayla roaring through the main thoroughfare below them and sweeping the multitude of dead and dying into the maw of the Canal Tunnel. 'There must be something more we can do, Maester.'

'Pray, Sergeant, pray.'

Chapter 34

Outside the walls of Dredgemarsh, close on one thousand Brooderstalt bowmen turned their backs to the city, flung their weapons to the ground and raised their hands high in the air. Spread across the Vildpline from east to west, Cesare's army approached them like wraiths out of the swirling rain. The Knights of Anselem and the Dredgemarsh Invincibles led by Cesare Greyfell, were flanked on one side by the mounted Lydian Bowmen and on the other by the Gliondar Hobelars. Behind them, with Captain Paine and Potens at their head, the Dredgemarsh troopers with their light lances and surcoats emblazoned with the Dredgemarsh hawk formed an impenetrable wall of menace through which there was no escape.

Agobard Luparellus and his cavalry, assigned by Pentrojan to kill all fleeing Dredgemarshians, were now the quarry and not the hunters. He and his men, followed the example of the Brooderstalt bowmen. They dismounted and cast aside their weapons. The crewmen of the two surviving Manchian war engines and the smaller mangonels stood down.

Dubnar Niells, Captain of the Gliondar Hobelars, spurred his mount forward. 'Kneel you dogs, kneel. His Majesty King Cesare approaches.'

All knelt except Luparellus who stood defiantly glaring at the approaching Cesare Greyfell. Without warning Dubnar Niells swung his bardiche from its saddle and buried it in the side of the Brooderstalt captain's neck. Luparellus, eyeballs bulging in disbelief, collapsed and expired. The Brooderstalt captives, kneeling in the mud and water, lowered their heads, not daring to even glance at Dubnar Niells or any of the approaching army.

They were herded together and forced to sit in one sodden mass along the esplanade of the castle.

'Why have they not killed us?' one whispered. The question echoed the thoughts of all the captives who in the reverse situation would have already slaughtered the enemy.

They stole furtive glances at Cesare and his officers who were inspecting what was once the main gateway of Dredgemarsh. Now it was closed off by a mountain of rubble behind which could be heard the roar of the Yayla and above which spumes of water shot into the darkening sky.

Like flickering stars, cresset lamps began to flicker into light and were hoisted on long poles by the Dredgemarsh troopers who surrounded the prisoners. Torches appeared at the embrasures above and snatches of conversation vied with the constant roar of the deluge. After one of these stuttered exchanges, Cesare, Aubrey of Vilspont and a small retinue of Anselem Knights rode eastwards along the esplanade at a fast gallop.

Fifty Brooderestalt were called forth from the main body of prisoners and ordered to go with a group of Gliondar Hobelars.

'We're finished.' A young Brooderstalt buckled at the knees and would have fallen had he not been helped by a companion.

'No, they have some other use for us,' an older man said.

They were taken to the siege cat and forced to wheel it back to the main entrance. Then began the slow exhausting work of tearing down the mountain of rubble and flood detritus that blocked the main entrance, using the cat's giant claw on its swinging beam. Time and again the claw stuck, and the Brooderstalt were whipped till they prised it loose. Huge granite blocks from the destroyed tower tumbled from the mound straight into the siege cat killing and maiming those within. The crushed corpses were hauled away by their comrades and more Brooderstalt from the main body on the esplanade were impelled to take their place. Crude repairs, adequate enough to keep the cat working, were made and their labours recommenced. They worked throughout the night. The task got more difficult with every passing hour. The floodwater began to seep through the barrier of rubble. Fissures opened, small at first but widening all the time, and the water sprayed through the gaps. The ground underneath the siege cat turned to sludge. The Cat had to be withdrawn. and more of the prisoners were forced to fill the quagmire with rocks and construct a rough platform onto which the cat was dragged back into position.

As the first glimmers of dawn appeared behind the Anselem mountains they started once again to claw through the muddy barrier. The weakened mass began to shift. Then the whole agglomeration slewed sideways and fell asunder. The siege cat and those operating it were swept away in a deluge of mud, stone, charred timber and ash followed by a flood of the drowned bodies of the Brooderstalt army, man and horse. They were disgorged through the main entrance over the esplanade and down the castle glacis onto the Vildpline where the grisly remains were scattered like an evil harvest.

The Brooderstalt prisoners, all nine hundred of them, horrified by the sight of the carnage wreaked on their mighty army, were marched east along the promenade. Captain Anvil Paine and Dubnar Niells led the long procession marshalled by the Gliondar Hobelars. Behind these rode the Knights of Anselem, the Dredgemarsh Troopers and the Lydian Archers. The supply wagons arrived then, with food, weapons, and cooking utensils, including those appropriated from the Brooderstalt. Following closely were the squires in charge of the Destriers and the sumpter mules. Bringing up the rear were four finely sprung coaches bearing the symbol of the healer: two snakes entwined on a winged staff. Tethered to the rear of the last coach was a striking black palfrey: the mount of Lia Celeste.

When they reached the breach in the curtain wall, the squires were gathering there minding the horses. One stepped forward and addressed Captain Paine. 'His Majesty, Sir Aubrey and his knights have gone ahead on foot.' He pointed to the great mound of the collapsed curtain wall. 'We are to follow with the horses when it is all cleared.'

'What news of the Prince?' Captain Paine asked.

'We have heard nothing, Captain.'

The Brooderstalt prisoners were ordered to sit facing the wall. The four coaches with the insignia of the healer were signaled to come forward. They were led by the field surgeon, Brother Eustace of the Knights of Anselem, and three of his acolytes. He took charge of moving all his patients up and over the breach into the castle environs. Some could negotiate the climb with help, others were strapped to pallets and carried by volunteer troopers. A litter with drawn curtains was the last to be transferred. Brother Eustace insisted on being one of the bearers.

'Is that Lady Lia Celeste, Captain Paine?' The squire pointed at the litter. 'His Majesty is most concerned about her.'

'Captain Niells,' Paine called out, 'I will go on with the wounded.' Dubnar Niells waved his acknowledgement.

As soon as the sick and Captain Paine were inside the castle wall, a hundred of the prisoners were set to widening and clearing the breach. When the first group had been worked to exhaustion, they were replaced. Each retiring group was force-marched along the deserted streets of Dredgemarsh and incarcerated within the vertiginous dreary walls of the leper compound of St. Lazarus. The compound, chapel and chapter house were long abandoned in favour of a more isolated settlement on the northern tip of Meregloom Gorge.

'Captain, Captain.' Sergeant Blazer rushed forward and flung his arms around Anvil Paine. 'You're alive, you're alive.'

'Steady, Sergeant.' Captain Paine stumbled backwards.

'Sorry.' Blazer released his bear-hug and stepped back. 'I can't believe … but how … it's, it's …'

'A long story, Sergeant.' Captain Paine reached out and grasped the sergeant by the shoulder. 'It is good to see you too, Sergeant. The angel of death has feasted well here, but you are still with us.'

'So many have died, Captain. So many. Good men. Brave men. Why I …' Blazer's voice deserted him and he turned aside for a few moments.

'Sergeant, the Prince; what of the Prince?'

'Saved us all, the city, the whole kingdom,' Blazer said in a stifled voice still facing away from captain Paine.

'Where is he?'

'The infirmary. Wounded. It's bad. We don't know if he will live.'

Chapter 35

The white storks returned from their southern wintering grounds, some to their habitual nesting platforms on disused turrets and chimney stacks; thousands more settled onto their rough nests of sticks on the sparse trees along the eastern side of Meregloom Gorge. Their distinctive bill clattering and bustle as they reclaimed their nests sounded joyful in this city and plain of decaying corpses. But the rains had stopped and the skies were blue and cloudless as if to welcome home the feathered wanderers.

Cesare Greyfell stood in an oriel window facing north on the top floor of the infirmary. On the left the destroyed western wall was just visible and straight ahead he could see the Firedrake platform and one tower of the main gate where the flood waters still flowed unto the Vildpline.

It was two weeks since the great drowning. The barriers constraining the floodwaters to the North Parade were reinforced and built higher by pulling down all contingent buildings. The Grand Plaza was a lake that emptied its polluted waters through Canal Tunnel to the subterranean network of canals below the city. Thousands of carcasses of men and beasts now lay exposed on the plaza and clogged up the roadway down to the canals. The icy weather had delayed the decomposition of the dead, but, within the last couple days, a sultry sweetness was beginning to foul the air.

From dawn to midnight, the Brooderstalt captives, using all available carts and supply wagons, were forced to haul the decaying carcases from the Grand Plaza and surrounding streets through the temporary gateway hacked out of the breached curtain wall. The bodies, stripped of their armour and war accoutrements were dumped in Meregloom Gorge.

Out beyond the curtain wall, the floodwaters flowing out through the demolished main gate was turning the Vildpline into a vast marshland where buzzards and white-tailed eagles, wild boar, wolves and jackals fought over the carrion of the once invinciple Brooderstalt army.

For Cesare Greyfell the task of returning Dredgemarsh to some semblance of normality was an onerous one, but a welcome diversion for brief moments, from the guilt that assailed his mind and gave him little peace night or day. He turned away from the oriel window and sat down at the head of a large table around which Aubrey of Vilspont, Ranulf Halfhand, Dubnar Niells, Andret Longspere and Captain Anvil Paine sat in respectful silence.

'Where were we?' Cesare looked to Aubrey of Vilspont.

'Another few days should see all of the bodies removed, Sire. The cold has delayed decay and our medical men assure me that there will be no major outbreak of sickness. You had started addressing the rebuilding of the Western wall.'

'Ah yes. The Western Wall.' Cesare, leaned forward on the table and cupped his brow in both hands. 'I have talked with our military engineers and yours, Sir Aubrey. They have completed the design of coffers dams. We will need many ells of timber from Rim Wood and Grak's Forest. Waldgrave Benedek and his foresters are ready to help. That needs—'

'Sire, Sire.' Bella Crumble barged through the door. Everyone stood. Dubnar Niells drew his sword. 'Sire, the Prince is awake.'

'Sirs,' Cesare leapt to his feet and rushed towards the door. 'You know what's required.'

Cesare slipped into the sickroom. Harry, half propped up on a bolster and pillow was staring up at Maester Aidan, a look of desolation on his face. Matron Judith stood to the side. Her face mimicked the emotion on Harry's face. Her left hand cradled the clenched fist of her right that she pressed against her breast.

'It grieves me to say it, Sire,' Maester Aidan was shaking his head from side to side, 'but there is no certainty that she will ever recover.'

'Does she remember nothing?' Harry's voice was weak and constricted.

'Nothing, Sire. Nor does she recognise anyone. She does not know where she is. She clings to Rebecca who is with her at all times. That is some comfort.'

'Her father, General Hawksfoot … does she not …?' Harry's voice trailed off into a broken whisper.

'She has no knowledge of any thing or person.'

Harry lay back on the pillow and closed his eyes. 'Where is Grunkite?' he whispered.

'I'm afraid—' Maester Aidan began.

Cesare stepped forward. 'Chancellor Grunkite sacrificed himself for Dredgemarsh … for us … for our people.'

Harry opened his eyes and stared at Cesare. He struggled to raise himself but fell back on the pillow. 'How did he die?'

'My son, you should rest, regain your—'

'How?'

'Sire,' Maester Aidan interjected, 'your father is right, you must—'

'How? How?' Once more Harry tried to rise but failed.

'Grunkite died on the western wall.' Cesare said. 'The flagpole marking the nephryte fell under the Brooderstalt barrage. He alone raised it again and remained holding it aloft until the end.'

'No.' Harry cried out. 'I killed him.' He began to jerk his head from side to side.

Maester Aidan rushed to his side. 'Hold his head still, your majesty.' Cesare, from the opposite side of the bed, with gentle but firm hands, held Harry's head and tilted it forward. Maester Aidan put a small beaker to Harry's lips and forced him to drink. Within moments, Harry relaxed, and Cesare laid his son's head back on the pillow.

'Harry, my son, we will speak later.' Cesare put his hand on Harry's shoulder. Just the lightest of touches.

'There is nothing to be said. I'm tired. I was never your …' Harry jerked his shoulder away from Cesare's touch and rolled onto his side.

'He will sleep now, your Majesty,' Maester Aidan said. 'Do not concern yourself with his talk or manner. It is the hellibore in the tissane makes his mind wander withershins.'

'Perhaps you are right Maester, or maybe your medicine unencumbers his mind from polite formalities and he speaks the truth. I am inclined to believe the latter.'

'He has shown a generous, brave and noble spirit in our awful travails, Majesty. I do not believe he will or can discard his own nature. All will be well.' Cesare reached out and laid a hand on Aidan's shoulder. He opened his mouth as if to speak, hesitated and turned towards the door. 'Join me, Maester.' As they walked away from Harry's sick room Cesare spoke. 'Is there no hope for the girl?'

'There is always hope, Sire, but experience cautions me to be temperate in my expectations. For all our sakes.'

Cesare stopped and faced Aidan. 'Do not take what I am about to say amiss, Maester, but have you consulted with our field physician, Brother Eustace of Anselem. He is much more than a bone setter.'

'There is no offence taken, Sire. I am well aware of the skills of my esteemed brother and his knowledge of alchemy. He has prepared an electuary of baladhur which we have begun administering. It is a subtle and dangerous medicine that may help, or, if administered too profusely, will condemn the sufferer to a madness that craves above all else the medicine rather than the cure.'

Chapter 36

Harry paced up and down outside the door of the belvedere of the late General Hawksfoot where Lia was now convalescing. His arm and shoulder were encased in tight bandages.

'Relax, Harry, relax, you're just out of your sick bed, which is where you should still be.' Potens leaned against a pilaster paring his nails with his seax.

The voice of the maid who slipped into the belvedere to announce Harry was reduced to an indecipherable murmur behind the heavy oak door.

'If you find it so tedious to be here, go elsewhere.' Harry glared at Potens.

'Would that I could, Harry,' Potens slid the seax into its sheath on his belt, 'but your father, you know, the father you have so willfully rebuffed, ordered me to guard you day and night.'

'Father?' Harry raised his voice and stabbed his finger towards the door. 'He did this.'

'Unfair, Harry. You know it and I know it.'

'It may be your duty to dog my every step, but spare me the lecture.' Harry spat the words out.

'My misfortune, Harry, to be appointed wet nurse to a spoilt—'

The door opened a few inches. 'Quiet, quiet.' Rebecca's furious whisper silenced them. She opened the door wider. 'Come in, but quietly.'

'You stay here,' Harry said to Potens.

'My pleasure.'

Harry entered the room. The maid servant scurried out before the door closed.

'Forgive us, Rebecca. You were right to chide us,' Harry said.

'Maester Aidan said peace and calm are as important for her as the medications.' Though speaking just above a whisper there was still a tone of admonition in her voice.

Harry scanned the room. Where was she? Radiant sunshine beamed through the arc of lancet windows in the north-east facing wall. In the centre of the room a table with a diaphanous orfray-edged covering displayed a bowl of blue and yellow gentians. Beside it a silver tray with glistening filigree was set out with a decanter of vernage, two delicate glass goblets and a basket of wastel bread and cheese. Everything was bathed in the ethereal light of the morning sun rising above the snowcapped Anselem mountains. Where was she?

There, there she sat, in the centre of the arc of lancet windows, where it opened onto a small semi-circular balcony. What alchemy caused his heart to expand as if to embrace the whole world in an act of pure love, he could not fathom, but the sight of her golden hair, a shimmering halo, caused the breath to leave his body and, for a moment, he leaned on Rebecca's shoulder lest he fall.

'Lia, Lia,' Rebecca said, 'you have a visitor.' Lia rose to her feet and gazed at Harry. Those eyes that mesmerised him from the first moment he beheld her, matched the silk bliault of the palest azure trimmed by dark blue samite. For an instant he was sure she recognised him. He took a step towards her and whispered her name. She backed away from him.

'Lia,' he said, 'don't be afraid. It's me, Harry. You remember—'

'Rebecca,' Lia called out.

'Please, sire. You are frightening her. Leave now.' Rebecca hurried to the side of her frightened charge. 'Have no fear, Lia. The Prince is a dear friend.'

Harry backed away, turned and fumbled at the door latch. There were tears rolling down his cheeks. His hands were shaking.

'I can't …' The door opened. Potens stood there holding the latch.

'Harry, what's wrong?'

Harry rushed past him, his head bent and hand shielding his face.

'Wait.' Potens reached out, grasped Harry by the upper arm and steered him to a bench seat set between two marble pilasters. Even if he had wanted to, Harry could not resist the powerful grip of Potens and he stumbled to the seat. Potens knelt down in front of him, reached out and placed a hand on his shoulder 'What is it, Harry?' The voice and the touch of the big man was now both gentle and awkward. Harry, for the first time in his life, cried and surrendered himself to the grief in his heart.

Chapter 37

It was two weeks since Harry's futile visit to Lia, two weeks since he shut himself away in the royal quarters. Indifferent to the sumptious surroundings, he spent most of his days in his solar. He knew he should be helping with the damming of the Yayla and the reconstruction of the West wall. But every ring of the stonemason's hammer and shout from the carters ferrying rocks and timber to the wall added to his sense of remorse and guilt that silted up his days. So many dear friends had died helping and protecting him. Sleep, if only sleep would come. But every time he closed his eyes, Lia's face, lost and frightened, was there.

'Harry you must eat.' Potens said. The big man, deft and powerful on the battlefield, was awkward in the midst of the refined trappings of power. 'This is not good, Harry, not eating,' he said in a hushed voice as if Harry's "not eating" was a secret that must not be spoken out loud. The tray of food just delivered by Bella Crumble looked small and delicate in his massive hands.

'You look tired, Potens,' Bella had said, 'How is the poor boy?' Potens just frowned and shook his head. Bella reached out and squeezed his hand.

'It will be all right, give it time dear,' she said and he turned away so that she would not see the distress on his face. He carried the tray of food to Harry's solar and laid it on the table where the disconsolate Prince sat.

'Later, ' Harry said, and shoved the tray aside.

'Grak's piss, Harry, what can I do. Give me a hundred Brooderstalt to fight; anything but this. This fart catcher job, I can't …' Potens slammed his fist onto the table.

'I'm going to see her.' Harry, without warning, rose up and his chair clattered to the floor.

'No you're not. You'll frighten her even more than last time.' The big man moved with surprising speed to place himself between Harry and the door.

'Let me pass. I order you.' Harry spat the words in Poten's face.

'No,' the big man said in a calm voice. Harry raised two clenched fists. His face was red. He sucked air through clenched teeth and stepped in close to Potens. Potens did not flinch.

'Aghhhh, curse you, Potens.' Harry clasped his head in his hands. Potens picked up the fallen chair and sat Harry down at the table and took a seat opposite him. 'I have to do something. I feel useless.'

'You'll be even more useless if you don't eat. I've given my word to the King that I will look after you and that is what I mean to do. Now eat or, by God, I'll shove this down your gullet.' Potens pushed the tray of food back in front of Harry.

'You can't—'

'I can, and I will.'

Harry glowered at Potens. The big man stared back, resolute.

Without looking at the food before him, Harry began to eat. Potens pushed a goblet of mulsum towards the lone diner. Harry grabbed the goblet and in one long swallowing, drained it. Potens refilled it.

'Go on, drink,' he ordered his sullen charge.

Harry, nostrils flaring, took the goblet and drained the contents in one draught. 'Are you happy now?'

Potens pointed to the food on the plate and filled the goblet once more.

The chore of eating and drinking appeared to make some impact on Harry's state of mind. The contours of desolation on his face mellowed into those of sorrow, vulnerability.

'It's unfair. She saved us all. Saved Dredgemarsh. If she had just gone to Anselem and not ...'

'I understand, Harry.' Potens poured himself a good measure of Mulsum and topped up Harry's goblet again.

'And now she's lost, terrified, knows no one. And it was me. It was me ... my fault. If I hadn't worn that stupid disguise or— '

'No, it wasn't your fault. It was nobody's fault. The King blames himself more than anyone. He can't bear to think of what it's doing to you and yet he was just defending his son, or so he thought. It was no one's fault, Harry, no one's.'

For the first time since Lia's tragic accident, Harry did not bridle at Poten's defence of his father. His demeanor changed to one of troubled reflection. Potens refrained from speaking further.

'Since coming here, Potens,' Harry spoke at last, 'I have been thinking, dreaming perhaps, of my real mother. It could not be memories of her, but …'

'My father,' Potens, poured a good measure of Mulsum into his own goblet, 'often said that she was the most beautiful woman he had ever seen, Harry. Father was the King's fewterer. Loved and cared for those hounds better than he looked after me.' Potens chuckled and drank half the mulsum in one draught. 'No, he was a good man. But he told me that when she died, your father abandoned everything. His mind went astray. I don't understand it, Harry. Maybe you have some idea now of what it was like for him.'

The pair lapsed into silence.

After some time, Potens, having shared the last few drains of Mulsom with Harry, leaned forward, planted both of his great hands flat on the table and said 'Harry, lets you and I go to the west wall now. Just to see the work, nothing more. The walk and the air will be a tonic and your father; it will help him, Harry, just to see you out. He has been where you are now and it near destroyed him.

Harry stood up. 'So be it.'

'What?' Potens, still seated, stared up at Harry.

'I'm ready,' Harry said.

Potens scrambled to his feet. 'After you, your Majesty.' He bowed and extended his arm in a flamboyant sweep towards the door. Harry shook his head in mock irritation. His good friend laughed.

The Dredgemarsh Spring came, as it always did, abrupt and in full force, banishing within days the last pockets of snow from the Vildpline. The sun warmed the low-lands which were already showing the first signs of luscious green vegetation. Above, the unseen skylark thrilled.

'Ah, that air,' said Potens breathing in and closing his eyes, 'blowing straight from Anselem.' He pointed towards the mountains glistening with their snow-capped peaks that appeared so unnaturally close to them in that crystal clear light.

'I swear I can smell that delicious bread they bake in the Anselem monastery. Do you remember. Harry?'

' I remember.'

'Let's take the market route, Harry. The flood didn't get that far.' Harry followed Potens. The streets were empty and the marketplace was deserted except for the burly figure of Frambert Fullfare, who was painting the outside of his inn and humming some tuneless ditty.

'Preparing for the lovely Hiltrude's return, Frambert?' Potens shouted to the proud owner of The Slaughtered Horse.

'Well blast my black soul, there's just one voice like that. Potens, did they not kill you after all?' Frambert said before he even turned around.

'If your stale braggot didn't kill me, Frambert, what chance has a Brooderstalt army?'

'None, I suppose, you great ox.' Frambert laughed. 'Harry … I mean Sire … sorry?' Frambert mumbled. Harry waved away the apology.

'How are you, Frambert?'

'Rampant, Sire, rampant.'

'Poor Hiltrude,' Potens whispered aside.

By the Gods,' Frambert, continued, 'you saved us all, Sire.' He grabbed Harry's hand and shook it vigorously.

'We all did our part, Frambert and you did more than your share. I have not forgotten,' Harry said.

'No more than the next man.' Frambert blushed. 'Now gentlemen, will you come and join me in a little toast.'

Harry looked at Potens whose face lit up at the mention of a drink in the Slaughtered Horse.

'Yes, we accept, Frambert. This great ox, as you called him, looks thirsty.' The three made their way into the inn. Harry half listened to the conversation between Potens and Frambert. The Slaughtered Horse brought back so many memories; in particular his mother, Maisie Fairgame. Not his real mother but he could not think of her otherwise. She loved him and he loved her. That was the strange puzzle: how could there be love when she and her worthless father stole so much from him. He remembered the day — it was so long ago — when he came home to their small hovel on East Canal Way and told her that Professor Quickstrain chose him, above all others, for special studies at the University. How proud she was. Even now he smiled to himself remembering the glow of sheer delight on her face. He recalled the exact words she used: "You deserve it and so much more, Harry".

Potens and Frambert talked about the rebuilding of the West wall, the clearing of the canals and the problems of getting fresh water. There in Frambert's inn, amongst the bottles and flagons, the comforting drone of conversation between his two friends and the crackle from a blazing fire, Harry began to drift into sleep.

'And what of that poor lass, Hawksfoot's daughter, Lia. What a tragedy,' Frambert said to Potens who screwed his face into a grimace, tapped his forefinger on his lips and kicked Frambert in the shin. It was too late. When Frambert said the word, "Lia", Harry opened his eyes and, in an instant, the slumberous prince rose from his chair

'We must go.' Harry said.

'I'm sorry, forgive me, sire, I should have …' Frambert slapped his hand over his own mouth..

'Thank you, my friend.' Potens patted Frambert on the shoulder, 'Another time.'

They strolled to the West Wall, their footsteps the only sound in the empty streets. They climbed to the highest walkway which was some distance from where the stonemasons, carters, soldiers, and Brooderstalt prisoners laboured to repair the great gap blown in the wall by Firedrake. As they got nearer, Harry looked in amazement at the extent of the work already done. An enormous coffer dam was in place diverting the Yayla away from the damaged section of the West Wall. Huge wooden ducts, built into the coffer dam, siphoned off water to feed the conduits supplying the canal network below Dredgemarsh. Three double width treadmills driving a single axle was hoisting massive granite blocks with a triple pulley crane onto beds of mortar being prepared and spread by stone masons. On the inside of the wall two lighter capstan driven cranes were supplying the mortar. Every living soul in Dredgemarsh appeared to be working there and once again Harry felt a pang of guilt for not being amongst them.

His attention was drawn to a man standing on a granite block which was being lowered into place. He wore a muddy smock and mason's cap. At a casual glance one might take him for just another labourer, yet there was something about the man that compelled Harry to look again. The block settled with a satisfying thud into place and the men cheered and clapped.

'Bravo,' said Potens. The tall man standing astride the block removed his cap and his long dark hair streaked with white fell about his shoulders. Harry shook his head in disbelief. It was his father.

'It's no wonder they love him.' There was a catch in Poten's throat. 'Damned dust,' he said and rubbed his sleeve across his face.

'No wonder,' Harry repeated and there was no anger or resentment in his voice.

Cesare at that moment directed his gaze up to the walkway. He saw Harry and Potens. He began to climb down the scaffolding on the inside of the wall.

'Come Harry,' said Potens and the pair made their way down the stone stairways of the tiered walkways. They arrived at street level the same time as Cesare stepped from the scaffolding.

'Harry!' he said.

After a short delay, Harry replied, 'Father.'

Cesare reached out with both hands and took Harry's right hand. Harry did not resist.

'Forgive me, Harry,' the King whispered. Harry gazed into his father's eyes and after long moments, with a barely perceptible nod, he touched the enclosing hands of his father with his left hand.

'I must get back to see …' Harry mumbled the words, disengaged and walked away.

'Thank you, Potens,' Cesare said to the big man, who smiled, nodded to his King and followed Harry.

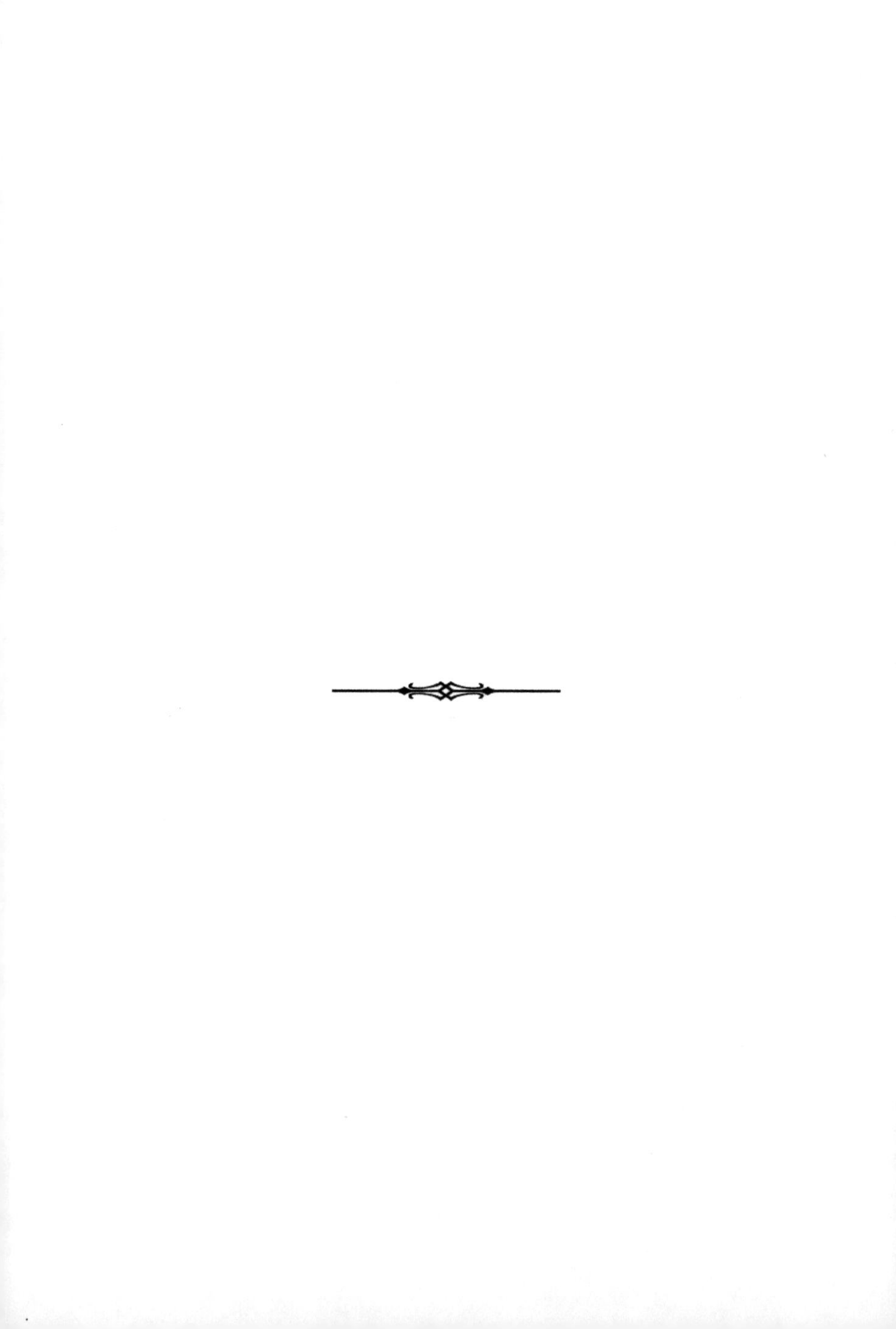

Chapter 38

Judith Engar entered the vestibule of the Great Hall of the infirmary. She hesitated at the door into the hall, sighed, turned away and stepped into a tiny alcove with a piscene and marble seat built into the wall. She washed her hands and dabbed water unto her furrowed brow. Lowering herself unto the seat she closed her eyes and leaned her head against the cool marble of the wall. She was on the cusp of sleep when the door to the hall burst open. The clamour from within disgorged into the vestibule along with Sigbod groaning under the weight of two covered pails as he staggered towards the main door..

'What.' Judith's eyes snapped opened.

'Sorry to wake you, matron. Didn't see you there.'

'I was not asleep, Sigbod.' She stood and brushed down her kirtle.

Sigbod plonked the two pails onto the floor and gasped for air. 'We all need rest,' he said. 'And why we're running around after those Brooderstalt curs, I don't know.'

'We treat every sick person the same, Sigbod. Now be careful, don't spill anything.' Judith smoothed back her hair and stepped into the main hall.

'Madness,' Sigbod muttered. He heaved the two pails up off the floor and tottered out the main door.

'Matron.' Maester Aidan beckoned Judith even before the door behind her closed. He was instructing a young oblate on how to clean the cautery instruments. 'Remember the water must be boiling.' He pointed to an iron pot of water on top of an athanor, and then led Judith towards the kitchen off the main hall. They picked their way through the confusion of beds, paillasses and stretchers upon which the wounded lay unconscious, struggling for life or calling out in the final throes of death. Brother Eustace, his assistants and oblates of St. Jerome were weaving their way through the labyrinth of suffering with water, food and medicines.

In the relative quiet of the kitchen, Maester Aidan waited for Judith to answer a question that he had no need to give voice to, because it was foremost in everyone's mind. And that answer was plain to see in her face. Aidan bowed his head and sighed.

'She is still in the wilderness, Maester. Lost to the world. Lost to everything and everyone. All I can see is terror in her eyes.'

'You administered the electuary of baladhur?' he said.

'Yes, of course. It's made no difference.'

'She should have remembered something by now. Brother Eustace is of the same mind. It would be wise to prepare for the worst, Matron.'

'But she did speak!' Bella Crumble interrupted the sombre exchange between Maester Aidan and Judith. They looked to the source of the interjection: Bella Crumble peering from a small scullery off the main kitchen.

'She did what?' Aidan asked.

'I couldn't help overhearing your conversation, Maester, Matron.' Bella stepped out from the scullery. It's just that, Lia did remember some words from the past.'

'When was this?' Judith said.

'Just after you left the belvedere. I left shortly after that'.

Judith covered her chin and mouth in her cupped palms her eyes wide and alert, her drowsiness banished.

'I must go to her at once.' said Maester Aidan. 'Matron, you will have to take charge here.'.

Maester Aidan tapped on the door of the belvedere where Lia convalesced. He did not wait to be admitted but slipped inside like a shadow. The room was suffused with morning light. Rebecca was arranging a posy of fresh gentians on a richly carved chest of drawers set against the back wall. Lia, sitting by a lancet window facing the Anselem Mountains looked around at the intruder. She shrank back, her eyes wide with alarm.

'Do not be fearful, Lia. I am Aidan, you know me.' He spoke in soothing tones. But still she looked fearful.

Rebecca rushed to her side and held her hand. 'You remember Maester Aidan, Lia? He is a good friend.'

Lia stared with intense concentration at Aidan. She diverted her troubled eyes away from him and, still holding onto Rebecca's hand, she turned her gaze once more to the snowy peaks of Anselem, a remote world as desolate and empty as her own heart. Rebecca shook her head.

'I must speak with you, Rebecca,' Aidan whispered and gestured towards the balcony off the belvedere. Rebecca disengaged her hand from Lia's.

'You are safe, Lia. I must talk to Maester Aidan for a moment.' She joined Aidan who took her arm and led her onto the small balcony.

'You look tired, child.' He cupped her hands in his. She shook her head. 'We have neglected you in our concern for Lia.'

Rebecca wiped tears from her cheeks, breathed deeply a few times and then stood resolute before Aidan.

'Thank you, Maester, but I am not the one who needs help.'

Aidan nodded. 'It is a matter to do with Lia that brings me here. Mistress Crumble tells me that Lia remembered something from the past?'

'Eh … not really, Maester. It's just that twice she said something from the past but when I asked her about it, she didn't know why she said it. That is all.'

'What was it she said?'

'Tramp boy,' Maester Aidan looked bemused.

'And this refers to something in the past?'

' Yes, it happened a long time ago.'

'Rebecca, please sit down, I want you to tell me exactly what these words mean to Lia. When and where did she hear or use these words. '

'Will this help?'

'It may; I can't promise anything but ...'

'Tramp boy was what she called the Prince the first time we ever saw him. We were only seven or eight years old. I think.'

'Continue Rebecca. Every detail is important.'

'He was a poor canal boy then on his way to Meregloom Gorge with a dray of canal rubbish. It smelled horrible. She was unkind but regretted it, especially when she threw a stone and it hit his pony.' Rebecca turned her head and looked out unto the Vildpline and smiled. 'Such happy days, Maester. We were on a picnic with nursie. But Lia did regret that day so much.' Once again Rebecca became tearful and her voice faltered. Maester Aidan leaned forward and patted her hand.

'Later, when he became a student and a soldier, she came to love him. I know he loved her too, even though they met but a few times. That was before anyone knew who he really was.'

'Rebecca, Rebecca. Where are you,' Lia called out.

'I'm here, Lia. I'll just settle her and come back, Maester'

'I'll wait. Do what you need to do.'

Rebecca moved Lia to a seat within the Belvedere with a view of the balcony. 'See. I'm on the balcony talking to our friend Maester Adrian.' She hugged Lia and returned to the balcony. 'There's not anything more I can tell you, Maester.'

'The baladhur may have triggered her memory. That's good. I have no wish to prolong that treatment.'

'But if it's working, why —'

'It's dangerous medicine. We must wean her off it now lest she succumb and be enslaved by it. We will use a more natural healing strategy, now that we know the past is not entirely lost to her.'

'What must I do, Maester.'

Aidan explained the details of a plan for Lia's treatment. He had Rebecca repeat it to him step by step before bidding her good day.'

Chapter 39

The afternoon sun warmed the old walls of Dredgemarsh. A small ornate one-horse carriage with its curtains drawn passed through the portal gate and out onto the Castle esplanade. It took a right turn and after a short journey descended a gentle sloping escarpment to the left and stopped in a small coombe between the esplanade and the Vildpline. The curtain on the little carriage was drawn back and Rebecca looked out.

'We are here now, dear Lia. Don't be frightened, it's just you and I. We will have a wonderful picnic just like we did when we were small and nursie was with us.'

'Please, I don't want to go out there.' Lia shielded her eyes and turned away from the carriage window.

'You remember how we talked about this place earlier. You always loved it here. Please, just for me, for a little while. Take my arm.

Lia grasped Rebecca's arm with both hands.

'Yes, that's it. The sun is shining for us, don't be afraid. I will tell the coachman to wait for us.'

As they emerged from the coach Rebecca kept up a stream of conversation. Lia clung to her companion. She wore a fine linen caftan the colour of lilac and over it a fitted surcoat of samite that glistened and sparkled in the sunlight.

'Look, look Lia, our picnic, all set out and ready just like nursie used to have it.'

There in the heart of the small coombe a sumptuous picnic was laid like a work of art on a dazzling white cloth. They sat close to each other on two soft bolsters. Rebecca enticed Lia to eat some comfits made from anise seeds and drink a sweet quince cordial.

'Nursie always made these comfits and you loved them, Lia. You always ate too many and felt sick on the journey back. And this cordial, oh the aroma, I have not tasted it in years.'

'I liked it too,' Lia said in a faraway voice.

'Yes, yes, you did, Lia. You remember?' Rebecca could not hide the excitement in her voice. Lia hesitated.

'I don't know,' she said, 'I don't know.'

'Never mind Lia, never mind. Shall I tell you about nursie and the awful things we did on her.' Lia nodded.
Rebecca talked on. Lia ate the comfits and sipped the cordial. The sun gathered the two girls in its warm embrace. The meadow pipits filled the air with their busy chattering and Lia was smiling

The portal gate of Dredgemarsh opened for the second time that afternoon. A small pony pulled an empty canal dray accompanied by a tall young man dressed in the clothes of a canal cleaner. He also turned right and made his way along the same route that the coach travelled earlier.

'What is that sound?' Rebecca said and stood up.

'Oh, let's go back, Rebecca, please,' Lia said.

'Don't you worry, I'll see them off, you just sit there.' Rebecca walked back towards the castle esplanade.

The young man and his pony came into view.

'Be off with you, tramp boy', Rebecca shouted. 'Be off. This is Lia's picnic.' She picked up a stone and threw it at the intruders.

'I said go away, tramp boy, get out of here.' She stooped to pick up another stone.

'Rebecca,' Lia called out,' 'Rebecca, don't be cruel.'

'Tramp boy. Tramp boy.' Rebecca continued to shout and made ready to throw another stone.

'No, no,' Lia rushed forward and stayed Rebecca's hand. Rebecca stood aside. Lia stared at the young man and his pony. She looked bewildered, like someone waking from a vivid dream. She stepped towards them with a quizzical look on her face.

When she was a few feet away she pointed to the little pony and whispered 'He likes potatoes.'

Harry leaned forward. His whole body was trembling. 'What, what did you say?'

'He likes …' The tears streamed down her pale cheeks, 'he likes potatoes.' She put her hand out and patted Pingo on the muzzle.

'Yes, oh yes. Pingo likes potatoes.' Harry could hardly speak. 'He loves potatoes … Lia. He loves potatoes.'

'Ha … Harry?' she said.

The End

Glossary of Antique Words

A

Alquerque

Medieval board game like chess

Allure

An **allure is** an architectural term for an alley, passage, the water-way or flat gutter behind a parapet, the galleries of a clerestory, or sometimes even the aisle itself of a church. It may also be used to refer to a wall-walk on a castle wall.

Arbalest

A heavy cross bow

Arbalester

Cross Bow soldier

Athanor

Furnace used to produce uniform and constant heat.

B

Baladachin

Canopy held over a king or queen.

Baladhur

A medieval drug to strengthen memory

Ballista

An ancient form of large crossbow <u>used</u> to propel a spear, bolt or other missile. Anti-siege weapon.

Bardiche

A long bladed, crescent shaped axe used in battle

Beard-splitter

Slang for a man who has sex with many women

Botargo

Roe of mullet salted and pressed into rolls

Braggot

A brew made with honey, beer and spices

Braies

Medieval underpants

Brattice

A Brattice, also known as a bretèche or an oriel, is a projecting wooden or stone balcony or gallery that protrudes from the upper stories of a castle or other fortification. The purpose of a brattice was to provide defenders with an elevated position to observe and attack enemy troops.

Browis

Bread soaked in broth or gravy

C

Camaline Sauce

One of the most common medieval sauces for meat based on red wine, vinegar and lots of spices.

Canonical Hours

- Matins (nighttime)
- Lauds (early morning)
- Prime (first hour of daylight)
- Terce (third hour)
- Sext (noon)
- Nones (ninth hour)
- Vespers (sunset evening)
- Compline (end of the day)

Capuchon

A hood, which may be attached to a cape, permanent or detachable

Catamite

A boy kept by a pederast

Charlette

A dish of milk and meat

Clarrey

White wine with honey and spices.

Clotpole

A blockhead or stupid person

Chitterlings

The entrails of animals or offal cooked for eating. Great care required in washing chitterlings before cooking. Usually reserved for the lower classes or slaves in ancient history.

Clunch head

Slang for a lump head

Coombe

A deep narrow valley or dip in thr landscape.

Cony

Rabbit but also had sexual connotations: female parts.

Crennelations

A rampart built around the top of a castle with regular gaps for firing weapons

Crustade

A molded or hollowed bowl-like crust of pastry, or bread, used as a serving container for another food.

Cullion

A despicable person

Custorin

In hospitals the custorin (woman) supervised all housekeeping, kitchens and essential purchases.

D

Dowcette

Custard tart sweetened with honey and coloured with saffron.

E

Ell An ell (from Proto-Germanic *alinō, cognate with Latin ulna) is a unit of measurement, originally a cubit, i.e., approximating the length of a man's arm from the elbow (elbow literally meant the bend (bow) of the arm (ell)) to the tip of the middle finger, or about 18 inches (457 mm).

F

Falchion

A one-handed, single-edged sword

Fortilage

A small fort

Frumenty

A sweet spiced porridge

H

Haywain

A large heavy cart for farm work

Hobelar

Light cavalry, or mounted infantry, used in Western Europe during the Middle Ages for skirmishing.

J

Jongleur

A wandering minstrel, poet, or entertainer

K

Kirtle

A one-piece garment that was worn by men and women in the European Middle Ages and sometime later only by women.

L

Lazrol

A language (Dredgemarsh invention)

M

Machiolations

A projecting gallery at the top of a castle wall, supported by a row of corbeled arches and having openings in the floor through which stones and boiling liquids could be dropped on attackers

Mangonel

The mangonel is a class of medieval siege engine that hurls stones and other missiles by means of its single arm.

Mazer

A special type of drinking vessel, properly made of maple wood

Medovukha

Slavic honey-based alcoholic beverage very similar to mead

Merlon

A merlon forms the vertical solid parts of a battlement or crenellated parapet

Moile

Bread warmed under roasting meat and soaked in dripping.

Montero

A cap with a spherical crown and flaps which can be drawn down to protect the ears and neck.

Muff

A woman's sexual parts.

Mulsom

A drink made from wine and honey.

N

Nephryte

A mineral referred to as jade

Nones

Ninth hour (3pm) of prayer in christian liturgy

Numbles

Heart, lungs, liver, etc., of a deer or other animal, cooked for food

O

Orache

A plant of the goosefoot family with leaves that are sometimes covered in a white mealy substance. Several kinds are edible and can be used as a substitute for spinach or sorrel.

P

Paliasse

A thin straw-filled pallet used as a bed.

Pattens

Type of clog worn over soft indoor shoes.

Piscene

A shallow basin often near an altar or in a holy place.

Podex

An arsehole.

Purliu

An outlying or neighbouring area

Puttock

A prostitute

Pyment

A drink made from fermented grape juice and honey.

Q

Quintal

The quintal was a traditional unit of weight in medieval Europe. 44.5 Kilograms (100lb)

R

Rebec

Medieval stringed instrument

Rumareth grass

Rumareth contains a powerful drug which stops bleeding and also makes the user drowsy

S

Sabots

Clogs

Samite

A luxurious and heavy silk fabric worn in the Middle Ages, of a twill-type weave, often including gold or silver thread

Scramaseax

The sax, seax or scramaseax is a large knife that was worn by European men in the 5th until the 11th century

Scrip

A small bag

Seax

See Scramaseax

'Slids

Contraction of God's eyelids (a swear word)

Soffit

The underside of any construction element on a building, like a protective covering under the eaves of a house, or the surface of an arch as seen from below.

Telemons

A figure of a man or woman used as a supporting column

Triforium

A shallow arched gallery within the thickness of an inner wall

Tupped

Have had sexual intercourse

Vernage

Sweet white wine

Vespers

Evening prayers

Vestibule

A lobby, entrance hall, or passage between the entrance and the interior of a building

Wain

A large open farm wagon

Waldgrave

an officer with jurisdiction over a royal forest

Wastel Bread

Bread made from very fine flour

Widdershins

In a left-handed, wrong, or contrary direction